Knock on Wood

Leslie Tall Manning

ISBN: 978-0-9600177-3-7 (paperback)
ISBN: 978-0-9600177-4-4 (digital)
ISBN: 978-0-9600177-5-1 (audio)

Publisher's Cataloging-In-Publication Data
(Prepared by The Donohue Group, Inc.)
Names: Manning, Leslie Tall, author.
Title: Knock on wood / Leslie Tall Manning.
Description: [New Bern, North Carolina] : [Leslie Tall Manning], [2019]
Identifiers: ISBN 9780960017737 (paperback) | ISBN 9780960017744 (digital)
Subjects: LCSH: Brain damage--Patients--Fiction. | Memory--Fiction. | Disco music-
    -Fiction. | Man-woman relationships--Fiction. | Home--Fiction. | LCGFT:
    Domestic fiction.
Classification: LCC PS3613.A5653 K66 2019 (print) | LCC PS3613.A5653 (ebook)
    | DDC 813/.6--dc23

Cover layout and typography Copyright © 2019 by J. Kenton Manning Design
Inserted chapter wallpaper photos by Shutterstock.com
Book formatting by Polgarus Studio

Available at Amazon.com and other book stores.

Other books by Leslie Tall Manning

GAGA
Maggie's Dream
Upside Down in a Laura Ingalls Town
i am Elephant, i am Butterfly

Knock on Wood Discussion Questions can be found at the end of the book followed by an excerpt of the novel *Maggie's Dream*.

For Debbie Engle:
You, the music, and the memories will always be with me.

"Our memory is a more perfect world than the universe;
it gives back life to those who no longer exist."
~ Guy Maupassant

"Let him step to the music which he hears,
however measured or far away."
~ Henry David Thoreau

PART I

Summer, 1978

Chapter 1

Stephanie

"Come on, Stephanie! I'll prove to you who can hold their breath longer!"

Billy's lanky arms and legs pumped extra hard as he raced to the end of the narrow dock and stood on the edge, barely keeping his balance. His shirtless torso was already picking up the sun. I wondered when in the world his mama was going to buy him a new pair of swim shorts. His cutoffs were the same ones from the summer before. As he stood on his toes with his back to the pond, his mop of dirty blond hair bounced away from his head then righted itself again. By the time the carnival came to town, that yellow hair would shine as bright as my grandma's waxed kitchen floor.

He wiggled his skinny body like a jelly fish. "I got me a groove thing," he sang and shouted at the same time. "Shake shake shake it!"

I laughed from my belly as I sat with my legs stretched out on the horse blankets near the tall pines and firs, and gazed at my pink-polished toes. Donald sat on my right and Lance on my left. The first day of summer surrounded us. The air lay thick and still with humidity, the cicadas buzzing happily, the portable radio playing *Casey Kasem's American Top 40*. I licked my lips and breathed in freedom and sunshine and the familiar smell of the pond only a few yards away.

"You go in, Billy," I shouted sweetly. "I don't have the gopher guts to try that cold water. Not yet, anyways."

Donald, Billy's older brother, whispered something in my ear, but I shooed him away like an annoying gnat. I was busy watching Billy, who was giving me the most adorable grin.

"Y'all are a bunch of chick-chick-chickens!" He crazily flapped his arms, jumped out into space, and disappeared over the edge of the dock. Water droplets leaped into the air, mingled with streams of sunshine, then fell back into the pond like rain.

Donald stood up and pulled off his T-shirt. "A chicken can't hold his breath as long as I can!" His bare feet kicked up clumps of damp earth as he ran, covering the tracks Billy had made moments before. Donald ran down the dock and stopped at the edge, turned his head to give me one of his stupid I-know-you-want-me-baby looks, and dove in.

The moment Donald vanished, my head became clear again.

It was my plan to marry Billy Baker. I had loved him since our eyes first met in the cafeteria vaccination line the August before first grade. He never cried like the other boys when the school nurse jabbed him in the arm. Billy was the bravest boy I'd ever known.

By the time the summer between middle and high school rolled around, my love for Billy became stronger than those silly crushes my girlfriends couldn't shut up about. My heart was filled with all the grand things a grown woman feels when she's in love. A constant aching for him to kiss me like he did that first time at the drive-in. Raw, jealous pain when he tossed a casual look toward Debbie in square-dance class, or Tina in chorus. That unexplainable emptiness when Billy was absent from school, a stomach virus or a winter cold keeping him home. Those nonstop flip-flops that sent my stomach up to high heaven every time I heard him imitate one of the Bee Gees, or caught him giving me those baby blue goo-goo eyes. I kept on having to throw away my book covers, driving my mama absolutely insane, because I couldn't help scribbling all over the insides: *Stephanie Taylor Loves Billy Baker; Stephanie Caroline Baker; Stephanie Taylor Baker; Mr. and Mrs. William Baker; S.T. + W.B. TOGETHER FOREVER!*

I lay back on the blanket, a stream of sunlight peeking through the clouds and massaging my face, and pictured what my wedding dress would look like. The band on the radio program kept singing about shaking their booty, and I smiled as Billy's best friend Lance sang along, his voice cracking in all the best places until the song ended, and the deejay blared Coca-cola commercials and ads for the new movie *Grease,* which Billy and I planned on seeing opening day.

I turned down the radio. A moment of silence followed.

A very long moment.

Lance stood up and looked at his watch, trying to read it without the sun's glare. "They've been down there for over a minute." His eyes darted from his wrist to the water. His Adam's apple slid up and down.

Another twenty seconds drifted by.

"Shouldn't they be up by now?" I asked, standing next to my friend. Together we watched for any kind of movement, any rippling in the water. Anything.

Lance took off his watch and threw it onto the blanket. He started to untie his sneakers just as Donald's head appeared at the end of the dock.

"Man, that was one long hold," he said between coughs. "I thought my lungs would explode." He heaved himself onto the pier and strutted toward the blankets. "How'd I do? Break last year's record?" He grabbed his *A-Team* towel from where it lay on the grass. "Did I kick his ass?" He shook his head like a wet mongrel and dried off his legs and feet.

"Where is he?" Lance said.

"Huh?"

"Where's Billy?"

"Guess he's still holding his breath."

For a moment I thought Lance would punch him; his fists kept clenching and unclenching. Then, as if someone had called his name, he ran across the grass and down the dock.

Donald hung his towel over a shoulder. "You hungry, Steph? Ma can make us tuna fish on saltines."

Lance's voice drifted to me. "Holy Jesus."

"What?" I asked, barely loud enough for my own ears to hear. My head still didn't want to comprehend what my intuition had been itching to tell me. Panic rose in my throat.

Lance shouted, "Steph, get Mr. Baker. Tell him to call an ambulance. And to bring a knife!"

Through the woods I ran in my flip-flops, trying not to step in any mud dauber nests or trip on any roots. I screamed, "Mr. Baker, Mr. Baker!" at the top of my lungs. "It's Billy! Call an ambulance! Bring a knife! Hurry!"

Once I heard him coming, I ran back up the path, across the grass, and down the dock. My flip-flops flew off my feet as I dove in. The icy water should have shocked my body, but I barely felt it. My heart raced, pumping loud and hard in my throat until it nearly choked me. Underwater, the rickety dock groaned like it was in pain.

I opened my eyes. Billy floated next to a piling from a dock that no longer existed. We were warned to watch out for those old pilings, but no one had ever said anything about looking out for nets. I tried to help Lance free Billy's ankle, but it was no use. It was as if that net was a part of his foot. I needed more air, but still I tugged. Billy's arms floated next to him. His face was blue and had taken on a peaceful stare, like a mentally ill man I had seen once in a movie. Vacant and calm.

I could no longer hold on. As I rose to the top, I looked back to see Lance placing his lips against Billy's, desperately giving him his own air, and I wished to God it had been me giving him those breaths.

The moment my head broke through the water's surface, the choking in my throat began, my oxygen spent, my lungs aching for air. As I coughed up water and closed my eyes to stop from vomiting, preparing to take another journey back to my Billy, Mr. Baker came storming down the planks, carrying a deer-gutting knife in his hand. The afternoon sun bounced off the blade. Mrs. B was right behind. I felt my heart searching for its regular rhythm. Everything would be all right now.

But then I caught the look on Mr. Baker's face and quickly turned away. It was the look of a man out of control. And dads aren't supposed to be out of control. Dads are supposed to know how to save the day.

Mr. Baker kicked off his work boots and jumped into the water. He, too, disappeared below the surface. Mrs. Baker reached down to pull me up, my knees and shins grazing the edge of the dock good and hard, tiny splinters digging in. Little tracks of blood dotted my shins, but I never felt a thing. My body was numb, like someone had pulled me from a freezer and stuck me on top of a Popsicle stick. I shook uncontrollably. Mrs. B wrapped a towel around my shoulders. As she dried me off, I did a slow-motion pivot.

Donald sat behind us on the horse blankets. His silver braces flashed in the summer sun, his wide smile like a cartoon hyena. I almost laughed out loud at the absurdity of it all: Billy trapped underwater; Lance and Mr. B like alligators, taking turns coming up for air then slipping under again; Mrs. Baker clutching the hem of her apron and shaking it like a dirty sheet as she paced along the dock, screaming that the ambulance was on its way, the police and fire department too.

As she paced, she repeated over and over again under her breath, like a chant, until her words echoed in my ears, even hours after she'd stopped saying them, "Everythin' will be fine. My baby will be fine. My favorite boy will be just fine..."

Chapter 2

The water entered my throat, my lungs, my ears, my stomach. Somehow there was a comfort in becoming one with the water. I stopped struggling to free myself from the net which held onto my ankle; no longer needed the body which had belonged to me for fourteen years. I heard a song, muddled and far away. My head turned toward the sound and a smile crossed my lips. In what seemed like a moment of instant magic, I broke free from the net and zipped through the water, like a dolphin on *The Wonderful World of Disney*. I breached the surface and exploded into the air.

Holy moly, hot ravioli! I can fly!

My arms stretched out like a giant bird. I soared over the trees and up to the clouds on my belly, my side, my back. I performed loop-de-loops, spun in circles, dove in and out of the jet stream. My fingertips nearly touched the wing of a lazy hawk, I flew so high!

Then I looked at the world below me: Lance, Mom, and Dad were like little ants crawling around. And there was Stephanie, my girl, kneeling on the dock. Oh, how I loved my Stephanie.

I'm gonna marry her, I thought as I soared over her head. *I'll ask her on her eighteenth birthday, that's the right age to do it, and she'll kiss me with her bubble gum-flavored lips and I'll spin her around and around on the dance floor until the sun comes up over the biggest disco club in the city. We'll have babies and watch them grow up to become little pieces of me and her, and they'll live with us in our big farm house on the other side of town with our horses and chickens and garden...*

But for now, I was flying like a bird. I didn't have wings or feathers, but I was still doing it.

Up in the air, junior birdman, up in the air, upside down…up in the air junior birdman, get your wings up off the ground!

From the sky, I watched the scene below. What was happening down there? Why couldn't they see me fly?

Look up here, guys! Look what I can do!

No one noticed my flips and fancy twirls, my loop-de-loops, my air dives. Fear, like too much mud after a flashflood, slid into my belly.

Two men in white jackets carried a stretcher to the dock.

Did someone get hurt while I was busy showing off my silly bird tricks?

The weight from the fear in my belly forced me to drop a little. And that's when I saw what the fuss was all about.

On the dock lay my bluish body. The men pushed and prodded, their quick hands pressing against my chest, turning me on my side, then strapping me onto a stretcher and placing a contraption over my face.

Mom pressed her hands against her eyes. Dad shouted at one of the ambulance drivers, his heavy-weight hands moving violently through the air. The man ignored him. Lance ran behind the stretcher. Donald sat Injun-style on the horse blanket. And Stephanie…

Stephanie!

There she was, still kneeling on the dock, staring into the water. I watched as her tears fell into the pond, distorting her reflection.

I flew down and landed beside her, placing my arms around her waist.

I'm sorry, I told her. *I didn't mean to…*

I squeezed her so tight I knew it would be hard to let go. So tight I never felt the darkness as it overtook me and dragged me to a place I'd never known before. A place I'd never want to go back to again.

PART II

Spring, 1994
Sixteen Years Later

Chapter 3

The old house rocked as if spelled by angry gods of thunder. The soft earth rippled to the outer edges of the property all the way to the apple trees on the sides and the stream in back, like a huge piece of green carpet being shaken out by a pair of giant's hands. The vibrating mailbox became a snare drum on the top of its post. The front door begged to be let loose from its hinges. Windows from the first floor to the attic threatened to pop from the seams which held them and shutters vibrated. In the kitchen, there was the constant rattle of dishes, pots and pans, food in the fridge, the fridge itself. Canned goods and boxes vibrated in the pantry, as did the dozens of jars of blackberry jam and pickled onions in the cool basement. Twenty empty Avon perfume bottles, angels, princesses, fairies, danced haphazardly in their window boxes in the living room, and cheaply framed photos trembled next to the clock on the mantel. Robins and finches chirping in their nests or hanging out on telephone wires ceased their gossip, and any squirrel or rabbit or deer which happened to choose this unfortunate time to go digging in the early spring garden, contentedly nibbling on the seedlings of sweet flowers and new buds, ran for cover the moment the music started to play.

The moment KC, accompanied by his lovely Sunshine Band, took hold of William Baker's bedroom and didn't let go.

Chapter 4

I gripped that wheel pretty tight cuz I could see them kids settin' there on the curb, pretendin' to toss pebbles. But I knew better, and I'm sure you woulda too. They stared at me the way my ol' German shepherd did when he got the distemper, that devil's look in his eye. My Buick protected me like a green suit of armor. I pulled into the driveway and looked in my rearview. Them kids still settin' there, starin' at me like I was a circus freak.

Or the mother of a circus freak.

No matter, I told myself. *Life can only be lived forwards.*

Four bags of groceries. Easy enough to get inside. I opened the car door and the music hit me in the face like a hailstorm. The whole house was a-rattlin'. All my things inside probably rearranged again. One time, my favorite vase, that flowered one I got for a weddin' gift umpteen years ago, had moved from the center of the coffee table to the edge, just about ready to take a leap to the floor when I caught it just in time.

But as much as I wanted to scream, as much as I wanted to take my son and strangle him for being so doggone dense, I also found comfort in that loudness. In the expectin' of it. Like knowin' my toes would throb before I slipped off my work shoes in the evenin'. Cuz that loud music belonged to me a little bit as well.

With the bags in my arms, I used my hip to hold the kitchen door open. I stood for just a second in the doorway, watchin' as the chairs danced a little, a type of kitchen chair square dance, them thin metal legs shimmyin' on top of my poor linoleum floor.

The bags fell out of my tired arms onto the ol' pine table, and I did what I done at least five hundred times over fifteen-plus years: I stormed up the back staircase extra hard on the chance he might hear me. Outside William's bedroom door, I dug my fingers into pillows of fat hidin' beneath my soilt work uniform, mumbled a quick prayer, and pushed open the door.

Chapter 5

I still wore my faded denim cutoffs. My hair was forever wet. My skinny torso remained bare, as did my feet. I sometimes looked at my long thin toes. The toes of a growing boy. Or a boy who had *stopped* growing, depending on how you wanted to see it.

Nobody knew I was there, had never left. Most of the time that included William, though on rare occasions he would suddenly hear my thoughts like they were his own—after all, they really were his own—and sometimes he even understood what I was trying to tell him. But most of the time the music, whether playing on his eight-tracks or albums or in his head, was turned up so loud it would've taken an explosion to get him to pay attention to anything else, least of all me.

Nearly every day at the same time, I sat watching William dance around the room in front of his two backup singers like a man caught in an electric fence, dressed in one of his polyester shirts with the wide collar, a pair of tight bell bottoms, brown platform shoes.

I was still fourteen. He was turning thirty. I was him. He was me.

No one could see me.

But sometimes they could feel me.

It wasn't so bad hanging out and listening to disco music. I loved disco. Always had. Could have probably started my own band, if I hadn't gone and—

Anyway, I had all but given up trying to crawl back into William's skin.

Sometimes I'd feel warm, other times cold, depending on what was happening around me. Say it was Christmas, or maybe a birthday, I'd get all warm like a Pop-tart just out of the toaster. But then, say that William got into a row with Mom. Those goose bumps would cover my skin like a blanket. And I don't think the chills had anything to do with the way I was dressed.

So there I sat, half-naked, on the edge of the twin bed in the early evening like always, my legs Indian-style, watching all two-hundred pounds of William bop around the bedroom like a maniac in his super tight white bellbottoms and matching vest. Today he wore a black satin shirt underneath, but sometimes he went for more sparkle. His platform shoes sat by the bed, so he danced in his socks.

Whenever William danced, the two talented backup singers in his head would groove behind him, snapping their fingers, swaying to the beat, keeping his rhythm in sync. For the millionth time William wiggled his bottom, pointing his finger straight to the ceiling, and for the millionth time I looked up, as if there were suddenly an angel up there, or maybe an extraterrestrial being.

I didn't flinch when the loud knock came to the bedroom door. William didn't hear it, of course. When his music was on, even if it wasn't turned up too loud, he couldn't hear anything else. Only the music.

Mom opened the door, her cheeks puffed out like she was preparing to blow out a fire. Then, as always, she watched William spin around in circles like an oversized ballerina, and I could tell she was fighting off a smile.

But she was still Mom. "William! Turn down that music! The neighbors..."

William didn't hear her. He skipped around while his leisure suit backup singers moved beneath the speckled glow of the never-ending disco light.

Mom's eyes took in the room William used to share with Donald before Big Brother decided to join the Big-Time League, the only difference being one bed instead of two. Ancient posters of Farrah Fawcett, the Bee Gees, and Earth, Wind & Fire hung on the walls, fighting off sixteen years of mites. A broken lava lamp, with its 1970's innards floating like animal fat, sat on a red plastic Parson's table in the corner. Dozens of trophies and ribbons covered the dresser, most of the statues dusty, the cobalt and red ribbons faded to sky blue and light pink. The window near the dresser was open.

Mom hesitated to stop William while he spun around on the outside chance he might swing back and hit her by mistake. It had happened before, back when he had started his bedroom dancing. So Mom sat on the twin bed beside me, hoping her grownup son would eventually open his eyes.

When he finally did, he smiled.

He said some words but they were drowned out by KC and his Sunshine Band. William sneaked a peek at his two perpetual dancers, still grooving and jiving to the beat.

Mom held her hand up in the air. Her fingers imitated a turning motion, a signal nearly worn out over the years. William nodded and went to the old eight-track player. Abruptly the music stopped. His dancers took a simultaneous bow and vanished, taking the disco ball with them.

Mom poked her fingers into her ears and moved them around. Finally, she rested her hands in her lap and stared at her son. William, that is.

"What did you say?" she asked.

"I said, 'Hi, Mom'," William said.

"Hi."

William popped out the eight-track tape and carefully tucked it back into its cardboard pouch.

"William…son…"

He kept his back to her, making sure the tape was secure as he squeezed it into the row on the low shelf, right above his overcrowded album crate.

The scenario was the same every time. Mom *wanted* to yell, but she didn't. She *wanted* to tell William there were kids in the neighborhood who hung out on the curb while his music drifted through the open window. Cruel kids who jerked about in deliberately uncoordinated dance steps, laughing and hooting, "Woody is a retard!" She knew those children didn't understand. Just silly kids with nothing better to do after school than pick on somebody different. And she didn't mind his dancing, really. She only wanted William to play his music a bit softer, that's all.

She could have said these things out loud, but she didn't.

"Supper's on in a half an hour," she told him. "Come on down and set the table."

"Okey-dokey," William said as he rearranged his eight-tracks.

I followed Mom down to the kitchen and watched as she unpacked the groceries. She rubbed the web between the index finger and thumb on her right hand. She must have felt a pinch there, from hours of spooning tasteless mashed potatoes and gravy and red Jell-O to whining children and grumpy teachers.

But that night she had to cook, and she was fixing up our favorites: hot dogs and mac-cheese.

"A birthday supper fit for a king," she said out loud to the kitchen.

Seeing as how she didn't know I was there, I didn't reply. I only felt warm all over.

"Lance and Stephanie'll be here soon," Mom told William. "Help me do them supper dishes so's we can get ready for your birthday dessert."

"Lemon cake, lemon cake," William sang. "I'm gonna have me some lemon cake."

He rolled up the sleeves of his shirt, turned to the sink, and poured liquid detergent onto the sponge. I sat on one of the kitchen chairs. I loved hanging out in the kitchen. It made me feel more real.

Mom disappeared into the walk-in pantry and came out again with a large wrapped gift. Her muscles flexed with the weight as she placed it on the table.

When William turned around to collect the last of the dishes, he stopped. Suds dripped from his hands to the floor. "Yowza yowza yowza!" He turned off the water, dried his hands on a dishtowel, and sat at the table across from me, even though he didn't pay me any mind. "What did you get me?"

Mom smiled. "Open it and see."

William stared at the gift like he was waiting for it to open itself. Then he untied the ribbon and tore off the paper. He put his face close to the box.

"It's a CD player," Mom explained. "The salesman at Crazy Moe's said it's top of the line. You can buy CDs and play 'em without that eight-track interruption, or scratches on them albums. It'll fit in your room—perfect size, just a little bigger than your ol' stereo system."

William started to touch the box but jerked his hand away.

"What's wrong?" Mom asked.

William didn't say anything.

Goose bumps popped out on my skinny arms.

"We can trade it in for a bigger one," Mom said. "So long as you don't take it out of the box."

"I don't want a bigger one," William said.

"Well, I suppose you could go smaller, though it won't hold as many CDs—"

"I'm gonna leave it in the box."

"No, sweetie, you take it *out* of the box if you want to keep it. Only leave it *in* the box if you want me to take it back to the store."

"I'm gonna leave it in the box."

"You wanna exchange it for another one?"

"No."

"Then what?"

"I don't want this." He stood up, all six-feet of him, and pushed back the chair, a bit too rough.

"I don't understand—"

"I don't like it."

Mom turned the box and read the back like she was auditioning for a television commercial: "The Ferralight Super CD Player comes with remote control…has quality sound…limited warranty…you can put in up to fifty-two discs…I know that's gonna take time, since CDs are expensive and all, but in a few years—"

"No!" William took a step back, whacking his tailbone against the sink.

"William—"

"I don't want it! I like my records. And my eight-tracks."

"I worked hours of overtime to get this for you. It wasn't cheap, you know." Mom looked brave, talking about money, her chin tilted a notch, her bottom teeth jutting out. "If I had my druthers, you'd give your ol' stereo equipment to the Goodwill or somethin'—"

"N-n-n-no! I w-w-won't. It's mine, and you c-c-can't make me throw it a-w-w-way." He kicked the chair and it skipped across the floor, crashing onto its side.

A cool breeze swirled around the small kitchen as I stood up.

William chanted under his breath, "That's how you do it, uh-huh, uh-huh, we shake it, uh-huh, uh-huh…" He wished his dancers would come and lend a hand, but they must have had another engagement. He sang alone, the words mixed up as they often were, an overlapping of two or more seventies tunes: "That's how you do it, uh-huh, uh-huh, we shake it, uh-huh, uh-huh…"

Mom picked up the fallen chair but didn't go to him. She lowered her voice to a whisper. "Alright, son. Calm down and breathe."

William's nostrils flared as he closed his eyes.

"That's it—breathe."

The tears began as soon as his eyes opened again. Open sobs, with no shame, like the way a three-year-old cries when he doesn't get his way.

I moved next to William and patted his arm.

"I—" William said. "I want to make up my own mind. It's m-m-my birthday."

Our birthday.

Mom's voice cracked. "Please don't cry, William."

Mixed-up lyrics poured through his sobs as he sang: "At first I was afraid…I want to fall in love and settle down, down, down…we were born…born…born to be alive…" William snapped to the ground, touched the floor, and bounced back up again. "I was petrified, but now I need to be alive, be alive, be alive."

He froze in place. Mom stared at him, wondering.

"I'm thirty," he finally said.

"Bless your heart, I know you are."

He spoke the words slowly to keep himself from stuttering. "And I'm not a retard."

"Course you're not. That's an awful word to use."

"Then I should make up my own mind."

"Yes, you should."

"And—and I should get a job, like a real thirty-year-old."

"You already have a job takin' care of the two of us."

Three of us.

"I want a *real* one," William said between sobs.

"Honey, we tried that before, and you—"

"It wasn't my f-f-fault—"

"—landed yourself in the ER."

"I thought it was my Kool-aide. It tasted sweet."

"Yes," Mom said. "I remember."

"I'm gonna get a real job this time. With no mistakes."

Mom pinched the spot above the bridge of her nose, the place where her bifocals sat whenever she balanced her checkbook or read one of her paperback romances. She picked up the overturned chair and slid it back to the table.

"Doin' what, William? What is it you'd like to do?"

"Train horses."

"We haven't owned a horse since before you—"

"Since before I turned into a retard."

William sat on the bottom step of the narrow staircase leading up to the small bedroom. I stood close by, near the pantry door.

"Just stop it now!" Mom suddenly shouted. "You get ugly like this every birthday! Just once I'd like to throw you a party where you're actually enjoyin' it."

William spread his arms out in front of him. "I want to make m-m-money—"

"We're doin' just fine."

"—so I can get m-m-married and buy a house and have horses and a t-t-tire swing."

A backup singer appeared a few steps above William. His shiny black skin glistened with sweat, and his greasy afro shimmered like a Fourth of July sparkler.

"A tire swing," the man sang, showing perfect balance as he spun around in his white suit while holding onto the oversized collar. "A tire swing..."

The bags under Mom's eyes looked like gray cocoons. She placed the last of the dishes in the sink. "Your brother looked in this town for two years before he finally moved to the city," she said.

"I'm good with horses," William said.

That's true, I added.

"I know you are, son. There just ain't too many opportunities here these days."

"Then I'll work in the city."

"And how you gonna get there?"

Singer number two, who could easily have been the twin of singer number one, popped onto the step above the other. He and his partner swayed together as they sang in perfect harmony: "How you gonna get there, get there, get there…"

They waited in freeze-frame for another cue.

William didn't answer Mom's question, and she didn't press.

She turned on the faucet as I sat next to William on the step. She stared out into the dark through the window as she soaped up the remaining dishes. "Feels like rain. Perfect for them bulbs I planted last week." She wished rain for her plants, but the damp weather hurt her arthritis to bits. "Rain or no rain," she said to the night. "Either way somethin' will end up sufferin'."

"I'll move there," William told her. "I'll move to the city."

The fork Mom was washing slipped from her soapy hands and landed on a supper plate with a loud clank.

She turned to William, keeping her dripping hands over the sink. "You ain't gonna move to the city."

"Donald did."

"That's different," Mom said.

"Why?"

"Cuz your brother is better off in the city than he is here."

"Maybe I'm better off there too. You ever think of that?"

"You know what, Billy? You're exhaustin' me." Mom rinsed the last dish and put it in the drain board. She shook out the dish towel and hung it in the handle of the refrigerator, then looked at the miniature cuckoo clock next to the pantry: 7:45. "What could be keepin' them, anyways?"

William stood up. "You called me Billy."

"What?"

"You called me Billy. Billy with a capital B."

The backup singers sang: "Capital, capital, capital B!"

"Well," Mom said, "if I did, it was an accident."

Accident.

William said, "You and Daddy used to call me Billy when I was little."

"Your daddy loved stories of Billy the Kidd, remember?"

"I don't like that name. I want you to call me William."

"Of course. I know that." Mom walked over to William on the stairs and cupped his chin in her hand. "I always thought of you as a true fighter, not some mean ol' cowboy. You remember who I named you after?"

"I think you told me once…"

"When I was back in grade school we read about a famous warrior. He was strong and brave, and took on lotsa challenges. He stood tall and had big muscles. To me, that's who you are: William the Conqueror."

"William—" he flexed his biceps on both arms, and I reached up and lightly touched one of them— "the Conqueror!" He grinned and kissed Mom on the cheek.

"Why don't you go on upstairs and change? They'll be here any minute."

William said, "Maybe Stephanie'll move to the city with me—she can take care of me like you do, cuz she loves me just like you do."

He ran up the steps two at a time, straight through his backup singers, who turned to follow him.

I went to Mom, put my arms around her, and gave a squeeze. She walked to the kitchen door and opened it up just a bit, putting her face close to the crack so the night air would cool her off.

Chapter 6

Stephanie sipped her coffee across from Mom at the kitchen table. I let her long brown hair run between my fingers. I put my nose inches from her neck and took a whiff of wild rose.

"He sure is taking a long time," Stephanie said. She gently rolled up the sleeves on her blue cardigan.

Beautiful beautiful Stephanie.

"Always takes extra long when he knows you're comin' over." Mom lowered her voice. "He threw one of his fits about movin' to the city."

"He goes through that every year. He'll forget about it by tomorrow."

Mom rubbed the edge of her saucer. "I don't know...he seems different this year. More...stubborn."

"He's always been stubborn," Stephanie reminded her with a soft smile. "He's had lots of practice."

As Mom stirred more cream into her coffee, the back door swung open. Lance stepped into the kitchen. He scuffed his work boots on the kitchen mat.

"Hey, Mrs. B," he said, taking off his baseball cap and readjusting his ponytail. "Sorry I'm late. Construction on the highway. Hey, Steph."

"Hey."

Lance took a seat across from Stephanie as William's voice rolled down the stairs.

"Ready or not, here I come!"

Heavy feet clomped down the back staircase. Into the kitchen jumped William, his backup singers leaving him to go solo. He still wore his white pants and vest from earlier, but he had added his platform shoes and a white leather jacket. He offered a fancy turn and sang, "Shake it, uh huh, shake it now, do it and shake it…" He slid across the linoleum on his knees, landing at Stephanie's feet. Spreading his arms wide, he said, "Whatcha think? I bought it at a yard sale for a dollar."

Stephanie let the fringe of his jacket tickle the palm of her hand. "You look like Elvis."

William stood and gave an exaggerated pout. "I'm supposed to look like KC."

"Even better," she told him.

"Okay, Mr. Sunshine Band," Mom said. "Let's get on with the real reason everybody's here." She disappeared into the living room and reappeared with a yellow frosted cake, thirty lit candles sprouting up from the lemon icing. She set it down on the kitchen table.

Everyone, including William, sang happy birthday. I sang as well. After all, it was my birthday too.

William leaned over the cake. "I wish—" Then he stopped. "I wish—" he said again, shaking his head.

I whispered in his ear, *I wish I could be me again.*

He didn't always hear me, but I wished it for him anyway.

He blew out the candles. "Okay," he said. "I'm ready for my presents."

Lance and Stephanie laughed. Mom did not.

"William," she scolded. "Be polite. Let's have some cake first."

She cut slices with a long knife while Stephanie pulled the milk container from the fridge. Lance grabbed the special flowered plates from the china cabinet and forks from a drawer. Each person knew what his or her job was. After all, this wasn't the first birthday they'd shared with William.

I made my way around the table as they ate, always excited to see my friends.

William dug into his piece of cake without waiting for anyone else to begin. "This is good," he said with his mouth full.

Mom's face turned peachy.

After wolfing down the piece, William shouted, "Present time!"

Mom motioned with her hand for William to wipe his mouth, which he did.

William turned to Stephanie. "Well?" he asked, checking out her lap and the floor under her chair. "I don't see a gift anywhere."

"William," said Mom. "Don't be rude."

"It's alright," Stephanie said, smiling.

God, that smile…

She put her left hand into the pocket of her cardigan and pulled out a chain. A gold medallion hung from the end. "I found this at an equine convention a few weeks ago. I completely thought of you, William."

He slid his chair closer to Stephanie's. "What is it?"

I stood behind them.

She held out her open palm and laid the gold coin in the small pile of chain. "It's a horse medallion. Well, the head of a horse, anyway. An artist over in Greenmount makes them. He stamps them himself and casts them in fourteen-karat gold. Here. Hold out your hand."

"Yowza," William said.

Stephanie turned her hand over and let the necklace fall from hers to William's. William held it up by the clasp. The coin dangled over the table.

Lance said, "Where'd you get that?"

"I just told you," Stephanie said. "At an equine convention—"

"Not *that*," Lance said, nodding his head toward her hand. "The *ring*."

Stephanie's hand dropped to her lap. A pink veil covered her cheeks and neck.

"What ring?" William asked. The medallion still swung back and forth over the table. His smile tilted when no one responded. He lowered his hand. The chain clanked against the edge of a dessert plate.

"Let's put that gorgeous necklace on," Mom said. "Come here, William. I'll hook it for you." She held out her hands, waiting.

But William didn't move. His eyes never left Stephanie's. "You got a ring?"

"I wanted to wait to tell y'all," Stephanie said. "I really didn't want to say anything on your birthday, William."

"Show me," he demanded.

"Son—" Mom began.

"Show me."

Stephanie pressed her lips together as her left hand reappeared above the table. She splayed her five fingers, the silver sparkling, the diamond facing outward like a laser beam.

I put my face close to the ring. Together, William and I stared at the shiny stone.

William took her hand in his. "Where'd you get it?"

"From Gerald," Stephanie said. "You know, that friend of mine I told you about a few months back."

"The fireman?"

Stephanie nodded.

"Why'd he give you a ring for?"

Stephanie's sideways glance begged for help from Lance or Mom, but neither one met her eyes. She pulled her hand from William's and brought it back to her lap, twisting the ring around her finger as she spoke. "It just about floored me when he proposed." She let out a nervous laugh. "I nearly fell over."

"You and Gerald are getting married?" William asked.

"Yes, William. We are." She spoke to him softly. Kindly. Which only made her words stab harder. "I want for the two of you to get to know one another. You'd adore—"

"He's a jerk," William said, sliding his chair back a few inches.

"No, William, he's not. He's a very nice man who—"

"An asshole j-j-jerk!" William stood up hard and fast, his thighs banging against the table. Stephanie's coffee spilled over the edge of her cup into the saucer.

"William!" Mom shouted. "You apologize to Stephanie right now."

"N-n-no!" William shouted. He glared at the woman he loved, the girl he believed she still was. "She's g-g-gonna marry a j-j-jerk cuz he has a j-j-job and makes m-m-money, and buys her diam-m-monds and things!" Tears streamed shamelessly. Spit dribbled down his quivering chin as he pushed his feathered hair out of his face.

"Don't say those things," Stephanie said, her voice still calm. "They're not true. I can take care of myself just fine, like I have all these years. I'm marrying Gerald…because I love him. We love each other, William." She fleetingly looked at the three sets of non-blinking eyes.

Maybe this would be the final breaking point to push William into realizing his childhood sweetheart hadn't waited around for him. That the occasional Christmas card or birthday visit was about all he could hope for. That she wasn't getting any younger, and he definitely wasn't getting any smarter.

She's 20,000 leagues ahead of us, I told him.

William shouted, "Gerald l-l-loves you? Well, g-g-good for him, cuz I hate you!"

He threw the necklace onto the table. The horse's image landed face down on the cake platter and sank into the yellow icing.

William's two backup singers popped into the kitchen, twirling behind him as he closed his eyes. He cried and sang at the same time, the mixed-up lyrics tumbling over one another: "You were the girl that changed my world…you were the one for me, uh-huh, uh-huh…you lit the fuse, but now I'm used…you were the first for me, uh-huh, uh-huh…now you drop this bomb on me…" William opened his eyes and glared at Stephanie. His thumb pointed to his chest for emphasis. "On *me*!"

With his singers at his heels, William stormed out the back door, letting it slam behind him. It was no secret where he was headed. He always went out there to think, make sense of things. Out to the tree house Daddy had built before he went away.

A tear rolled down one of Stephanie's blotchy cheeks. "I should go after him," she said.

Mom grabbed her wrist. "Don't."

"Somehow I believed he'd be happy for me. Gerald's a wonderful man. He even offered to take William on a tour of the fire station."

I glided to her side, my fingers touching the softness of her blue sweater.

"Let me talk to him," Lance said. "I'll take him to a movie or something. I'm happy for you, Steph. And I'm sorry I asked about the ring. I didn't know." He stood up and pushed in his chair. "Don't worry about William, y'all. He'll be fine."

Mom followed him to the back door, gave Lance a hug, and shut it behind him.

"I don't know what to say," Stephanie said, wiping her smeared mascara from under her eyes with a paper napkin. She stared at the brown smudges. "You know how I feel about William. He's like a brother to me."

"And you're like a daughter to me," Mom said. She lifted the sheer kitchen curtains, placed her face close to the small window, and breathed wet circles onto the glass. "After your Mama died, I bathed you when your daddy needed help, bless his heart. I wiped your tears and sometimes your blood with my own spit. Even gave your bottom a good smack now and then when you and William—*Billy*—got into mischief."

Stephanie wrapped her sweater more tightly around her. "I'm so sorry."

"He cares for you more than anything in the world, you know." Mom's voice mellowed to a whisper as she stared into the dark. "You and Lance were the only ones who came to see him every day. I don't think he woulda made it through without y'all."

"Mrs. B, that was a million years ago. We were children."

"Nothing's changed for *him*."

Nothing.

"But everything's changed for me," Stephanie said. "I'm not that little girl anymore no matter how much he needs or wants me to be. I'm about to start my own veterinary practice. I want to get married, have a family…"

"I only wish he hadn't found out. Least not tonight. Not on his thirtieth."

"I'm truly sorry," Stephanie said again.

Sorry.

Mom let out an extra big sigh. Her vapor covered the whole window. "So am I."

Chapter 7

Honey, let me tell you, them girls on stage that night were the ones I don't frankly care for. Tasha needed her three hits of smack a day so she wouldn't toss her cookies backstage. Keri was lipstick lesbo and figured everyone else was too. I mean she was hot, but not *that* hot. Then there was Natalie, the most beautiful black woman I'd ever come across in all my years of dancing. She always wore a different wig, because she had some weird disease that made all the hair on her body fall out, so her skin looked like black wax, and when she sweated, that black wax was super shiny.

The night I met William for the first time, Natalie wore her strawberry blond wig, like the one Glenda the Good Witch wears in the *Wizard of Oz*. But I don't think the men cared whether she was bald or not. They didn't care about nothing except tormenting her and us other girls for their own perverted satisfaction.

The audience was made up of mobs of men from all over creation. White, Black, Chinese, Mexican, herds of cowboys, snotty yuppies, too many suits to count. The club always smelled like sour apples mixed with wet cigarette butts.

I used to waitress at Dirty Burt's, back when I first started taking classes over at the community college. The tips for serving beer were great, but the tips for dancing were better. My first night on stage was on my twenty-second birthday, and my last day sitting in those mind-numbing classes was the very next day. Although, I gotta tell you, they threw out some pretty cool vocab words in that hoity-toity English class. But a girl's gotta be careful who she's using those big words on—men don't whip out their gold Amex cards for spiffy conversation, if you know what I'm saying.

All of the men stopped talking when I came out. I could feel their eyes on my body, my face, my moves. They'd throw money at me, or slip tens and twenties into my garter. I even learned to snatch bills with my toes—I have very talented feet, or so I've been told. And very talented other parts, which I don't have to be told.

Mostly men loved me on account of my hair. It's red and natural and curly, and back then it fell all the way down to the bottom curves of my butt cheeks. I had to use a gallon of Aqua Net to keep it in place, and I sometimes lost my little butterfly hairclips in the curls. A royal pain to take care of, but it was my number two asset. My number one asset was my ass. No fat or cellulite like some girls who danced. I mean, who wanted to pay to see that Jell-O wiggle in your face? Some guys seemed to dig the flab, but not my men. My men were cream of the crop—doctors, lawyers, professors, stockbrokers—who wanted to get away from their nagging wives and screaming kids and fantasize about what their hard-earned money could buy them. And at Dirty Burt's, money could buy them 'most anything.

That night—the night I met William—started out the same as any other, the men calling out dirty words to the girls on stage, drooling into their beers, keeping their hands in their laps and rearranging things every so often. Should have been just another night.

But it wasn't.

I stood backstage, spraying sparkles into my hair—a pain to get out later, but well worth the trouble—and peeked into the audience. I had just bought a new outfit at Looky-Lou's, and man did it make me feel scrumptious. Sheer white, shimmery, tight-fitting, completely see-through. Velcro connected the front to the back. I wore white fish-net thigh-highs with white satin four-inch heels, and a shiny silver halo attached to my headband. Small feathered wings were strapped to my back, and when I twirled around, those feathers moved like there was a magical breeze blowing.

So there I was, ready to go on in three minutes or so. I didn't usually look past the curtain before I went on because getting out of character in the theater is very unprofessional. But I was in a nosy mood, and Frank the manager was in the back office, so I eye-balled the audience.

A couple of regulars sat down in front, and a few new faces lined the bar. Then I spotted these two guys in particular: late twenties, maybe early thirties, sitting in the middle of the room at one of the tiny round tables. One of them was your typical rural dude: faded jeans and a T-shirt, baseball cap, hair tied back in a pony tail, cute in a country boy sort of way. Like stick him under a cowboy hat and maybe he'd turn a few heads. The other guy looked like a blond-haired David Cassidy, who my mama used to love, had just stepped off his music bus for a visit. He wore white bellbottoms and a white jacket with fringe on the sleeves, and his black shiny shirt was unbuttoned almost down to his navel. But he did have a nice jaw line, and his eyes were awful pretty.

I stared through the sliver of the curtains, thinking maybe he was someone famous. At the same time, he looked up and stared right into my eyes for shit's sake, and I had this weird, what's the word…psychic feeling…like a…premonition—that's it, a premonition—that we were connected somehow. And don't ask me why I felt that. I mean, the guy was dressed like a pimp from a seventies cop show.

It was time for me to go on, so I waved my arm to the deejay to play my opening song, *Lady Marmalade*. I know this was 1994, but that song is one of the best in the world to make a girl feel sexy no matter what she's doing or who she's doing it to.

The moment I stepped into the light, the whole room changed. It was like electricity bouncing off the walls. I'm not bragging or nothing, because it's the truth.

As I danced, Mr. Fringe didn't take his baby blues off me, even when Tina the waitress brought him and his buddy shots and let them lick salt off her cleavage. The waitresses could be touched, but us dancers had a force field around us because of the law. I danced along the center of the stage, took that pole between my legs, slid deliciously up and down, slithered toward the audience on my belly like a white snake, and gracefully reached out for those bills from the suckers in the front row. When my song was almost over, and most of my clothes in a neat pile on the floor, Mr. Fringe's buddy whispered something to Tina. When the song ended, I headed backstage and waited for Tina to come and get me.

"Room number four," Tina said like an excited kid. She helped me get my wings back on. "Tyrone's back there already."

I gave Tina a ten dollar bill. She was very young and looked up to me like a big sister.

We had five private rooms at the club, but room number four had the least amount of skanky smell, and anyways, I always wore an extra squirt of Tommy Girl perfume. Under the spotlight, Mr. Fringe sat on a chair in the center of the tiny room, waiting.

"Hey, Tyrone," I said to my guard. He just nodded. Tyrone hardly ever said nothing.

I closed the door behind me and walked up to my client. "My name's Cecilia."

My real name, of course, didn't matter. When you danced for a living, and sometimes even went out of your way from time to time, real names didn't matter. I liked the name Cecilia because my biggest dream was to visit Sicily one day, and they sort of sound the same.

"My name's William," my client said.

I could tell he was one of the shy ones by the way he stared at his hands which were folded in his crotch.

"Hi, William," I said in a sweet voice to help out his nerves. "I'm so glad you chose me tonight. You want a lap dance, sweetie, or a total strip?"

We called it *total*, but really it was just down to my g-string. The state had a strict law about showing all your goodies. Even though half the guys who handed me twenties worked for the state. "Them tax dollars at work," the boss used to say.

William shrugged. "Both, I guess."

Just before Tyrone started the music, William said, "Stephanie's getting married. She said she loved me, but she's a damn liar."

"Well, who needs her then?" I told William, putting my face so close to his our noses nearly touched. William's heavy breaths pushed the smell of tequila into my sinuses. "I'm gonna show you the time of your life," I said. "You ready, sweetie?"

He looked down at his lap again. "It's my b-b-birthday. I'm thirty."

I took his face in my hands and tilted his head up until his shy blue eyes met mine.

I grinned and whispered, "Then you certainly are ready."

The music began, and for ten minutes I did my thing. By the time I was done, the connection I'd felt with William earlier sort of faded and wouldn't come back again until another time.

When I got off work later that night, I'd made over four hundred dollars. Not too shabby for a girl without a boyfriend, a sugar daddy, or a college degree.

Chapter 8

He had left me behind. This happened sometimes, when William made a conscious effort to keep me away. So I stayed in the dark kitchen and waited.

Time meant nothing to me. It was as useless as a driver's license or a fishing rod. There was no reason to be impatient, no reason to look at clocks. Time was for the living, not for those trapped in the in-between.

A car door slammed shut. I listened as William fumbled with the key, trying repeatedly to get it in the lock. The car drove off as he entered the kitchen. He held his fringed jacket in his hands. His shirt hung outside his pants. I caught a whiff of alcohol and cigarettes.

William put his finger against his lips and said to the kitchen, "Shhh! Momsleep!"

He closed the door and moved across the linoleum. Tripping on the first step as he headed upstairs, he let out a loud, "Oof!" like someone had socked him in the gut.

It was hard not to laugh.

As William stumbled up and around the bend of the staircase wall, Mom came into the kitchen in her robe. I stopped on the second step as she went to the door, jiggled the handle, and locked it.

She stood at the bottom of the staircase and peered over my head. She whispered, "William? That you?"

A muffled voice floated down from his bedroom. "Yeah. Tired. Night."

"You boys have a good time?" Mom stepped on the first step, her face only an inch from mine. "Lance give you your surprise?"

I laughed, more loudly this time, and for a moment Mom looked directly into my eyes, then shifted her focus again.

"Uh-huh" was the reply.

"You tell me all about it in the mornin', okay?"

"Uh-huh."

"Goodnight, son." Mom stood there a moment longer, pulled her robe more tightly around her, headed back to her bedroom, back to her paperback romance, or late date with David Letterman.

I ran up the steps. The bedroom was dark but moonlit. Retching sounds came from the tiny bathroom. I waited patiently on the bed. When he entered the bedroom, William's feathered hair jutted out in funky angles all over his head and his shirt dragged behind him like a baby's blankie. He looked like an intoxicated Baby Huey.

You're drunk as a skunk!

"Skunk," William said. He started pulling off his trousers over his shoes, lost his balance, then fell onto his rear on the edge of the bed, missing me by inches. Somehow he managed to get out of his platform shoes and his bellbottoms. He reached into one of the pockets and pulled out a thick roll of lottery scratch-off tickets. He climbed the rest of the way onto the bed, not bothering to take off his socks, and pulled a pillow to his chest. The roll of tickets unraveled beside him. I stared into his face. He was already snoring, his breath loud and obnoxious, but somehow gentle at the same time.

I know what happened tonight, I scolded, speaking to his dead face. *You got hammered, saw a girl take off her clothes, and jerked it in the restroom afterwards, right? A little booze, some tits and ass, and now you're a man.*

He rolled over, squashing the tickets.

Feeling lucky this year?

William let out the snore of a bear.

Good for you, I told him. *You won't be feeling so lucky in the morning.*

37

Mom always worried she'd be cast to hell for arriving at church after the organist had finished playing the opening song. It embarrassed her to walk in and have the women from the Jefferson Country Club or the Ladies Christian League staring at her, wearing their frou-frou hats, saturated with the latest perfume they bought on sale at Belk, sucking up to the clergy like that would help get them through the Pearly Gates.

I could have told them there weren't any gates made of pearl or otherwise.

I sat on the bottom step as Mom paced back and forth across the kitchen floor.

"William!" she suddenly shouted. "Come down for breakfast now or we'll be late again!" When he didn't answer, Mom rearranged her simple blue hat, grabbed the cross around her neck, and shouted one more time. "William Baker!" She put her foot on the first step and tapped it loudly, as if that would set off an alarm in William's head.

"I don't feel good" drifted down the staircase.

Mom's low black heels just missed my fingers as she flew up the steps. I followed behind.

"Jiminy Christmas. You got a fever? Is it your tummy?" She nearly threw herself onto the bed, playing with his blankets and pillows.

William's face was a peculiar shade of yellow. I hadn't seen that color since he was seven and accidentally poked a finger through a rotten robin's egg he'd found beneath the apple tree in the backyard. The area around William's bed smelled almost as bad.

His lips quivered. "It's my stomach. And my head. And my body. I ache all over."

Mom put the back of her hand to William's forehead. "You don't got a fever, but you're perspirin'. Let me get you some Pepto—"

"No. I'll throw it up."

Mom took off her hat, systematically removing the two Bobbie pins which held it in place. "I won't go to church. Reverend Thomas'll understand."

"No, Mom. I just wanna sleep and be alone. Please."

Mom looked confused. William had never sent her away while he was sick. If anything, he'd whimper until she waited on him hand and foot, make her fill up a hot water bottle, rub Vick's on his chest, or make a pot of homemade soup.

But not this time. This time he was asking her to leave.

"Well…" she said. "If you're sure. Are you sure?"

William shut his eyes and nodded.

"Well," she said again. "I'll be back right after. Won't even meet in the hall for donuts."

William rolled away from Mom, pulling the pillow over his head.

Mom stood up and wiped any wrinkles out of her dress that may have crept into the material, hurried back down the stairs, closed the kitchen door behind her, started up her Buick, and headed off to Saint Bart's.

I leaned over his lifeless body.

Look at you. Pathetic.

The string of lottery tickets hung down from beneath the covers. The bottom one scraped the floor.

Play with your tickets yet? It's probably the only thing you'll have the energy to do today.

William pulled the pillow from over his head and rolled onto his side.

There's a penny on the floor.

He shimmied to the edge of the bed, leaned his body over, reached his arm to the floor, and closed a fist around the coin.

Go ahead. Why should this year be any different?

William leaned his back against the headboard, wound up the roll of tickets, and placed them in the valley of the blanket between his legs. As he put the edge of the coin against the first little card, the telephone rang. He cocked his head to the side, wondering if what he was hearing was real or part of the ringing in his ears. He tossed his tickets onto the Parson's table, crawled out of bed, and held onto the railing as he made his way down the steps in his black socks and BVDs.

I followed him across the kitchen as he grabbed the telephone on the fifth ring.

"Hullo?"

Who's calling this early on a Sunday?

39

"Donald!" William suddenly shouted.

More than a cool breeze tore through the warm kitchen. I watched as goose bumps sprouted along his arms. He did a little dance, wrapping and unwrapping himself in the telephone cord, his size twelve feet sliding back and forth on the floor.

"Wow," William said. "It's great you called. I'm home sick from church…yeah, lucky me…what am I having for dinner? I don't know. You thinkin' of comin'? You haven't been to Sunday dinner in a long time…my birthday was yesterday, not today…I know, always busy…okay, Donald, I'll tell her…yeah, hold on…I'll write it down…" William unwound himself from the cord and dug for a pen in the junk drawer. Carefully, he began writing on his palm. "6:30—I forget how you spell tonight. Okay…t-o-n-i-g-h-t. Got it. Bye, Donald!"

William hung up the phone and stood staring at his hand, his lips softly repeating what he'd written.

So. Big Brother decides to make an appearance. When did we see him last? Ah, yes. When he was behind on his rent and needed the emotional support of his beloved family, then disappeared five seconds after burying the check in his pocket—

William tore up the stairs.

Where are you going?

Of course he didn't answer. William used to listen to me all the time back in the beginning, just after the accident. But over the years it had become hit or miss. Sometimes he heard me, other times he didn't, and still other times he chose to block me out.

I shouted up the staircase, *Four months of rent! Remember?*

I sat on the bottom step and put my fists under my chin, my elbows on my knees.

I'm happy you're feeling better.

Chapter 9

Waitin' for Donald was like hunkerin' down for a tornado: You know it's on the way, so you prepare, tighten down the stuff that might break, brace yourself and your home. But no matter how much you do that, it don't matter. Donald shook up the house every time. Didn't even need to say somethin' to get us runnin' around like we was nothin' but a bunch of anxious chickens.

I talked to myself a lot before Donald's visits.

"What if he don't like what's for dinner?" I'd say to the frozen roast. "What if I say the wrong thing, and he gives me that same look my daddy gave when I done somethin' wrong?" I'd ask the pot of collards. "What if William says somethin' to upset his brother?" I'd say to the empty kitchen chairs.

What if, what if, what if?

I opened the oven door and poked the roast with a fork. Light pink juice streamed out. I stabbed a cubed potato which was just gettin' soft and shut the oven door. As I put the flame on low under the collards, the little red cuckoo bird poked out his head and chirped one time, meanin' it was 6:30.

"William!" I shouted. "He'll be here any minute!"

One thing about Donald: he was mostly on time when it came to a home-cooked meal.

"William!" I shouted again as I grabbed the fine silver from the sideboard.

He finally appeared at the bottom of the steps, his orange shirt sparklin', his feathered hair sprayed so flat against his head it looked like a wig. I'd tried for years to get him to cut it short, knowin' as the styles had changed. The boys in the lunch line all had short hair, some of 'em like little GI Joe's. And Lance pulled his back in one of them ponytails. But William refused to go near a barber shop or tie his hair back. He liked it feathered, and that was that, bless his heart. And the good Lord knows I could stand his whinin' even less than his hairdo.

"Help me set the table, son." I watched as he set a plate on each placemat. "You've been hidin' all day. You feelin' better?"

His cheeks had taken on some color.

All's he said was, "Uh-huh."

I wasn't gonna ask, but since he wasn't offerin' no information, I went on ahead and did so anyways. "Where'd y'all go last night?"

"Nowhere."

I pulled the roast out of the oven and set it on top of the stove to cool. I fanned the smells to my face.

"Well, you must've went somewhere," I said. "Lance wouldn't have stayed with you in your tree house half the night." Lance had a wife and a family that kept him tethered.

My son concentrated on where to put each piece of silver. I wanted him to figure it out on his own, but it was one of them things he couldn't remember. Like the letter *K* when he wrote out the alphabet. Or the "Gettysburg Address" which at seven years of age he'd practiced in the bathroom mirror to recite on parent night and then performed it without one mistake.

But some things left him that summer back in '78. Things like knowin' how to roller skate, understandin' the rules of a football game, how to set a table. Them things just faded away. Others stayed with him, though. Like his dancing, or his affections for Stephanie.

I made my voice casual-like. "What was your surprise?"

"Lottery tickets."

"That all?"

I covered the roastin' pan with a large piece of aluminum foil.

"This time it's thirty," William said.

"Lance always gives you the same number as your birthday." I watched as

William stood unmovin', three forks in his hand. "Fork goes on the left, son."

He put 'em down, one at a time.

I grabbed three tall glasses from the hutch and placed them on the table.

"So," I said. "You win somethin'?"

"Haven't scratched yet."

"We can do it after supper. Good job settin' the table. Now be a gentleman and fetch me a can of cranberry sauce from the pantry."

I watched my grownup son move like a clumsy bear across the kitchen and disappear through the doorway. A few moments later he came back, his hands empty.

"Forget what I asked for?"

"Yup," he said, not like he was sad or sorry, just matter of fact.

"One can of cranberry sauce, please."

William headed back into the pantry.

I knew Donald was comin', that he'd show up on the dot, stick his head through the doorway and say, "Hey, Ma," in that deep but somehow nervous voice of his. And yet I still jumped when the kitchen door opened.

I caught my breath and went to my eldest, wrappin' my arms around him. He was shorter than William near about four inches but somehow seemed taller, at least when I looked at him. Never understood how that could be.

"Donald," I said, holdin' my first-born at arm's length.

His green windbreaker was a size too small—the zipper hardly made it over his belly. He and William looked so much alike, except Donald had a thick line of stubble on his chin, like he deliberately shaved it that way. In his left earlobe sat a tiny ruby earring. His long blond hair had a new spatterin' of gray at the temples. I wondered how William would look with gray in his hair, feathered the way it was and all.

"God, Ma," Donald said. "Let me put down my things."

He pushed me away from him, not hard or nothin', he was just showin' off his independent side. He put his briefcase on the floor by the table and his travel phone on one of the dinner plates. Then he hung his windbreaker on the back of the chair where his daddy used to sit. I stared at his skinny arms.

"What?" he asked.

He always could read me pretty good.

"It's just that you…look washed out. You eatin' alright?"

"Lay offa me, Ma. I just walked through the door."

"I'm sorry," I told him. "It's just that it's been a long time. You look so different every time I see you."

"You look the same," he said. "More gray, I guess."

That was Donald, always one to say what was on his mind.

"Well," I told him. "I am a bit tired these days. Seems like I'm always tryin' to catch my breath."

He looked toward the staircase. "Where's Woody?"

"Shush. He hates it when you call him that."

A terrible draft was givin' me the shivers all of the sudden, so I walked over to shut the kitchen door, but it was already closed. I thought, *I gotta get me some of that weather strippin' they sell at the hardware store.*

I went on back to the stove. For a moment I felt as though William was standin' right at my shoulder. Not my William like he is now…more like he was *before* the accident. It had happened many times, thinkin' my little Billy was right behind me, or starin' at me from the foot of my bed on a Saturday mornin', the way he once did, waitin' for me and his daddy to wake up and make pancakes. A couple of times at night, when I was puttin' moisturizer on my face, I saw his reflection standin' behind me in my vanity mirror. But after turnin' around the first few times it happened, I realized how silly I was. I'd even gotten sort of used to it, so I had stopped lookin' over my shoulder a long time ago.

"Hey, Woody!" Donald called out.

"I'm here," William said, comin' through the pantry door. His cheeks shined bright pink.

Donald sure had a crazy effect on people.

William handed me the can of cranberry sauce, never takin' his eyes off his older brother.

"Hi, Donald."

They shook hands, just like a couple of lawyers.

"What up, dog?" Donald said. He ran his hand along William's orange satin collar. "You're looking fly."

"You look groovy." He rubbed the sleeve of Donald's black T-shirt between his fingers.

Donald sat in his daddy's chair. He motioned with his hand for William to sit. It was time for my boys to become reacquainted with each other. It had been too long. At the counter, I opened the can of cranberry sauce.

William pointed to the briefcase on the floor. "What's in there?"

"Paperwork," Donald said.

I dumped the cranberry sauce into a bowl. Then I stirred the gravy slow, actin' like I wasn't payin' them no mind, but I kept my ears on Donald to make sure he didn't say nothin' that might upset his younger brother, in case William was still feelin' sensitive, like when he saw Stephanie's engagement ring.

"How's the city?" William asked Donald.

"Dude, life is crunk. Hot girls, business meetings, power lunches. I'm slammin' it every chance I get. Making so much cheddar I could make a thousand pizzas."

"I'm getting me a job," William said.

"Really? Where at?"

"Never mind that now, William," I said as I checked the collards. "Donald, how's your work goin'? You still sellin'…what was it…timeshares?"

"As if," he said, puttin' a finger against his travel phone's antenna and spinnin' it around on the plate. "I'm into real financial deals now. You know. Consulting and stuff like that."

"Your phone is funny," William said. "Where's all the wires and stuff?"

"You living in the Ice Age? It's a *mobile* phone. In case clients need to reach me. In case there's an emergency."

"On a Sunday?" I asked. "Who would call on a Sunday?"

"You never know, Ma."

"I suppose…"

"You staying for a while?" William asked.

"Got a meeting in the morning," Donald said. "Just came by for some good eats and to chill out with my family. And to wish Woody here a belated happy birthday." He scruffed his brother's hair and William smiled.

I placed the roast in the center of the table. "Why do you stay away so long?" I asked Donald. "Even a phone call sometimes would be nice once in a while. You aren't so busy that you can't—"

"Quit trippin' about my personal life, would you, Ma?"

William said, "Guess what Donald? I got a CD player for my birthday." He jumped up, ran to the sideboard, and picked up the box. "You can have it."

My stomach twisted.

"For real?" Donald asked.

"I don't want it," William said, grinnin' like he'd just solved the hardest math problem in the world. Like I should be proud of him.

"I'm down with that," said Donald, still twirlin' his phone around in a circle on the plate. "My apartment can use one."

"No," I told Donald flat out. "I bought that for your brother." I tried to find the gold cross I always wore, but it had somehow slipped to the back of my neck. I was goin' crazy, tryin' to find that thing. I threw the potholder off my hand and finally found the cross, squeezin' it and prayin' right on the spot that what was about to happen wouldn't.

Donald's voice was as smooth as a wild rose petal. "It's up to Woody here. At thirty, dude should be able to make his own decisions. Right, Woody?"

Sometimes William took a second or two to mull somethin' over. He'd tilt his head back and his eyes would glaze over as he stared at the ceilin'.

I held onto my cross so tight I about ripped it from the chain.

William brought his eyes back to Donald. "I'll let you have it if you promise not to call me that ever again. No more Woody. Ever, ever, ever. Cross your heart."

Donald stood up and shook William's hand. Now they really did look like lawyers, only Donald was a lot better at winnin' a case.

"Deal!" Donald said, tappin' a fist against the top of William's head. "Woody!"

William grabbed his brother by the wrist.

Donald let out a nervous laugh, the one I was mostly used to, and said to

William, "Psyche, dude. I was only kidding!"

William let go of Donald's arm and smiled like he'd just won a blue ribbon at the 4-H fair.

Chapter 10

William sat drinking hot chocolate on the faded green living room couch. Mom sat next to him with her own mug, her apron still around her waist from washing dinner dishes. Next to the end table, Donald was overly comfortable in Dad's old leather Lazy-Boy, sipping extra-strong coffee. I drifted around the room like the cartoon Funky Phantom, only instead of an eighteenth-century costume, I was stuck in twentieth-century cutoffs.

"Be sure to take home some leftovers," Mom told Donald. "I already put them in a Tupperware container."

"Cool."

William said, "I got lottery tickets."

He set down his mug on the wooden coffee table and left the room. Mom took the mug and put it on top of a *Cross Stitch* magazine.

I moved beside Donald and blew against the side of his head. He jabbed a finger in his ear, trying to shake out whatever had crawled in there. I laughed and took a seat on the ottoman.

"He misses you, Donald," Mom said. "He still don't remember things good, you know that. Only bits and pieces. Sometimes while we're settin' around watchin' reruns, when he's relaxed, somethin'll pop through. But most times he don't remember too much. Every day is a chance for you to start over with him."

"Start over how?" Donald said. "I live in the city. Y'all live out here in the sticks."

"You're his older brother. Lookin' up to you is somethin' he's never forgot how to do. William needs more than just me. He needs to have a man in his life."

"Whatever. You should have thought about that before Dad left." Donald set his coffee cup down on its saucer on the end table. The sound of china tapping against china made Mom flinch.

Son of a bitch.

"Don't be ugly," Mom said. "I only tell you this cuz I think your brother is lonely."

"You know what?" Donald said. "You do this every time I come for a visit. That's why I don't hardly come out here anymore."

Mom sank back in the sofa and pursed her lips together.

"You need to chill out, Ma. Seriously."

William came back into the living room, tickets dangling from his hand, the row of them spilling behind him like a tail.

"Okay," he said excitedly. "Everyone gets to scratch. But first you gotta make a wish."

Under his breath, he started counting off the tickets.

"Let's see…" Mom said, putting on a smile for William. "I wish for perfect weather this spring so's my garden looks extra spectacular."

We waited as William struggled to figure out how many to give each person.

"God, give 'em to me," Donald said, jiggling his fingers in the air as William collected them from the floor. Donald quickly counted them out, splitting up the rows into three sets of ten, keeping a row for himself and passing the other two back to William.

William handed a row to Mom, who dug three dimes out of the end table drawer.

"William, give this dime to your brother."

As William handed him the coin, he said, "It's your turn to wish, Donald."

"Let's see," Donald said, tapping the coin against his chin. He leaned back against the leather, allowing the footrest to pop up under his feet, and closed his eyes. "I wish…I wish I lived on a private island with sweet golf courses and more hotties than I can count and sunshine all year 'round."

Standing in the middle of the room, William said, "Now it's my turn. I wish…"

I moved beside him and whispered in his ear: *Go on…say it…I wish I could remember…*

William said, "It's a secret." He took his place on the couch next to Mom. "Let's scratch!"

One by one the tickets fell onto a lap or the floor. Scratch, tear, drop. Scratch, tear, drop. The same every year.

"I got a winner!" Mom shouted. "Two dollars!" She kissed the ticket and tucked it into her apron pocket.

"Oh, boy," Donald said, whistling. "Don't spend it all in one place."

I'd tried so many times to give Donald a punch in the gut or a rap upside the head, but the best I could do was give him the chills or that bug-in-the-ear trick. Both of which had lost their charm over the years.

"I never win anything," William said.

"What about all them ribbons and trophies in your room?" Mom said. "You've won lotsa times."

"Not since—"

"Check it," Donald said. "I got two SPINS. One more and…aw, bummer." He tore the ticket away from the rest and flicked his wrist, sending the sparkly piece of cardboard clear across the room.

"Three tickets left," William said.

Mom neatly stacked her non-winning tickets, put them in an apron pocket, and flattened the material down again. Donald dropped the dime into his shirt pocket and used the last ticket to clean his teeth.

"Two more," William said.

I stood next to him, looking over his shoulder. He scratched the first ticket. $500. $500. $25. $50. $25. William held his breath and let it out in a rush as the sixth number appeared: $10.

"Damn it all," William said.

Donald snickered.

"William," Mom said, frowning. "Language."

William concentrated on scratching off his last ticket while I looked over his shoulder. $2 appeared once, then twice. He smiled and blew the cardboard crumbs away. He'd be happy to win anything.

Next scratch: $5.

Next: SPIN.

Next: SPIN.

William closed his eyes and scratched. When he opened them and looked down, he read the word, silently spelling out the letters with his lips: S-P-I-N. But he didn't move. He stayed glued to the edge of the couch, calculating in his head what he was seeing.

You've won, I told him.

William held the ticket close to his face. He spelled them out in a rush: "S-P-I-N, S-P-I-N, S-P-I-N…"

Mom slid out of her comfortable position against the worn sofa cushions and leaned forward, taking the ticket and inspecting it.

William said, "I won, Mom."

"Yeah, right," Donald said.

"Glory be," Mom said. "Oh my dear, dear Jesus…"

Donald took note since Mom never said Jesus' name out loud unless she was praying. He slammed against the footrest and nearly jumped over the coffee table. He grabbed the ticket from his brother's hand and glared at it, as if daring William to be wrong, to be pulling his leg.

A huge grin broke out across his face. "Little brother got three spins! Three spins! Holy shiznit! You get to spin the freakin' *Lotsa Luck* wheel!"

Donald almost stomped on me as he paraded across the room, and I tumbled backward off the ottoman and onto the floor. I didn't think it would hurt for someone to fall on me, but I wasn't taking chances.

Mom's voice again: "Oh dear Jesus. Oh my goodness. Oh my goodness…"

From the floor, I watched while Donald shouted to the walls that there were things to be done, haircuts to be had, suits to be tailored, shoes to be bought, newspapers to be called.

Mom leaned back and let the cushions take her once again. Her hand touched her throat.

William grinned. "I did it, Mom. I won somethin'."

"Dear, dear Jesus in heaven…"

"And a new tie," Donald ranted. "Definitely a new tie, brother. And maybe we can get you to grow a moustache before you go on. I mean, there'll be God knows how many people watching you on television. *Primetime* television. Maybe a manicure. And a facial. I know a hottie downtown who's pretty good, plus she owes me a favor. This is so dope! I can't even believe it! I guess we gotta call the *Lotsa Luck Wheel Show*—let 'em know they got themselves a winner!" He took a breath and scratched his head. "Damn! This is tight. But there's so much to do…"

"It's my lucky day, Mom," William said.

Donald danced around the room like a groupie at a rock concert. I wanted desperately to trip him, but before I had a chance to try, he froze in the center of the living room. He rubbed a hand across his sweaty forehead, wiped his palm on his jeans, and snapped his fingers. "Yoyo Homie Jo! Do you know what this means? We could all become millionaires!" He grabbed the ticket from William's hand and shook it in front of his face. "*Millionaires!*"

The three of us turned to William, who was staring at the television, a dark and silent box in the corner of the room. We followed his gaze.

William's stunned whisper fell gently into the room like a balloon that had lost its helium: "I'm gonna be on TV."

Chapter 11

We kept them lights out durin' the show and sat through dozens of commercials. The new Ford pick-up truck. A movie preview. The excitin' new tennis bracelet at Justin's House of Diamonds. Another Craftsman one-day-only sale at Sears. Dog food. Cat food. Cat litter. Must have been lots of pet owners watchin'.

The show was pre-taped in front of a live audience, like *The Price is Right*. Microwave popcorn sat in a bowl on the coffee table. Donald brung a six-pack of Dr. Pepper. I guess you could say it was a party. For William's winnin's. Funny to be watchin' ourselves on television, 'specially since he'd won the money a week before.

"God, they show a lot of commercials," said Donald.

"It's so's the advertisers can make money," I told him.

Donald handed me a look that said he already knew that, but he didn't say nothin'. He hadn't said nothin' ugly in a week. Not since William's ticket had showed three spins. Donald was watchin' his P's and Q's. Openin' the door for me. Showin' up for dinner two nights in a row, both times with a bottle of Martinelli's grape drink, knowin' as how I forbade alcohol in the house. Callin' William every mornin' to make sure he'd kept his appointments with the barber and the nail lady. And spendin' money! Never thought I'd see the day when Donald would foot the bill for nothin'. He musta spent near about three hundred dollars, and that's not includin' the after-celebration dinner at Joe's Rib House.

William dipped his fingers into the popcorn bowl, poured some into his mouth, and wiped his hand on his bellbottom jeans. On TV, the *Lotsa Luck Wheel Show* played music. William started gigglin'. So much so that he choked on a piece of popcorn, coughed on it, then took a swig of Dr. Pepper. He burped out loud, and then Donald burped out loud, and then the two of them laughed.

"Alright you two," I told 'em. "Enough of that now."

I only pretended to be angry. I smiled the whole time I said it. My two boys, for the first time in what felt like eternity, were actin' like real brothers. I sipped my soda and celebrated to myself. Then the music on the TV ended and that dapper Mr. Lotsa Luck strolled onto the stage, glowin' like he was an angel sent from heaven…

Chapter 12

I thought William would get to hang out in a sound-proof booth or a green room like rock stars do, with donuts and cookies and soda. Instead, he was told to sit on a metal folding chair on the side of the stage next to a broom closet, while a handful of stagehands hurried back and forth.

On the stage in front of the studio audience, Mr. Lotsa Luck beamed a smile so blinding it looked like he'd rinsed with a bottle of Wite-Out.

"Let's hear it again for Mr. Juan Ernesto Fernandez, tonight's winner of Ten. Thousand. Dollars!"

The audience barely clapped as a blond woman with huge breasts escorted the Fernandez family offstage. I looked at the man's three small children as they passed by. They were pouting. The mother dabbed at her eyes with a lace hanky she pulled from her sleeve.

But I wasn't interested in the Fernandez family or the fact that they'd only won ten thousand. I was mesmerized by Mr. Lotsa Luck in his Hollywood thousand-dollar suit and his Bob's Big Boy hairdo. The show took a commercial break. A man in army fatigues and a Braves baseball cap pushed Lotsa Luck onto a stool and patted tan crap all over his face. Then he rubbed pink stuff on his lips and cheeks, like a clown in the Hatfield Brothers Circus. When Lotsa Luck brushed him away, the makeup guy picked up the stool and disappeared behind the curtain on the other side of the stage.

Lotsa Luck shot William a serious side glance that said, "You'd better be ready to shine, Mr. Baker—I'm losing my audience!" Then he headed toward the bottom edge of the stage as a man standing next to a camera on the floor put up his fingers: Three…two…one…

Music blared from speakers hiding in the walls, and Mr. Lotsa Luck came back to life, sliding across the stage like a Sunday morning evangelist, microphone in his hand, the funny doo-dad on top of his head bouncing up and down like a trained pet.

I gave William a final onceover. He'd thrown a fit when the barber tried to cut off his pretty feathers, and threatened to flush his winning ticket down the toilet if Donald didn't leave him be. At least William had agreed to wear his dark blue suit, but only if he could wear his silver dress shirt underneath. He kept messing with his tie, pulling the knot away from his throat. He ran his fingers through his hair, played with his buttons, wiped a palm across his forehead.

Just smile a lot, I told him, hoping my words might break through the nervousness.

From the backstage monitor, we checked out the audience. Mom and Donald sat in the front row. That's where they kept all the family members so they could join the contestant onstage afterward.

Mr. Lotsa Luck whispered into the microphone. It seemed like the whole room leaned in to hear what the TV host had to say.

"Our last, but not least…" His voice started to climb. "…guest is from…can you believe it…" His voice louder still. "…right here in my hometown!"

Electricity charged through the audience as they clapped and whistled.

Lotsa Luck shouted, "Let's give a warm welcome to our own local yokel, William Baker!"

The whole room shook with applause and stomping feet as Big Boobs took William by the elbow and led him from behind the curtain onto the lighted stage. I followed by his side as trumpets sounded from the speakers. A small camera on a crane panned over the heads of the audience. Mom sat with her hands folded tightly in her lap. Donald sat beside her, absently playing with his watchband.

In the center of the stage, William did a funny little dance, a toned-down version of the Electric Slide, ending it by spinning around in a tight circle.

Big Boobs whispered something in his ear before exiting, and William shoved his hands deep in the front pockets of his slacks. His eyes darted around the room and landed on the monitor at the foot of the stage, where he could see himself.

"Welcome to the *Lotsa Luck Wheel Show!*" Mr. Lotsa Luck said.

I thought William was going to eat the microphone as he shouted a muffled, "Hi!"

The audience laughed. Mom beamed. Donald sunk down in his seat. I stood close to William, in case he needed me. Which, of course, he almost always did, even if he didn't know it.

Mr. Lotsa Luck pumped William's hand up and down. "Wonderful to have you on our show!" He flashed a smile, his teeth like bleached-out piano keys. "Tell our audience a bit about yourself!"

William stared at himself on the monitor and froze. Mr. Lotsa Luck, who was obviously used to dealing with stage-frightened contestants, gently put an arm around William's shoulders, guiding his focus away from the monitor.

"Do you work, William?" he asked, his smile never ending. "What is it that you do exactly? Our lovely audience wants to know."

William looked out at the dozens of strangers' eyes staring up at him. He grabbed the microphone and put his mouth against the top. "I'm a really good dancer. But I used to—"

"A dancer!" Mr. Lotsa Luck shouted, taking control of the microphone again. "Ladies and gentlemen, we've got a dancer here!" Mr. Lotsa Luck slid to the end of the stage, then back to William again. "Tell us, William, what kind of dancing do you do? Are you in the ballet? Vegas review? Local theater troupe?"

Mr. Lotsa Luck extended the microphone but held onto it so William couldn't grab it.

"I'll show you," William said. He unbuttoned his suit jacket, took hold of each lapel, and spun in a circle. The audience laughed. William jutted out his left hip and aimed his right hand toward the ceiling. The audience grew wild as he shook his hips from side to side, his finger pointing from the air to the ground, a near-perfect imitation of John Travolta.

"Fan-TAS-tic!" Mr. Lotsa Luck said, his smile never faltering. "Nothing wrong with some fancy footwork to get your motor running! How about that, beautiful audience!"

Donald sunk deeper into his seat as the audience stomped and clapped and hooted. William blushed.

Mr. Lotsa Luck spoke again in his deep radio voice. "William? Do you feel lucky tonight?"

"I never win anything," William told him.

Mr. Lotsa Luck touched William's arm. "Tonight could change all that." He walked away from William, leaving him alone in the center of the spotlight, and leaned over the edge of the stage. He whispered, "What do you say, audience? Would you like to create a millionaire tonight?"

The crowd thundered with excitement, their feet stomping against the floor, their hands clapping in unison as Big Boobs entered again, pushing the gigantic wheel in front of her.

The famous *Lotsa Luck* wheel was beyond spectacular. It stood on a tall post, the grand circle stretching five feet across. Different colors separated it into sections, like the slices of a giant rainbow pizza. Each slice offered a dollar amount, a trip, a car, or a restaurant coupon. The only section *not* a rainbow color was the ONE MILLION slot. That slice had been painted in heaven: bright glittery silver like it had somehow captured a lightning bolt. When the stage lights hit it the right way, I had to cover my eyes.

"Alright, William," Mr. Lotsa Luck said. "It's time for you to become a winner. You ready to spin?"

"Okay."

The host placed his hand against the side of the wheel. "Spin it nice and hard, and step back so everyone can see where it lands."

William nodded.

"Wait," Mr. Lotsa Luck said. "There's one more thing I need to say before you spin."

William stared at the man with his cartoon hair and white horsy teeth.

"Lotsa luck!"

William took a deep breath and leaned up to get a good grip on the wheel.

He brought his hands down as the wheel took off, spinning fast enough to make the colors blur to black, like a giant version of a vinyl record. William watched it spin, his lips pressed together, his fingers patting his cheeks. The audience continued to stomp their feet. Some people rhythmically slapped their hands against their thighs. I stood close to William, nearly touching his hand.

It took a whole minute before the magic wheel slowed enough to read the blurry words and actually hear the click-click-click-click-click as it passed HONDA ACCORD, TEN THOUSAND, FIVE THOUSAND, TRIP TO DISNEYWORLD, TWO HUNDRED AND FIFTY, ONE THOUSAND, ONE HUNDRED, FIFTY, OLIVE GARDEN COUPON, CHILI'S COUPON, IHOP COUPON. It went past them all again and again, including the segment I'd ignored until now. The one slice that, if William landed on it, would destroy the smattering of confidence he barely held onto: LOSER.

"If I get L-O-Z-E-R," William had announced on the way to the show, "then I'll know it's true."

Without correcting his spelling, Mom had tried to convince him that a silly word on a wheel couldn't ruin someone's life, but William only snorted.

If it did happen, if the wheel landed on the worst slice of all, it would be a setback. The worst setback yet. And after what had happened with Stephanie...I didn't even want to think about it.

Click-click-click-click-click flew the spinning wheel—each and every click causing William to twitch, that same tick that had appeared in the hospital and didn't go away for a year. But now that tick was back, working on the left corner of his mouth like someone had attached a thread and was tugging on the end of it. Not enough for anyone in the audience to notice. But I saw it. That little tick was William's fear that the wheel was going to land smack dab on LOSER, marking him for life in front of Mom, Donald, the audience, the whole state.

As the room wound into a frenzy, I could only hear the clicking. I moved in between William and the giant wheel. The clicks grew slower, like the wheel was getting tired. It was time to choose a slice of pizza.

William's destiny.

Our destiny.

Unless there was something I could do.

Click-click-click-click-click...

But what?

Click-click-click-click-click...

William's lip was trembling now. His eyes were filling with water. So I wished it for him. I wished it with my mind and pushed the wish into his mind, knowing that wishing might not be enough...

And then it came to me: I could blow! When the wheel landed on the word LOSER, I could blow it to the next slot. I didn't even care what the slot was, just as long as it wasn't that awful word; a word that could bring on more than just a nervous tick.

I once had strong lungs, and now I let them fill with air. Just when I thought I couldn't take in anymore, I sucked harder. Then, in a rush, I started blowing, picturing my exhale like the breath of Zeus. I blew until I believed my cheeks would explode and my head would fly off. I took another deep breath and blew again.

The wheel was crawling to a stop. I rubbed my hands through my wet hair as I stared at the pizza slices. Panic entered my belly. My breaths weren't working. Blowing on a big plastic wheel wasn't the same as blowing in someone's ear.

William's backup singers appeared on the corner of the stage. They dipped to the floor and spun around in their shiny white shoes, fanned out an arm in the direction of the wheel, and then froze in place like two statues, waiting under their disco ball.

The wheel stopped hitting the rubber ticker. The audience gasped. In what felt like minutes but was only a split second, I took my hands that were invisible to everyone but me and pushed. In over fifteen years I hadn't used my hands this way, and even though I couldn't exactly feel the texture of the wheel, the sensation was purposeful and filled with desire. I pushed harder, staring at William's anxious face at the same time, listening to the cries of the audience, the exaggerated heavy breathing of Big Boobs, the "Tsk, Tsk, Tsk" of Mr. Lotsa Luck himself.

For the first time since 1978, I could feel sweat as it ran down my temples and dripped onto my skinny bare chest. Harder, harder, harder, harder. I nearly cried with exhaustion when my fingertips suddenly *felt* the wheel...*felt* the wood.

Could this really be happening? Was it *me* making this happen?

And then it *did* happen!

The wheel moved, only a fraction, but it was like pushing a half-ton truck uphill for miles—miles that were compressed into inches.

I heard the stomping feet and a hundred voices coming together like the cries on a roller coaster. "Ooh!!" then "Ahh!!"

The wheel moved one more inch.

One little inch to the next slot.

One freaking inch that would change William's life—*our* life—forever.

One. Final. CLICK!

ONE. MILLION. DOLLARS.

The audience was stunned into silence until someone in the back row shouted, "Wahoo!" and the rest of the room followed like a hungry pack of wolves.

Donald jumped up and high-fived the strangers sitting behind him. Mom stayed in her chair, her pale face staring up at William, her hand clutching her cross necklace. Big Boobs ran down the stage steps as fast as she could in her five-inch heels and fancy tight gown. She grabbed Mom by the arm. Donald grabbed onto the woman's other arm. She led them onto the stage. Confetti and balloons poured from the ceiling. A couple of kids in the audience stomped on the weaker balloons which drifted into the seating area.

Trumpets sounded from the speakers as Mr. Lotsa Luck shouted over the wildness into the microphone. "Congratulations, William Baker! You've won a million dollars! Tell everyone here and at home—we're dying to know—what are you going to do with the money?"

His backup singers sang, "Money...money...money..."

William looked at me, standing by his side. *At* me. Not around me, or through me. His thirty-year-old eyes stared into my forever child's eyes, and he whispered, "What are we going to do with the money?"

I shrugged.

William grabbed the microphone and shouted enthusiastically, "We don't know!"

The host moved to the edge of the stage as a couple of stagehands and Big Boobs quickly escorted William, Mom, and Donald to a private room backstage. I drifted along behind William's backup dancers as Mr. Lotsa Luck enthusiastically told the audience, "Don't go away, folks. We'll be right back after a word from Doggie Do Diapers—the diapers for doggies that doooo!"

Chapter 13

"I got to see me on TV," William said from the livin' room floor where he'd been settin' for half an hour. "I looked pretty cool."

"As if." Donald said. He shuffled from one foot to the other in the middle of the room, like he didn't know what to do with his energy. "Why didn't you say something catchy, like you want to go to Disneyworld?"

"That's not important right now," I told Donald. "William, we have some decisions to make."

"You got that right," Donald said. "A million bucks is a lot of beans."

"William," I said, mostly ignorin' Donald. "Come on over here and sit." William got up from the floor and sat hisself next to me on the couch. I took his young man hands in my callused ones. "Son," I told him, "this is an awful lot to be handlin' on your own. Understand? You and me gotta decide as a family what to do. Why don't I call that accountant who was helpful a few years back, when your daddy—"

"Are you trippin'?" Donald said. "That guy was a freakin' loser. He raked you, Ma."

Donald stood in the middle of my small livin' room, his hands curled up into fists. Sometimes he scared me. But not right then. Not even a little.

"What do you know about it?" I asked him. "You were nowheres to be found back then."

William said, "I think—"

Donald interrupted. "You saying I bailed on the family? Is that it?"

63

I was startin' to feel lightheaded. Sometimes Donald had that effect on me. "No," I told him, speakin' slow and soft, like that doctor on Oprah said to do when tryin' to reason with someone. "That is not what I'm sayin'."

William said, "I want to—"

Donald went on. Once he got started, it was hard to shut him off. "You think I abandoned y'all. Just like Dad."

"I did not say that," I tried to explain. "Stop puttin' words—"

The nausea crept up out of nowhere. I put a hand to my mouth. Too much happenin' in so few days.

"Listen," William tried again. "I know what I want."

Donald was red in the face now. "You can't lay offa me for two seconds, can you, Ma?"

William stood up. "I have something I want to say!"

I felt small, settin' there on the couch, comfortin' myself with the sofa cushions.

"Well?" Donald said to William, standin' with his arms crossed and his head bobbin' with impatience.

William was quiet for a couple of seconds, and in that silence my heart dried up like an apple left on a window sill, for with the Lord as my witness, I knew before he got them words out exactly what he was gonna say. Just like that time when he'd crashed into a tree while ridin' his dirt bike out on Old Forks Road, and I had a true feelin' in my heart that somethin' awful had happened, even before I saw the blood drippin' down his forehead. Knew it the way a mother knows if her child is sick, or lonely, or angry, without ever havin' been told. And in that moment of knowin', I wished I didn't have the power that a mother has to see things ahead of time.

William, just as grown up as could be, like a brave man fixin' to tell his family he was goin' off to war, said, "I'm gonna move to the city and live with Donald."

Chapter 14

In her bathrobe, Mom paced back and forth from her bedroom to the kitchen door. Back and forth like a wooden duck in a shooting gallery. She knew the time was coming, and more than once she stopped at the bottom of the steps like she was about to go up there and tell William to stop being so silly, to put away his notions of living an ordinary life like an ordinary man. But she didn't. In silence she stood with a hand on the railing, eyes red and puffy, her face looking older than usual.

I put my arms around her in a tight hug, but she started crying harder, so I had to let go.

On the bottom step I sat, listening as William showered and readied upstairs. Mom hadn't said more than two words in the last four days, and William remained suspended in his own world, the music in his head never turning off, the boys behind him dancing, their steps mismatched as though William wasn't communicating with them clearly. He had spent those days filling up two worn out suitcases from the attic, shoving clothes and shoes in one, eight-tracks in the other, unpacking and repacking them until everything fit.

Just as William dragged the heavy suitcases from his bedroom to the top of the staircase, Mom disappeared into her bedroom and shut the door.

A horn honked outside.

William and his suitcases thumped down the staircase.

How can you leave without saying goodbye to Mom?

William didn't hear me. He hadn't heard me since that day he'd spun the wheel. Or hadn't *wanted* to.

You're a jackass!

He slightly flinched before hauling the bags to the kitchen door.

His dancers and I watched from the back stoop as Donald tossed the suitcases into the trunk of an old rusty Mustang. William hesitated before getting in. As soon as he did and the doors slammed shut, his two backup dancers faded into nothing. The Mustang's tires dug into the gravel as it headed down the driveway, spitting up chunks of rock that struck the back porch railing, missing me by inches.

I hung out in the house a while longer. I'd have no problem finding William. He could only be without me a few hours at a time. There were times I yearned to leave him altogether. But as long as he needed me, even a little bit, I had no choice but to follow.

Mom suddenly stormed through the kitchen, past me, and onto the stoop. Into the evening air she shouted, "William! William!"

Of course it was too late.

And just like the day when my cold blue body was pulled from the pond, Mom fell to her knees, pressed her palms against her face, and cried like the world was coming to an end.

PART III

Chapter 15

The movie *Coma* was a huge hit during the summer of '78. Lines wrapped around the Red Carpet Theater for months. I saw it four times. Three with Lance and once with Stephanie. But Hollywood's *Coma* never prepared me for the hole I was about to plummet into on that fateful day, back when I was happy, love was a gift, and summer days seemed endless. The memory of each moment had remained with me, as tangible as my wet hair or denim shorts. And somewhere, buried in a deep well, each memory was still a part of William.

That day, down on the dock, Stephanie was sobbing as my arms wrapped around her.

No, babe, don't cry...

I couldn't bear to see her like that.

What can I do, Steph?

She couldn't hear me. She was staring at the blue boy on the stretcher.

I knew what had to be done: I slammed back into my body.

The searing pain that attacked my lungs made me wish I was dead.

A part of me *was* dead.

My eyes were glued shut. Heavy fists thumped against my chest. Three of my ribs cracked under the pressure. Liquid gushed out of my burning lungs. My throat felt like it had swallowed fire instead of water. The men threw me onto my side and repeated the process. I heard cries and moans and wondered if the sounds were coming from me. All of my senses were magnified, every pore opening toward the warm summer air as it moved across my cold body, my skin smelling and tasting the sun. I could feel every strand of hair on my head, each drop of sweat which slipped down my neck and onto the thin mattress beneath me.

Half dead. Half alive. Body on the stretcher. Soul buried miles deep in the center of that black hole.

I wished to be taken. I begged. There had to be a place better than this. There had to be a place where the pain would end and darkness would become light.

My pleas were answered.

Hundreds of invisible hands, the size of mountains, gathered around me and plucked me from the hole, pulling me up toward the sky, past where I'd been zooming through the clouds; past where an airplane can go; past where Apollo 13 had traveled; past the moon and the planets in our solar system; out into a place that no living human being is allowed to see. I don't know how I knew this, but I did.

The gentle hands deposited me along a bright beam of light before they disappeared. I looked around for Luke Skywalker, thinking maybe I was a character in the *Star Wars* story. But I didn't see Luke. Instead, I floated alone toward the end of the beam where a group of people—*shadows* of people— waited for me, like moving sepia-tone photographs or characters from the black and white Charlie Chaplin films. Shadows of both men and women surrounded me, but it was the women who spoke to me—spoke around and through me.

"You are safe now," they said in one voice.

It was true, I felt safe. Safer than I'd ever felt in all my fourteen years. Safe and loved. This love was different than earth love. With no strings attached. It was a million pieces of endless love that were somehow joined together. All the love in the universe wrapped itself around me, flowed through me, became one with me. The black hole was far, far away.

"We will guide you," the women said, their beautiful voices coming together like a chorus. "But you must choose to stay with us. We cannot decide for you."

These shadows loved me, protected me. I had no choice but to stay with them.

A woman's shadow from the center of the circle took me by the hand and began leading me toward the other end of the beam's path. I tried to turn around to remind myself of what I was leaving behind, but my body wouldn't obey. My earth life as I knew it grew hazy.

I floated along beside the woman as images of my short life rushed through me. My *entire* life, not just random bits and pieces. I could see *everything*, from the moment I was born, until the moment my breathless body was pulled from the pond, my lips blue, my eyes rolling back in my head. The images bound me tightly like a piece of twine, refusing to let me look away:

Being placed as a newborn on Mom's sweaty belly. Taking my first baby steps. Throwing my head back and laughing while sitting on Dad's shoulders as he roared across the living room shag carpet like a dinosaur. Riding bikes without training wheels. Shooting cans with a BB gun. Playing with dogs. Running barefoot down dirt roads. Feeding sugar cubes to horses. Reciting lines in a President's Day play in elementary school. Gagging on a sip of Miller Highlife from one of Dad's almost empty cans. Blowing candles out on each and every birthday cake. Climbing the brand new ladder to a tree house Dad had built as a surprise while we boys were away at Christian summer camp. Catching butterflies in nets. Setting them free. Listening to music. Kissing Stephanie. Trying to act cool while slipping my naive tongue into her mouth for the first time…

With these images came emotions like none I'd ever experienced on earth. Feelings that filled me with a joy I'd never known possible. I overflowed with elation and peacefulness, and prayed that the feeling would last forever…

But then the memories changed.

I saw myself hitting my brother square in the nose with my fist. Arguing with Dad about curfew. Yelling at Mom for not understanding why I felt the need to play my eight-tracks so loud. Donald daring me to pull the lighted belly off a lightning bug, then taking the dare and watching the tiny bug starve to death in the jar on the end table between our beds. Burying my favorite pets. Donald running away twice because he thought I was loved more than him. Daddy leaving, explaining how he'd be back after he figured things out. Then waiting…and waiting…for Daddy to come home…

Not only did I feel joy and pain of my own life, but of others' lives as well. Lives that I had deliberately or unintentionally influenced in some way. Relatives, teachers, friends, strangers, animals, insects: all were mine to know and understand as a part of my current existence. My body and heart and mind had become one with every living thing. Time disappeared yet went on forever. All beauty and ugliness in the universe swirled around me, an infinitely churning funnel cloud which suspended me in the center.

A shot of electricity jolted through my hand, and the woman holding it abruptly let go. The funnel cloud stopped spinning, but I remained floating in its center. Human fear filled me.

The unearthly woman's voice floated nearby, but it had changed from joy to pity: "You must go back. I cannot take you with me."

Confused and consumed by the feeling of abandonment, I pleaded with her. "Please. Let me stay."

She repeated, "I cannot take you with me."

"I don't understand."

"You have an earthly purpose. You must go back. A hole needs to be filled. There is much learning and teaching to be done. You have no choice." She turned from shadow to nothingness, leaving only a trace of her voice behind: "Goooo…baaaack."

The same collection of invisible hands that had pulled me into their world now gently pushed me back toward the other.

"No!" I shouted as the beautiful light began to dim. "I want to stay here! I want to float! I want to be safe! I don't want to go back! Please—"

The hands opened, dropping me into the looming shadows. I spiraled downward, out of control. Into a deeper hole I tumbled, completely forsaken. The hole had the depth of the entire universe. It sucked me into its center. I fell and fell, but the ground never came…and yet I knew I was attached to the earth again. I heard voices, human voices, and the sound of crying. Men arguing. More sobbing.

I continued to plummet until my descent eventually tapered off and I floated again, but this time I wasn't able to soar above puffy white clouds, or spin with my face tilted toward the summer sun. There were no clouds. There was no sun. Which way was up or down? There was no gravity in the dark world to which I was cast. I stayed there, floating, suspended in a cave that had no visible entrance or exit, no top, no bottom. In a constant state of nothingness, the core of my being was trapped, curious as to who or where or why I was. There came with the darkness a lack of pain and sorrow, but also a lack of joy and understanding. There was nothing. Only an infinite emptiness that no human being deserves to feel or understand.

And that is where my soul remained for thirty-nine days.

Chapter 16

Nothing like waking up to a dumbass smacking Lucky Charms to get your day going.

The first morning went something like this:

I was sound asleep on the sofa bed in my studio apartment while Woody waited like a human fly on the arm, buzzing in my ear.

Him: "Donald…" Smack!

Me: "Unh."

And then, a little louder: "You…" Smack! "Awake?"

Me: "Unh."

I buried deeper under the blanket, but I could tell he was grinning. Could feel it the same way I could picture milk drooling down his chin.

Him: "Wanna watch cartoons?"

Me: "What time is it?"

Without waiting for an answer, I grabbed my watch from the end table and took a peek under the blanket: nine-thirty.

"Crap," I said, jumping out of bed, grabbing my pants from the floor, and putting them on. I pushed my hair out of my eyes while trying to pull on my ratty sneakers.

"You…" Smack! "In a hurry, Donald?"

I tied my laces and headed into the bathroom. I was supposed to be at work by nine-thirty. Monday mornings were always big cleaning days at the church, especially if Friday and Saturday spit out more sinners than usual.

Most Sunday congregations left behind wads of dirty tissues on the pews, muddy footprints across the carpet, and overflowing trash in the bathrooms. One time I found a baby bottle filled with spoilt milk in between the hymnals.

Woody said something to me from the living room, but I could barely hear him with his mouth full of cereal and the water running in the bathroom.

I stuck my head through the doorway. "What?" Toothpaste dribbled down my wrist. I wiped the back of my hand against my pants.

And now he sat at the kitchen table eating his cereal. "I made breakfast. You gonna eat? There's orange juice and milk. It's not non-fat like Mom's, but it's okay when you put it in cereal." He wolfed down another spoonful. Smack, smack, smack! Holy shit, I wanted to open a can of whoopass on him.

I took a deep breath. *Patience, my man,* I said to myself as I smiled my toothpaste smile in the mirror. I spit and rinsed, splashed water on my face, dried it with my only towel, and walked back into the living room. From the chair in the corner, I grabbed my undershirt and my faded blue T-shirt.

"Breakfast is gonna have to wait," I told him as I brushed my hair. "Can't afford to miss the bus."

Woulda been nice keeping Sherri's Mustang, but I could only take it at night when I knew she was too drunk to notice it was missing. I got a hold of her car key one time when she dropped it next to the mailboxes, and I real quick had a copy made. That landlord bitch didn't have a clue. Her wrinkled lips were usually sucking hard on a bottle of Jack before the TV guy gave the morning weather report. But I couldn't take no chance no how grabbing the Mustang while she was sober. I'd maybe go to jail over a sweet Porsche Carrera or a Mazda RX7, but not over that rusty piece of metal.

I put my briefcase on the sofa bed, opened it, and shuffled through the hand-made graphs and newspapers Old Man Charlie had given me, knowing as how I sometimes liked to make a quick stop after work.

"It's a numbers game," Charlie had always said.

And I kept those papers in order, man, because I was one badass organized mother-fucker.

"See this?" I said to William, dangling the apartment key like the Queen of England's necklace. "It's called a *key.* I will be locking the door behind me.

Do not for any reason, so-help-you-God, open the door for anyone. You hear me?"

He swallowed the last of his cereal, slurped the rest of the milk out of the bowl, and then slammed the bowl on the table. "Ta-da!"

I took a deep breath to keep from exploding. If things were to work out the way I wanted, I couldn't go postal.

"Dude," I said. "Did you hear what I said about the door? Yes or no?"

A small marshmallow moon stuck to William's chin.

"Yes or no?" I repeated.

"Yes," he said, wiping his chin with the back of his hand, the little marshmallow falling somewhere under the table. "When will you be back, Donald?"

"Tell me what I told you to do."

He looked up at the ceiling. "Do not let anyone in no matter what, so-help-you-God." He grinned again.

I wanted to go over there and pop him a good one.

Maintain...maintain.

"Keep the door locked," I told him. "If anyone comes, like, say, the mailman with your *Lotsa Luck* check, he'll drop it through the slot in the door. See? This is called a mail slot. Just hold onto it till I get home. Then we'll deal with it together. You need somebody smart like me to handle your finances. You got that?"

"Got that."

I looked around, sort of afraid to leave him alone. There was a good chance he might break something. "What are you gonna do while I'm gone?"

He shrugged his shoulders like a total numbnut.

"Well," I said. "Since you're gonna be living here for free, eating my food, using my TP and electricity and water and shit, maybe you could clean up the place. It'd be sort of like a trade. Whatcha think?"

"I'm a good cleaner."

And he wasn't lying. I left for work, locking the door behind me, and when I got home at six o'clock, I couldn't believe my eyes. The place looked like a freakin' shrine. My *Playboy* and *Forum* mags all stacked up nice and neat on the end table. The stove, which I don't think had been cleaned since three tenants before me, looked like it belonged in the Sears appliance section. And don't ask me how he did it, but it even looked like the carpet had been vacuumed—and I didn't own a vacuum.

So, at first, other than his eating habits, it wasn't so bad having my idiot brother around. I was getting antsy about the check not coming yet, but there wasn't nothing I could do about the fucking postal service. I was making ends meet, and Woody was down with our trade agreement. I'd buy some groceries, he'd make dinner. I'd rent a movie, he'd clean up the dishes. I'd share my bathroom, he'd make sure the toilet was spit-shined. It was like living with a brainless male version of Mrs. Cleaver.

One morning, a couple of weeks after he moved in, I bought a newspaper so I could real quick check out the favorites. In Charlie's honor. The old guy had finally kicked it. His funeral was in a couple of hours, and even though I didn't love him or nothing, it was only right to pay my respects.

My brother looked at the funnies while I went through the sports section to see who was doing what in the wonderful world of ponies. As I passed by the "Around Town" section, a picture caught my eye.

"Hey," I said. "Check out who's in the paper."

The wedding photo hardly did Stephanie's body justice. She looked like she belonged in one of those old-school catalogs with her hair in a bun and a frilly collar up to her chin. But it was easy to imagine the fine gems she had hiding underneath.

I barely had a chance to read the caption when Woody grabbed the paper out of my hands.

He read out loud. "Mizz-Steph-a-nie-Car-ter-of-Tay-lors-v-v-ville—"

At the rate he was reading we'd be sitting there till the fucking Fourth of July.

I grabbed back the paper and continued: "…weds Mr. Gerald Simpson of Harrington in a small ceremony at the Harrington Country Club. Seventy-eight guests attended. The bride plans to become a veterinarian locally. Her new husband is a fireman with fire station #58 in Morton. The couple met while at the local university together when they took a class—"

"Stop it!" Woody stood up and pushed back his chair. "You d-d-don't need to r-r-read any m-m-more!"

I started laughing. My little brother really was a funny guy sometimes. "Why're you freaking out?" I put the newspaper on the table and stood up. "So, Stephanie married a fireman. Big effing deal. What? Did you think she'd wait around for you to get better? The poor girl could only hold out so long. Hasn't it been like fifteen years since the two of you—"

Woody's fist came at my shoulder faster than a World Series curveball. I tried to get out of the way, but there wasn't enough time. My spine landed against the refrigerator, knocking a box of cereal off the top and onto my head. I fell to my knees, grabbing my shoulder in agony, and spotted a hundred Lucky Charms on the linoleum. Tiny marshmallow hearts, moons, stars, and clovers scattered everywhere.

"What the fuck?" I said. "Are you crazy?"

"I'm not crazy!" my brother screamed. "You don't call me that again. I'm not a r-r-retard, and I'm not crazy!"

His shadow loomed over me. I tucked myself into a little ball. I wasn't afraid of him, I just didn't have any energy that morning, you know, with a funeral to go to and all.

I raised my good arm and held up my hand. "Okay, okay—you're not crazy!"

"And I'm not a retard."

"I never said you—"

"I'm not a retard!"

"Fine! You're not a retard! You're a walking encyclopedia!" My shoulder throbbed. Shit. I hoped they didn't ask me to help carry the damn coffin.

Woody snatched the newspaper from where it fell on the floor. Then he opened the apartment door and threw the paper into the hallway.

"And I'm not staying in this room anymore," he told me. "You don't have no hi-fi or no eight-track player. You don't have no CDs to play on the CD player I gave you that Mom gave me. I'm gonna find me a job. I'm gonna show Stephanie who's better than a stupid fireman...shake it shake it shake it, that's right..."

In the living room, he spun around in a circle and shook his hips. I swear to God, you could almost see a couple of backup singers behind him getting jiggy with it.

Then Woody stopped in the middle of the room. "I'm gonna shake my booty!" he shouted. "It's my booty and it's my life!"

He grabbed his silver disco jacket, slammed the door behind him, and left me on the kitchen floor. I picked up a yellow marshmallow moon, stuck it on my tongue, and counted to fifty as the pain in my shoulder turned into a dull throb and the moon dissolved in my mouth.

Chapter 17

I floated beside William through the downtown district. It had changed a lot since the eighth grade when we took a field trip to see *The Wizard of Oz* at Center City Park. No place to take a kid today. On every corner, women with their clothes barely hanging on to their skin approached William. All of them wore thick lipstick, some wore wigs, and most had dirty nails.

"Hey, Baby, wanna feel real good?"

"Come on, sugar, you look so uptight—let Mama take your worries away."

"See these lips? Only five dollars to let 'em make a new man out of you."

Addicts slept in doorways, sad faces and bony bodies hidden underneath their choice of camouflage: an old blanket, a Hefty bag, a newspaper. Others were more open about their desperation, getting in William's his face to ask for a handout, speaking like they'd memorized lines for a school play.

"I ran out of gas, can you spare some change…"

"My daughter is ill and I lost my job, just one dollar…"

"I haven't eaten in three days…"

It was obvious by the peeling skin, chapped lips, swollen fingers, and bloodshot eyes, these people lived right there on the sidewalks. Waiting in doorways, sleeping, peeing, trembling, waiting until some chump came by. A buck here, a pinch of heroin there. Whatever it took to help carry them through to the next minute.

William didn't have much money, only a thin stack of fives he'd saved in a shoebox from past birthdays. He'd shoved the bills into his wallet before leaving Mom's. Even if he had money to spare, he didn't pay attention to his scummy surroundings. He was on a mission and nothing would stop him. Not even the shit of the city.

Five blocks. Seven. Ten.

Where are you going?

No answer.

Except for that morning, after his fight with Donald, when his backup singers popped in for a moment, barely any music had played in his head since leaving Mom's.

And he only let in my voice in bits and pieces, like an AM radio station nearly out of range.

At City Park, bums slept on benches and sat in rows along the vandalized water fountain, and more beer cans than flowers lined the sidewalks. Cats meowed in alleys, some in heat, others crying for food, rattling through trash cans as we hurried by. We moved past empty buildings with "For Sale or Lease" or "We Quit!" written in magic marker on sun-bleached signs in the windows. I peeked into the dark spaces to see the empty shoe store chairs and cash registers and shirtless hangers like ghosts behind the soaped-up glass. Every once in a while, we'd pass a neon palm print with "Madame Extraordinaire" or "$25.00 Readings" posted next to it, the smell of pot and cigarette smoke floating through the open doors. Across the street, you could barely read the faded JC Penney sign at the top of the three-story building, the windows boarded up, the foundation beyond repair.

The sun hung overhead in a clear, blue sky, a warm and beautiful spring day, yet this was the dreariest place I'd ever seen.

Where are you going? I tried again.

William stopped and turned, staring over my head.

"There," he said, pointing.

Excited that he'd heard me, I followed his gaze toward the staircase heading down beneath the city. By the time I'd turned back to William, he'd already begun moving again.

The subway was just like the other parts of the city: filthy, scary, and ridden with slackers looking for a handout. But there was a different energy beneath the streets. Men in business suits ran to catch subway trains like their lives were at stake. Women with babies or shopping bags moved more gracefully than the men, but just as fast, and kids skipping school hid beneath their hooded coats so security guards wouldn't spot them.

William stood in the center of the action, frozen. He read the signs above the tracks: NORTHWEST; NORTHEAST; UPTOWN; CENTRAL.

Now what?

I followed William to a black man in a uniform sitting behind doubled glass at the token booth.

"How many tokens?" the man asked.

"I want to get a job," William told the man.

"As a token collector?"

"No."

"Then what ya tellin' me your business for? How many tokens?"

William dug into his bellbottom pockets and pulled a five-dollar bill out of his wallet. He placed the bill in the metal scoop.

The man looked at the bill. "You need to tell me where you goin', so's I can sell you the right amount. You don't tell me where you goin', I can't sell you no tokens."

William looked up at the signs again. "North-west...no...Cen-tral... um...I mean..."

"Aw, come on, buddy. There's a line behind you."

Uptown, I said, trying to help him out.

"Uptown," William repeated.

The man took the five. "Uptown she is." He pushed a handful of tokens, two ones, and some coins into the scoop.

William didn't move.

The man said, "Just take your tokens and push 'em through them slots over there, next to that turnstile. Then push the bar to let you through. Go to track number two. It's right there. Train'll be here in about three minutes. Stand on this side of the red line. We don't want nobody fallin' onto them tracks. At least not on my shift." The man laughed and William laughed with him as he shoved his change into his pocket and held the tokens tightly in his fist.

As I followed William away from the booth, the token man said to the next person in line, "That fella's slower than ketchup!"

We pushed our way through the turnstile, stood at track number two, and waited for the subway train.

"Gotta get me a job," William said.

Why? When your money comes in, you'll be set. You can live with Mom and buy a horse or two. Shit, with all that dough, you could buy a couple of—

"Can't live with Mom no more. Gotta grow up. Gotta act my age."

A woman, standing a few feet away from William, grabbed her packages to her chest and moved to the other end of the crowd.

The tracks rumbled as the train came barreling through the tunnel and screeched to a halt in front of the platform. The doors opened and the crowd forced William and me into a car. The doors shut again. William held onto a dirty plastic loop which dangled from the ceiling as the train picked up speed.

For a moment he looked just like any other city man, making his way uptown to grab another day's wage.

Except, of course, for the polyester.

Uptown was way busier than where Donald lived. Stores were still open for business. McDonald's and Burger King had lines out the door. Two security guards stood in front of the Museum of Art, watching as people came and went through the big glass doors. The kiosks on the corners selling hot dogs, sausages, and bags of kettle corn were surrounded by dozens of people, most of them glancing at their watches. A wrinkly man sat on a stool in front of his newspaper stand selling papers, magazines, cigarettes, and candy. People walked dogs, strollers, mini grocery carts. Black and yellow taxi cabs honked their horns. Tourists with cameras posed for each other in front of the old theater. On one corner sat the Best Coffee House, across the street the Coffee

Clutch, two doors up Cafe Mocha's, and across from that the Uptown Beanery. You could smell coffee in the air three blocks before and two blocks after.

William kept walking.

You'll have to stop somewhere. You can't keep walking, hoping someone'll come up to you and say, Hey, wanna come work for me? I think you have to go inside and actually talk to someone.

William stepped inside a men's clothing store called the Gentleman's Gentleman. Before he was barely through the doorway, a salesman rushed up to him.

"Good afternoon, sir. Is there something special I can help you with today?"

"I need a job."

The salesman, whose nametag said Robert, looked William up and down, his eyes taking in everything from the half unbuttoned shirt to the white pleather shoes.

"A job? Selling clothes?"

"A job doing anything. I'm real good with stuff. I can groom horses, I can clean stuff, paint stuff. I keep my room real neat, and I painted my bike last summer."

The man jerked his eyes around the store as though there were cameras hidden somewhere, maybe behind the eyes of a mannequin or in one of the sprinklers on the ceiling.

"Navy blue," William said.

"What?"

"My bike."

"Oh." Robert looked around again, but the only other person in the store was another salesman at the register ringing up a pair of socks for an older man.

"Well," the salesman said, "as you can see, we aren't too busy right now. I don't think we'll be hiring until…next year sometime. Maybe you could come back then." He smiled a perfect smile that looked way too much like Mr. Lotsa Luck's.

"Okay," William said.

We left the Gentleman's Gentleman.

The next four stores on the block gave us the same hype.

We continued up the street and across town.

I don't think this is going to work. Why don't you go back home and talk Mom into getting you a job at a local farm, taking care of horses or something—

William stopped dead in the middle of a busy intersection. "That's it!" he shouted, snapping his fingers as best he could. A long line of elementary school students following their teachers gave William a curious look as they marched past.

In the middle of the street we pivoted, heading back the way we'd come. Even after that cruel summer day at the pond, William's sense of direction was spot on. We inched through mobs of people to the newsstand. The wrinkly man still sat on a stool in the middle of the newspapers. The smell of fresh ink filled the air.

"I need a paper," William told him.

The man, who had no front teeth, sucked on a toothpick. He pulled it out to speak, holding it in between his thumb and forefinger, twirling it around as he spoke. "What kind ya lookin' to read?"

"The kind that'll help me find a job." William let his eyes wander over the papers in the piles before him.

"Well, you could get the *Gazette*. That's got lotsa jobs in it, listed in them classifieds."

William stared blankly at the man.

"It comes in the center of the paper," the man said. "Here, I'll show ya."

The man pulled a ratty paper from under the plywood counter and opened it to the center. He pulled out a section, pointed to the word "Classifieds" and said, "This is what you want. It begins with the A's, and runs all the way to the Z's. But I don't think I've ever seen no Z jobs in there before. And I've gone through this thing every day for twenty-three years. Even them X's get a chance, what with x-ray technician being a job and all."

"How much does it cost?" William asked, pulling out his change.

"How 'bout ya just take this one? I won't even ask ya to pay. I've read today's ads already, so I don't mind if ya take it. I already got me a job, but it don't hurt nothing to keep my options open." He handed the paper to William, carefully folding it over. "Carry it under the arm like so, and ya won't even know it's there."

"Thanks," William said.

"Good luck. It's a dog-eat-dog world out there."

"I wanna work with horses, not dogs."

William turned and headed back toward the subway, the newspaper tucked under his arm like the man showed him.

And, once more, I followed.

Chapter 18

Everyone at the middle school knew somethin' was off. While I was servin' up pizza and corn nibblets one afternoon, a fifth-grader told me I looked like one of his bug-eyed fish he'd found floatin' on top of the tank that mornin'.

My son left me twice: once as a child and again as an adult.

When you raise a child to thirty and get used to him always bein' there, either dancin' in his room, settin' in front of the television, or headin' up to his tree house that reminded him of better days, there's no way around bein' lonely once he's gone. It was all I could do not to call the police and have them drag him back home. But that wasn't possible. He wasn't no ward of the state. And I had no rights, even though I was the only one who could take care of him proper.

On top of everythin' else, Stephanie got married. Sent me an invitation to the weddin'. I sent back the card sayin' I couldn't make it. Didn't see how it would be possible to sit in that chapel and not feel torn between being happy for her and sad for William. After their honeymoon—seven days in the Bahamas—Stephanie came by to introduce me to Gerald formal-like. Nice man. A bit older than her, some gray in his sideburns and thick ruddy hands, but who was I to judge? Anyhow, you could tell by the way he looked at her, sayin' nice things to her, listenin' to her when she talked, they were a good match.

Stephanie and Gerald and me sat in the kitchen drinkin' coffee and eatin' cookies, and they told me all about their plans: she'd finish up her trainin' at a nearby vet clinic, and he'd keep on fightin' fires the next town over. Them two had their whole lives laid out like a map of the world.

I asked if they were gonna have babies right away and they both blushed, sayin' as how they were goin' about it the ol' fashioned way, with nature takin' its course. As if it was any of my business. I just nodded out of respect.

They left a little while later after huggin' me like we was family and all, and I sat at the kitchen table alone for two hours, till the sun disappeared behind the house and I couldn't hardly see the cuckoo clock tellin' me it was way past suppertime. I cried in the dark like I was in mournin', cuz it shoulda been William sayin' the "I-do's" and kissin' Stephanie in a church before Jesus. It shoulda been William becomin' a fireman or whatever he wanted. It shoulda been William talkin' to me about havin' or not havin' kids, about me someday becomin' a grandma. *Grandma Francine*—always thought that had a nice ring to it. Shoulda been my son who came back to me that day at the pond instead of gettin' caught in that net; instead of comin' back to me as a child I never knew, one I could hardly tell used to be my Billy.

And him insistin' that everyone call him William. I think that was on account of the fact that deep down inside, in a place he could barely reach, he knew he wasn't no longer the same person.

I sat in my dark kitchen and thought about all them fine days when we were a regular family. Birthday parties in the backyard, limbo contests at Felton's Roller Rink, and bowlin' down at Knock'em Dead Lanes. Shoppin' at the JC Penney for school clothes, Dad goin' into the dressin' room with Donald, me goin' in with Billy, tryin' to get him to stop his fussin' whenever I tightened the belt to get those Levis to stay up around his waist. Such a skinny child. So much smaller than other boys in his grade. But he sure could run fast. Beat Donald and Lance in every race they ever had, and whoever else wanted to challenge him. Ran as fast as them boys over at the high school when he was only in the eighth grade. I'd heard through the grapevine that the high school coach was already keepin' his eye set on Billy Baker as a shoe-in for the track team. But Billy never did brag about it. Always kept a modest head on his shoulders.

When William was a boy, he was good at so many things. He climbed trees as quick as a lizard. Pitched the fastest ball at the Rec Center. And he used to read books just for fun. When he was twelve or so, I climbed up to the tree house to make sure them two-by-fours were still strong enough to hold my growin' boys, and there, settin' in the corner, part covered by one of my afghans, was a stack of *Hardy Boys* and *Nancy Drew* books I'd bought at a garage sale years before. I honestly thought them books had disappeared somewheres in the attic with so many other things the boys had tired of. I knew Donald wasn't readin' 'em, he was too proud to read anythin' like a schoolbook, 'specially in the summer.

One day, while hangin' out the sheets on the line to make 'em smell like sunshine, I overheard Billy's voice up in that tree house, readin' out loud. Later, when I called him down for lunch, who climbs down that ladder after him but Stephanie. He'd been readin' to her! I think that's one of the reasons she was so smitten: Billy was smart and didn't mind sharin' it with people.

And Lordy, could he dance. How could so many dance moves come out of one person? I offered to sign him up for the Rec Center's jazz and tap classes, but when Donald and his friends got wind of it, they never let the poor child hear the end of it. That's when dancin' became a private thing for Billy. I could hear him practicin' in his room when Donald was out with his gang of ruffians, and he'd turn off the music as soon as his brother or his Daddy came in the back door. He didn't want them thinkin' he was a sissy.

But his daddy knew Billy wasn't no sissy. That child loved all the things boys love: horse-back ridin', rock-climbin', hikin', swimmin', tumblin', gettin' all scratched up and dirty, and mischief-makin' in general.

And did he ever love fishin'. Their daddy would drag my two boys out of bed at three-thirty in the mornin' some Saturdays in the summer, and they'd cry like babies, complainin' they were too tired. That is, until I fed them pancakes with real blueberries and whippin' cream on top, and they'd come back proud later that evening, their coolers filled with catch, smellin' to high heaven like worms and dead fish. I hated that smell then, but now I know it was the sweetest smell in the whole world.

What I wouldn't give to have that smell around me now. Even if it was just dead fish.

Chapter 19

All you had to say was that one word—*pony*—and I'd get a shiver down my neck as electric as feeling a girl's titty.

My very first bet at the track won me six grand on a horse named Bo-Bo Clearing. Quarter horse, way too young, odds stacked against her big-time. Got a little inside help from Old Man Charlie, who taught me the ins and outs of horseracing. He smelled something terrible and his teeth were the same color as the lunch bag he carried his cheap bourbon in. But he was pretty tight, that Charlie. Rolled his own cigarettes and could turn a good trick if you let him. He'd fire one up, stick it all the way in his mouth, twirl it around in there for a sec, bring it back out with his teeth, and that stogie would still be lit. Thought for sure lung cancer would get him, but instead he keeled over from a heart attack in the lobby of the hotel where he lived.

It's all a numbers game.

Anyhow, Charlie knew the ropes. Me and him worked together cleaning the church on Seventh Street, the one with the nineteenth-century bell still hanging in the tower. They don't use the bell now, since they got a computerized one, preset to ring at certain times throughout the day through a speaker. But the old bell's still up there, I guess for decoration.

Me and Charlie cleaned that church just fine. Mopping up the basement that smelled like dirty diapers from the daycare they had down there; polishing the rails around the altar, using that expensive lemon polish to shine up the pews. Eighty rows of 'em. That's some major ball-busting work. But me and Charlie, we made a good team.

Old Man Charlie knew the ponies like he was a horse himself. Said he'd bought a four-bedroom house in the suburbs from his first-year's winnings. That was back in the good years, he said. Back before he got careless with his bets.

A few weeks before he died, just after quitting time, we sat in the last pew. Charlie pulled out his wallet. "This here's a photo of my Belinda."

She was as old as Charlie and a total fugly, but I smiled like she was a hottie. You don't want to offend no one.

"She's gone now," Charlie told me. "Got the cancer real bad. Probably from my cigarette smoke. It landed in her bones. She was in so much pain, but I couldn't afford no hospital or nothing. I thanked God the day he finally took her."

When it's someone's grandpa who dies, you get over it pretty quick. Sometimes I even ask how they died. But when it's a woman or a kid or something, I always mumble, "Sorry," under my breath, cuz I can't think of nothing else to say.

Charlie whispered, "Only cheated on her once in all our years together, God forgive me." He looked up at the large cross hanging in the shadows behind the altar. "And do you know what? I think she knew. But she never said a word. That's the kind of classy woman Belinda was. Couldn't give me no kids though. We always aimed to have a son, but that dream wasn't to be ours."

He looked at me when he said this, and I knew he was thinking he wished he could have been *my* dad. I thought, better to have Old Man Charlie than a man who didn't have the freakin' balls to stay with the family he was given.

Charlie and me, we worked together for about a year before his ticker froze. Spent every weekend at the track drinking, betting, winning some, losing a little. Not a dime to his name when he died. The church took up a collection and buried him as a freebie. Even had some of the church members help carry the coffin to the gravesite, thank God for small favors.

Besides the pallbearers, there was only the minister, me, and a greasy-haired three-hundred-pound circus act in an Armani suit. The fat dude didn't look anywhere but down at that coffin. Gave him three chins with his head bowed like that. He didn't look sad, but he didn't look happy neither. I guess you could say he didn't look like he was feeling nothing either way.

When the short funeral was over and most of the people had left, I whispered into the hole, "Peace out, my man." Then I headed across the lawn and back to the church. I still had a few hours on the clock, and until they hired someone to take Charlie's place, I had a lot of polishing and mopping to do on my own.

A voice shouted, "Hey you, kid!"

I said to myself, *Who the hell thinks I'm a kid?*

It was the fat guy.

"Yeah?" I said over my shoulder without stopping. Four hundred pairs of finger smudges waited for me in the church.

"Stop a sec, will ya, kid?"

I stopped between the weeping willow and the church steps.

"I'm not a marathon runner," the fat man said, stopping to catch his breath.

No shit, I thought.

"Your name Donald, that right?" he asked.

"Depends on whether or not that'll win me a prize."

"Sarcastic. I like that. Just like your old man."

I paused, wondering. "You know my dad?"

"Up until he died."

"My dad—" but I stopped myself fast. He wasn't talking about my *real* dad, he was talking about Charlie. Had Charlie told him I was his kid? I had to watch what I said. Charlie lied almost as much as me. And even though he would never hurt a flea, he didn't have a lot of friends. When the ponies are involved, your only true homey is your bookie. And sometimes your accountant, depending.

"Sorry about your old man," the fat guy went on. "A whole lot of people gonna miss that guy."

Then a whole lot of people must not have known about the funeral today, I thought but didn't dare say out loud.

"Yeah," I said, still not letting on that I wasn't no relation to Charlie, trying to feel out the situation. "He was a good man. Heart of gold."

The man in the Armani suit reached out his sweaty hand. "I'm Roland Polcheki," he said, shaking my hand. "Some people call me Roly-Poly." He saw my smile. "Punk in the eighth grade gave me the nickname and it stuck. You know, like dog shit on your shoe."

Charlie had never mentioned no one named Roly-Poly. That's not exactly the sort of name you're likely to forget. I had to act chill. Needed to tiptoe around this butterball like a ballerina on feathers.

"Oh, *Roly-Poly*," I said, not wanting him to think I was stupid. "Now I remember."

"Charlie told you about me?"

"Oh, sure. Pop didn't keep nothing from me. He was as open as a—"

Thunder cracked in the distance as gray clouds suddenly moved in. A raindrop fell onto Roly-Poly's nose. He wiped the wet from his face with a fat finger.

"No secrets, huh?" he said.

I wasn't sure if he was asking a real question, so I didn't answer.

Roly-Poly eyeballed me. "You don't look anything like him," he said.

"Adopted." Lying had always come easy for me. An inborn talent. Stories slid off my tongue like kids heading down a sliding board on soapy water. "He and my mother, Belinda, God rest her soul, couldn't have none of their own. Took me and my brother in when we were teenagers. Saved us from the streets."

"That's nice. Your old man ever tell you about the favor good ol' Roly-Poly did for him a little while back?"

"Can't remember. Ol' Pop said a lot of things." I liked this game. Pretending I had a dad who gave a rat's ass.

"Charlie asked me to help him with a—project," Fatso said. "On the condition that he would pay me back. Get what I'm saying?"

"Not really."

"Your old man is dead. But the favor he owes me—please forgive my crudeness—didn't get buried with him."

The cold drizzle turned into real rain. Goose bumps rose on my arms underneath my faded cotton shirt.

"I don't understand," I said.

"I did something for Charlie that took months of research and time. With the promise that I'd be paid back. Now, how we gonna do that without your daddy being here? Maybe bring out a *Ouija* board? Have ourselves a little *séance?*"

"What kind of favor?"

"Why don't we go someplace dry. And private."

Roly-Poly wobbled toward the church stairs. He gripped onto the railing to support his weight as he lugged himself onto the first step.

"Tell me what the favor is," I said, following behind him.

He leaned on the railing and turned around, the rain flattening his thin black hair, his red cheeks bulging like he'd been blowing up balloons. "Something only you and me and God can know about."

We sat in the middle of the empty church. Stained glass windows of baby Jesus and the Virgin Mary stared down at us. Reverend Miller was doing paperwork next door at his house, and after polishing I was to snuff out the candles and turn out the lights before locking up. In the old days, we could leave the doors open cuz nobody would have dreamed of robbing a church, afraid of going to Hell and all. Then again, back in the old days, two grown men wouldn't have the balls to sit in a church and discuss things like murder.

We kept our voices low, as if by whispering, the baby Jesus wouldn't be able to hear us.

"I can't do that," I said after he told me what he wanted. I played with my ruby earring, a habit I had when I was nervous.

"*Can't* is not a word I'm used to hearing," Roly-Poly said. He took off his jacket and put it over his lap, one hand underneath, the other on top.

"I was trippin'," I said. "Charlie didn't actually adopt me. He was *like* a dad to me. I thought that's what you meant…"

"Is that right? You sure seem to know a whole lot about a man who wasn't your father. Awful nice of you to come to his funeral."

"But we don't even have the same last name—"

"If you're telling me you lied, well, I like liars even less than the word *can't*. You understand what I'm saying, kid?"

I could run. Jump over the pews and up the aisle and out the church doors. I'd be halfway across town by the time Roly-Poly could get off his fat ass.

But something told me I might not make it past the donation box if this fatso decided to pull his hand out from under his coat and happened to have one chunky finger resting on the trigger of a gun. Not a pretty sight, getting shot in the back and dying slow in one of the pews. Might not be found for a week.

I tried to reason with him.

"How am I supposed to kill someone in front of all those people? You ever see the racetrack crowd? You can't even move most of the time. You ever see pin day? Anyone who places a minimum twenty-dollar bet gets a pin. That's a big deal to a lot of people."

Roly-Poly said nothing.

"Pin day's popular," I rambled on. "I've never skipped one. I've collected over forty. I keep 'em in a box." I rubbed my shoulder. Three Ibuprofen and the damn thing still hurt. Last time I help carry a coffin, I can tell you that.

Roly-Poly said, "I will let you show me your collection. *After* you do what I ask."

"But—"

"Your old man got the kind of help from me that even I had a hard time managing." Roly's voice grew softer, kinder. "Your mother. Remember how sick she was?"

I remembered the fuzzy old lady photo of Belinda that Charlie had shown me.

"Look, kid. I'm gonna lay it to you plain. Charlie needed my help taking care of a little business. I have a friend who plays golf with the coroner. We got Charlie hooked up real good. Your mother had the kind of pain I don't wish on my worst enemy. Truly. And Charlie wanted her to be at rest. That's where I came in. You understand?"

"You helped her…"

"From being in pain."

"Did she know?"

"What does it matter? She's in a better place. And now she has your pop to keep her company. Things couldn't have turned out better for the two of them. Except for one thing."

"The favor."

"You're a smart kid."

"And now you want me to kill someone." In my younger days I could take on anyone anytime. Beat up kids on the playground every other day. But this wasn't no playground, and if it had been, Roly-Poly would have been king of the whole mother-fucking hill.

Then he said, "I never said you had to kill a *person*, did I?"

"Well, if I'm not killing a person, then—" And it hit me, right between the eyes. By the smile on Roly-Poly's face, he saw that it'd hit me. "You mean kill one of the—"

"Don't go jumping to any more conclusions, understand? Jumping to conclusions could get somebody killed." He grinned, showing me a half dozen or so silver fillings.

Racehorses had kept me going for years. If all of a sudden I was to kill one, wouldn't it be like killing off part of my livelihood? Part of my manhood?

"You can make a shitload of money, you know," Roly-Poly said.

"Money?"

"One pony dies, another wins. You place your bets accordingly and you'll be sitting pretty, eating caviar, drinking *Dom Perignon*, getting a little tang from the sweetest ho-bag you ever set your eyes on."

My eyes blurred as I pictured myself sitting in an Armani suit, eating expensive mixed nuts, sipping champagne—then she walks in. A fine hottie with legs to her neck, lips shaped like a heart, blond hair down to the hem of the miniskirt that barely covers her perfect ass. She slowly takes the champagne from my hand, drinks what's left, and throws the glass against the wall, making everyone else in the room leave. When we're alone, she loosens my tie, undoes the tight button at my throat, then inch by inch she travels down my body, her long red nails reaching for my zipper…

"Yes or no?"

I was back again, sitting in the pew next to the fat man. "Yo. What?"

"Jesus H. Christ. Yes or no?"

"Yes," I blurted. But what I really meant was *Maybe*. "Yes," I said again, to sound convincing.

"Good," Roly-Poly said, smiling like a crazy mother fucker. "Meet me at the track tomorrow morning so I can explain the details. The Dellshore's about to get their new employee of the month."

Chapter 20

Donald got home after midnight. I heard him belch as he worked his key in the lock and let himself into the apartment. He looked down the dimly lit hallway, closed and locked the door behind him, then dropped his briefcase to the floor.

William was crashed out on the sofa bed in his underwear, the room dark except for the television playing another rerun of the *Partridge Family*.

"Fuckin' *Nickelodeon*," Donald said, clicking off the television. He headed into the kitchen and turned on the overhead light. The dank smell of beer and whiskey followed after him.

William sat up, scratching his face. "Donald?"

"Yeah."

"What're you doing?"

I sat on the arm of the sofa bed, pushing my wet hair out of my eyes. Donald wasn't only drunk, he was in a hurry. He readjusted something in his wallet and pushed the billfold into his back pocket.

Something was up.

"Tell me your money came today," Donald said.

"Not yet." William got out of bed. In his underwear, he went into the kitchen and grabbed the newspaper from where it lay on a kitchen chair. "Got me a class-i-fied." He held it up. "I'm getting a job."

"What the hell you need a job for?"

William sat at the kitchen table. I stood close to him as he raked his fingers through his flattened hair. "You sound like Mom."

Donald suddenly shouted, "Why didn't your money come? What the hell's up with those people?"

He picked up the phone on the end table next to the couch. His fingers stumbled as they dialed 411. "Gimme the *Lotsa Luck* people." With the cord stretched between the two small rooms, Donald sat across from William at the kitchen table and spoke under his breath. "Twenty-four-hour hotline."

Donald pressed a number on the key pad. "Yes," he said into the phone. To William, he said, "What was your number on the show?"

William put both feet flat on the floor and both hands flat on the table. He closed his eyes and smiled. "Number 7-9-2."

"7-9-2," Donald repeated to the prompt. "William Bernard Baker." He whispered, "What's your social security number?"

William rushed to his suitcase in the closet, pulled out a small folder from the front flap, and read the nine digits out loud.

Donald repeated the numbers slowly, his words still slurred from whatever it was he'd been drinking. After a moment, he hung up. "Your check's been processed. That means it'll be here soon. Sweet."

William nodded from where he knelt over his suitcase and carefully put his social security card away.

"I gotta go somewhere," Donald said. "You chill out and stay in the apartment till I get back."

"I don't wanna stay here," William said. "It's boring."

"Well, you gotta guard the place. At least until the check comes. Can you be on guard duty?"

William jumped up, excited. "Is that a kind of job?"

"Sure it is. A real job for you."

"Okay."

"When that check gets here, you find a hiding place for it, and when I get back, we'll go to the bank."

"Where you goin'?"

Donald didn't answer as he headed into the bathroom. I floated toward the doorway, watching him as he collected his razor, deodorant, toothpaste, and toothbrush. Back in the living room, he shoved everything into a ratty backpack. Next, he pulled clothes out of the only dresser, cramming underwear, socks, T-shirts, and a pair of faded jeans into the bag.

He told William, "If a big fat dude comes by looking for me, tell 'em you don't know where I am. Tell 'em you haven't seen me in over a week. You down with that? Just play dumb. That should be easy for you."

"But that's lying."

"Shut the fuck up and go back to bed. And stop keeping the TV on all night. I'm not paying a double bill so you can get off watching Marcia Brady play with her brothers." He stopped before opening the door. "Don't leave the apartment, got it? You might miss the mailman. And we wouldn't want anything to happen to your check, would we?"

William said, "No."

"Word." Donald flung the backpack over his shoulder. As he closed the door behind him, he added, "Later, gator."

Chapter 21

William's breath deposited little puffs of steam onto the glass. I stood beside him and tried to breathe my own vapor onto the window next to his, but nothing appeared. Together, we gazed down into the morning street. A cat ran along the gutter and disappeared into a side alley. Trash blew in funnel clouds over the steel grates.

You've been sitting on that kitchen chair for two days. Stop staring out the window. Get out of here. Call Lance. Maybe he'll take you to a movie or something. You have the right to leave.

God, I hated how he ignored me. I had a mind to leave him, I swear I did. But I couldn't. As long as he needed me, even if I was the only one who knew he did, I was destined to stay.

An aggressive knock against the apartment door made me jump.

William stood up. "Who is it?"

A deep voice came from the hallway: "Mailman."

William ran to the door and pressed his forehead against it like he was trying to see through the wood. He said nothing. His shoulders traveled up and down with his nervous breathing.

"Hello?" the voice in the hall tried again. "Got a certified letter here for a—William Bernard Baker."

"I'm William."

"Gotta have a signature."

"I can't open the door."

"What?"

"I can't open the door."

"You contagious or something?"

"My brother said so."

After a pause, the man's voice said, "I'll put the slip through the mail slot, you sign it, then give it back so I can get on with my route."

"Okay."

A small yellow piece of paper dropped onto the floor. William picked it up, ran to the kitchen for a pen, then back to the door.

"Where do I sign it?"

"On the line at the bottom, where it says *sig-na-ture.*"

William placed the form against the door and signed it, careful to triple hump his *m* and loop his *l's*. He sent it back through the door slot.

After a moment, an envelope fell into William's hands. He carried it to the kitchen window. He tilted his head toward the morning clouds.

It's our prize, I told him, leaning against the counter.

He sat down and placed the envelope on his thigh. He caressed the rectangular cellophane window where Donald's apartment address was neatly typed.

What are you waiting for?

William looked down at the envelope. He turned it over.

Open it.

I moved behind him, peering over his shoulder as he carefully opened the envelope and looked inside. We stared at the number on the check: $697,432.04. I couldn't tell if he comprehended how much money it really was. But I did.

To help him get the gist, I said, *You could buy an entire team of horses with that kind of dough.*

William lowered the check to his lap and lifted his face toward the window again. The morning clouds were burning off and the sun was shining.

Whether he was speaking to me directly I wasn't sure, but I hoped he was when he smiled and said in a hopeful voice, "Horses."

Chapter 22

Being friends with William had drained me over the years. Not on account of he was forgetful or had lost so much of who he was before the accident—none of that mattered much to me. It was draining on account of I felt so damn sorry for him. And I was tired of feeling sorry for him, you know?

It was the three of us from the beginning: me, him, and Stephanie. From first grade on. Not too many people can say that.

Even if Steph and I had reminded William of the truth of that day, it wouldn't have mattered. William didn't remember any of it.

I can tell you this: I would *never* forget. Not that day, not any of the days following.

While he was in the coma, his lips sometimes moved like he was trying to say something. His fingers would even grab at the blanket. The nurses and doctors said they were neurological twitches. But I knew better. I also knew he could hear me, on account of that first week in the hospital I brung in my portable eight-track player with some Led Zeppelin, and his forehead crinkled up, sort of irritated. But the second I put in an Earth, Wind & Fire track, his toes started wiggling. I could see them vibrating under the covers, all happy, moving around like he was on a dance floor. So I never stopped believing he'd wake up. I knew it the same way I knew I'd marry my wife the second I laid eyes on her. Knew I'd love my babies even before they were born.

What I didn't know was how much William would behave like a newborn when he came out of the coma. How he wouldn't be able to walk or talk for six months. Or feed himself, or drink by himself. Had to wear a diaper and get changed and bathed by the nurses. And he cried all the time. Just like a baby.

He did get better, in time. He learned to walk and talk again, and even dance. In some ways, William hadn't changed at all. He never left that day at the pond, even though he refused to remember it. In his mind, he was still fourteen. Still talked about horses like he owned one. Still loved Stephanie. Acted like we were still the Three Musketeers. Like he still believed in fairy tales.

But life goes on. I got married, had two little ones, worked hard to move up the ladder at work. And Steph, well, she moved on as well. No one would have expected her to not to.

Sometimes I felt the need to leave William. To make him understand by leaving that he had to move on as well. But then guilt would eat me up, and I knew I would stay in this town forever, raise my kids down the street from where I grew up, not too far from William's house, in case I was ever needed. After all, they needed me that day at the pond, but there wasn't a damn thing I could do. Even though I wished there was.

In some weird way that even I didn't quite understand, I sort of owed him one,

didn't I?

It's important for outsiders to know that William never became a ward of the state. He almost did when William's dad first left and Mrs. B couldn't take care of him by herself. But when they made her manager at that cafeteria, and she got a raise, she decided to do it all herself. She took him to speech people, psychologists, psychiatrists, and some kind of motor skills center. Helped him relearn stuff when she wasn't at work. Spent every spare second getting William back on track, so she could get the stares of the neighbors off her breaking back.

"Poor Mrs. Baker. First her son nearly drowns, then her husband leaves."

They didn't have to say those words out loud for her to know what they were thinking. And Mrs. B wouldn't stand for anyone pitying her *or* William. She was all right, that Mrs. B.

"William Bernard Baker is, by law, independent," the state told us when William decided to move in with Donald. "No one has the right to tell him what to do. He is his *own person*."

If he was his own person, then why was he cooped up in that shithole with only TV dinners and cereal to eat? I'll tell you why. Because his older brother, Donald, was just like their old man: weak, angry, and felt the world owed him one. As far as I was concerned, the only thing owed to Donald *and* their daddy was the steel toe of my work boot in their behinds.

Donald's an asshole. Told William he wasn't *allowed* to go out. Wasn't *allowed* to open the door. Not *allowed* to talk to anyone.

I got off work early and took William to Southern States Bank & Trust to take care of some paperwork. The gal there was super helpful. After that, it was time to celebrate. William deserved to have some fun, even if it was only for a little while, and even if I couldn't tell my wife about it.

Some things are better left unsaid.

Chapter 23

They came into the club around nine o'clock. William headed to the men's room, and his buddy, the one with the ponytail, sat down at a table in front of the stage. I was actually serving drinks for an hour or so, since one of our waitresses didn't show, and the floor was packed. Wednesday night was Skirt Night. Half-priced well drinks and one dollar beers, even though there weren't any ladies in the room. Every once in a while you'd get some dikes, or maybe a kinky couple, but not too often.

The guy with the ponytail said his name was Lance and told me to pay a little extra attention to his friend, William.

"There something wrong with him?" I asked.

Lance touched my wrist and pulled me close. He smelled like peppermint aftershave.

"He's just a little depressed," he told me in confidence. "The girl he's been in love with since he was a kid got married. He deserves some attention. He's never been—you know—*close* to a woman before. You know anyone who'd be willing to help out? Someone who could remind him that he's a man? Maybe *after* work hours?"

Lance handed me a crisp one-hundred-dollar bill. I've never been the type of girl to let down a person in need. Being obliging is part of my personality.

I nodded and headed to the bar for the next round of tequila, which I was happy to partake in drinking a couple of.

Lance and William sat at the table a couple of hours, downing shots, laughing, pointing to and whispering about certain girls on the stage. When Belle, the only Asian dancer, told the deejay to play some Bee Gees, William pushed his chair back, stood up, stuck his chest out like the pigeons that strut on the ledge outside my condo window, and started shaking it. His ass rocked from side to side, his arms taking turns pointing up and down, his pelvis moving like he was on that prehistoric *American Bandstand* show my mama watched when she was a teenager. The whole room started clapping for William, which did not go over well with Bitchy Belle. She made the deejay stop the music and shouted for him to play a slow song by Madonna, who I personally cannot stand. While the deejay was digging out the other record, William danced a little longer, like he thought the Bee Gees were still singing, and then he realized the music stopped, so he stopped too. He sat again and downed another shot of tequila, making his friend laugh.

They were a happy duo.

But here's what was interesting: the next dancer moved onto the stage. The lights came up, and there stood Maryanne. Maryanne should have been a man. She had everything going for her but a dick. Short GI Jane hair, more earrings than skin showing on her face, and quads and deltoids that looked like she pitched hay in somebody's back forty. Well, when William whistled at Maryanne, a pit opened up in my stomach, and an itty bitty seed of jealousy began to sprout. I don't have a clue where it came from or why, only that it was growing in there.

I traded spots with the next dancer, Helena, to get my ass up on stage as soon as I could, sure to dance extra special for my two boys in the front.

And I planned to give a little something extra to William once my shift was over.

Chapter 24

"You got a key?" a girl whispered outside the door.

"Lance made one for me," William said. "My very own."

They laughed and fumbled about for a minute, trying to get the key in the hole, dropping it, picking it up, starting over.

The door finally opened.

"Fuckin'-A," the girl said as she stepped into the living room. She had wild red hair and wore a black mini skirt with a slinky top and a pair of the highest high heels I'd ever seen.

It's after two. What's up with the chick?

The girl began to giggle. William giggled with her.

"This is my brother's apartment," William told her, shutting the door behind him. "Everything's spinning."

The girl stumbled across the room and fell onto the folded sofa bed.

William opened his arms wide. "This is my brother's apartment."

"You said that already."

I hovered behind the girl and leaned over the sofa. She was pretty, in a Metallica groupie sort of way. I watched the goose bumps cover the flesh on her freckled arms. A tiny mermaid tattoo lay on the inside of her left arm, above the wrist.

"Damn," she said, taking the tan jacket she had on her lap and putting it on. "It's freezing in here. You got a window open or something?"

William went to the living room window and looked at it carefully.

"Window's closed," he said, his words slurred.

The redhead stood up, shifting her weight from one foot to the other. "Where's the toilet? For real, I gotta tinkle-winkle something fierce."

William pointed.

The girl disappeared into the bathroom. She spoke from behind the half-closed door.

"I'm sure you're wondering why they call me Cecilia. It's because I want to visit Sicily so flippin' bad, I can hardly stand it. I'm saving money for it now. I've always felt like I belong there. One time, at the club, I met a guy from Italy, and he said I would fit in there perfectly, that I could pass for Northern Italian. Even with my hair. Isn't that wild? Did you know they have a volcano in Sicily? Mount Etna…"

Why the hell did you bring her here? Do you know what Donald will do if he comes home and finds her in his apartment?

It was getting hard to tell if William's snubbing was deliberate or not. I had followed him out the door earlier in the evening, but as soon as they stepped into the strip club, I found myself back at the apartment. Sometimes that happened when he was being especially stubborn.

If you'd let me come with you tonight, I would've stopped you from doing something so stupid. But no. You have to do things on your own. Always trying to prove you don't need me. Well, I have news for you, Master William. You do need me. You may not need me forever, but you do right now. You'd be nothing without me. Do you understand? Nothing!

"Nothing," William said, as the girl came out of the bathroom.

"What?"

"Nothing."

Cecilia looked around the tiny apartment. "You got any wine? Or maybe some vodka?"

William went to the fridge and opened it. "Nope."

"Any bottled water? Drinking city crap'll give you brain cancer."

"Got orange juice."

"Okay." She sat on the sofa again, kicked off her high heels, leaned back her head, and stared up at the water-stained ceiling. She twirled the end of a long red curl. "If this is your brother's place, how come he isn't here?"

William carefully poured the juice, set the container on the kitchen table, and brought the glass into the living room. He handed it to Cecilia.

"He's mad at me," William told her.

"What for?"

There's the question of the hour. He's been mad at you since the day you were born, for God's sake. Since the day he found out he'd have to share Mom and Dad.

"Just mad, is all," William said. "He's a businessman."

"What's he do?"

"Goes to business meetings."

"Oh." Cecilia patted the sofa cushion and waited as William sat beside her. "Let's talk about you, sweetie. Your friend Lance says you're a nice guy. That true?"

I moved next to the arm of the couch. A mixture of sweet perfume and stale smoke swirled around me.

"I'm nice," said William.

Cecilia drank the rest of her juice and set the glass on the end table. She tucked her bare feet under her bottom and leaned forward, exposing a deep cleavage. "I'll bet you are." She caressed his arm. "You sure do like soft shirts. Sort of silky, huh? You like silky?"

William shrugged and leaned over to grab the remote control from the floor next to the couch. He pressed the red button.

The girl looked from the television to William. Her hand left his arm and flopped by her side.

William changed a few channels, finally landing on a cable network that showed reruns of old TV shows.

"What's this?" Cecilia asked.

"The *Dick Van Dyke Show*."

"It's in black and white."

William didn't say anything.

"Who watches shows in black and white?"

William smiled as sitcom husband, Robert Petrie, shouted something funny to his sitcom wife, Laura.

Cecilia spoke over the canned laughter. "Your friend tells me that you're kinda special."

William turned to the stripper.

She went on. "That you're kinda…slow. That true?"

William didn't answer.

"He asked me to take care of you tonight, William. Ever had a woman take care of you before?"

"My mom does."

Did, I reminded him.

"That's not exactly what I mean," Cecilia said. She carefully tried to pry the remote from William's hand, but his fingers held onto it like a baby bottle. "You ever…had a girl make you…feel good before?"

"One time me and Stephanie kissed for a whole minute. Lance timed us."

"Hmm."

"She got married," William told her. "To a fireman."

"That's too bad." Cecilia placed one long leg over his thighs. "You ever, you know, touch her? Like this?"

Cecilia took William's hand and tucked it inside her blouse, then cupped his fingers around her breast.

William dropped the remote.

"N-n-n-no."

"Ever have a girl touch you before? Like this?" She placed her hand in between his legs and gave a squeeze.

"N-n-n-no!"

"Well, mercy, sweet William, maybe it's time you did."

Like a sleepy cat she moved to the floor and kneeled at William's feet, unbuckled his white belt, and tugged on the zipper of his pants.

On the television sitcom, Robert Petrie and Buddy and Sally were up to their antics in their downtown office. William and I both closed our eyes as the audience roared.

Chapter 25

It was still dark as I moved along the sidewalk with the windbreaker hood covering most of my face. I kept my hands tucked inside the thin pockets. Those freakin' pigeons were just starting to make their noise up on the window ledges and it wasn't even five AM. In through the building's front door I went like a regular I-Spy, checking the alley first, then under the staircase. I didn't have a gun, but I was good to go with an army knife, and all it would take was a jab in the throat to turn a dude into dust.

My brother usually slept like a baby, but I still wasn't taking no chances, not with a million dollar check waiting for me. I was as quiet as a dead mouse.

I put my key in the lock and pushed the apartment door open. There he was, asleep on the sofa bed, the television on with the volume down. Either he was watching those stupid seventies shows, or doing his fucking dances in the middle of my living room when one of the channels showed disco flashbacks. This was almost the new millennium, for Chrissake. Only a freak would choose the Bee Gees over Nirvana or Dr. Dre. Even the dumbest tools in the box were listening to grunge or rap.

In the blue light with his hair across his face, he looked like little Billy. And he was freakin' hilarious wearing a satin shirt with his tighty-whities, the sheet wrapped around his ankles, snoring like a lion.

But this was no time for laughing. This was serious business. I needed to stay tight.

It only took me two seconds to spot it on the kitchen table on top of the pile of overdue bills. I opened the refrigerator door so I could see the outside of the envelope better: *Mr. William Bernard Baker.* I smiled. The name wouldn't be a problem. No problem at all. I took a quick peek inside the envelope and spotted the most beautiful number in the world: $697,432.04.

Out of nowhere, my bladder cramped. Sometimes it did that when I got excited. I'd take a quick pit stop and then get the hell out. As I started to shut the refrigerator door, I spotted something funny in the dim light. Through the kitchen doorway on the end table sat a dirty glass with dried up orange juice in the bottom. But that wasn't what was funny. I picked up the glass and held it up to the refrigerator light. A lipstick mark. On the rim. Ruby red. Plain as day.

Yo. What up with—

A banging noise out in the hallway. I shut the refrigerator door, knocking out all the light except from the television. I put the glass in the sink, folded the envelope in half, and shoved it into my back pocket.

My apartment sat in the middle of a long, narrow hallway, with four apartments on either side. It was sort of like living at the Holiday Inn, but without room service or elevators. Across from my door, a staircase led down four flights to the lobby. At each end of my hallway was an emergency door, but the alarm on both doors hadn't never worked since I lived in the place. It was hard to tell over Woody's snoring, but I convinced myself that someone had come through one of the emergency doors and was headed up the hallway, looking for the number on my apartment door.

If Roly-Poly knew where I worked, then he sure as hell knew where I lived. My backpack sat in a locker at the bus station. I'd have chosen the church pews over those hard benches for sleeping, but I didn't have no choice. My job at the church had to be sacrificed. No job, no paycheck.

But who gave a shit about a measly paycheck, I thought to myself as I patted my back pocket.

The second I stepped back into the living room, I realized the fucked-up mistake I'd made. The front door. Open a foot. My keys still dangling from the outside lock. Did I have time to go back and grab them? What if whoever was in the hall caught me taking my keys and introduced a fist to my face or a knife to my gut?

Wait, wait. Just chill a sec. Enough shit had happened lately to make anyone paranoid. I thought an old lady on the bus was following me earlier that day, because I ran into her again downtown when I paid a visit to my connection on Tenth. There she was, sitting on the bus stop bench, reading a lady's magazine, a wrinkly thing that looked like she belonged in someone's kitchen baking cookies. She never even looked up at me.

Paranoia sure is a creepy thing. Especially when it's yours.

But deep down I knew this wasn't paranoia. Someone was out there in the hall; I could sense it the same way I could sense that my landlord, Sherri, had the hots for me, even though she acted like she hated my guts.

Number one problem: there was nowhere to hide in this shoebox. No normal bed to crawl under, a closet barely big enough for Woody's two suitcases, a bathroom shower the size of a birdbath.

It would have to be a window. The only two windows were the large one in the living room over the window seat, and the one in the kitchen. The kitchen one had bars on the outside.

I ran to the living room window, unlocked the twist bolt, and freaked. The damn window had been painted over a million times. Nothing budged as I pushed with my hands. Tiny flakes of lead paint flew into my face. I lay down on the narrow window seat and stretched my right leg into the air. Then I kicked. The window gave a bit.

I heard the jingle of keys. I kicked again, this time harder. Who gave a shit if I broke the window? Send me a fuckin' bill. But I didn't break it. The frame rose an inch as my ankle twisted sideways. I'd pay for it later, but who cared? A sore ankle or my life? I got on my knees and pushed the window the rest of the way up. *It's go time!* Like fucking Spiderman, I jumped onto the escape. I struggled to get the window down, but it stuck halfway.

That's when the dude entered my apartment: a giant villain straight out of a comic book. In the light of the television, his skin glowed bluish black. I ducked down and crawled to the edge of the fire escape. I swung my body around, lowering my feet onto the top rung.

There was no top rung. There also was no second, third, or fourth. The ladder was gone. My bladder throbbed. My feet were falling asleep—that always happened when I got nervous. Arms and legs just froze.

I could either take a chance sliding down the rusty support pole to the apartment below or stay put. On my belly, I looked through the grate of the fire escape. The pole was jagged and looked like it would crumble if someone breathed on it. I rolled onto my back and saw the clear sky above me, the twinkling stars. This would have been a great place to chill out and smoke some doobage if I could have afforded it. And if I wasn't praying for my life.

I pulled my hood tight around my head. A plane zoomed high overhead. The stars kept twinkling. I rolled back to the side of the brick building and lay as flat as I could against the wall, right under my apartment window. I breathed real slow and concentrated on feeling my limbs. And that's where I hung out for a long time.

PART IV

Chapter 26

Sometimes we became one while William slept. That's how I knew he remembered. Because I could see things in his dreams. Not as much as in the early days, when he had just come out of the coma. Back then, the dreams came to him in vivid colors, the scene playing over and over.

Cecilia the stripper girl left the apartment around four in the morning. She had turned down the volume but left the TV on. William fell asleep while watching an old rerun of Lassie, an episode where a farmer's young son was drowning in a nearby pond. Sometimes that's all it took to bring on the memory.

If we ended up back at the pond, he'd beg me to wake him. But I'd refuse. He needed to see, no matter how much it hurt. Needed to see again and again until he believed it. Until he got it right.

The dream always started out the same:

I'm at the edge of the dock. Donald and Lance and Stephanie are sitting on the horse blankets. The radio is blaring. I know the water is ice cold, but there is no way in H-E-double-hockey-sticks I will let my girl see me as a chicken. We're madly in love. Grownups think we have something called "puppy love," but that's not what it is. Stephanie and I are meant to be together forever. We're gonna get married and have children and grow old together. We'll buy a big farmhouse, load up our stables with horses, and teach our kids to ride. We'll even boogie down in the kitchen after supper just to drive our children crazy.

This is *not* puppy love. But only Stephanie and me know that.

KC is singing on the radio and the early summer sun falls across my face and shoulders. I am in love with Stephanie. I am in love with this moment. As I prepare to jump in, I'm wearing a big grin and give my girl the sweet eye. Donald is whispering something to her. Duh. He thinks his asinine comments will make her like him, but I don't worry. She'll never give him what he thinks he can have. Stephanie is a good girl. We're gonna be each other's first. We've already discussed it—it's gonna be on her sixteenth birthday, and since Lance's older brother is assistant manager at Tyson's Drug Store, rubbers will be easy to get.

I look at the pond. You can't wait too long or you become a sissy before you ever hit the cold water, and that'd be no good, since a guy can't turn chicken shit in front of his girl. I suck in air, hold my breath, and become a human cannonball.

It takes only seconds for my body to get used to the temperature. I've always been that way. Always the first one in the pond every year, always the fastest swimmer, always able to hold my breath the longest.

I had saved a boy's life the year before at Lake Towodi. That was one scary day, the day that little kid almost drowned.

Dad had taken me and Donald on a two-day fishing trip. There was no lifeguard on duty at Lake Towodi until Memorial Day two weeks away, but Dad wanted to get some camping in before the crowds hit.

We arrived in mid-afternoon and planned to start fishing at sunrise the next morning. Once our tents were standing, we headed down the wooded path to the sand. The day was warm and breezy. Only a handful of people sat on the narrow strip. As I helped spread out our blanket, I looked at the trees that lined the back of the beach as they moved together in the wind. Dad asked me and my brother to play cards, but I wanted to check out the water. I walked to the edge of the lake and watched some kids throw rocks from the shore while Dad and Donald played "War" on the blanket.

A little boy, about five or so, took an inflatable dinosaur into the water, even though it was chilly. The wind was his enemy that day. Within minutes he had drifted beyond the safety buoy, about a hundred yards from the beach.

His mother sat on a blanket not too far from ours, her legs stretched out in front her, a wide floppy hat on her head, chatting with a bunch of other ladies. When she saw her boy, she yelled, "Get your tiny butt back here, young man! You know you ain't allowed to go out that far!"

I heard her say to her friends, "Just like his father, stubborn and immature."

The ladies laughed as they pulled sandwiches out of their bags.

The kid looked like he knew he'd be in trouble if he didn't obey his mother, but as hard as he kicked, he couldn't get the floatie to come back to shore. The wind whipped through the trees behind me. I glanced at the boy's mother again. One hand was on top of her hat, holding it down. With her other hand she poured green liquid from a large thermos into her friends' red plastic cups. Dad and Donald kept playing cards.

I turned back to the boy. All that floated on the water now was an empty dinosaur, bobbing up and down.

The spot where the boy had disappeared was only ten feet deep, but I'd learned in a lifesaving class at the YMCA that it takes less than two inches of water for a kid to drown. I ran into the frigid water like a tiger was after me and started swimming.

Voices on the shore started shouting. Screams rose into the air.

I made it to the dinosaur and wrapped my arms around the inflated neck. I stared beneath my treading feet but could only make out the reflection of the sun on the water's surface.

I breathed in a lungful of air and only let out enough for my body to sink. The water was murky. My hands felt along the bottom. The clay was covered with twigs and rocks and other things I couldn't make out. It took only seconds before my left foot kicked him in the head. I put my face to his, turned him around, placed my arms under his arm pits, and pulled him to the surface. As we rose, I thought, *This is easy. I ought to be a lifeguard one day.*

Those thoughts disappeared as faces and hands were all around me, pulling the boy from my arms, and pulling me as well. I was dragged to the shore and tossed onto the beach. The boy, only a few feet away from me, lay on his side, his mouth open. An older man pressed on his stomach. The boy's mother, no longer interested in her girlfriends, knelt beside him and panted "Toby" over and over. I shut my eyes. When I opened them again, the boy was spitting up dirty water and whatever he had eaten earlier that day. He started coughing and crying and shaking all over. Someone wrapped a big Snoopy beach towel around him and carried him off, the spectators following behind. As I stood, Dad's arms suddenly wrapped my own towel around my scrawny shaking shoulders. He held me tight.

"I'm so proud of you, Billy," he said.

"I didn't want him to die," I said, unexpected tears streaming down my cheeks.

"Let's go cook some chili. I think someone needs to warm up."

Dad grabbed my stuff and we headed toward the path.

Donald paced a step behind me. "Pussy show off," he hissed in my ear as we made our way up the narrow trail.

For a whole year Donald used that phrase whenever he didn't get what he wanted.

I shake those angry words out of my head now as I fall like a boulder into the pond, knowing that when I get out, Stephanie will come to the edge of the dock and wrap my towel around my shoulders like a king who's just come home from a long journey.

My body is instantly shocked. It takes about fifteen seconds to get used to the temperature. The icy water shoots through my cutoffs and freezes everything tucked away inside my underwear. My balls fold themselves into my gut, and the tips of my ears feel like they've been sliced off with a pair of machetes.

I let some air escape through my nose. One of my favorite parts about being in the water is watching the bubbles rise. I can hold my breath longer than anyone I know. Even longer than Donald, and he's older than me. But he always wants to compete. Sometimes I let him win, when we're alone, to get him off my back.

But not when Stephanie's around.

I swim underwater toward the inner tube which works as a buoy not far from the dock. I keep my eyes open in case I should come across a water moccasin or an alligator, even though no one's seen an alligator since 1970.

The last one I'd heard about had ended up in someone's toilet, but I think that was a made-up story to get kids to keep the seat down.

Swimming is never an effort, just like riding horseback, sprinting, or imitating those disco moves the Manhattans and Kool & the Gang do on television. It all comes easy to me. I'm lucky that way.

I reach the inner tube, swim around it, and head back to the dock. Thin streams of bubbles sneak out through my nose, but I'm careful to leave as much air in my lungs as possible to help me stay under longer.

Through the murky water I can barely see the dock about twenty yards away, when I realize I'm not alone. He must have jumped in while I was by the inner tube, because I never heard the splash. There he is to my left, grinning like a stupid sea creature. *What a goob*, I think, as I swim toward the dock. Donald grabs my arm but I don't want to stop. I want my king's robe around my shoulders. He points to his nose, then his wrist. He is offering a challenge to see who can hold their breath longer. But that wouldn't be fair. He jumped in way after me.

I shake my head and break from his grasp. Stephanie's waiting for me. We're supposed to go roller skating at Felton's. Mom's going to the church for a meeting, so she'll drop us off at seven and pick us up at nine. A real date! It almost hurts to think about making out with Stephanie behind the lockers.

When I am only a few feet from the dock, I hear an underwater shout. Donald is suddenly on my right, struggling to get out of what looks like a fishing net. Nobody fishes in this pond. There are only mullets and other gross fish, but somehow a net has wrapped itself around a piling from an old dock that years ago washed away during a hurricane. I swim to Donald. His arm is tangled. With the tiny bit of air I have left, I begin to unwrap the net…

The first jolt was the hardest, like a baseball bat being whacked against a jug by a professional hitter. We opened our eyes to a dark apartment. A fist flew into William's skull, his right cheek, his right ear. Another blow. And another.

An angry man's voice broke through the quiet. "Scum bucket. When the boss is mad at you, he will take it out on everybody else."

William covered his head with one of Donald's pillows.

"You think someone will protect you?" the man asked. He grabbed the pillow from William and threw it across the room. "Who do you think you are, Donald Baker, Mr. Fucking President of the United Fucking States?"

"I'm not D-d-donald!"

I jumped out of the way as the tall dark silhouette grabbed William by a wrist and dragged him from the sofa bed, taking the wrapped sheets with him. At the same time, the stranger closed the front door and pushed William against it. William crumpled to the floor and sobbed, touching his bloody lips with a shaking hand. I ran to his side as the man kicked him in the thigh.

"I'm not bad," William screamed. "I'm g-g-guarding the—"

The man's fist connected with William's right eye.

William believed that if he could prove he wasn't Donald, all would be fine. But before he had a chance to say anything more, the man's fist sent William's stomach into his spine. William rolled onto his side in a little ball. Before the darkness became one with his brain, he caught movement across the room. There, from the other side of the window, a hooded face peered through.

Chapter 27

For a friggin' hour I lay shivering out there on the fire escape, freezing my *garbanzos* off. The temperature was in the mid-forties. Under my cheap-ass windbreaker with the cheap-ass hood, I only wore a T-shirt and a pair of jeans. Forget about me being found in the alley below. They'd find my thawed body come summer.

When the comic book villain finally left, my numb hands grabbed the bottom edge of the window. It slid up easy this time. I straddled the window sill and let myself back in, careful not to put too much pressure on my ankle, and left the window open behind me in case I had to get back out in a hurry.

My bladder was begging for mercy, but peeing would have to wait a little longer.

I could have ignored my brother altogether. Could have pretended he wasn't even there. But it's like passing those accidents on the highway, when you gotta strain your neck and have a look-see. He was a big lumpy scarecrow in a heap on the floor. I pushed him with my good foot. He didn't move. I bent down and put my face close to his. "Yo. What up dog? You dead?" Gurgled puffs of air came from his throat.

The fear of doing time in prison went through my mind again. Here I was, in my own apartment, my bloody brother lying at my feet, and I'm about to walk away from the crime scene. Try explaining that one to the neighbors.

But no one would call the police. The losers in my building were drug dealers or state check alcoholics. They didn't give a shit about me. And

William wouldn't call anyone. He'd forget within twenty-four hours that anything unusual had happened, unless he looked in the mirror and saw his swollen face.

"Sometimes we gotta take a fall for one another, don't we?" I patted the envelope in my pocket and smiled. "It's called brotherly love."

A small squeak came from the floor. I played with my earring and waited, but he went back to making those gurgling sounds.

The new Sony Super CD player still sat in its unopened box under the end table. A few quick bucks until I got to the bank wouldn't be a bad idea. I'd already pawned my damn mobile phone. I grabbed the box and tucked it under my arm. I stepped over William. In the hallway, I looked both ways while I closed the door behind me. My keys, of course, were gone.

Were they on their way to Roly-Poly? Was there a plan to come back again? Hadn't that monster already done what it was he had come here to do? How much more could there be?

With no key, I had no choice but to leave the door unlocked.

Whatever. I'd be chillin' down in paradise before anyone realized they effed up the wrong guy. Besides, did I really care about not having keys to get back inside this dump? I could hire my own chauffeurs, my own maids, my own damn butlers. As I limped down the four flights of steps, I reminded myself of something I'd always believed: a rich man should *never* have to carry his own keys.

Chapter 28

After vacuuming my condo, I took out the trash, scrubbed the bathroom, and washed the windows with citrus cleaner. I spent most of my days off cleaning. I like a tidy home. It's one of my best qualities. There's something about scrubbing things until they shine after helping out a man you hardly know.

Janet and LaToya, my sweetie-pie canaries, chirped up a storm as I pulled their yucky paper out of the cage and slid in the Sunday comics.

My panties and teddies soaked in the kitchen sink in Woolite—I'd swear my life on that stuff—and a pot of homemade chicken soup sat simmering. Most people wouldn't have thought that I had a life outside of that club, but I did. I had subscriptions to *Vanity Fair* and *Rolling Stone* and had been taking guitar lessons for a year. I learned to play some pretty mean Eagles tunes. The cooking thing, well, that was something to feed my creative side. Chopping up veggies and tossing everything together in a pot, keeping it on the stove all day so the house smelled toasty. Like my granny's house before she died.

In my bedroom, I gathered up the clothes I'd worn the night before. My black leather skirt and my tan jacket sat on the rocking chair in the corner. As I picked them up, I spotted one of my turquoise earrings in the carpet beneath the rocker. I had taken them off while sitting on the toilet in William's apartment and slid them into my blazer pocket. I'd lost too many earrings to speak of, and these happened to be authentic turquoise from Mexico, a gift from a pro soccer player. Pretty much my favorite pair, even though I liked my half-carat diamonds a lot too. Can't never go wrong with diamonds.

I bent down to find the other earring, but it wasn't anywhere to be seen. I picked up the jacket, feeling around inside both pockets. One turquoise earring, MIA.

I recounted all my steps from the night before, even though I was still tipsy by the time the cab driver had dropped me off at my condo complex, and I barely remembered saying goodnight to the doorman before heading upstairs. I stood in the middle of my living room, thinking it through.

Maybe I'd sucked it up in the vacuum, I thought, ready to pull my Eureka out of the closet and dig through the revolting bag. But I knew I wouldn't find it in there. I would've heard the clickety-clack.

There was only one possibility: I'd dropped it in William's bathroom. And hopefully not in the toilet.

"Shit," I said to Janet and LaToya. They chirped so pretty when I spoke to them direct. I put my finger through the slat in the cage and wiggled it. "What should I do? Should Mama go all the way across town on her day off just to find a silly earring?"

My precious babies stared at me with their little black eyes.

Sighing, I got out of my sweats and into my stonewashed jeans and a sweater, pulled my long hair back with a Scrunchi, and slid on my flats. Then I turned off the stove, scooped some chicken soup into a thermos, and screwed the cap on extra tight so it wouldn't spill onto my Camry's leather seat.

Chapter 29

"Where is he, Emmanuel?" Roly-Poly asked, sitting all comfy in his big black chair in the basement office.

Ten or twelve boxes of Hostess cupcakes sat in a neat stack on the corner of the metal desk. I stood before him trying not to gag. No windows in the room and barely enough air for a tit-mouse. Just the smell of mold and rat poison and the fat man's sweat.

At six-foot-two, and strong from years of survival, I still shook like a Haitian flag in a hurricane.

"I did what you asked of me, sir," I told him. "I brought him to his senses."

I worked hard to bury my Creole accent, which was always floating along my tongue. In front of the mirror in my apartment, I often practiced my "this" and "that" to make sure they did not sound like "dis" and "dat." The words were clear in my head, and in America I made sure they came out that way.

"That right?" Roly asked.

"Yes, sir."

Roly-Poly pulled out a cigar, bit off the end, and spit it at my feet. It landed on the floor between my legs. When he made no effort to light the cigar, I took the lighter from his desk and lit it for him. He took a deep drag and exhaled. Smoke sucked up any hope of healthy air in the room.

Roly told me, "You know, Manny, when I first brought you and your mother and that little runt here, you seemed so extraordinarily gifted. You could sense things before they happened. You amazed me."

"Yes, sir."

"Why did you decide to stop amazing me?"

I did not know how to answer his question, so I kept my mouth shut. My fist was sore from punching bone, but I held back the desire to rub it in front of my boss.

"All I did was ask you for a favor," he said. "One simple little favor. How do you expect your debt to be eradicated?"

Roly-Poly leaned back in his chair. For a minute, I thought his weight would carry him and the chair tumbling backwards. But he had an unusual skill of balance for a man of three-hundred-plus pounds.

"I did as you asked, sir. I roughed him up. You should see his face. Like a rotten coconut."

"I asked you to persuade him to keep his promise. What if he isn't fazed by what you did to him?"

"I will go back later today. After he has had time to think about it."

"What if his thinking leads him to the bus station? Or the airport? What then?"

I said nothing.

Roly-Poly's lips barely moved while he spoke. He looked like a ventriloquist's oversized dummy. "You get your shiny black ass over to that man's apartment and pray he's still there. If he is, then you'd better pray he's changed his mind. Because if he hasn't, you might have to tell your happy family to start packing their bags."

Fat fucker. I would have liked to slit his throat with my *kouto* just to watch the lard pour onto the ground.

Roly had ordered me to "Go over there and give him a pounding. Make him pay for Charlie's debt." He never specified I was to give him an interview. Who did I look like, that skinny white ass, Barbara Walters?

The only saving grace was that Roly didn't want *me* to do the final deed.

I was too close to both him and the horse. He wanted at least two degrees of separation. He also believed in debts being paid by their rightful owners. Maybe that old Polish fatso and I had something in common.

The Public Transit Authority was crowded. Every passenger who stepped onto the bus took one look at me and moved as quickly and as far away as possible. I was used to it. Sort of liked it as well.

Ten blocks. In the rain. A cold rain, not tropical like in Haiti. Seemed like the bus was moving backwards, stopping at every bus stop.

I found myself praying that the sonofa*bouzin* was still passed out on the floor. I prayed as much in America as I did in my homeland.

I jiggled the set of newly acquired keys in my jacket pocket as the bus brakes squealed. Another stop. And another. I almost shouted to the bus driver, but I held it in. There were no papers yet to protect me. Illegal alien. *Imigran.* I had to keep my foreign nose clean, at least until I finished doing everything Roly-Poly asked. But if this Donald fucker did not cooperate, or if he had already skipped town, the only papers I would be getting were letters of deportation.

Chapter 30

I was getting impatient waiting for William to answer. After all, I had driven all the way over there on my day off. With soup.

After the third round of knocking, I said, "Screw it."

I was headed back toward the stairs when I had one of them premonitions I told you about. I remember having my first one when I was fourteen, about my mama. She went to the doctor because she was tired all the time, and the doctor told her to eat more red meat, as if we could afford it, but I knew that wasn't gonna cure her. I knew there was something worse going on. A year later, a week after Mama died of cancer, my second sight came to me again when Carl, her boyfriend, decided to crawl into my bed. He told me he was lonely and missed my mama bad, but I knew that wasn't why he got under the covers. Especially when he shoved himself inside me and told me I would enjoy it, though most men wouldn't know how to make a woman happy even if they were paid to.

At the top of the stairs I stopped. I glanced behind me.

William was in there.

I walked to the door again and put my ear against it. Loud snoring, like it was really close to the door and not across the room.

Part of my mind shouted for me to walk away, that if I went in there I was pretty much in this for the long haul, whatever that meant. Sometimes it was hard ignoring that smarty pants brain of mine.

Tucking the thermos in the crook of my arm, I placed my other hand on the knob and turned it.

Chapter 31

When our eyes finally opened, everything was blurry. Sunshine streamed through the windows. The television had been turned off.

A girl's voice was saying, "Come on, honey. Let's get you onto the couch." She placed a thermos on the table by the door and threw her jacket and purse on a chair. She locked the door and bent down, wrapping one arm around William.

He looked up at her without recognition. But I remembered who she was.

"My face hurts," William mumbled through his swollen lips. "Where am I?"

Cecilia helped him onto the unmade sofa bed. Blood was spattered on the bottom sheet.

"Your apartment," she told him as he sat. "Looks like you were in a chicken fight. What the hell happened after I left?"

William touched his mouth and winced. "My lip is broken."

"I'll get you some ice."

While she rummaged through the freezer, I knelt on the floor beside the sofa bed, next to William.

Do you remember anything? I asked.

"I don't remember nothing."

"That's okay," Cecilia said, carrying a folded dish towel from the kitchen. "We'll get you back to new. Put this against your eye. It'll hurt a little, but we gotta get that swelling down." She placed the homemade ice pack against his eye. "Let me take a look at the rest of you."

"Cecilia," William said, finally recognizing her.

"Yeah, baby."

"You were here last night."

"Move your right arm for me. Good. Now your left. Good. How about your neck?"

William showed her that he could still move everything without too much effort. "My head hurts real bad."

Cecilia knelt on the bed and leaned over William, her fingers moving through his long hair. "Looks like you got at least one nasty bump. Right here." She touched the top left side of his skull. "Once your eye numbs up, we'll put the pack against your head." She carefully opened his shirt, looking over his chest and stomach. She traveled down his body until her fingers landed on the grapefruit sized bruise on his thigh. "Who did this to you?"

"I dunno." William sniffled and put his fists to his eyes.

"Oh, hey," Cecilia said. She took his hands away from his face. "Don't cry. It'll be okay. You got any aspirin?"

He shook his head.

Cecilia got up and went to her handbag. "I always carry Midol with me. It's for cramps, but it works for swelling too. And moodiness." She shook a couple of pills into William's hand and headed into the kitchen. She came back and handed him a glass filled with water. "Here you go."

William took the pills and leaned back against the sofa. He pulled the blanket up to his chest and held the ice pack against his eye. "I wasn't supposed to leave the door unlocked. Guarding the door was my job. Donald said so."

Donald...

"No, William," Cecilia told him. "I'm the one who left. I thought you'd lock it behind me. We were sort of drunk last night. Do you remember last night?"

Donald...

Something was coming to me, but what? What was it we couldn't remember?

Cecilia's voice was soft and kind. "It's my fault, William. I should have made sure the door was locked. I'll take care of you till you get better. I was almost a Girl Scout, you know. Well, I would've been if they'd liked me." She stroked his hair. "If you think you might know who did this, or why, I have connections."

William didn't understand what *connections* meant. He sat very still, concentrating on keeping his one eye open, which was hard because of the throbbing in the other.

"Someone hit me. In my head and my eye. I dunno why."

Ask her to call the police. That's what she should have done the second she saw you on the floor. Ask her.

"Police?" William asked out loud.

"I can call them if you want," Cecilia said. "I don't know what they'll do exactly, take a report I suppose. They'll probably have you go to the hospital for—"

"No!" William took the ice pack from his eye. "I d-d-don't want to go to the hospital."

"Calm down, William, it's okay. I won't call them. Unless you have something broken…"

William shook his arms again, then his legs. "Nothing broken. Nothing broken."

"That's good," Cecilia said. "Now stop wiggling and put the ice back on your eye. To help the swelling go down."

William did as she asked.

"You like chicken soup?"

William nodded.

Cecilia grabbed her thermos. "You stay put. I'm gonna add a little water to this and reheat it on the stove." She rattled around in the tiny kitchen for a moment before coming back to the living room. "While it's simmering…I think I lost an earring in your bathroom last night. Back in a jiff." She disappeared into the bathroom, closing the door behind her.

William tried to grab the remote control from the end table, but his body was too sore to stretch that far.

I leaned down next to his ear. *Did you notice the open window?*

William slowly turned his head and looked at the window, open about two feet.

Who opened it? A ghost? I don't think so. Who did you see out there on the fire escape last night? Do you—

I was interrupted by the click of a key sliding in the front door lock. The lock turned.

William eagerly sat up on the couch. "Donald?"

It's not Donald! I screamed.

The door opened.

"Donald?" William repeated, his voice less steady, as the dark stranger once again enter the apartment—this time like he owned it.

Chapter 32

I found one of my butterfly hairclips, even though I didn't know one was missing, and it didn't matter since I had about fifty. But I stuck it in my pocket anyway as I looked around for my earring. On the sink, in the sink, under the worn bath mat, behind the john. Right when I was about to give up, I spotted it. There my little blue stone sat, in the stained bottom of the toilet, near the hole.

"How the hell didn't you swim away?"

I didn't see any rubber gloves or toilet scrubber, just a tube of toothpaste on the sink next to a ratty toothbrush, a roll of toilet paper on the tank, and a towel hanging on the back of the door. I decided to look in the kitchen for something to help me dig out the earring when I heard voices in the living room. At first I thought William had turned the television on, but then I realized it was him talking.

"I'm supposed to g-g-guard the door," William said. His voice was sort of muffled because of his swollen lip, but the panic was clear.

"What is it you talk to me about?" A man's voice slid under the bathroom door. He had an accent.

"It's my j-j-job."

"Asshole," the man said. "Your job was to be at the track when you were supposed to be. Your job was to clean up Charlie's debt." The man pronounced the word *job* like *jobe*.

I opened the bathroom door a sliver and peeked into the living room.

The dark man, who wore a denim jacket, a pair of stiff jeans, and work boots, leaned over William like a giant. William pulled the blanket over his head.

"Does Roly know what a fucking *coco* his henchman is? Huh?" The man sat on the edge of the sofa bed and shoved William through the blanket with his large hands.

My heart cried. I put a hand over my mouth.

The angry man said, "You and I are going to have a conversation, man-to-man. I am not going to beat you anymore—I must keep you in good shape, boss's orders, lucky for you. Come out, Donald. Let us get this fucking show on the road."

William stuttered under the blanket: "I'm not D-D-Donald."

The man yanked the cover from William's head. "Okay then. I will play along on this game with you." He looked around the room then behind the sofa bed. "Where did our Donald go? He was here only last night, and he looked just like you. Is that not strange?"

"D-D-Donald's on a business trip. I was g-g-g-guarding the door. I was watching Nickelodeon." William pointed to the dark TV screen. "N-n-nick-o-lo-de-on!" He began to cry.

"What the fuck?" The man held out the palms of his hands like he had an audience. Then he laughed. "You are *estipid*? A...numbskull?" He patted William on the cheek.

William blubbered harder, making my stomach sick.

"Stop crying now, little sissy, and tell me who you are."

"W-W-William."

The man put his face up to William's. Their noses just about touched. He whispered, "And who is William?"

"Donald's brother."

"Brother?"

William rolled his knees to his chest wearing nothing but his wrinkled satin shirt and underwear. As he lowered his head and cried into his arms, his hand let go of the towel and the ice cubes rattled to the floor.

I wanted to go to William. Wrap my arms around his shaking shoulders.

I'd never felt so sorry for anyone in my life. But I couldn't go out there. There was no telling what the man would do to me.

"You telling me I cracked my knuckles over a man with an empty head?" he asked William.

No answer.

"What are you doing here?"

Still no answer.

"Answer me!"

William flinched. "I live with Donald. I'm an independent. The s-s-state says so."

"Where is your brother? And do not lie to me, or I will make sure your other eye does not open for a week."

"A b-b-business trip."

"Where?"

William shrugged and wiped his nose with the back of his hand. "I'm g-g-guarding the door."

The man stood up. He pulled a pen and a small notepad from his jacket pocket. "I will write a message to give to your brother." He scribbled something and handed the piece of paper to William. "You make sure Donald gets this phone number, understand? If he thinks the horses are running for him only, he is wrong."

William wiped his cheeks with the sleeve of his shirt. "Horses?"

"You tell him if I do not hear back within twenty-four hours, he will be finding his own ass at the glue factory."

William said nothing.

"You are deaf now?"

"No."

"Why do you look at me that way?"

"Where are the horses?" William asked.

"Why do you ask this question?"

"I train horses."

The man's shoulders relaxed. He smirked at William. "Do you now?"

"I won seven trophies in 4-H."

"What is *4-H?*"

"I got over ten blue ribbons and some red ones," William said, "but the red ones aren't as good as the blue ones, but I only got me three red ones anyway."

"That is an incredible story." He looked at his watch. "Make sure your brother gets that note. Perhaps I should staple it to your forehead so you do not forget?"

William touched his forehead. "No."

"I need some water," the man said.

I opened the bathroom door an inch more. William sat on the couch, staring at the blank television screen. The faucet in the kitchen turned on and off.

The man appeared in the kitchen doorway. I ducked back.

"Who makes this soup?" he asked.

My stomach dropped.

William didn't say anything.

That's it, William, sweetie. Stay silent. Play dumb. If you feel like you owe me something for last night, well, this would make us even…

"You know how to make soup?" the man asked William.

"N-n-no."

"Well, I do not think you hired a personal chef."

I shrank into the corner behind the door.

"I hope for your sake you did not lie to me, William."

"I don't lie."

"Maybe Donald is here after all? Maybe hiding in the closet?" I heard a door open and shut. "Maybe he takes a bubble bath while his homemade soup waits for him?"

I braced my hands to stop the bathroom door from slamming into me, but the slam never came. Instead, the man opened the door real slow, until the tips of my pretty flats stopped it from going any farther.

He stepped one foot into the bathroom. His cold black eyes caught my reflection in the medicine cabinet mirror. He cocked his head to the side. "Well, now," he said, grinning to the mirror. "In America there is a surprise around every corner."

Chapter 33

Red-headed women lucky enough to be born with intelligence have tempers worse than my own. I had a feeling this one had both characteristics. The *pinda* didn't try to run away, she only stood behind the door with her arms folded across her chest as if daring me to come and get her. Showing defiance. Like my nephew Anthony when he turned three.

"Let's go have a seat," I told her.

Her hips swung her round bottom from side to side as I followed her out of the bathroom.

I stood in the middle of the room. The retarded one still sat on the couch. The girl sat on the chair beside the door. Getting people to answer my questions has never been a problem for me.

"Tell me who you are and where Donald is," I ordered.

"I'm Cecilia. And I've never met Donald. Only heard William talk about him."

I can tell if a woman is lying from a kilometer away. They blink fast, bite the lip, sometimes scratch the nose or chew the inside of the cheek. But she wasn't doing any of those things.

"How do you know this man here?" I asked her.

The two of them exchanged quick glances.

I laughed with surprise. "You two are fucking?"

The red-headed bitch said, "If it's any of your business, no, we're not."

"Then what are you doing here?"

"William and me are friends. I stopped by this morning to see how he was getting along and found his face turned into pulp."

Her eyes moved to my swollen knuckles, but I was not bothered by this.

"I don't know his brother," Cecilia said again, "and I don't know what you want him for. But I guarantee it has nothing to do with William."

"Nothing," William chimed in.

What was I to do? These two were as helpful as a pair of worn sandals. My brain started moving at quick speed. All kinds of possible solutions entered my mind.

I turned to the girl. "Go and get us some soup. I will like to see what kind of chef a stripper is."

Her stone face showed no surprise, but behind her eyes I could see that she wondered how I knew.

To William she said, "I'll be right in the kitchen."

William gave the stripper a small smile as she left the room.

Chapter 34

Once Cecilia disappeared into the kitchen, the man moved in on William.

"What does that whore want with you?" he asked.

William shrugged.

"Put on some pants—you are embarrassing yourself."

William grabbed his bellbottoms still hanging over the back of the sofa bed from the night before. Wincing, he slid them over his hips, leaving the fly open.

"I gotta pee," he told the man.

"Go and do your business then."

After William left the room, I floated over to the man and stared at his face. His uneven skin was the same dark blue-gray as the ashes the reverend used to smear onto our foreheads on Ash Wednesday. His eyes matched his skin. His black hair had the tiniest sprinkling of white above the ears. He was clean-shaven and smelled like Ivory soap. His nails were clean and filed. Not exactly the kind of guy who would beat up strangers while they slept.

A burst of thunder rocked the building. Outside, rain came down in a rush. The man turned toward the window. The *open* window. Raindrops sprinkled onto the dirty carpet.

I followed him across the room. He ran a finger across the lower sill. Chalky bits of white paint covered his fingertip. He stretched an arm through the narrow opening and held his palm upward, feeling the rain. With some force, he slammed the window shut before turning the rusty latch.

William came out of the bathroom.

The man wiped his wet hand on his jeans. "Did you open this window?"

"No."

"It was not open last night," he said. "If you did not open it, then who did?"

"I dunno."

Cecilia popped her head through the kitchen doorway and said, "Soup's ready."

"I will talk to William alone," the man told Cecilia as he spooned chicken soup into his mouth.

Cecilia stood next to William's chair. I floated next to her and begged, wishing I could grab her by the arm.

Don't go…please…

She placed her hands on the table and leaned over, her face barely a foot away from the stranger's. Her voice was low and even.

"You beat up this poor man for no reason."

"There are reasons for everything," he said between spoonfuls.

"I'm a pretty popular girl and I happen to have a lot of close friends. Friends who are cops, lawyers, judges…"

The man tilted the bowl of soup against his lips, ignoring her.

"Don't worry, William," Cecilia told him. "I'll be back in an hour." She shot the man a dirty look and held up an index finger. "One hour." She gathered her things from the living room and closed the apartment door behind her.

William and the man finished their soup in silence. When he was through, William pushed his half-empty bowl to the center of the small table. He took a napkin and wiped his chin, careful not to rub the crack in his lip.

"That's some good *kaka*," the man said. He tapped his spoon against the table top, a smooth repetitive beat—rat-a-tat-tat—like a drummer in a jazz band. "Do you know what an idea man is, William?"

"No."

"He thinks up new and better ways to get things done. That is what they call me: Manny the idea man."

"Manny," William repeated.

"When was the last time you take care of these horses you talk about?" Manny asked.

William had to think hard, always mixing up the past with the present. He couldn't remember which Christmas we got our new Schwinn bicycle. Which year at camp we learned to play flag football. Which entire summer we missed because of the coma. Barely remembered taking Special Ed classes so we could graduate with our class.

"I can't remember," he finally answered.

Rat-a-tat-tat, rat-a-tat-tat.

"If you could do anything, would it be to again work with horses?"

"I don't wanna watch the door anymore."

Unconsciously, William touched his swollen mouth. His overgrown fingernails were caked with dried blood.

"I owe you," Manny said. "After the accident last night."

"Accident?"

Accident...

"Mistaking you for your brother. What if I told you I could make it up to you? What if I told you, you can take care of horses again?" Manny changed his rat-a-tat-tat from the table to the empty soup bowl. Clang-a-clang-clang.

"I'm good with horses," William said. "I won lots of ribbons before. And I won other stuff too. Cuz I'm all of a sudden lucky."

"Well now, what makes you so lucky?"

"I got lots of money. I'm gonna buy my own horse. Maybe even two. But I gotta build a barn first."

"You have money? Now that does not sound like the truth."

No. Don't do it...

"I do so have money. On account of the lottery."

The man stopped tapping.

Oh shit-shit-shit.

I moved as close to William as I could without sitting on his lap.

"Lottery?" the man asked.

Stop talking!

"I was winner number 7-9-2 on the *Lotsa Luck Show*."

Manny tossed his drumming spoon into the bowl and leaned on his elbows. "How much did you win?"

"Six hundred and…and…" William tried to calculate but let out a sigh. "A million before the tax man. I was on TV."

Jeez Louise. Do you hear yourself?

The man narrowed his eyes. "Is this a lie you hand to me?"

"Nuh-uh."

"A million?"

"Uh-huh. But I can't have it for a few weeks. The bank told me."

William pulled his wallet from his back pocket and laid it open on the table. On the left of the fold under clear plastic was his State ID: *William Bernard Baker, 127 Stoney Brook Avenue*, followed by the city and zip code. On the wallet's right side, a slip of paper was tucked under the other plastic window: *If found, please call: 555-228-6997*. William believed the request was in case he lost his wallet, but it was really in case something happened to him. From the wallet's money pocket, he slid out a small photo of himself standing between the wheel and Mr. Lotsa Luck. He beamed as he handed it to Manny.

Manny held up the picture and spoke under his breath. "So, that is what that pinda wants…" He rubbed the wiry hairs on the tip of his chin. "William, you need some help. Your brother has deserted you, and you cannot trust a woman with hair of *rouj* as far as you can piss. You need me."

"I do?"

"We will call this good faith," Manny said, pulling his wallet out of his back pocket. He counted out fifteen twenty dollar bills. "This will tide you over."

"Tide me over?"

"To get you by. Until your first paycheck comes. I am going to hire you. To work with horses."

"Yowza," William said, splaying out the bills on the table.

"We were meant to come together," Manny went on. "I was sent into your life to help you."

"And the horses too?"

The man smiled. "Some of the most beautiful horses in the world. But they will not know you are alive unless I introduce you to them. They will love to meet you. Are you ready to let someone older and wiser help you?"

"Okey-dokey," William said.

There was nothing I could do but stand by and watch. Stand by helplessly the moment William started crawling to Manny, like a lonely baby crawling to a brand new pacifier.

Only I was sure this pacifier was dipped in poison.

Chapter 35

By the time I got back to William's apartment, the creep had left. The front door was unlocked. I stepped into an empty living room.

"William?" The shower was running. I stepped into the bathroom. "William?"

He popped his head out from behind the shower curtain. The crack in his lip had stopped bleeding. Soap suds ran down his dark blond sideburns and dripped onto the cracked tiles. "I'm taking a shower."

"William, you need to remember to keep that front door locked."

"I gotta wash my hair and shave and cut my fingernails. Manny said so." He disappeared behind the curtain again.

"His name is Manny?"

"Uh-huh."

"What does he need you to get cleaned up for?"

"He got me a job."

"What kind of job?"

"I'm gonna take care of the horses."

"Where?"

"At the track."

I closed the toilet seat and sat on the lid. "You ever done that before?"

"Not racehorses, but other kinds. I know how to clean them and brush them and feed them and everything. I won all kinds of ribbons. They're at my house."

"You have a house?"

"My mom's house."

"Oh."

"He gave me my own key. I can come and go cuz I'm an independent."

I was supposed to do something, wasn't I? I mean, it was my fault the door was left unlocked to begin with. Didn't I owe the poor guy something more than soup?

"William?"

From behind the shower curtain, he sounded like he was speaking with the water running over his face. "Yeah?"

"I don't think you can trust Manny. I mean, after what he did to your face and all."

"My face?"

"Your *face*. Don't you remember what he did to you?"

William was quiet for a moment. Then he said, "Yeah."

"Well, don't you think it's weird that this stranger beat the crap out of you last night and offers you a job today?"

"He thought I was Donald. He beat up Donald, not me."

"No, William, he beat up *you*."

"But he *thought* I was Donald."

"But—"

"He said he owes me one."

"Okay. He owes you one. So what are you gonna get paid for this new job? Are they paying you by the hour or by the day? Does Manny work there too? Will he be your boss? How're you gonna get there?"

"Manny's getting me a bus pass. He gave me tide money."

"Tide money?"

"Until I get my first paycheck."

I didn't know whether or not to repeat the other questions. The more important ones. If he didn't have the answers, he might get upset.

"William?"

"Yeah?"

"When you're through with your shower, I'll take care of your nails."

William sat on the couch with a towel around his waist. I had watched him shave over the sink. It surprised me to see how he slid the razor over his jaw line without nicking his skin once, his bicep moving with every stroke of his hand across his chin, slowing down when the razor got close to his wounds.

"How did you get such an amazing body?" I asked as I clipped and filed his nails.

William's cheeks turned red. Light freckles on his nose turned auburn. "I dunno. I dance a lot."

"You mean like you did at the club that night?"

He nodded.

"Can I ask you another question?"

He watched my face as I tried to put the words together.

"What happened to you? To make you—this way? Were you born like this?"

"I got sick from the pond."

"You mean like an infection?"

"They put me in the hospital for a long time. Then I didn't get all the way better. But it's okay, cuz tomorrow I start my new career."

I smiled. "So, you want to work with horses as a career?"

"Uh-huh."

"And Manny's gonna make sure you get a real paycheck and everything?"

"Yup. Even though I don't need to work. Cuz I already have—"

He stopped mid-sentence and closed his eyes.

"Already have what?"

Silence. Eyes still closed.

"It's okay, William," I told him as I clipped. "You don't need to tell me everything. A girl's gotta figure out some things on her own."

William opened his eyes. "Do you like me, Cecilia?"

"Well, I must or I wouldn't be sitting here in your living room clipping your fingernails, now would I? Sometimes it's just nice to have a new friend. Don't you agree?"

"Uh-huh." He thought for a moment. "Stephanie married a fireman."

"I heard."

"We wanted it to be special, not in a car or under the bleachers; we wanted to do it in a hotel room, on a bed, like grownups."

"You and Stephanie never got to do that?" I asked.

He shook his head.

"But you really wanted to?"

"Uh-huh. She loved me."

I finished clipping. A small pile of dead fingernails sat on the edge of the couch. I clamped the clippers between my fingers and my thumb, nervously snipping at nothing.

"Can I ask you one more question, William?"

"Uh-huh."

"If you hadn't got sick, do you think you and…Stephanie…would be married now?"

Club dancers gotta be strong, because we meet all kinds of people. Happy, horny, angry, sad, looney-tunes. But I wasn't prepared for William's tears. They came on all of a sudden, like he'd been saving them up, waiting for the perfect moment to let them out.

"I'm sorry, William. I didn't mean to make you cry. Please don't…I shouldn't have asked you that. It's none of my beeswax."

He wiped his wet face, on accident rubbing the black and purple bruise around his swollen eye. He jerked his hand away. He stared at me, like he was deciding what to do with me.

"Do you want me to leave?" I asked.

He took a deep breath and let it out. "No." He put the balls of his feet against my leg. I could see his personal belongings under the towel with his knees bent like that.

"You sure?"

"Uh-huh. You still gotta do my toenails."

He smiled as he wiped his hand across the bottom of his nose, and I smiled back as I started on his left foot.

Chapter 36

My fake license had a state seal and everything. In the diner's booth by the window, I laid it on the table and let my fingers rub the front. For the first time in my life, I thought it was dope that Woody and I looked so much alike.

But Lady Luck has a mind of her own, and she can turn on a man in a millisecond. "As quick as a confused whore," Charlie used to say about Lady Luck. And he was right.

I opened the *Lotsa Luck* envelope.

"Shit!"

A few old men, sitting at the diner's counter smoking their cigarettes while eating their greasy bacon and runny eggs, glanced in my direction. In the booth, I lowered my head and stared at the rectangular piece of paper: *a fucking check stub.*

I shook the envelope, hoping something more would fall out. Something did. A bank deposit slip. I read the name: Southern States Bank & Trust. He had already deposited the damn thing! How was that possible? The freak could barely tie his shoelaces, let alone handle a bank deposit.

With my finger, I tapped the saucer under my fourth cup of stale coffee and stared out the diner's window. Sun barely up and already people crawled along the sidewalks like hyperactive ants. Three skinny homeless dudes sat on a curb across the street, holding an open hand out to the suits headed to taxis or the subway. No one gave the hungry men a couple of bones to help them out. No one even looked at them. Those guys could've been pieces of trash for all anyone cared.

I wasn't cut out for a beggar's life. I couldn't sleep on the street. I deserved a bed. And a pillow. The YMCA wouldn't let me use their shower again unless I did some volunteer work in exchange. Screw them. Like they couldn't spare some friggin' hot water without me bleaching their dirty towels or digging gummy hair out of the shower drains.

The CD player got me enough cash for a day's worth of food. I'd pawned my earring, too, that beautiful ruby bought with my very first winnings.

Even more than a shower or a real bed, I missed the track. And I don't mean off-track betting cuz they aren't the same thing. There's nothing more exciting than the crowd of people waiting together for the first race, all breathing in and out at the same time. The hooves as they pound the dirt, making the stands vibrate. That feeling when my pony flies across the line right when I want her to, and pays out ten to one.

I shoved the fake ID, check stub, and bank deposit slip into my wallet. I threw just enough dimes and pennies on the table to cover the coffee, then joined the other ants on the sidewalk.

My knees near about buckled when the hottest bank teller in the world looked at the ID and said, "I'm very sorry, sir."

"Sorry?" I asked.

She knew. Gina, her name plate said. Gina, with her silky skin and happy boobs, knew. She'd call the manager, and the security guard would block my exit through the lobby doors. I'd be tackled to the floor, my wrists yanked behind my back and locked in handcuffs. The courts would throw me in jail for fraud, and wishing for a comfortable bed would be the least of my worries.

Glancing in the rent-a-cop's direction, my hands held onto the counter to keep me from falling over.

"Mr. Baker," Gina said, "I mentioned to you and your friend the other day that it could take up to a few weeks for the lottery funds to become available. Though sometimes it's sooner."

The bank teller slid the ID back through the scoop in the window. Even if Woody got help depositing the check, and even though the money wasn't available yet, she'd totally fallen for the fake ID. If she believed I was my brother, why was she staring at me like that?

"Do you want to speak to my manager?" she asked.

"No! I mean, no thanks."

She kept staring at me funny. Finally, she said, "Did you get your hair done different?"

"What? Uh, no, just letting a little of this grow in." I rubbed my blond whiskers.

"You can still get into your other account in the meantime."

"My other account?"

"Where you deposited cash. Don't you remember?" Then she started speaking extra slow. "You said your new boss gave it to you. To hold you over until you got your first paycheck. You were so excited—"

New boss? Paycheck?

"I never forget a face, and I never forget a great story," Gina the teller went on, smiling at me like a Special Olympics contestant.

Then it came to me. Here I was, hoping she'd think I was William Bernard Baker, idiot of the universe, and here she was thinking exactly what I wanted, even when I'd forgot the most important ingredient!

I slouched real fast. "Oh, yeah," I said, dropping the right side of my face like my brother. I began fidgeting with my ID, doing the Woody shuffle on the marble floor, which wasn't too hard with my sore ankle. "My *other* account."

"Do you want me to help you fill out a withdrawal slip?"

"Yes, please, ma'am."

"How much would you like to withdraw?"

"Two hundred dollars?" I said, hoping not to overshoot my limit.

Gina typed some numbers on the keyboard. "That leaves you with about a hundred. Until, of course, your lottery money clears." She pulled a rectangular form from beneath the counter, her fine breasts dying to pop the buttons on her blouse as she wrote the account number across the bottom. "Sign here and you're all set." She pointed with her pen along the black line and passed it through the scooped-out dish under the window.

I signed *William B. Baker*, my hand taking its time to write each letter, and passed back the slip.

"Would you like that in twenties?" Gina asked.

"Yes, ma'am." I smiled at her, a perfectly brainless smile. A Woody original.

The gal slid back the bills. I put them into my wallet extra slow, working hard not to let her see my anticipation growing. There was a good chance I could double the cash before noon.

She counted out the cash and smiled patiently as I put them and the receipt in my wallet.

"Thank you," I told her.

She caught me staring at her cleavage and crossed her arms in front of her. "Have a nice day, Mr. Baker."

Still grinning, I told her, "Okey-dokey."

Chapter 37

Mercy, it came to me like a bat outta hell, if you'll pardon my French. I was in the garden, pattin' some dirt around my tulips peeking their heads out of the early spring ground, and I knew, just like that.

I ran inside and picked up the kitchen phone and dialed the apartment. It rang twenty times before I finally hung up. Then I called Donald's other number, the one that belonged to his travel phone. It rang three times before an operator's voice said, "The mobile customer you are trying to reach is unable to accept calls at this time. Goodbye." I hardly had time to understand what she was sayin' before she hung up on me.

I'd thought a million times about drivin' down to the apartment, but William wanted his independence, and I didn't want to upset him none, have him thinking I didn't believe in him. He might not never speak to me again.

Then it popped into my head. I'd call Lance! He could go on over and find out if anythin' was wrong.

I read his number from the Post-it on the fridge and dialed it. His wife Julie answered.

"Hello," I said. "Can I speak with Lance, please?"

"Who's calling?" Julie asked.

"This is William Baker's mother. I'm afraid I need to ask a favor of your husband."

"I'm sorry, Mrs. Baker. Lance is on a fishing trip with his cousin and won't be home till tomorrow night. Is there something I can do? Is everything all right?"

A dog was barkin' in the background. A television blared a talk show. Montel, by the sound of it.

"Did William go fishin' with 'em?" I asked.

"No, ma'am, I don't believe so. Lance drove his truck, which only holds two people with any comfort, I can tell you that."

"Oh."

Julie said, "If you want, I could call the campground and relay a message. I'd be happy to do that."

The dog in the background started barkin' louder.

"No, thank you," I told her. "I don't want to go spoilin' his good time for no reason. It's not that important. I can speak with your husband when he gets back. Will you have him call me when he does?"

"Let me get a pencil and something to write on."

Even though Lance knew our number, I gave it to Julie, thanked her again, and hung up. Then I collapsed onto the kitchen chair, my stomach twistin' every which way, on account of I knew there was somethin' wrong, only I didn't know what.

Chapter 38

Life is all about who owes who what. It is a world of debts. If Joe does me a favor, I owe Joe. If I overpay the favor to Joe, then Joe owes me a bit more. It goes on that way until the debt owed feels equal to both parties. But only then.

Do you see what I am telling you?

Having this responsibility fall upon my shoulders gave me a weight I could not release, but this was the way it was to be. Once the job was done and the fat man handed me the cash, I was out. I would move to a bigger city. New York or Los Angeles, so my *manman* could feel safe not being targeted by officers of immigration. Who would notice a black woman with a Creole accent on the crowded streets of New York? Roly promised this was the last job. Then he would get me the papers to free my family. Those papers meant Anthony could get the education he deserved, and my manman could move into a high-rise condo with a garden on the balcony, like the rich ladies.

But I didn't want to handle any more jobs for Roly-Poly. Not even one, and not even if it was William who would ultimately take care of the task. I wanted to begin my life now. Eighteen months had disappeared since coming to America. Roly was no different than the Haitian government, giving me and my family a tiny taste of American freedom, then keeping us hungry enough to beg for more.

I would have killed not to beg anymore.

By now, William's chicken-*kaka* brother was probably in another city, maybe another state, scamming a distant relative or an old whore. Who cared? Having that *enbesil* out of the way was exactly what was needed.

William was as dumb as a potato and as sweet as a kiwi. He would never desert me like Donald had deserted Roly. It made me laugh to think of Donald feeding Roly-Poly that kaka about Charlie. He should have picked a man more dependable than that old drunk to play his *dada*. Someone who understood the meaning of the word "debt." Someone who understood how business is supposed to run. Of course, William would never know he was hired to pay back a favor—he did not need to have his brain cluttered with so much information.

As one of the smallest tracks in America, with only one barn, the Dellshore was relatively left alone, unless the owners popped in. There were the jocks and gallop boys and the trainers too. But they usually came early in the morning when it was cool, and were gone by noon. William would be working the later half of the day, into the night, when the horses were put to rest. Even if authorities asked William questions after the plan was executed, they would realize the moment he opened his mouth that he could not have come up with a plan so ingenious. He could barely remember I had beaten his face even as the bruises faded.

When I showed William's Dellshore ID picture to Roly, he thought it was Donald until I told him otherwise. His pudgy grin told me he was proud of my resourcefulness. It did not matter if Donald the asshole or William his brother did the dirty deed, since Roly figured they were both Charlie's kids. As long as the debt was paid. And I did not bother to tell him about William's numbskull brain. My boss did not care to get into personalities. He did not have much of one himself.

"Do not worry about filling out an application," I had explained to William that day in his kitchen before the whore came back. Slowly, so he would understand. "Sandy in personnel will know you are coming."

I thought about Sandy, her rear end jutting out behind her like it had its own mind. She would be quite accommodating after receiving her new earrings. All American women like diamonds, that is the truth.

"I will get you a bus pass and a schedule," I told William. "You cannot be late on any occasion and have the boss exploding. That is one thing you do not want to see." Then I added the most important thing of all: "Do not tell *anyone* about your lottery money. Some people will take advantage. Do you understand?"

He nodded, but his eyes seemed far away.

I used a sweet voice, like a teacher in charge of five-year-olds, along with a little leverage. "You tell anyone, and you might have to quit your job taking care of the horses. You see, William, if people think you already have money, they will give your job to someone else. Someone who does *not* have money."

William's eyes cleared. He shook my hand in agreement until I thought it would fall off. He stared at me like I was a movie star. I have been told by a few that I resemble Denzel Washington, only I had earned a few more wrinkles. Maybe William saw me as a dada. Outcasts like him are always hanging out on those American television programs like Oprah, with their sob stories of how Dada left them behind to start a brand new family with brand new babies. My dada left me for something less than that, so I can understand when a young man admires a person older and wiser.

Because no matter how much money a man makes, or how many wrinkles lie within his skin to prove how long he has walked this earth, one thing is for sure: he never stops wishing for another chance with his dada.

Chapter 39

The stables were ripe with fresh hay and manure. I could hear those beauties chomping on straw, snorting as William and Manny walked by the stalls. They snorted extra loud when I floated past.

I was proud of William, getting a job, taking the bus, showing up on time at the barn. But Manny frightened me. He kept a large knife in his waistband, and it showed whenever he leaned back. His dark weary face was the face of a man who tried hard to maintain control but couldn't always do it. What scared me most was how focused William was on Manny's words. He hadn't paid that close attention to anybody in sixteen years. And now Manny was all of a sudden his *friend*. His *boss*. After what he'd done to William's face.

Manny spent a lot of time explaining things to William.

"You are a stable hand apprentice. You report to me, always. The rules are many. We deliberately keep the horses in the dark, close and quiet, to make sure they get the rest they need. And no treats of your own. Only feed them when I tell you and what I tell you. If you feed them something else, and the vet tests the poop, you will be up a creek of kaka." He proudly laughed at his joke. "If a horse has a problem of any kind, tell me, no one else. As far as you are concerned, I am the head honcho around here, even if someone tells you otherwise."

William said nothing, only nodded his head and stared at each of the six horses as we moved past. Occasionally, he'd say hello to one. Manny either didn't notice or didn't care. He told William their names, described their different needs, explained their quirks.

"Here is the most important *bebe* in the barn," Manny said. "William, meet Neapolitan."

We looked into the stall. Before us stood a beautiful mare, decorated with colors of brown and white across her flanks and head, and streaks of auburn through her smooth mane and perfectly groomed tail. She stood at least sixteen hands high, with thick muscled thighs and a shimmering coat. Her eyes were black pearls. She was clean cut. Perfect. A mythical beast. I looked to see if she had wings.

It only took five seconds for William to fall in love.

"Yowza."

With his fingertips, he stroked the horse from her forehead to her nostrils, up and down, up and down. Her eyes closed halfway. So did William's.

"She is the one you will pay the most attention to," Manny told William. "And the reason you were hired."

A chill raced up my back, reaching for my skull. For a moment I was back on that summer day, sitting on the blanket with Stephanie, gearing up to jump into the pond. A thought that was more intuitive than intellectual went through me that something uncontrollable was about to happen.

And that's when the shaking began.

I reasoned that it was an earthquake, even though there hadn't been an earthquake in the state in over twenty years. Then I realized the shaking had nothing to do with the earth.

Neapolitan's eyes darted around the barn and landed on me. Her head pulled away from William's hand. He tried to get her to bring her nuzzle back to him.

"It's okay...it's okay." William's words came to me in muffled chunks, like he was speaking from underneath a mattress.

I held up my hands. They were vibrating, blurring in front of my eyes, like they were photographs of my hands and someone was shaking them back and forth. I leaned against the stall door.

Neapolitan began to whinny, little snorted whimpers, then cried out like a whip had walloped her flank.

William stepped back. "Something's wrong…"

Manny's dim voice was slow and even, his voice like thick syrup dripping into my ears: "All right, Neon, calm down." He pulled the horse to him and stroked her muzzle. "William is here to take care of you. What is the matter? You have got a spirit in there with you?" He looked at William. "What did you do?"

"Nothing. Just patted her head is all," William said, sniveling.

A thin line of drool dripped from Neapolitan's mouth to the stable floor. Manny stroked her, calming her down. After a few moments, the vibrating subsided, and so did Neapolitan's neighing. Now she only grunted in spurts.

But my tingling hands were nothing but ghostly images. I looked down. My bare feet had nearly faded as well. Drifting away from the stall, I shook my hands in front of my face. Then I jumped up and down, trying to get my feet to come back. They did not.

Through the years, my voice only entered William's head when he was open to it, or when I forced my way into his dreams. Sometimes he paid attention, sometimes he didn't, depending on the situation. I was used to being ignored. But now it felt like I was fading away. Evaporating like a puddle during a dry spell.

Manny continued to go over his list of do's and don'ts. William's head was cocked to the side, his eyes half closed, trying to absorb the rules.

As William and Manny talked about barns and horses and manure, panic filled what was left of me: what would happen to William if I suddenly disappeared?

And, for crimony's sake, what would happen to *me*?

Chapter 40

A credit card and a thin line of cocaine sat on top of Roly's desk. He offered me the line, which meant he not only trusted me but felt I deserved a small reward.

Instead of responding, I gulped from my bottle of green Gatorade.

"What's the matter?" Roly asked. "Don't feel like celebrating?"

Rich men's poison was not needed to make me feel empowered.

"Thank you anyway, boss."

"Suit yourself."

A hundred dollar bill appeared from nowhere. Roly rolled it into a small tube. He held it up to his eye and peered at me through the miniature telescope. Then he placed it against the line of snow and snorted. He leaned his head back, the rolled bill twirling delicately between his finger and thumb. "Now that's Italian!" He laughed, wiping up the remains with his chubby finger and rubbing it against his upper gum. He smiled at me. The same smile he offered when I was his personal bellhop at the Port-au-Prince Hotel in Haiti, where he vacationed with his whores.

Roly uncapped a tiny jar and tapped another small white pile onto his desk. He picked up the credit card and shaped the pile into a line. He stared at it like it was speaking to him, but he did not snort it. He said, "You're part of something greater than yourself, Emmanuel. Keep your eyes on the prize, say the men who are wise."

"Yes, sir," I said, not knowing what he meant or giving a shit.

Roly's sniffing and sighing could still be heard as I closed the office door behind me and headed up the tunnel to the other end of the track, where William was enjoying his new life with some of the most beautiful horses in the world. At least for the next few weeks.

"Life can only begin," my dada used to say, "where another ends."

And so the World of Debt would spin around and around.

My manman's *grann*, who lived to be ninety-three, believed that when a horse looks a man in the eye and goes mad, it is because it has witnessed the man's future. And the only time a horse can see a man's future is if it is dreadful. It took all my strength not to allow myself to believe those things. Ancient superstitions needed to stay in my homeland. There is no place in America for such ideas. Even if there is some truth to them.

I have seen unbelievable things in my lifetime. More poverty than America will ever know or feel the need to complain about. Tuberculosis and other diseases hit our rural community with a constant hammer. Orphaned children were left begging on the streets, hungry nomads wandering about aimlessly while the government decided who the hell was in charge. Debating about who would or should be the one to fix things. I watched countless presidents and generals take over, giving my people false hope with their false promises, making them believe that a better life is just around the corner. As a child, I listened to arguments taking place in the Saturday markets, about which philosophy would work to make Haiti the way it was before President Duvalier's twenty-year reign. Scores of my relatives disappeared into the horizon upon homemade rafts, in search of a better life in America. In search of riches the Great White Way convinced them they could have.

Many were never seen again.

My dada worked for the railways for a decade, but when they laid him off, and he knew that it was only a matter of time before the line would close indefinitely, liquor quickly became his companion—and not so long after, his enemy. My manman, even though she is a Christian, paid a witch doctor to cast spells to help him with his pain, but I knew they would not work. It is not easy to perform magic when Christian ritual exists all around you. My dada died in his bed, a gallon of dark liquor inside his belly, a drop of fox seed oil on his forehead, an open Bible on his chest.

Things in Haiti got worse for my family after Dada's passing. Food was scarce. Jobs invisible. My older brother joined the national police and began to believe in their corrupt ways. He moved to the other side of the island, where white tourists exhaled money like polluted air.

When I was a teen, my older sister Angelina disappeared into the suburb of Carrefour as a prostitute, every so often coming home to offer money and to ask for Manman's forgiveness. On Angelina's last visit, she gave birth to my nephew. She bled to death on the mattress in her old bedroom. We never knew who the dada was; it could have been anyone. She had known countless men. After Angelina was buried, we began to starve, my manman, baby Anthony, and me. We had no milk, no fresh water or bread, and the sugar cane and coffee which grew wild all around us offered no hope without the skills and resources to refine either.

One afternoon as I searched for roots, I was arrested, accused of stealing a pound of sugar from a neighboring farm.

"What would I do with a pound of sugar?" I asked the policeman who questioned me. "We do not have electricity for baking things."

A few times I had stolen fresh water from the tower a mile and a half away. The entire village was guilty of this. We had many droughts in our part of Haiti. We were thirsty all the time. It was fresh water, for God's sake.

Still, I was accused of being a sugar thief. They tossed me into a makeshift prison, along with another boy a few years younger but no more frightened than the seventeen-year-old that I was. Two days passed without being offered food or water. I had no way of telling my manman where I was. When the hurricane hit, and the policemen in the front office evacuated, they forgot about us in the cell in the back of the prison. Or perhaps they were in too much of a rush to be burdened by a pair of hooligans. Soon, I thought, we would be destroyed by the same element our people so desperately needed.

The holding cell sat in the center of town, and as the water rose into a muddy river, the other boy and I decided it was not worth getting upset over. We would die like many of the others in the path of the storm, and that would be that. At least we wouldn't be hungry anymore.

He and I held onto each other, like brothers, though we weren't related. We didn't have the same shade of skin or the same dialect. But we never let go of each other, even as the river poured into the cell, forcing its way through the front office rooms and down the dirt hallway through the bamboo bars. The boy and I held our breath and waited for the inevitable.

But there were angels in the prison that day.

Water rose to our knees as we stood in the corner waiting for fate to take its course. It swelled to our hips, our bellies, our necks.

As the water lapped at our chins, the cell wall behind us crumbled like a god had reached down from the sky and gritted it apart with invisible fingers. Afraid of drowning, the boy and I latched onto the bamboo bars of the prison door. But as the rest of the cell walls crumbled, we were propelled forward by the water's force, holding onto the cell door like a raft. Dirty water slapped my face until I could barely breathe. Much of it I swallowed. Through the street, the storm's river carried us past what used to be the town square. Past where the fruit stands and Colonial church used to be; the place where I had once fallen and torn my knee open when I played football in the street; the remains of the small hospital where European doctors gave free shots once a year. We rushed through the town on top of the water as dogs and chickens and goats washed under.

I do not know how long we held onto those bars. A large tree the height of an apartment building, which had fallen earlier, stopped us, and we somehow got nestled in its leaves and branches. My knuckles were bleeding. My eyes and sinuses were filled with dirt. We stayed on that bamboo raft for hours, until the rain stopped and the sun shone above us. When we were brave enough to crawl onto the fallen tree trunk, each seeing how badly the other was injured—his left ear barely held on, my right ankle was twisted like a piece of saltwater taffy—we looked behind us and saw that the town had been erased.

We limped back to my home, since his family had given him up when he was ten as they could no longer feed him. My mud-and-brush house stood leaning, its black bamboo posts bent over like skinny old men. Manman sat on a large rock on the hill behind our house, above the streams of drying mud, her head in her arms, crying and singing and praying all at once. I took the boy to her, and she hugged us both and told us it was my dada's spirit who had saved us.

Slowly, survivors cleaned up our village. We unearthed bodies, cattle, humble belongings of those who had perished. We were even more hungry and thirsty than before, but we had survived.

Then my prison friend got tetanus. Smelly pus oozed from his ear. Maggots found the pus and made it their home. A high fever took him. He knew he would die a slow and horrible death, so he stole a large knife from a sleeping rancher and brought the weapon to me in the brush a mile from my home. I remember the air was drier than I had ever known. My mouth was cracked from my lips to my tongue to my gums. Swarms of little black flies kept going for the last bit of water my body had, dipping their insect straws into the cracks in my face.

My friend handed me the sword.

"Do it, Emmanuel," he said to me. "I will be the one judged for making you do this. Not you. You are doing this from your heart. Do not be afraid."

"I am never afraid of killing," I told him. "I am only afraid of being left behind."

He lay on the cracked earth near a dead tree and stared into the sky. "Manman, Dada," he said, as I raised the kouto high into the air, and with the only strength I had, stabbed him in the heart.

Chapter 41

Each day, William showed up for work at lunchtime, even though he didn't need to be at the track until late afternoon. He could sense the workday ahead of him, the exact moment to head out to the bus. It was as if his whole life had led him to this point, working at the Dellshore Racetrack.

When he got back to the apartment each night, he didn't watch television—the cable bill hadn't been paid, and the service was disconnected. William didn't care about the TV anymore. He brought home horse magazines left sitting around the Dellshore employee lounge, articles about gambling, horse-brushing techniques, modern medicines for ailing studs, picking out the words he could read and comprehend. When he finally noticed the CD player had disappeared, he didn't let it bother him. He stopped thinking about Mom. Stopped pining for Stephanie. Nothing mattered but the horses. He was all consumed by them. He began to smell like the barn.

His muscles became more defined, like a WWF contender. His name could have been something like Wild William or Smack-Down Willie. His back was broader, like an Olympic swimmer's. His legs were beefier, like he was squatting hundred-pound weights every day. But he wasn't. He was pitching hay, cleaning stalls, scooping up manure with a shovel until you could nearly eat off the stable floor.

William hummed while he shoveled, shaved, and prepared his mac and cheese dinners from boxes bought in the vending machines at work. He smiled to himself while climbing up the bus steps, down the bus steps, across the track, through the barn, into the steaming manure that waited for him each afternoon.

"Your first payday," Manny told him one week after he was hired. "Go to personnel and they will give you your check."

"Yowza," William said.

"You have my permission to leave early. To celebrate."

Under the late afternoon sun, William ran and I floated across the grounds and down into the tunnel. At the personnel office, he put his face up to the window, his nose leaving a dime-sized dot of oil on the Plexiglas.

"It's my payday!"

The woman behind the counter had her lips permanently pursed together, like a sour pickle had somehow got caught in her mouth and there was nothing she could do about it. She peered over her bifocals.

"Identification."

She stared at a chipped nail while waiting for William to dig the ID card from his wallet. He handed it to her. She held the card up and looked from William to the photo. Without saying a word, she withdrew an envelope from a small file box and passed it through the little half-moon window.

William smiled at her. "I have a bank account, so I'm gonna put it in there."

The woman ignored him and scribbled something in a ledger.

William didn't need her acknowledgement. He grinned all the way to the bus stop.

The bus was empty except for the driver and a pretty blond lady sitting next to a little boy who looked like her. The woman read a magazine article while her son played with his toy truck, zooming it over his legs and across the back of the empty seat in front of him.

William opened the envelope and stared at the three-digit number on the check, as excited as the day he'd received his lottery money.

What do you care about a few hundred dollars? That check isn't enough to get you through one week, with rent and food.

Still smiling, William folded the envelope and stuck it in his back pocket.

Then he stared out the bus window, counting streets as the sun began to set.

The little blond boy, sitting in a seat too large for such a tiny bottom, stared in my direction. His toy truck sat on the seat beside him, momentarily abandoned.

He whispered to his mother, "I want to play with that boy."

"What boy, honey?"

"The one wearing shorts."

William wore his mud-spattered bellbottom jeans. I was infinitely stuck in my denim cutoffs.

"Sweetie," the woman said, "that man is wearing long pants."

She went back to her magazine.

Can you see me? I asked the child.

He nodded his head.

Can you see both of us?

The boy looked at William then back to me. He nodded again and said, "Where are your hands and feet?"

The boy's mother looked up. Her son was staring in William's direction.

"Honey, don't bother that man."

"But the boy don't got any hands or feet."

"Stop being silly."

"What's your name?" the boy asked me.

Billy.

"Trevor," the woman said. "I asked you not to bother that man. He's not listening to you. Leave him alone."

"I'm not talking to the man. I'm talking to the kid." Her son stood up, holding onto the seat to keep his balance as the bus stopped at a red light.

I thumbed toward William. *We're the same person*, I told Trevor.

Trevor nodded his head like he completely understood what I meant.

The mother closed her magazine. She looked at William again, trying to make sense of what her son was telling her. "Honey, there is no little boy over there. Stop playing games and sit back down."

"Why is your hair wet?" the boy asked me, taking a few steps up the aisle, his truck abandoned on one of the seats. "Aren't you cold?"

Not really. Well, I do get goose bumps sometimes—

"Trevor! I said stop talking to that man. Come back here and sit down. Now!"

Little Trevor did as his mother asked, picking up his truck along the way.

I floated until I was next to him. *Shh. Don't say anything*, I told him, wanting to hold my finger to my lips but not being able to. *Your mommy can't see me.*

I looked at Trevor's mother. Her nose was buried deep in the magazine. *Hold up how many fingers you are.*

Trevor held up five, then four, then five again.

I'm fourteen. But I was your age once.

Trevor whispered, "How can you walk without any feet?"

I don't have any idea, I told him. *I sort of float.*

"Are you an angel? Where are your wings?"

The boy's mother slapped her magazine against her lap and grabbed Trevor by the arm. "That's it! You may not say one more word until we get home. Do you understand?"

Trevor's eyes filled with tears as he nodded his head. He pushed himself back into the dirty seat beside his mother and pulled his toy truck to his chest, pouting.

Don't say anything, I told him. *We don't want you to get in trouble. Your mommy can't see me. It's our own special secret, okay?*

Trevor's eyes told me he understood.

We sat in silence for another mile until the bus driver pulled over and Trevor's mother stood up. She rolled the magazine and stuffed it into her pocketbook, then took her child by the hood of his jacket and dragged him up the aisle, his truck tucked in the crevice of his arm. He held out the other hand to touch my face, but his mother was moving too quickly. Off the bus they went.

The driver shut the doors and pulled away from the curb. I looked out the window. Trevor glanced up at me from the sidewalk.

Thank you, I said, hoping he would understand.

Trevor smiled and waved.

At Southern States Bank & Trust, William carefully filled out the deposit slip, exactly the way Lance had shown him when he'd deposited his *Lotsa Luck* check. Depositing such a large check was a big deal, even for a big bank like Southern States. And this time he was on his own, though he got a little help from a teller named Gina.

William walked up to the counter and pulled out his state ID card.

"Today's my first paycheck," he told her.

"Well, good for you," Gina said sweetly. "And you made it just in time. We're about to close. Would you like some cash back?"

"Okay."

"You need to write down how much you want, subtract it from the subtotal, and then sign right here."

"I need to buy milk and orange juice and eggs and Captain Crunch…" William looked up at the ceiling. "…and toilet paper!"

The other tellers, busy closing out their drawers, glanced in our direction.

"Okay," the pretty brunette said patiently. "How about twenty?"

William nodded.

She helped him write the amount and showed him again where to sign his name. She exchanged his deposit slip for a twenty dollar bill.

"Here you go, Mr. Baker."

William beamed. He liked being called *Mr. Baker*.

"I need to take the bus to the Piggly Wiggly," he told the girl. "Do you know how?"

"The one on Johnson?"

William nodded.

The girl spoke to another employee.

"The bus stop is right across the street," Gina said. "Just take the number seventeen."

William carefully placed the twenty in his wallet and left the bank. He stepped onto the sidewalk and breathed in the evening sun.

I followed William across the street. He sat on the bench. I sat beside him, wondering if my legs were swaying even though I couldn't see them. Together we waited for the bus that would take us to Piggly Wiggly, the only store William had ever been to for groceries. With Mom. Back in a time that felt like eons ago.

Chapter 42

My boss called me into his office.

"Wassup with your ass tonight?" he asked as he dug around in his mouth with a toothpick. "Those men aren't paying to see their granny up there on that stage. Get it together, girl, or take some time off."

So I took a week. Boss's suggestion.

What did I care if I missed out on a thousand bucks? I had over twenty-two thousand dollars in my IRA, and I owned two condos—the one I lived in and another I rented out down in the Keys. The year before I'd bought a bunch of stock in what I heard was a hot new company, supposedly the wave of the future, even though the name *Yahoo* sounded funny. My investment guy only expected a little hoochie-coo every once in a while for supervising my finances, so it worked out for everyone.

What? Did you think I'd be dancing till I was sixty-five?

Anyways, what the hell was going through my mind about William, I have no idea. I found myself thinking about him at the oddest times. The whole thing was driving me batty. I'd been with millionaires, cops, attorneys, professors, politicians. So why William? I wish I could say. I really do. Maybe I felt sorry for him. Maybe I was curious. Maybe it was being the soft-hearted fool that I was deep down.

He was working at the track for a while now, but I didn't know his schedule. So I decided to make a surprise visit.

I'd been sitting on the floor outside William's apartment for a few minutes, twiddling my thumbs, when a woman in a robe appeared at the top of the stairwell. She shuffled toward me like an ugly ghost. Her hair was greasy and looked like it had been teased with a pick and doused with a can of Aqua Net. Her robe was soiled around the bottom and dragged along the floor. Her feet were invisible. I hugged my pocketbook and cringed against William's door.

The creepy ghost stopped a foot away from me. The skin on her face was like a cracked leather chair at the Goodwill. She stared down at me and said in a scratchy voice, "Something y'all need?"

"I'm waiting for someone," I told her, "if it's all the same to you."

"That shithead borrows my car whenever it pleases him, never puts gas in it, never answers the door, and owes me rent. So, yeah, it is all the same to me."

I stood up. She'd seemed tall when I was sitting on the floor, but now, standing face to face, I saw how tiny and skinny she was.

Her breath smelled like whiskey and beef jerky. She nodded toward the apartment door. "You his new hooker?"

I bit my lip. "I'm a friend."

"Didn't know Donald had friends." She tightened her robe with the terrycloth belt. As the hem lifted, I spotted a pair of tattered slippers, which, thank God, covered her toes.

"I'm not friends with Donald," I said as if it was any of her beeswax. "I'm friends with his brother."

"Brother? Well, I swanee. Didn't know Donald dip-shit come from a real-live family. Always thought he growed out of some fungus on a cave wall or somethin'." Her sudden laughter pushed her into a coughing fit. Her face turned red as she bent over, her hand covering her mouth. When she was finished hacking, she said, "Y'all got any money?"

"For what?"

"For an itty bitty shot or two. Was fixin' to relax tonight."

"Why would I give you money?"

"Seems to me you'd be more at home in the apartment than out here with the rats…" She made a sick chirping sound with her lips. She pulled a set of keys from her robe pocket, holding them up for me to see. "I'm Queen Sherri, ruler of the building and all who live here. I could go in there right now, if I wanted. Snoop through the little shit's mail. Watch my stories on his TV. Open the medicine cabinet and see what kinda condoms he's using these days. Or…" Sherri clutched the top of her robe with her free hand. Her eyes opened wide. "Oh, no! What if he's hurt? What if he's fell down in the bathtub? I better go see if my tenant is alright!" Her teased hair stood frozen on top of her head as she jiggled the keys. "Y'all go on down to the ABC store, honey, it's right on the corner, and pick me up a bottle of Jack Daniels. A fifth'll do fine. You look like a workin' girl who could part with some cash. Let's say you put that bottle outside apartment 1-A and ring the doorbell, and then come on back up and this here door will be unlocked like it was magic."

Sherri turned away from me like we'd made an agreement, her robe dragging behind her, the echo of keys fading away as she made her way back down the stairwell.

Chapter 43

I was drownin'. A hill of rocks sat on my chest as I laid flat on the bottom of the pond. Donald was starin' down at me from the dock, his face blurry through the water.

I looked for my Billy. Searched for his blond wavy hair, his denim shorts. *Billy, where are you?* Bubbles rose up, but no other sounds came to me.

I tried to pull off them rocks that pinned me to the pond's bottom, but they were too heavy against my chest. My arms and legs were free, and I kicked 'em hard, hopin' to make the rocks fall offa me and let me go. But they weren't strong enough.

How did I get down here? Where is my boy?

The rocks grew heavier. My ribs were splittin' open. My shoulders felt like someone was standin' on them.

I began to sob, my cries fillin' the water with sound, the water fillin' my mouth.

Then a voice said, "Hey, Ma." I looked to my right.

Billy!

My baby boy was comin' for me, praise the Lord. He would save me. He would move the rocks from my chest and help me swim to the top, so's I could get some air. We would hold each other and cry on the dock and then our tears would turn to laughter when we realized it had all been a dream. No one really drowned, no one died, not me, not my Billy.

As he swum closer, his face got clearer.

It wasn't Billy after all.

Donald? I said, all of a sudden fearful, but not knowin' why.

He sat cross-legged next to me on the pond floor. He seemed to breathe so easy under the water.

Where's your brother at? I asked him.

Donald said, *He's in the net. That's where he lives now. I'll be your favorite son from now on. The only one you'll ever need.*

I need Billy.

No, you don't.

Yes, I do. Get him out of the net, Donald.

Donald swum away, and I felt relief that he'd gone to free his brother. But when he came back, Billy wasn't with him. He dragged a large bag behind him. The bag stirred up sand and silt as he dropped it between us.

What's that? I asked him.

Donald smiled. *You'll see.*

He opened the bag and began pullin' out more rocks. One by one, real slow and careful, he added them to the pile on my chest…

Just a crazy dream, I told myself a hundred times as I stretched the hairnet over my bun, spread strawberry jam on my toast, added sweetener to my coffee.

The dream faded as the day wore on, but the knot in my chest never left. I found it hard to breath, hard to lift my arms, as if they'd fought long and hard against my covers in the night.

The other ladies in the cafeteria told me I looked pale, that my lips looked white as Saltines.

"You feelin' okay, Fran?" Selma the head cook asked me. "You lookin' like hell."

I felt like hell, pardon my French.

It was a long day.

After I got home from work, I tried callin' Donald on his travel phone again, but the robot voice told me he still wasn't available. I called his apartment too, but this time the operator apologized and said, "We're sorry, the number you have reached is no longer in service. Please check the number and dial again." Well, I thought. Enough was enough. I couldn't take it no more. I had to see for myself that my William was okay.

Hardly ever drove downtown, what with the meters eatin' up all my dimes and the parkin' bein' so bad. I prayed I'd be able to squeeze my Buick into a space near Donald's apartment. And that no one would steal my hubcaps.

Only been to the apartment one time, back when Donald first got the place. A nasty part of town. Girlie clubs around the corner and homeless people sleepin' on the sidewalks. Wouldn't never figure out what the draw was. Been better off stayin' at the house, but he wanted to be on his own. Always was a spirited child, even if he didn't have much sense. Like a wild horse nobody could tame.

The sun was wantin' to set behind the trees by the time I got onto the highway. I thought my heart would explode with how fast it was runnin'. My stomach wouldn't settle. I worried about gettin' lost. What if I got turned around in that section where drug dealers and come up to your car while you're stopped at a red light? What if my car broke down? Sometimes she made this clankin' sound for no good reason. Vinnie, my mechanic, said not to worry none about it, just a sound an older car makes without havin' a reason. But it kept me on edge anyways. And what if I made it all the way to Donald's apartment and no one was there? Would I sit in the hallway waitin'? Would I sit in my car? And for how long? If I had my druthers, I'd drag my son back home with me. But what if I showed up, and William was there, and nothin' was wrong at all? He'd be embarrassed I was checkin' up on him. Maybe even be angry.

I would take my chances. The house seemed so empty since William left, cold and vacant and lifeless. Like it used to be a pretty box filled with Christmas presents, and now it was just an ugly cardboard box with nothin' inside.

Something else come upon me as I drove: what if William didn't remember me the way he used to? Time was a funny thing with William. He mixed up mornin' with night. Forgot different events, holidays. Would think his birthday was Christmas, or Easter was the Fourth of July, until I reminded him which was which. If somethin' was out of sight for more than a few days, it was usually gone for good, bless his heart. 'Cept for Stephanie and those damn songs, pardon my French. Of course, he never forgot Donald neither, so maybe there was a chance he wouldn't forget his mama...

Thirty minutes later, I saw yellow and white streams lightin' up the city sky.

Back when Mr. Baker and me was first married, we'd some nights head downtown for a drink at the Casper Hotel, smack dab in the heart of the business district, a few blocks from the China Garden, where they served real Chinese food. At the hotel, we'd listen to a wild black piano player named PJ Carmichael and dance till midnight. Sometimes we'd even have a martini or two, with extra olives. PJ would announce us when we entered the bar, sayin', "Here come my favorite couple, Fran and Frank!" But I don't think the Casper Hotel is there no more. I think it's condos now.

Then there were the days at the downtown zoo. Frank and me and the boys would head to the zoo on a sunny Sunday after church, with a can of peanuts to feed the elephants and a picnic basket filled with my crispy fried chicken. I think the zoo is still there, only I don't think it's as nice as it used to be.

Oh, don't let's forget the holidays! There's not much to see in the way of Christmas decorations out in the countryside, 'cept maybe a plastic nativity scene or a couple of flashin' lights. But mercy, if you could see downtown! All the shops' windows filled up with Christmas goodies, lights strung over every tree and doorway. Mannequins dressed up like elves. Salvation Army Santas ringin' their bells on the corners. And if it snowed, now that would be a real treat. You could almost hear Jimmy Stewart screamin', "Merry Christmas, Bedford Falls!" as you hurried with your bundles.

But Christmas was over. Spring was here, and the rain started hittin' my dirty windshield, a spatterin' at first, then harder as I took the Rogers Boulevard off-ramp toward Donald's apartment.

I hadn't planned on rain. Crud, I thought, pardon my French. Bad weather was the last thing I needed to add to my worries right about then.

Chapter 44

We strolled up and down the aisles at the Piggly Wiggly, hovering over each and every box of cereal: Lucky Charms, which William'd had enough of; Raisin Bran, no toy inside the box; Wheaties, not enough sugar for taste; and fifty other brands that William either hadn't tried or didn't care to try. He finally narrowed it down to Captain Crunch, with a do-it-yourself pin-wheel kit inside, and Fruit Loops, with a chance on the back of the box to win a college scholarship.

William tossed both into the cart and rolled over to the bread section.

Four long shelves were dedicated to dozens of different breads. Nature's Best Whole Wheat or Home Pride White? Sourdough or potato? English muffins or bagels? Raisin bread or cinnamon swirl? Donuts or éclairs? William grabbed two loaves of plain white and tossed them onto the child's seat in the cart.

Watch your money, I told him.

Shampoo, paper towels, toilet paper…

Hope you're adding this up.

Frozen Gionelli's pizza, frozen Eggo waffles, two chicken pot pies, milk, orange juice, sliced American cheese, brown eggs. Mom always insisted on brown, since she believed they tasted more like eggs than the white ones.

I floated next to him as he put his groceries on the conveyor belt. A spiked-haired girl with a tiny diamond on the side of her nose rang up the items while a pimply boy put them in paper bags.

"Twenty-four-seventy-six," the cashier told William.

"I got a twenty," William said, pulling the bill out of his wallet and proudly handing it to the girl.

"You still need four dollars and seventy-six cents."

The girl, whose name tag said to call her Mandy, didn't seem fazed that the line behind us was growing.

"I don't got any more," William said.

I thought how absurd it was that William would soon have access to over six hundred thousand dollars, but he didn't have five extra dollars in his wallet.

"Well," Mandy said, "let's take something out of the bag to lower your total." She reached into the bag. "How about one of these breads?" She took one of the white bread loaves out of the bag and put it on the counter. "Let's see…now you're down to twenty-two dollars and eighty-four cents." She rooted through the bag. "Do you need to have two boxes of cereal?"

"I love cereal." He began to sniffle.

Mandy looked up. Five people waited in line behind William.

"Look," Mandy said, "I'm sorry, but you gotta pick out something that comes to two dollars and some change, or we're never gonna get through this line. *Capiche?*"

"You already took a loaf of bread," William told her. "Now I only have one loaf. The bank said to get twenty." Splotches of red appeared on William's cheeks and neck. He looked down at his hands.

"Come on, buddy," a fat man behind us said. "Some of us have plans."

I looked at the items the man had put on the motionless conveyor belt behind William's: a large can of Colt 45, a box of imitation Wheat Thins, and a can of chicken-and-stars soup.

"I don't wanna take anything out," William said. "I can give you the money tomorrow. I can go back to the b-b-bank."

The girl tried a new tactic. "Why don't we use your ATM card? That way you can pay for it all now."

"I don't have no ATM card." William started to cry. "Why can't I give it to you tomorrow? I have lots of money. I was number 7-9-2. I was on TV!"

The line of customers grew silent. Men and women in nearby aisles looked up from their grocery lists. The store manager stared down from his raised booth behind the glass barrier.

A sweet voice floated over to us. A voice as unforgettable as the girl who spoke. "William? That you?"

Three people in line leaned back so William could see.

"Stephanie!"

She wore a peach-colored jacket with a pretty skirt. Her crimped hair was pulled back in a loose bun. She wore no makeup. And she was beautiful.

"Do you need some money, William?"

"I have money," he told Stephanie, drying his cheeks. "I got me a job training horses. I got me a paycheck. I got me a bank."

"Excuse me," Stephanie told the people as they moved out of her way. She stepped beside William. "I only have a few things," she told the cashier as she placed her items on the belt, a bottle of vitamins and a small rectangular box with the letters *EPT* on the side. "Whatever he owes, add mine to it. I'll pay for it."

William stared at Stephanie. I thought for sure he'd plant a kiss on her in front of everyone. Instead, he let her pay, then he grabbed his bags and followed her through the sliding doors. Under the store's awning, a scrawny kid put a quarter in an electric horse and climbed on its back as it began to move. The music sounded like a *Bugs Bunny* cartoon. In the distance, thick clouds tried to smother the sunset.

"What are you doing way out here, William?" Stephanie asked. "I thought you were living downtown with your brother."

"I..." William looked at the ring on her left hand. He straightened out his back, trying to stand taller, shifting the two bags of groceries. "I got me a job at the track. I work with Manny and take care of horses and get paid. I clean the stables, brush their coats, and feed them. My favorite is Neapolitan. I call her Neon. She smiles at me when I call her that. I do really good at work."

"What happened to your eye?" she asked.

The bruise had faded to a pale yellow circle.

"It was an accident," he said. After a pause, he said, "I saw you in the paper. Are you still married?"

Stephanie smiled. "Yes, William, I'm still married. You sound happy. Are you? I'd be really sad if I thought you weren't."

William shrugged.

"You need a ride somewhere?" she asked.

"No," he said, readjusting his grocery bags. "I know how to take the bus. I have a pass."

"You do?"

He nodded. "I gotta get home and make dinner. Chicken pot pie and a glass of milk."

"You cook for yourself?"

"I cook and clean and buy groceries. I have a good job. Manny gave it to me. He likes me. And I have a friend name Cecilia. She has long red hair."

"A girlfriend?" When he didn't answer, Stephanie said, "That's wonderful, William. You seem so…different. Maybe moving to the city was exactly what you needed."

William smiled.

"How's your mom doing?" she asked.

The smile faded. "Mom?"

A cool wind started to blow. Beyond the awning, raindrops sprinkled onto the parking lot.

Stephanie said, "You do keep in touch with her, don't you?"

"Yes." His face turned red with the lie.

"Be sure to give her a big hello from me, next time you talk to her. Tell her I'll stop by and see her soon, will you?"

William nodded.

"I should go," said Stephanie. "Cooking dinner and hitting the hay early. I have a meeting with another vet first thing in the morning. We're thinking of opening up a practice together. Over on Townsend. You know, in that strip mall next to the pet supply store."

"Oh."

"So," she said. "Take care, huh? I'm sure we'll see each other real soon."

As she smiled, she cocked her head to the side, like she was looking in the glass window of the Piggly Wiggly. I stood in her line of vision. Our eyes met.

She shook her head only slightly, but I caught it.

"Be careful going home," she told William, touching his arm before walking in the drizzle to her blue Honda Accord. William and I watched as she put the groceries on the passenger seat, walked around the car, and slid behind the wheel. She started the engine and tapped her horn, waving slightly as she exited the Piggly Wiggly parking lot, her tail lights shrinking to tiny red dots as she headed up the access road.

The rain fell harder as we jogged across the lot to the covered bus stop. When the bus arrived, William asked the driver which one would take him to Stoney Brook Avenue.

"Where my mom lives," he told the man.

The bus driver told him to hop on, he'd get him there.

So we did.

Chapter 45

I woke up to a soft tapping sound. Except for a neon light glowing outside the window, the room was dark. I was covered by a smelly comforter and sitting up on a couch. At first I thought maybe I'd gone home with a customer who drugged me. It had happened once to a dancer I knew.

Then I remembered where I was: William's empty apartment.

Stretching my arms into the air, I turned my head from side to side until my neck popped.

The soft tapping came again. Someone at the door. Maybe Sherri, asking for more booze.

A woman called from the hallway. "William?"

It didn't sound like the landlord's voice.

Another knock, this time louder.

I turned on the end table lamp. Pins and needles tingled their way down to my ankles as I slid off the sofa and limped to the door. I shook out my legs. "Who is it?"

"Do I have the right apartment?" the woman asked.

"Depends on who you're looking for."

"William."

"Who are you?" I asked.

"Who are *you*?" came the answer.

"A friend," I told the woman.

"Please open the door. If my son's in there, I'd like to speak at him."

Her *son?*

My hand squeezed the doorknob and slowly opened it.

In front of me stood a short and squatty pear-shaped woman with graying hair pulled back in a tight bun. Her dress was out of a 1950's Sears catalogue; her shoes were the ugly tan ones volunteer librarians wear. She wore a brown sweater across her shoulders, buttoned once at her throat. A large black pocketbook dangled from her hand.

"Can I come in?" she asked.

I stepped back and held the door open.

She took a look around, walking into the bathroom and the kitchen, then gazing out the window over the fire escape. She turned to me. "Where is he?"

I shrugged. "Maybe on his way home."

"Home?"

She stared at me, sizing me up the same way I was sizing her up. Only she was staring at my cleavage.

I said, "You know, *here*...to his home *here*." I pulled my messy hair from the Scrunchie, scooped it up like a tail, and retied it. "Why don't you sit or something? I've been here for a while. It doesn't help to pace around the room. Trust me."

We sat at the same time, each of us on either end of the couch.

"Who are you?" she asked me. "Why are you here?"

God, I was so lucky my mama never stuck her nose in my business, never cared what I did, as long as it didn't mess up her plans. She was always one to give me room to grow, even if she didn't always have food in the fridge.

"My name's Cecilia," I told her. "I was worried when I hadn't heard from William in a few days."

"*Days?*"

"It's not like we talk all the time. We only met a few weeks ago. I came by to see how he was getting along. The landlord let me in. She's a wacky—"

"Where'd you meet him?"

I was ready for the question, since I'd been asked this by a handful of other men's mamas in different situations. "At the nightclub where I work. He came in with a friend. You have a very nice son, Mrs.—" I drew a blank.

"You don't know my son's last name?"

"I'm not so good with names," I said.

"It's Baker. B-a-k-e-r. How do you know my son? Where's he at? Why aren't you tellin' me?"

"I told you, I met him at my work—"

A knock startled both of us.

"Shit," I said, as I got up and opened the door a crack.

Sherri.

"What?" I said.

"I was thinking that maybe you could give me the money Donald owes me. Then he could pay you back the next time y'all meet for a screw."

I could feel William's mama boring her eyes into the back of my head. "I told you, I don't know Donald. I only know his brother."

"I don't give a rat's ass who you know," Sherri said. "If I don't get the rent in one week, I will evict the sonofabitch." She poked her nose through the crack. "Who's that?" she asked. "You hire a maid?"

"You'll get your rent money," I told her, not answering her question. "Now go away and mind your own business."

"One week. After that, ya'll can't blame me for what happens."

Sherri's slipper pulled back as I closed the door.

"One week!" she shouted from the hallway.

I turned to Mrs. Baker. "She's an alcoholic. Ignore her."

"My William might be thrown out on the street, and you're telling me to ignore her? She began rooting through her pocketbook. "Just need to find my checkbook."

"I can pay the rent and William can pay me back when he gets his paycheck."

"What paycheck?"

"From his job."

"Job?"

"Taking care of horses—down at—"

"That's what he told you?" Mrs. Baker shook her head. "That he's takin' care of horses? He's been talkin' that way for years. What he's been tellin' you is wishful thinkin'. I know my son."

188

"Then you must not know him very well."

For a sweet-looking old lady, she sure could give a death stare.

"What do *you* do for a livin'?" she all of a sudden asked.

"Excuse me?"

"You're a prostitute, ain't you? Did you get my son a job workin' for you? Is he some sort of pimp or somethin'?"

"Are you kidding me?"

"Then why are you bein' so secretive?"

"Fine," I told her. "I'm an exotic dancer. I love it, I'm good at it, and your son paid money to see me do it." I picked up my jacket and pocketbook from the couch and headed to the door. "Feel free to hang out. I'm getting a bite to eat."

Just before I opened the door, Mrs. Baker stood up.

"Wait."

I waited.

"We're both worried about William, right? I mean, it's good that there's other people 'sides me lookin' out for his welfare."

"And your point is?"

"Well, it seems to me we should be workin' together, instead of workin' apart."

My stomach growled.

"I could make you some dinner," she said. "Maybe there's somethin' in this place to scrounge up." She glanced toward the kitchen.

"Look, Mrs. Baker," I said. "William's making a little money and feels like he's doing something useful. Don't you think that's a good thing?"

"What he does with his money is nobody's business."

I held out the back of my right hand. "See this emerald and diamond ring? Paid for, in cash, from the jewelry mart downtown. And this pocketbook? Ninety dollars. Also cash paid. I do quite well on my own, thank you very—"

"Are you...*spendin' time* with my son?" She glared at me, waiting for my answer.

"We're friends," I said. "That's all."

"You do realize he's slow?"

"Yes."

"Then why, if you have so much money and plenty of men waitin' to see you dance, do you feel the need to spend time with my son?"

"I've been asking myself that same—"

"And what'll you do if he falls for you? Just cuz he's slow, don't mean he don't got what it takes to fall in love."

"Thanks for the compliment," I said, "but you got nothing to worry about. William knows we're only friends. He really does have a handle on things. I know you think he can't take care of himself—"

"Did he say that?"

"Not in so many words. I can see you're worried about him. But William does pretty good by himself."

Mrs. Baker looked at her watch and then at the window. "It's dark. And it's rainin'."

"He probably stopped at the grocery store or at a restaurant."

"And how would he get there?" she asked.

"With his bus pass."

"My William?" she asked. "A bus pass? Grocery shopping? He wouldn't know what to buy. And he's never had no restaurant meal without me his whole life."

"Maybe it's time he did."

There was that glare again.

I sighed. "Why don't I call the track and see if he's working late? Then at least we'll get an idea of when he'll be home."

"The track," Mrs. Baker said, shaking her head. "I can't imagine…" She grabbed the gold cross hanging from her neck. "Go on then. Make the call."

I pulled my brand new Nokia mobile phone from my pocketbook, flipped it open, and got the operator to connect me.

A woman answered. "Dellshore Race Track."

"I'm trying to find an employee by the name of William Baker."

"Which department?"

"Stables, I guess."

"Please hold."

After three rings a man answered, and I knew it was the bastard before he even spoke.

"Emmanuel speaking."

"It's Cecilia," I said. "You know, the chicken soup girl."

Manny said nothing.

"I was wondering if William left work already."

"Why should I tell you?" he asked.

"We have plans tonight and he's late."

"Why does a bitch girl like you want to be hanging around with a man like William?"

"What he does on his own time is *his* business," I said.

"You fuck with him and I will make sure your legs never wrap around a pole again."

"I just wanted to know what time he's off. That's all."

Manny paused. "Over an hour ago. Probably went to that tits and ass bar to find another whore. One without your—"

I hung up on Emmanuel and said to William's mom, "He got off an hour ago."

Mrs. Baker sat on the edge of the couch. "He's takin' the bus to goodness knows where. He's livin' in this dump. No home-cooked meals, no backyard, no real bed, no one to look after him."

"What about his brother?" I asked.

"Donald? His travel phone don't work no more." She leaned over and picked up the apartment phone, listened a few seconds, then put it back in the cradle. "No dial tone."

"Is he supposed to be taking care of William?" I asked.

"I'm not sure what he's supposed to be doin'. All's I know is he ain't here neither." Mrs. Baker's eyes grew wide. "You don't suppose they're both in trouble, do you?"

"Worrying about them isn't gonna do much, right? Why don't we wait another half hour, then if William doesn't come home, we'll go out and try to find him."

"Yes. Try to find him."

"Don't worry, Mrs. Baker," I told her. "Your son is fine. I'm sure of it."

Sometimes trying to convince other people you believe what you're saying can be as hard as trying to make a gay man go straight.

But it sure can be interesting trying.

Chapter 46

Girls like that pinda get their money by fucking men and fucking *with* men. Money and sex are separate issues. Anybody can fuck, but it takes intelligence to make a dollar grow, to see potential in a financial future.

I taught William how to read a bus schedule and how to set an alarm clock. In exchange, William gave me his trust. He told me how he loved music as much as horses. About wanting his independence. About his brother telling him what to do and when to do it, locking him up for days in that stifling apartment, like a prison. He worked hard at the barn, sweeping, shoveling, doing as told, no complaining, no lollygagging. He even showed up to work early sometimes so he could spend extra time with Neapolitan. He knew that beauty from the tip of her snout to the end of her smooth tail. Knew what her different snorts meant. What her nodding head was saying. What her eyes were telling him as he brushed or washed her.

He was crazy about that fucking horse.

That was too bad.

I told him not to get attached. Sometimes things happen: they break a bone, get an ear infection, or end up with bladder trouble. But William was like a child who never listened when it came to those realities. He only lived in the moment. Like there was no yesterday and tomorrow was not yet printed on the calendar.

William did not know he was my ticket to freedom. He did not even understand what it meant to be rich. He only wanted to work, go home, sleep, then come back and do it all again. He did not want a day off. I told him the union would not allow that, so he would have to take a day off even if he didn't want to. In reality, we did not have a union. I was just making sure that nothing stood out regarding his employment. That he was just a regular Joe.

"I can still come down and pet them on my day off, can't I?" he asked me.

I told him I did not see the harm in that.

He wore a pair of my headphones while he cleaned, which I told him he could keep. Inside the cassette player was an ancient tape of some disco music I had loved as a kid in Haiti. I envied those men and women, especially the black ones, allowed to live a life of song and leisure in America. While listening to the music, William would brush Neapolitan's neck, then do a turn and drop to the floor in a near split, like she was his audience. Luckily, there had been no more incidents like that first day.

One night, after a ten-hour day in the stables, Roly called me down to his office. I was worn out. My fingernails were thick with filth, my black boots caked in manure and dirt. I nearly swayed before him, ready to fall over from exhaustion.

"You have an important meeting tomorrow," Roly told me. "The details will be explained to you then. Listen carefully to what you are told. Apparently there is some real science to all of this, and the littlest mistake could mean no more America for you. Understand?"

I nodded.

"In the meantime, I want to give you something to show good faith. You understand what good faith means?"

He always talked to me like because I wasn't born in America, I didn't understand a fucking word he said.

I nodded again.

Roly rolled back in his chair and opened the top drawer of his desk. He laid a white envelope on the desk and slid it in my direction.

"For you, Emmanuel. For working hard and keeping with the plan, even during adversity."

I picked up the envelope and quickly leafed through the wad of bills, counting the fifties.

"One thousand," Roly said. "The other nine grand will come as soon as our boy—*your* boy—does the deed." Roly-Poly sat back in his chair. "Get yourself a hooker. Buy some fancy grub. Take your mama to a show." He smiled. "And you thought I was all bad."

I rolled up the envelope and shoved it into the front pocket of my jeans. It looked like I was very happy to see Roly-Poly, if you know what I am saying. I headed up the tunnel and out across the greens, back to the horses.

Soon, I would be an American. Soon, my pay would be for hard work and not for servitude. I would finally have a life outside of a barn, in a world where I could make something of myself without stinking like a pile of kaka afterward.

Chapter 47

Julie gave me Mrs. B's message the second I walked through my back door on Monday evening. The crew had been given a long weekend on account of they were doing some repairs on one of the machines at the plant. I was more tired after fishing than after a nine-hour shift.

I set the cooler of fish on the back porch as I stepped into the mudroom. "What did she say, exactly?"

Julie said, "That she was worried about William, she hadn't heard from him in ages, and…"

"What?" I sat on the mud bench and pulled off my sneakers, then my sweaty socks.

"She seemed so sad, Lance. So…lost."

I pulled my dirty shirt over my head and tugged off my jeans, throwing them into a pile on the floor.

"Where are the kids?" I asked.

"James has wrestling practice until five, and Shelby's over at Tammy's trying to get their science project to blow smoke."

Julie bent over and picked up the smelly pile of clothes, pulled the pocketknife and lighter out of the pocket of my jeans, poured detergent into the washer, dumped the clothes in, turned the knob, and shut the lid. It never ceased to amaze me how she did things like that without even thinking.

She sat beside me on the mud bench and put her hand on top of mine. "I think you should go and see what you can do. Maybe after dinner? I know where I can get some fresh trout to cook."

I smiled.

She gave my hand a squeeze, then let go. Her fingers crawled like a spider down my leg to my crotch. "You got time for a little bit of me while the kids are out?"

Twelve-plus years together and my wife still made me horny. She squeezed me where it counts, and I could feel myself grow. Her eyes had that dreamy look that I knew to take advantage of before the house was busy with kids and homework.

"I need a shower," I told her. "I'm all slimy."

Julie scratched her nails against the scruffy two-day whiskers growing on my chin. "That's okay," she said. "I can clean you up after."

I drove on the highway in the tail end of Monday rush hour as the sun disappeared behind the tall buildings. Julie and I loved going downtown but hadn't much since my management promotion at Morris Plastics. Plus, the kids always had somewhere to be, and of course we were their shuttle service.

The new arena shot beams of lights high in the sky, one sports game or another going on, though I wasn't sure what exactly. Always been a Nascar fan. And the occasional weekend bowler.

Working long hours and trying to maintain a family life don't give a man much time to think, but I thought about William as I headed down the darkening highway, about how his life had changed so much since turning thirty. Winning the lottery. Getting a job. Opening a couple of bank accounts. Living with his brother.

If there's one thing William really lost that awful summer day it was the caution he'd always shown with Donald. Somehow, the childhood fear that Donald would do something ruthless had drowned right along with William's senses.

The doctors said he'd be a vegetable. That he'd live at home in a bed, probably for years, with tubes feeding him sugar and protein, and Mr. and

Mrs. B taking turns reading to him, sponge bathing him, talking to him, on the outside chance he might wake up one day.

When he did wake up, the doctors called William a miracle. Even stuck his name in a medical book. He spent two years re-learning stuff. Not everything, but enough to be a real person, not some vegetable lying in a soiled bed, his muscles withering away.

Back in the days before the pond incident, we called him Billy. That stopped after he woke up and got his words back. He wouldn't let no one call him Billy again. Said to call him William, that was his given name. And everyone did. 'Cept his dad. Mr. B had a hard time letting go of the old Billy. Couldn't relate to the new one at all.

Imagine losing a son, then getting him back as a different person. It'd be like having your kid replaced by an alien. You know it's him. It looks like him, feels like him, sounds like him, but he's not the same person who disappeared. Still, there's no excuse for leaving your family.

Some folks in the neighborhood whispered behind the Bakers' backs for a long time, about Mr. Baker disappearing on account of his son being brain damaged and all. Disappeared one Sunday morning while Mrs. B and William were at church. William had just turned sixteen. Donald was hanging out with the wrong crowd, living in some lady's garage on the other side of town. He never visited the family much after Mr. B left, so I tried to help 'em out, mowing the lawn, staying with William while Mrs. B went to the grocery store or the doctor. Stephanie came around a lot too, for a while.

Money was tight. Mr. B didn't write or send money or nothing. And Mrs. B ended up working two jobs: one in the middle school cafeteria and the other at home as William's caregiver. I did what I could in the beginning, but after James was born, and then Shelby two years later, there wasn't much I could do without sacrificing my own family.

Julie was mostly patient with me before our kids entered our lives, even got a kick out of telling her friends how sensitive I was to be spending time with my brain-damaged friend I'd known since the summer before first grade. But once my babies came along, there was no way I could explain to my wife, or my kids, why Daddy wasn't gonna be home for supper, or why Daddy wasn't around for a fun video on a rainy day on account of it happened to fall on William's birthday.

At first, I tried to mix my own family with William's, but that didn't work out. Last time was more than a few years back at the Fireman's chili cook-off, William with Mrs. B, and me and Julie with our two little ones. I think they were two and four at the time, still in the stage of grabbing hold of our knees when strangers were around. We ran into each other at the Dalmatian Fire Prevention booth. My kids loved those dogs after seeing the Disney flick, did everything but climb on 'em. Believe it or not, William and his mother and my wife had only met once before, at our wedding reception, and that was such a crazy night, so many guests, Julie wouldn't have recognized William if she'd tripped over him on her way to the limo.

Anyways, William was checking out the Dalmatians near the fire trucks, and when we showed up and I introduced him to Julie, he gave her a big bear hug. But when he saw my kids, he froze. Shelby was sitting in her stroller, playing with the little spinning toys hanging on the front, and James was holding my hand. William stared at the two of 'em. James kept squeezing my fingers.

I said to William, "These are my kids, James and Shelby."

William didn't say a word. Maybe he was trying to figure out how come James looked like me and Shelby looked like my wife. Whatever the reason, he just stood there, like Baby Huey, staring down at my two kids.

Shelby got to crying and James hid behind my legs.

"William," Mrs. B said, "say hello to Lance's children."

"It's alright," Julie said. "He doesn't have to…"

I think my wife was perfectly happy not having a giant teddy bear tower over her children.

When William finally spoke, he asked me, "Where'd you get 'em?" He was in awe. Like my kids were real live angels. "They look just like you."

I tried to break the tension. "Well, as long as they don't look like the UPS man."

Nervous laughter moved around our little circle.

"Just like you," William repeated, his eyes going back and forth between Shelby and James and Julie and me.

"Looks like there's some great food here today," I said. "Can't wait for a bowl of chili."

William said, "I want one."

"There's plenty for everyone," Mrs. B said. "Fourteen booths this year."

"I want one of *them*." William pointed to James, still hanging on for dear life behind my knees, his fingers digging into my thighs, his tiny forehead pressed against my buttocks.

"He wants *what*?" Julie said, pulling the stroller closer to her.

William set his eyes on Shelby and leaned over her like a scientist examining a bug. She started whimpering.

"Lance," my wife said under her breath.

"He won't do nothing," I whispered back.

Mrs. B said, "Of course he won't do nothin'. Whatever would he possibly do?"

Silence.

William knelt before the stroller in the dirt. "She's so pretty." He reached into the stroller to touch her curly hair. Shelby started to cry.

"Don't!" Julie shouted. "Don't touch her!" She hopped backwards three feet or so, taking the stroller with her.

William stayed crouched on the ground.

"Jules—" I started.

"It's alright," said Mrs. B. "William, stand up, you're gettin' dirty."

William stood.

Mrs. B said, "There's a live band startin' in a few minutes, there's chili and french fries and ice cream, and there's a Ferris wheel. So much to see and do, ain't that right William? We'll be fine by ourselves. Always have been." She pushed William's bangs out of his eyes, gently took his wrist, and led him away into the crowd.

"Thank God," Julie said.

"What the hell is wrong with you?" I said.

"What?"

"He was being nice, is all."

"Nice! Lance, he was eyeing Shelby like he was gonna eat her for dinner!"

"He was not!"

Shelby cried louder. James came out from behind my legs and looked up at me. It was rare to hear daddy yell, especially in public. A few people stopped petting the Dalmatians long enough to give a noticeable glance. Julie glared at me.

"Look," I said, lowering my voice. "William wouldn't do nothing. Wouldn't hurt a flea. Never has and never will."

Julie crouched beside the stroller and popped a pacifier into Shelby's mouth.

"You saw the way he was staring, Lance," she said. "It was not normal. Not normal at all."

I wanted to explain that William wasn't normal about anything, but he wasn't no monster like she was making him out to be. And I knew what was going through his mind, though I wouldn't tell Julie. Some things are too deep to share with your spouse. But I could see into William's heart that day. He wanted what I had. A wife, kids, a normal life. Something to call his own. Little ones who looked like him. But he knew in a place deeper than his damaged brain that it wasn't never gonna happen. Not for him.

James climbed onto my hip and we followed Julie through the crowded fairgrounds, gripping onto the stroller, suspicious of any stranger who came too close. How could I tell my wife she had no right protecting our children the best way she knew? What kind of husband would I have proved myself to be?

The most important thing I learned that day was this: no matter how good a friend I was to William, the most important job I had was as a father and a husband.

One of my favorite Journey songs came on the radio as I headed closer to downtown. I cranked it up and tapped the steering wheel like a drum as I made my way toward Donald's apartment.

Chapter 48

Girls like Cecilia think because they take off their clothes for money, they have all the power. Well, I had news for her. William was *my* responsibility. I was taking care of him, because he would soon take care of me. I would go to his apartment and tell him why the bitch was no good for him. Explain to him the seduction of money, what it does to women, how it makes their head spin in the wrong direction. He had no choice but to listen to me. I held his job in my hands, and he held my freedom in his.

The bus moved quickly that night, so getting there at a reasonable hour would not be a problem. Roly had given me a mobile phone, but I hardly ever used it and kept it in my backpack. I had a phone in the stables, and Roly had hooked up a telephone in Manman's kitchen. This time, however, I used the one without wires, a miracle to be on a telephone while riding a bus.

Manman answered. Her voice sounded wary. "Yes?"

We spoke to one another in our native Creole.

"It is me, Emmanuel. I am going to be home late. Fix yourself and Anthony some dinner. Do not wait for me."

"You are to work late in that barn?" she asked.

"No, Manman. I have a friend counting on me to be somewhere."

"Oh, Emmanuel. I am so happy you have found friends. Go and have a good time. Bring them to dinner soon. I will like to meet them."

"Yes, Manman. Give a kiss to Anthony. Be sure to make him read that Silverstein book."

Anthony would not be enrolled in a real school until we were free from Roly, but Manman and I saw to it that he learned to read in English.

"You come home safe," Manman said.

"I will."

Chapter 49

I followed William about a mile from the bus stop to the old neighborhood. The sun was nearly down, and the bullfrogs and crickets croaked and chirped in the muddy ditches lining the road. The smell of springtime night flowers jumped out at us. The rain had stopped, but low clouds made the lightless road seem even darker.

The gravel underneath William's sneakers crunched each time he stepped. I looked down. Did my invisible feet make a sound? I wasn't sure. Background sounds only came to me when I was listening for them. And right now I didn't feel like listening to anything other than the frogs and crickets.

We passed Timmy Shafer's house up on the left, the porch light on, the family seated around a table in the lighted dining room. William gazed at the house and shifted his grocery bags.

This makes no sense, I told him. *You pretend you're independent, now you're heading to Mom's. What's she going to do? Make you a home-cooked meal? Beg you to stay? Maybe you should have brought your suitcases, cuz I can tell you right now, if you tell her about your job and that Manny character, she'll have a conniption. Anyhow, she might not even be home. What if she's out with one of the ladies from Saint Bart's? Maybe she's playing Bingo at the fire hall or eating a bowl of beef soup at Denny's. You should've called first. Should've used the payphone outside the grocery store...*

William stopped at the end of the driveway. He opened the mailbox and peered inside. "No mail."

The front porch light was on, but the rest of the house was dark. It began to sprinkle again.

We headed up the drive to the back of the house. The driveway was empty. *See? She's not home.*

William stood in front of the cement stoop and stared at the kitchen door. Raindrops and tears streamed down his face. It was hard to tell one from the other. He put his grocery bags on the steps, dug his house key out of his wallet, and opened the door. We stepped into the dark kitchen. Out of habit, William stomped his feet against the door mat. Then he flipped the switch, turning on the overhead light.

It was as if someone had caught the room in a photo. The table, chairs, and curtains looked like they hadn't been touched. The smell of celery and apple pie hovered in the room.

Well?

William put the grocery bags on the table and moved through the archway into the living room. The light from the kitchen cast a yellow glow across the room. Nothing had changed in there either. The television, the couch, the tables, the clock on the mantle—all there, all the same.

What did you expect? That she'd hire a decorator the second you moved out?

Back in the kitchen, he made his way up the narrow staircase. In his room, he pulled the chain that turned on the orange shaded light hanging over his bed. The room could have been a showcase in a seventies museum.

William sat on the edge of the perfectly smooth bedspread and began to cry again.

"Mom," he said out loud.

You should have called her at least a dozen times by now.

William wiped his nose with the back of his hand and stood up. He went to the shelf where he'd left stacks of eight-tracks that wouldn't fit in his suitcases. His finger traveled along the tops of the boxes, leaving a clean line through the dust.

A loud thud came from the backyard.

"Mom!"

William tore down the stairs, skipping the last one, and ran out the back door. I followed behind. The driveway was still empty. On the porch, he stared into the backyard, absently wiping the drizzle from his forehead. All was eerily quiet. Even the crickets had quieted down. He squinted into the dark across the property to where the old tree house stood guard. The same tree house he'd spent countless hours as a child. The same one he'd found refuge in after Stephanie's engagement announcement.

His feet stepped through the newly sprouted green fingers here and there, over puddles where the earth was uneven. He walked past the dozens of tulips growing on the side of the fence, ones that sprouted up each spring. Beneath the tree house, twelve splintered rungs lined up crookedly, barely holding onto the trunk with the rusty nails Dad had hammered in over two decades ago. William stepped onto the first rung and stopped. A crunching noise came from the trees lining the back of the property.

"Deer," he said out loud.

He continued up the ladder and pulled his weight onto the small landing. He crawled to the center of the room on his knees, since the ceiling height only allowed for a five-foot person. I floated up but remained near the entrance.

"Smoke," he said.

I couldn't feel my limbs, but I could still smell. I took a whiff. He was right. Candle smoke.

William grabbed a flashlight sitting on a shelf by one of two square window holes. He pushed the switch and slammed the bulb against the palm of this hand. A dim light flickered before brightening. Across the six-by-six room, a curl of smoke rose up from a candle sitting on an upside down apple crate in a corner. The pale stream made its way out of the nearest window.

"What?" he said out loud.

Goose bumps traveled across my arms.

"I gotta protect Mom," he said, shaking the flashlight when it started to flicker again.

Maybe it's just some neighborhood kids.

But I didn't really believe that. And neither did William.

He turned off the flashlight, set it next to the doorway, and headed down the ladder. I trailed after him across the yard and back through the kitchen door, which he closed and locked.

Call the police if you're worried.

Without stopping to wipe his feet on the mat, he marched across the kitchen floor, picked up the telephone, and pressed "0."

Chapter 50

I had just placed my ear against the apartment door when a woman's throaty voice said, "What ya listening for? Termites?"

She stood at the top of the stairwell. Her hair was wild and dirty, her long robe hiding all but the tips of her filthy slippers. A large kitchen knife, the kind used for chopping vegetables, dangled from her hand. The other hand held onto the neck of a liquor bottle. She swayed a little, like the earth was rolling beneath her feet.

Ignoring her, I put my ear to the door again.

"Take your ear offa that door," she said, moving closer. She reeked of alcohol and something like sauerkraut. "I ain't fuckin' around." Knuckles out, thumb up, she held the knife in front of her, the sharp tip pointed toward the ground.

I stood up and pulled back my jacket to show I had a kouto of my own.

"I am not drunk," I told the woman. "So my aim will be much more accurate than yours."

"Where ya from, anyhow?" she asked. When I did not answer, she said, "Maybe I'll call the police. They ain't so kind to the Blacks around here. Or the Mexicans. Or the whores."

"Do what pleases you. I will tell them there is a lunatic woman roaming the hallways, threatening people, carrying a knife in one hand and a bottle of scotch in the other."

"It's whiskey if you're so smart." She looked at the label on the bottle as if to make sure. "I can tell ya what's goin' on in there. You don't haffa eavesdrop."

An unshaved leg was suddenly thrust through the gap in her robe. The slipper fell off her foot. Her toenails were yellow. She wiggled her leg back and forth.

"Fine," I told her. "You may tell me who is in there. That way when I knock, I will not be surprised."

"It's Donald Shithead's mother," she whispered. "But Shithead's not there. Neither is his brother. That red-headed slut. She's in there. And some guy with a ponytail. Keeps a chain on his belt loop to hold his keys. I enjoy a redneck man now and then. They don't have no expectations."

"Did you talk to this man?" I asked.

"No. But I'm a pretty good spy." She grinned. "I have a place to listen without being seen. I do it all the time. Well, not all the time…I have a life, ya know."

"Tell you what," I said. "Take me to your secret listening spot, and I will buy you another bottle of your favorite. Wine, champagne, whatever your heart—"

"Champagne's for fucking blue-hairs."

She wobbled up the hall, clumsily opened the emergency door, and held it open for me. She held onto the knife, the bottle of whiskey, and the railing at the same time, so I climbed a bit to the side in case she tumbled down.

At the top of the stairs, a rusty sign marked "ROOF ACCESS" hung above the door. We stepped through. Cold drizzle fell and a thin fog blurred the nearby buildings. It was dark except for some light drifting up from streetlamps below.

"Ain't I a real-life Mary Poppins?" she asked as her robe dragged through a puddle.

I pulled a knit cap over my head as she led me to a thin rusty pipe sticking up out of the flat cement roof.

She pointed to a wire stretching across the ground and disappearing through a small hole. "Free cable." From a dark corner she dragged a faded blue beach chair, some of the straps missing and the rest ready to split at any moment.

"Sit," she said.

As I sat, I lifted my hat an inch and put my right ear to the pipe. Voices echoed through the pipe and into my ear.

"You gonna buy me that bottle before or after ya listen?"

"Here," I told her, pulling a twenty out of my stash. "Buy what you please."

"I can't go out looking like this. What'll the neighbors think?" She started laughing and squatted into a ball when the laughter turned into a deep cough. When she was through, she stood back up, wrapped her robe more tightly around her, and said, "Buy it for me after. I'm cold. I'm going back downstairs. Apartment 1-A. There's a troll wreath on my door. Ya better make good."

She staggered away and slammed the roof door behind her.

The drizzle continued as I listened through the pipe. The man's voice came to me first: "If anything bad happened, you or me would have been notified. He's keeps both our numbers in his wallet. I made sure of it."

"It's dark and it's raining," the woman said. "I need someone to keep a better eye on him. Donald ain't doing such a good job. He might be my son, but sometimes that boy…"

"Mrs. Baker," the man said, "you should go on home."

And then another woman spoke, and I knew in an instant it was the stripper.

Cecilia said, "Leave your number with both of us."

"I already have her number," the man said. "We've known each other for more than twenty years."

"Well," Cecilia said, "here's my number then. Just in case."

After a moment, William's mother said, "Lance, do you really think William's okay?"

"I do, Mrs. B. Why don't you go on home before it gets too late to drive? I'll take it from here."

The rain grew steady, pouring into my left ear. I shook my head and stuck in a finger to plug it up. Then I put my right ear back to the pipe.

Down in the apartment below, a door closed, followed by silence.

Chapter 51

The name tag on his dark blue uniform said Officer C. Powers. His hair was gray on the temples, his moustache almost completely white. He looked like he should've been wearing a cowboy hat, boots with spurs, and a sheriff's badge, maybe dropping his fishing line in a creek somewhere instead of standing in Mom's backyard. Tall pines and aged oaks cast shadows across the far edge of the property. Except for the officer's flashlight, darkness filled every corner.

"What exactly did you hear, Mr. Baker?" Officer Powers asked William as we made our way to the tree house.

"It might have been a deer or a dog."

"You didn't actually see anyone?"

"Just smoke."

"Where'd you see smoke?"

William stopped below the tree house. "Up there," he whispered, pointing. "From a candle. But I'm not the one who blew it out. I didn't even light it."

The officer glanced toward the back porch. The glow from the kitchen light made the house look safe and cozy.

"Does someone live here with you?" Officer Powers asked.

"I don't live here anymore," William said.

"Then what are you doing here?"

"My mom lives here, but she's not home right now. I don't know where she is. I moved to the city. To live with Donald."

Officer Powers' voice grew deeper. "I'll ask again, sir, what are you doing here?"

William fiddled with the cuff of his long-shirt sleeve. "I d-d-dunno." He began to sniffle.

The officer shone the flashlight in William's face. "Have you been drinking, sir?"

I laughed.

William said, "I went to the Piggly Wiggly for milk and cereal. Then I came out here." His bottom lip trembled. "Just wanted to see M-m-mom is all."

"William Baker...you the same Baker who nearly drowned back in the seventies?"

William nodded. "I was Billy. Now I'm William."

The cop removed the light from William's face and shone it on the driveway where the police car sat alone.

"How'd you get out here, son?" Officer Powers asked.

"Took the bus from the Piggly Wiggly. All the way. One bus. No transfers." William opened his wallet and proudly showed his ID and bus pass.

"You don't live in a—a place where you can be looked after?"

William shook his head.

"Well," Officer Powers said, "let's see what might be going on here." He patted William on the arm. "Don't worry, son."

The officer climbed up the ladder, the equipment around his waist clanking against the rungs. William and I listened below as he shuffled across the small wooden floor. After a moment, he leaned out the doorway. "Looks like someone's been using your tree house as a private party spot." He held up an empty can of Colt 45.

"I didn't drink that," William told him.

"It's possible it's been up here a while." Officer Powers came back down the ladder, still holding the can. "To be on the safe side, let's file a report. We'll be sure to get a record of trespassing and possible nuisance."

William led the cop back across the yard to the house.

Once in the kitchen, the officer said, "Mind if I have a look around?"

"No."

I followed behind as the police officer checked out the rooms on the first floor, then upstairs, and finally down in the basement. When he was back in the kitchen, he asked, "You notice anything missing?"

William shook his head.

"You mother lives out here alone?"

"Uh-huh."

"You plan on spending the night?"

"I gotta go back to my apartment downtown. I work tomorrow."

"You have a job?"

William nodded. "At the track."

"Well, good for you, son."

"I help take care of the horses."

"That right?" Powers said. "I just read an article about a horse they got over there named Neapolitan. She's expected to break all kinds of—"

"Neon's my favorite," William said. "I get to brush her and pet her every day."

"You're a lucky man."

William smiled.

Powers said, "Let's leave a note in case your mother sees or hears anything suspicious. I'll make sure a squad car drives by the next few nights. As a precaution."

They sat at the kitchen table while the officer filled out a report in his book. When he was finished, he wrote a note and left it in the center of the table.

William picked up his grocery bags and followed the officer onto the porch.

After locking the back door, Officer Powers said, "You going downtown on the bus tonight?"

William nodded.

"It's getting late," the officer said, looking at his watch. "My shift is over in ten minutes. What say I drop you off? It's on my way home."

The three of us rode together, William listening carefully as Officer

Powers explained the different instruments on the police cruiser dash, and me like a prisoner floating behind the bullet proof glass that separated the front from the back.

Chapter 52

Leaning over the roof's edge, I watched as the red-headed whore and who I assumed to be William's manman headed up the sidewalk. But there was a man in the apartment too, someone called Lance. And Lance was not with the two women as they made their way up the block. I ran back to the pipe and listened again but could hear nothing.

The rain had stopped, but my clothes were wet and sticking uncomfortably to my skin.

Enough of this, I thought. *Being a babysitter is not part of the plan—*

Lance's voice echoed through the pipe.

"Hi, babe," he said. "No, he hasn't come home yet. Everything's alright, I'm sure. I'm gonna wait around a while longer, see if he shows up. If he doesn't get here by the time I leave, I'll file a report. Okay. Give them kisses for me. Love you too."

I could have waited on the roof a while longer, but I was soaked to the core and wanted nothing more than to spend the evening with my family. I was sure William was fine. The same way I was sure that the plan would turn out perfectly.

My knees popped simultaneously as I stood. I went back through the roof door, made my way down the staircase, walked past William's apartment, and down to the lobby. On the first floor, I stopped in front of apartment 1-A with its grotesque wreath of tiny trolls and slipped a twenty dollar bill through the crack beneath the door. That drunken fool could buy her own bottle of poison.

I had just stepped onto the sidewalk when voices came to my ears. Like a jackrabbit, I ducked behind a van parked along the curb, covering myself with as much shadow as possible.

"This is me and Donald's apartment," I heard William saying. "But he's not around anymore."

"Where'd he go?" another man asked.

I peeked through the van's windows and spotted the police uniform. A gun was holstered on his hip. His badge reflected light from a nearby motel sign. I inched my way along the back of the van as the two men walked toward the apartment building. My fast food dinner bubbled up, burning my throat.

"He went on a business trip," William told the officer.

Their conversation cut off as the front doors shut behind them.

I took a deep breath. My bladder filled.

A police officer? Bringing William back from where? He had left work hours ago. And since when did William have officers as friends? How many did he know? Then my brain rattled out of control: what if this officer was his uncle, or his dada? What if Donald was an undercover cop and not the lowlife gambler he pretended to be? What if William was faking his mental incapacities, planning to bring down Roly's house of cards? Had he really won all that money on the *Lotsa Luck Wheel Show*? Or was that part of the scheme? Could it be I had been fooled all along, too exhausted to see the signs? Too wrapped up in the business at hand to notice?

Crazy thoughts slammed into my head from different angles, paralyzing me. Hidden behind the corner of the van, I stared at the brick building toward the only first floor apartment with a light on, and caught a silhouette moving behind the barred window. I looked a few floors above and located William's apartment. The light was on there, too, filtering through the blinds in the window over the rusty fire escape. Even with the window shut, I believed I could hear voices.

"Good work," my imagination heard the cop telling William. "You'll get a promotion. And tell Donald, that partner of yours, he's up for a raise too."

But this was not my manman's favorite mystery program, *Murder She Wrote*. William could not have known I was going to offer him a job at the track. Even I didn't know this was going to happen until it did.

No. William was legitimate. And Donald was still chicken kaka.

Then who was this cop, and why was he here?

I would not let paranoia get in the way. *Could* not. These kinds of thoughts would only deter me from the plan. From saving my family.

But the questions in my head spun into a cyclone. I could not think clearly. I suspected that sleep would not be mine until the job was finished.

Out of the darkness, I stepped onto the curb which ran in front of the apartment complex, pulled the tattered bus pass from my wallet, and started across the street. I hopped over a puddle and onto the cracked sidewalk. Once more, I glanced up at the building. Before I had a chance to look away, the blinds in William's living room lifted halfway. A shadowed face appeared behind the glass.

Though the eyes were as dark as the shadow, I knew they belonged to the cop.

I pulled my hat down to my eyebrows and scurried away, pretending to be just another bum looking for something to do on a drizzly night in the city.

Chapter 53

Like a Christmas gift, there it was, that beautiful note! My William had been right there in my house, and the officer too. I looked around, half expectin' to see my son jumpin' down the staircase, two at a time, landin' square in the middle of the kitchen.

I can't tell you the relief I felt. It was like I'd got a newborn baby all over again. My William was safe. Maybe not in my arms like when he was a baby, but safe anyways.

I called the number the officer left and told 'em down at that station thank you, thank you, thank you. They were kind enough to explain what'd happened, and told me they'd send a patrol car to my neighborhood every hour or so throughout the night.

But I wasn't worried none about the tree house. If there were some neighborhood boys wantin' to spend an evenin' or two in that ol' shack, more power to 'em. I even liked 'em bein' there a little. Be like when Donald and William were young'uns and slept out there on steamy summer nights. The Colt 45 can the officer wrote about tightened my jaw a bit, but what kids don't try beer at one time or another?

I was gonna sleep tighter than a caterpillar in a cocoon, knowin' my son was alright. Knowin' that a nice policeman had seen William home by now, and that Lance would be waitin' for him when he stepped inside the apartment.

I changed into my nightgown, crawled under the covers, and set the alarm clock for six-thirty AM, so I could spend another day at the middle school zoo.

Chapter 54

I used to hate the cops in our neighborhood, always in our faces, expecting us to be driving drunk, believing we were aiming to grab some tail from a minor in the back seat of her daddy's car. Made me feel like a hoodlum even though all we townies did was smoke a little weed some weekends while listening to Led Zeppelin or Pink Floyd. By the time I was nineteen, I was already married with a baby on the way, and I wasn't about to get into no trouble on account of becoming a daddy and all.

What's funny is that after James and Shelby came along, I felt appreciation for the cops who stuck their noses into our neighborhood's business to see who was burning trash on a non-burning day, or to find the person who'd dumped a pile of pee-stained mattresses down the hill behind the park.

You had to sort of forget how those cops made you feel when you were a kid, and keep in mind how they made you feel once you had kids of your own.

Officer Powers was friendly enough. And it was cool of him to bring William downtown, sort of like a front-door limo driver. Only for free.

He entered the apartment and wasted no time asking me who I was.

"Lance Jennings. Friend of William's. Known each other since before elementary school."

"Name doesn't ring a bell."

Officer Powers moved around the apartment, eyeing everything. It must be a built-in cop thing to want to know what's hidden inside every closet, under every pillow. But he didn't touch nothing, probably since he didn't have no court order. He walked around the place, occasionally patting the revolver on his hip, as if making sure it was still there.

"What kind of business your brother in?" Powers asked William.

I wanted to tell the cop that Donald worked as a professional asshole, but I bit my tongue.

William told him, "Donald does power lunches with businessmen."

"Where'd he go exactly?"

I said, "No one knows."

At the living room window, Officer Powers pulled the cord, lifting the blinds. He gazed down below.

"If y'all don't mind," I said, "I gotta get back home. Wanna kiss the kids goodnight before it gets too late."

"Sounds like a good idea, Lance," the officer agreed, pulling the bent blinds back down as best he could. At the door, he shook hands with William. "It was nice meeting you, Mr. Baker."

"Thanks for the ride in your police car," William said.

"Anytime. Be sure to lock the door behind you."

The officer and I waited in the hallway until we heard the click of the lock, then headed downstairs. As we walked past apartment 1-A, the door slipped open a crack, and a sliver of a woman's face peeked through. A skinny gray cat tried to make its way through the door, but the woman shooed it back with her dirty slipper.

"Something the matter, Officer?" she asked.

I could smell her dragon breath from ten feet away.

"No, ma'am," Officer Powers said. "Sorry to have disturbed you."

We continued walking.

"Ya'll didn't disturb me!" she shouted after us. "I was just eating dinner. I'm eating late on account of I had so much to do around here all day. God knows ya can't accuse me of being a slumlord, no way, José. Had to change light bulbs, paint a railing, fix a broken window—"

The front doors closed behind us.

Outside, Officer Powers said, "I'd like to ask you some more questions, Lance. Without William around."

I looked at my watch.

"I know it's late," he said. "Won't take but a few minutes."

I followed him to his patrol car and sat on the passenger side. All those years as a wild teen, and I'd never sat inside a cop car. I looked at the instruments on the dash and had to fight the urge to grab the handset and shout, "Adam 12, Adam 12!"

Officer Powers started the car and turned the heat to low. He switched off the radio, placed his left hand on top of the steering wheel, and turned to me. "You ever worry about your friend?"

"William? Sure. I mean, sometimes." *But not enough*, my conscience gnawed.

"How'd he come to living on his own, with his faculties—you know—the way they are?"

I said nothing at first, not sure how much the cop already knew. Plus, the story was so long, I wasn't sure where to begin.

"I know what happened to him, son," Officer Powers said. "Used to work your old stomping grounds. I wasn't around when the accident happened. I was on vacation that week, down in Florida with the wife, but I remember when I got back, the hoopla down at the station. Our department helped raise money for William's physical therapy. I even vaguely remember his father, Frank. I understand he left the family some time ago."

I nodded. "Barely a year after William was released from the hospital."

"Shame," Powers said. "His mother deserves a medal."

"Mrs. Baker asked the courts to make William a ward of the state, to help her take care of him and all. But a social worker convinced her to let him keep his independence. Told her if she made William the state's responsibility, and then found out that she couldn't take care of him, he'd be put in an institution. No way was she gonna let that happen. She has a certain amount of guardianship, but he's still his own person. He can pretty much do what he wants."

"And what exactly is he doing, living down here in this cesspool?"

"That's a good question." I looked up at Donald's apartment. The light was already out. William never was one to mess around when it came to

221

bedtime, even before the accident. I smiled to myself. I told Officer Powers, "He got sort of lucky a few months back."

"Lucky how?"

"Got a three-time scratcher that let him spin the *Lotsa Luck* wheel," I said.

"No kidding."

"And then he won a lot of money."

"How much?"

"A mil."

"Why come down here?" Officer Powers asked. "Why not use it for travel? Or invest it?"

"William sort of does things simple," I said. "Far back as I can remember, he never strayed too far from home, never wanted to see Italy or France or China, just wanted to live a simple life. Get married, have a couple of kids. Be independent."

"And his brother?"

"Don't even get me started," I said. "That rat was supposed to be watching William, but no one's seen him for weeks. Actually, that might be for the best."

"Why is that?"

"Donald tends to have an obsession with other people's things. Things he can't have himself. Someone has a car he can't have, he wants it. Someone has a girl he can't have, he wants that too."

A glimpse of that day at the pond came back to me so suddenly that I felt the cold water as it traveled over my body, freezing my eye sockets as I reached for William...

"Why did Donald leave?" Powers asked.

"My guess is he went MIA on purpose. Probably owes his bookie."

"A gambler?"

"Horses. Big-time."

Officer Powers said, "William mentioned he got a job at the track."

"Yeah," I said. "He and his brother both love horses. Only for different reasons. Funny that William would end up working around exactly what Donald loves the most."

"How'd he get the job?"

"Met some guy who hired him on the spot."

"Have you met this man?" Officer Powers asked.

"No. But he seems to be treating William alright."

"Does he know about the money?"

"Don't matter if he does. I helped William set up a couple of accounts. He can't touch the lottery money till it clears. Once that happens, no one but William will have access to the money. Ever. As I told you, he's independent. Just like you or me."

"That's good." The officer looked at his watch. "Well, I know you're tired, Lance. I've had a long day as well. I appreciate your time." As I opened the car door, Powers added, "Let's keep an eye on William for a little while, shall we?"

"You worried about something?"

"I have a pretty good sense of when something odd is brewing. Not sure what it is, or why, but I've learned over the years to listen to my gut. It's pretty dead-on. Most of the time."

"Sometimes your gut is wrong?"

"Sometimes," Powers said as he turned on his headlights. "But rarely."

Chapter 55

A cop car and Lance's truck were driving away when I walked up to the front of William's apartment complex for the second time that day. Something was wrong, otherwise why would a cop have been visiting? Was William in trouble? Should his mama have stayed after all?

Every window was dark, except where Sherri the landlord lived. Television light bounced around behind her window blinds, probably a shopping channel or a *Star Trek* rerun.

I sighed and burped at the same time, Denny's fried shrimp coming back to haunt me.

I could stand out there on the spooky sidewalk all night, or I could go home, or I could go up to William's apartment.

The wind hit me in the face as it blew up the street, bringing with it smells of rotting garbage and pee. God, I hated that part of the city. Always felt like I had to take a shower just from standing on the curb a minute.

I went through the front doors of the apartment building and took the steps two at a time. Outside William's door, I raised my hand to knock then stopped. I leaned my forehead against the door.

What did I want from William, anyways? This man who could barely tie his shoes, wouldn't know an encyclopedia if he tripped over it, and probably didn't remember me breaking him in.

I reminded myself that life is short, as I often did whenever I thought I was doing the wrong thing. Too short for questions that might not have any answers. I raised my hand again. With a long fingernail, I tapped five times. When no one answered, I used a knuckle.

William's sleepy voice said, "Who is it?"

"It's me. Cecilia."

After a moment, the door opened.

Greenish yellow from the hallway light entered the apartment. William was shirtless and wore a pair of tighty whities. His hair lay flat against one side of his head. I wanted to reach out and rub my fingers through that blond mess, tousle it with my hands, make it even messier.

When he didn't respond, I said, "You gonna invite me in?"

"I'm sleeping right now."

"I know…I'm sorry…"

Jesus H. Christ, I thought. *What kind of fool am I?*

William stepped back. When he closed the door behind us, we stood in darkness.

"I was sleeping," William said again. "I work hard. Gotta lot of responsibilities at the stables."

"I know you do. But your mom's worried about you."

"My mom?"

"We spent some time together," I explained.

"Did she see you?"

"Of course she did—I just told you we spent some time together, waiting and worrying about—"

"Is she mad at me?" he asked.

"Why would she be mad?"

I was confused, not only by his questions, but because standing in a dark room makes me feel out of control. I wiggled my fingers in front of my eyes to see them, but my eyes hadn't adjusted yet.

I asked again. "Why would she be mad?"

"Cuz of you."

"What?"

"I don't want to make her mad," he said. "Even though I'm an independent, she's still my mom."

"Honey, I don't understand—"

William giggled in the dark. "You called me 'honey.'"

"Yes, William, I did. Would you rather I not call you—"

"You're a hooker."

"Excuse me?"

"A hooker."

"No, William. You met me dancing. Remember? I'm a *dancer*."

"Lance said you're a hooker," he said. "Cuz you gave me...you know..."

"Are you saying you didn't like it?"

William breathed heavily in the dark. I thought he might cry, but I didn't care. I was sick of being called certain names just because I like to please a man now and again. As if educated women with trust funds kept their snatches locked in a safe.

"Didn't you like it?" I asked again. "If you didn't, then it won't happen again, I can tell you that right now." I dropped my pocketbook to the ground and reached for him in the dark, letting my hands touch his bare chest. "Are you telling me you don't like *this*?" I licked my lips and put them against his chest, letting my tongue move through his light chest hairs. His skin covered with gooseflesh. So did mine.

"Tell, me William," I said, pushing against his body, urging him to the sofa bed. "Tell me you don't like what I did."

He said nothing. Instead, he took my face in his hands and pressed his mouth hard against my own. His hands moved quick and powerful down my body, grabbing my breasts and my crotch, squeezing my ass. It was like being mauled by a very sexy bear.

"Whoa." I took his hands off my bottom. I reached in between his legs, feeling the hardness through his underwear. "Sit on the edge of the bed."

The cheap mattress springs squeaked under his weight. I slipped off my shoes. Standing in front of him between the open "V" of his legs, I took his hands and led them to the bottom of my sweatshirt. Together we pulled it up and over my head. His hands immediately moved to my breasts, but I stopped them. "Not so fast." I guided his hands to the top of my jeans, helping his fingers undo the buttons one by one. I slid them down to my ankles and kicked them aside.

With my small hands cupped around the back of his large ones, we slowly moved my panties from my hips, down my thighs, and to the floor. I kicked them away. Still facing him, I helped him unclasp the front clip that made getting out of my bra a snap. Cool air moved across my breasts as the bra fell to the floor.

I leaned my body on top of his and pushed him onto the sofa bed. I rolled to my left, and he rolled with me, his body towering over mine. I couldn't barely make out the outline of his face. As long as he wasn't speaking, William was just like any other man. Healthy and horny. But I had to hold back from crying, because I knew the universe had cheated this man. He'd never have the same chances as other guys, would never get married or have kids. Not that I wanted either of those things myself, but at least I had a choice. William's destiny was already set.

Feeling sorry for him made me want him even more. Made me want to wrap my arms and legs around him and hold him tight while he entered me; made me want to kiss him while he came, but in a tender way, not the way most men like it, with their tongue shoved down my throat and their cigar breath in my face. William made me want to make love for real. And I don't honestly think I'd ever done that before. Know what I'm saying?

"William," I whispered, holding his face in my hands as his warm breaths filled the space between us.

"Huh?"

"I know this is your first time. Don't go too crazy though. Make it last. So I can feel every inch of you."

Even though the room was black, and I still couldn't barely see a thing, I knew there was a part of him that understood completely.

And he did make it last. Well, at least longer than some I'd been with. He was gentle, like there was a chance I could break, even though there wasn't nothing left to break. And I didn't care about using a condom. I was on the pill, and I was as clean as the inside of a bottle of rubbing alcohol, just ask my G-Y-N. And William'd never been with anyone before me. I was his first.

For a few minutes we rocked together, and my orgasm hit in almost an instant, which blew my mind, because I usually don't get to have one by the time the guy has finished his own business. I moaned out loud, something else I don't normally do, and William moaned with me, and our lips pressed together. It was magnificent, I can tell you that. Like in the movies. The only thing missing was the sound of crashing waves.

William rolled onto his side. His breathing shook the bed. I touched the side of his face with the back of my hand. I swear he was grinning.

"Did you like it?" I asked. "Did you like being inside me?"

"Uh-huh."

I put a cheek against his chest and listened to his heartbeat. I thought, maybe his life would be wonderful now since I'd taught him something he could use. All he needed was the right girl to give him a chance. But then I thought with sadness, *What girl would do that?*

"William," I said, "what's your biggest dream?"

"Dream?"

"What do you want more than anything else in the world?"

"My own horse."

"Yeah?"

"Mmm-hmm."

"You don't wanna get married, have kids and stuff?"

He thought about it and said, "If I had a horse, I wouldn't need kids."

"Where would you keep it?" I asked. "At the track?"

"No. I won't let her race."

"Why not?"

"Just won't."

"Where would you keep her then?"

"In the backyard," he said.

"There's no backyard here."

The only thing behind the building was an alley. I may not know much about horses or nothing, but I'm pretty sure you can't keep one in an alley. Especially with all the bums sleeping back there.

"At my house," William said.

"You mean your mom's?"

"Uh-huh."

"But you don't live there anymore."

Silence.

"William?"

My head was still on his chest listening to his heartbeat. I reached up and touched his face again. His cheeks were wet.

"Oh, no. Why're you crying?"

"I gotta go h-h-home," he said.

"What do you mean?"

"My mom needs m-m-m-e."

"Oh, William, I think all moms feel bad when their kids up and move away."

Most moms, anyways.

"She needs m-m-me," he said.

"You could visit her, couldn't you?"

"I don't have a car. The bus takes too long. When I get there she's not there."

"I don't think you need your mom as much as you think—"

"*She* needs *m-m-me*! I told you that already!"

I sat up and pulled the thin sheet to my chest. "Okay, okay. Nobody said you had to yell. Shit, William."

He didn't say anything.

I waited a long moment before speaking again. "If you move back to your mom's, can you keep your job?"

"I don't even need my job."

"Doesn't working make you feel independent?"

"I don't need to work," he said. "On account of my money."

"What money?" I asked.

"I'm not supposed to tell you. Manny said so."

"Manny?"

"He's the only one who would give me a job. He likes me."

"What money, William? I promise I won't tell. I swear." I held up my right hand like I was a ten-year-old giving a Girl Scout oath, even though William couldn't see me do it in the dark.

"*Lotsa Luck*," he whispered.

"The lottery show?"

"I won."

All of a sudden William seemed like an oversized cartoon character, straight out of the Sunday comics, with dreams of owning a horse and winning the lottery.

"How much did you win?" I asked.

"A lot."

"How much?"

"One million."

"Holy crap," I whispered under my breath. "Then why...how...why...?" I didn't know what to ask first. There were so many things that didn't make sense. I finally asked the obvious: "Why are you living *here*, William? Why are you working at the track?"

"Manny likes me."

"But you don't need to work there if you have all that money."

"I don't have it," he said.

"Your money?"

"I don't have it."

"Yes, I heard you, William. Who has it?"

William was silent.

"Who has your money, William? Your brother?" I could feel my face turn hot as I gripped the sheet tightly in my fists. "Manny?"

"Manny likes me. He gave me a job."

"William, did Manny take your—"

"I'm tired. I gotta go to sleep. It's already past bedtime."

He pulled the sheet away from me and rolled himself up like a burrito. My skin chilled. I reached my hand out to touch him, but I'd overstayed my welcome. Again.

In the dark, as William's snoring filled the apartment, I gathered my things together and dressed next to the door.

A few minutes later, as I stepped onto the damp sidewalk, Sherri's smoker voice whispered through the blinds of her apartment: "Slut."

As I turned the first corner, I thought to myself, *That drunk old bitch might just be right.*

Chapter 56

"Do your normal duties," I told William as I put on my jacket. "I will only be away for an hour."

William smiled, put on the headphones, and went to work hosing down the barn floor.

Now, I sat in the smelly booth at the Twelfth Street Pub. A biker couple sat at the bar drinking whiskey, and two young men played a game of pool. I sipped my ginger ale, watched the news on the silent television, and waited.

I didn't see him come through the door, only as he slid onto the leather seat across from me. He was a tall pale man in a large overcoat, a golf cap on his head, a briefcase in his hand.

The man pulled his hat from his head and placed it on his lap. He smoothed down his thinning hair. "Are you the man to which I will explain about the horse?" He had an accent, stronger than the one I tried to hide. He pronounced his *S's* like *Z's*—*horze*, not *horse* and his *W's* like *V's*—*vill* instead of *will*. He did not reach out his hand to be shaken. Perhaps in some business ventures handshakes have no place.

"Yes," I said.

"I am Doctor Meyers," the man told me, though I was sure this was not his real name.

The bartender called from where he stood behind the bar. "Need something, buddy?"

"Sweet vermouth with a twist of lemon," Doctor Meyers said.

We said nothing else until the drink was placed on the table and Doctor Meyers had taken a sip.

"Do you know this horse well?" Meyers asked.

I nodded.

He opened the briefcase on the seat next to him and pulled out a photo. Neon stood in the corral, tall and beautiful, her trainer with a hand on her nuzzle.

"This is the one?"

Again, I nodded.

"Even-tempered?" he asked.

"She has her moods like any female," I told him.

He spoke quietly, gently, even though I could tell there was something sinister lying beneath the calm. "I will put this in layman's terms, so there won't be any confusion. If there is one step missed, one step overlooked, the entire mission will fail. And we both know what will happen if things go wrong."

The doctor regarded me as if we were two average men having an average Joe conversation. We could have been talking about trout fishing, the weather, or baseball.

"The virus is incubating," Meyers said.

"Virus?"

"Do not worry. It is safely contained in a live host."

"A live host?" I asked.

"A dove."

I knew that Neon was the sacrifice that would ultimately save my family. And I knew that one day another horse would have to be saved in order to appease Karma. But now that the plan was unfolding, my stomach fell into my groin. I could not tell this doctor that in my tiny Haitian village a *pijon* was only killed to worship ancestors or to feed the people. Karma wrapped itself around my neck like a snake, and there it would stay until the universe was again balanced.

"Why not keep it in a mosquito?" I said. "Like malaria or the *Dengue*."

"A mosquito offers too many difficulties. For example, if it should fly away

232

and land on another horse, or a human, then we would have a real problem on our hands." Doctor Meyers smiled, but it was hardly a warm Welcome-to-America smile. "We've found in lab studies that the dove is the most conducive to this particular situation. Chickens and crows die within a short amount of time. And most mammals do not incubate the virus the same as birds, for reasons we do not yet understand. But give us time."

The doctor spoke as though he were teaching me biology instead of how to exterminate a perfectly healthy horse.

He continued. "When the dove is delivered, it will have been sedated, to keep it from—how do you say—chirping?"

"Cooing," I said.

Meyers' eyes never left my face, even as he sipped his vermouth. "Yes, alright, cooing. That night, before you leave work, you are to take the dove out of the box, inject the needle into the bird—"

"Needle?"

"Please let me finish. You will draw out the blood and inject the horse. I will help you to understand."

The doctor reached into his briefcase and took out a large white envelope. From it he pulled a thick stack of photos, 5 x 10's, black and white. He handed me the stack and reached for a pair of reading glasses in his pocket. As I flipped through the photographs, he explained what each picture represented.

"Here, one of my partners is growing the virus in live tissue cell cultures, since viruses replicate within living cells. This one is a microscopic view of the virus. Notice from this photo to the next how much the cells have divided." His face lit up while talking about this miracle of cell division as though he had conceived the process himself. "The needle is easily inserted through the bird's skin, directly under the facial bones, and another, in this picture, under the wing." He pointed at specifics in the photos. "Here we see the bird's blood under the microscope. Notice the cells from the first to the last. A considerable change. The virus is growing heartily, just as we'd hoped. And that was only the first bird. Subsequent experiments using over three hundred doves worked as well. We tried on mammals later, though I did not bring photos of those trials. Dogs and cats carrying the virus were unaffected. Hamsters, rats, guinea pigs, and other rodents were the same as dogs and cats. But many of the sheep died within twenty-four hours. We found that to be quite interesting. Then we had a few human subjects, but we don't need to get into that at this time, hmm?"

I flipped to the next photo of a beautiful black stallion.

Meyers said, "Once you have drawn the live virus from the bird, you will immediately inject the horse. If more than a few seconds are wasted, the virus could die, and we can't have that. Like the bird, the needle is inserted into the horse, in the neck muscle there..." He tapped the picture. "But again, this has to happen directly after the blood is drawn from the bird. If this doesn't happen in an immediate fashion, we can all kiss our futures goodbye."

The last photo caused my ginger ale to bubble up in my throat. The horse from the previous picture, tall, dark, and grand, was now lying on the ground, its nose and mouth frothing, his eyes disappearing into their sockets. Even though it was only a photo, my imagination felt the horse trembling with convulsions.

"Unsettling, yes?" Meyer's said.

My voice belonged to another man. "What if Neapolitan doesn't...take to the virus?"

"Science can be tricky indeed, as conditions are often volatile. Over the course of our experiments, four percent of males and three percent of females did not expire, for reasons we do not understand. But the odds are ninety-seven percent this horse will respond accordingly. Good odds, yes? Once the virus has coursed through her body and into her spinal fluid, her brain will swell, and she will become recumbent. Once she lies down, the virus will move quickly to the lungs. Death can be counted on within seven to ten days. But incapacitation should occur within only a few days."

"What happens if the veterinarians try to keep her on her feet?"

He glared at me, his dark eyes like tinted glass behind his bifocals. "By the time they figure out what has happened, it will be too late."

I looked at the photo of the fallen horse again, disoriented and immobilized, a great mare diminished to the likings of an earth worm trapped on a sun-bleached sidewalk. I pictured our magnificent Neon, her pretty painted spots, her dark eyes. My stomach cramped again at the thought of such a vigorous horse being struck down by something as tiny as an angry cell.

"What if someone finds a cure?" I asked.

Doctor Meyers laughed sardonically. "A cure? Think, man, how many people have died from AIDS since the virus was given a name." He swallowed the last of his drink and slid the photos back into his briefcase. "I will leave some clean syringes for you. Use an orange for practice. Its skin is thick like a horse. You are responsible for disposing of the needles. And the bird, of course."

"The bird?"

"It must be burned, buried, tossed into a receptacle, whatever gets rid of it." The briefcase swung by his side. "Do you have any questions?"

I shook my head.

Doctor Meyers pulled a paper bag from his coat pocket and handed it to me. "What you need is in this bag. The bird will be delivered in two days. That should give you plenty of time to prepare." He stood up, tossed a ten onto the table, and put his hat back on his head. "Do not forget," he said, leaning in and touching my arm, making me want to punch him, "we are all expendable. But some of us are more expendable than others."

Chapter 57

William sprayed the hose back and forth across the stable floor, pushing stray pieces of straw and feed and manure out toward the edges of the pavement and into the cement gutters running along either side. Black flies buzzed around his head, but he didn't notice; he only heard the music coming through the headphones. It should have only taken him thirty minutes to wash the floor, but it had already been an hour. The sprayer was deafening. Like being trapped inside a car wash.

William shuffled his feet as he worked, listening to an old ABBA tune, a group he'd never cared for until Manny gave him the tape. His backup singers had popped up alongside him for the first time in weeks, stepping to the beat and twirling across the cement floor, waiting for William to join them. Egging him on with their sparkly suits and beaming black faces.

My legs had vanished up to my mid-thighs. I floated next to William and his dancers, a cast-off balloon with an invisible string attached to keep me grounded.

I was disintegrating a little more each day. William was losing me.

Or visa versa.

Take off the headphones, I tried for the twentieth time. *Something's going on. Why would Manny leave you here alone?*

But William only heard the music.

Maybe I had used up too much of my power on the *Lotsa Luck* wheel. Maybe that's why I was disappearing.

What if I hadn't tried helping out William to begin with? We wouldn't be standing here right now if I hadn't blown on that damn wheel, if he hadn't won the money and then moved in with Donald. If I'd left things well enough alone, we'd still be hanging out in our old bedroom, digging through albums and eight-tracks, listening to Sister Sledge or the Bee Gees or KC, dancing to their greatest hits, waiting for Mom to get home from work and shout for William get ready for supper. Roast beef and potatoes, chicken and dumplings, or maybe homemade stew. Nothing better than having a home-cooked meal, followed by dessert and the *Cosby Show*.

Crimony. If I'd left things alone, I'd still have my hands and feet.

And William would still listen to me sometimes.

Even if I could somehow climb back inside his head, it wouldn't change his brain. This was where I'd been since the blackness took over and spit me out. This was where I belonged.

Wasn't it?

I started to cry, but it didn't matter, because who would have known?

I wanted to see Mom. Float behind her while she pulled bobby pins from her bun and let her hair fall past her shoulders, brush the gray lines into the jet black ones, creating stripes I always loved. I'd follow her as she knelt next to the left side of her bed and pressed her hands together in prayer. She never prayed out loud, but I knew what she prayed for.

She'd get into bed, turn out the light, and turn on the television, sometimes falling into a dreamless sleep while late-night programming played in the background. I'd watch her, sometimes for an entire night, until William unknowingly called me back to him. He used to need me more than Mom.

Manny came back to the barn after about ninety minutes. With his long strides, he made his way over to us. His dark finger tapped William on the shoulder.

William turned around and smiled. He removed the headphones from his head and stood waiting, the water from the hose spilling off into a drain.

"Turn that off, William. I have something important to discuss with you. Something that will make you happy."

William turned off the sprayer and dropped the hose. He slid the headphones down around his neck and hit the STOP button on the side of the tape player.

"Let us go sit for a moment," Manny said.

William and I followed Manny to a tiny room next to the back entrance of the stable. The room was the size of a large broom closet and looked like it was once an office but hadn't been used in years. Spider webs hung from the rafters. The only window in the room had been boarded up.

"Sit," Manny said.

William sat on an old crate.

Manny pulled a paper bag out of his pocket, placed it on top of a rusty desk, and leaned against its front. He looked relaxed. *Too* relaxed. Like he was faking how relaxed he was.

"William, how would you like to do some of the things a veterinarian does?"

"Help the horses have babies?"

"None of our horses are carrying at the moment, so that will not be part of your responsibility."

William pouted.

"But, you will get to do something most stable hands only dream about. Do you know what proteins are?"

"Like vitamins?"

"Very good. Have you ever taken vitamins before?"

When we were little.

"When I was Billy, I took Flintstones Chewables."

Manny thought about this for a moment, then went on. "Some racehorses need special vitamins, just like people. They need special care to keep them healthy. All the extra training can weaken their immune system."

He's lying...

"They could get colds and stuff?"

"You catch on quick. All we have to do is give the horse a vitamin and she will be jet set and ready to go. Oh. But there is a problem..." Manny thoughtfully rubbed the hairs on his chin.

Even without my legs and arms, I could feel the goose bumps...

"What problem?" William asked.

"Well, it is difficult enough to give a pill to a child, or a dog, or a cat. But a horse, well, that would be almost impossible."

"Why?"

"How will you get your hand into the mouth to make sure it goes down?"

"Can't we mush it up in their food? My mom did that with my Benadryl when I was sick one time. She opened up the plastic pills and sprinkled dots on top of my apple sauce. She told me it was candy, and I got better."

"Hmm. We could do that, but this type of vitamin needs to be taken all at once, without breaking it up. Otherwise it will not work."

"Oh."

"The best way is to use a needle."

No...

"I have a needle on my record player," William said. "But it's still in my old bedroom. Sometimes it scratches my albums, so I like my eight-track better." He turned his head slightly, picturing what our bedroom looked like instead of panicking about what he was being asked to do.

"Not a record player needle," Manny said. "The kind a doctor gives you in the arm for vaccinations. I'm sure you have seen a needle before, yes?"

William frowned. "I hate the hospital. It's bad there." He began fidgeting with the tape, ejecting the cassette, turning it over, and hitting "play" again. The miniature wheels moved around as the tinny sound of music blared from his hip.

Manny leaned over, stopped the player, ejected the tape, and held it in his hands. "You will not be putting the needle in your arm, William. You will be putting it into the horse. The best place to do it is in the neck or the thigh."

No...

"Ouch." William slapped his forehead with his hand.

Manny laughed. "A horse's skin and muscles are extra thick. It will never feel a thing."

"That's good," William said. "Cuz I wouldn't want to hurt any of 'em."

Never, ever...

"Later on today, we will practice," Manny said. "That way you will be able to do it on a horse without any problem. We will practice on an orange."

William giggled. "An orange?"

"You can help me to teach you."

Tell him no, William. Tell him you refuse to do anything like that.

"Okay, Manny." He held out his hand and shook Manny's. "Just like a business meeting."

"Right," Manny said.

As they stood up, William added, "When Donald comes home I can tell him about my new responsibility."

"No," Manny said quickly. "You cannot tell anyone about this."

"Why not?"

Because it's a crime! Because you are about to hurt a horse!

"Because we do not want to scare the owners. If we tell them their horse needs a vitamin, they may think something is wrong. If word gets out that something *is* wrong, they may pull the horse out of the race." Manny touched William on the arm and whispered, "Or something much worse."

"What worse?"

"We do not need to talk about that, now do we?"

William looked confused.

"They could send her to the glue factory," Manny said. "That is where they send horses too weak to race. Or ones they *think* are too weak. You do not want to be responsible for that, do you? Responsible for Neapolitan being turned into Elmer's glue?"

William whispered, "No."

He's lying…he's trying to scare you…

"Good," Manny said. "Then we keep this task to ourselves, we keep the horses strong, and you become the reason they stay healthy."

"Do all the horses get a shot?"

"We will start with Neapolitan."

"Neon's not weak," William said. "Her trainer says she runs faster than ever."

"It will be up to you to make her even stronger. People will be more amazed than ever."

"Yowza."

"'Yowza' is right. Go on and put away your cleaning equipment. As soon as you are ready, we will get started on those oranges. We want to make sure we do things perfectly. For the horse's sake."

Manny led William out of the room. I followed close behind.

Please, don't do this. Please...

"I wanna help keep Neapolitan strong," William said.

"Of course you do," Manny said, as he walked with William back to the sprayer. "We all do."

Chapter 58

The first try was rough; the orange rolled away from William and he ended up jabbing the table, breaking the tip of the water-filled syringe. William laughed, and I laughed with him, overdoing my grin to hide how nervous I was.

"That is okay," I told him. "Again we will try."

I handed William another needle filled with water and held the orange for him so it did not roll off the table, as he carefully and slowly inserted the tip. He held the instrument like a doctor with a steady hand, narrowed eyes, pressed lips.

"Use your thumb like I showed you."

He did as I told him.

"Now what?" he asked.

"Simply pull it out again, like this." I held his thick white hand under mine as together we guided the needle back out of the orange.

William smiled and held the syringe a few inches from his eyes. "It's empty!"

"Yes. You sent the water into the orange, exactly as you will send the vitamin into the horse. I am very proud of you."

William still held the needle up to his face. "I'm proud of me too. Let's give her the shot now!"

Carefully, I took the needle from his hand. "Shh. No need to get excited. We must keep especially quiet. Do not want our baby sent to the glue factory."

William silenced.

"Let us practice a few more times," I told him. We had two days before the bird was to arrive. "Just to be sure."

After six more tries, each time a bit smoother than the last and filled with more confidence, William had the task down to a science.

Almost like a true veterinarian.

Chapter 59

I rubbed my neck as I almost sleepwalked past empty tables and the skank of old cigar smoke. Sleeping on the tree house floor made my neck hurt like a mofo, but it was way safer than sleeping on the street. At least I had a good breakfast. Never could go wrong with a Denny's Grand Slam.

I stood in front of my lucky window at the Lounge Lizard OTB Bar and Grill. OTB stands for *off-track betting*, in case you didn't already know. Most athletes, especially the greats, are superstitious. There's a major league pitcher who eats grits with honey before every game. Another guy, pro-football running back, listens to the same opera over and over again while he sleeps the night before playoffs. Then there's an Olympic ice skating chick who has a lucky pair of underwear. Wears the same damn panties for every competition. Gamblers are superstitious, too, so I ain't so different from the sports greats. Always had a lucky window, whether it was at the Dellshore or an OTB joint.

The girl behind the glass took the money, handed me a receipt, and I was good to go. Twenty dollars on a three-year-old beauty from California named Jumping Jack Betty. I ordered a rusty nail. Another superstition. Pretty early to be drinking scotch and Drambuie, but who gave a shit? After too many nights of crappy sleep and ducking behind cars every time I spotted a fat guy in an Armani suit, I was ready for some action. Not to mention a little reward for being so damn patient.

Only seven customers sat in the Lounge Lizard at eight o'clock that morning, and that included me. A pair of chunky girls wearing crew cuts sat at the bar. In the corner, on the other side of the pool tables, four Asian dudes sat drinking orange juice, staring at the replay of the dog races on the screen behind the bar. Dog races. What a racket. Ponies always give more for your money, any red-blooded American knows that.

I sipped my rusty nail, letting the liquid burn its way down my throat. I leaned back in the booth, closing my eyes for a minute, and when I opened them again, my bookie was sitting across from me.

"Morning, sunshine," Sherm said, taking his grimy straw hat off his head and laying it on the table. He flattened out his thick gray hair. "Sorry to wake you."

"What are you doing here?" I asked, pretending like I wasn't surprised to see him.

"I was about to ask you that same question." Sherm rubbed his gnarled fingers on both hands, his knuckles like parrot claws.

I shrugged and took another sip of my drink.

The waitress came to our table. Sherm smiled his disgusting snaggle teeth and ordered a Bloody Mary. As soon as the girl walked away, his smile disappeared. "Word on the street is that you got something big in the works."

"Yeah? Says who?"

"What does it matter? My sources ain't never wrong."

"Well," I told him, "you *heard* wrong then." I mixed my drink with the red swizzle stick and glanced up at the television screen. The thin, wiry greyhounds ran the track like they were being chased by a pack of hungry wolves. That's why I liked ponies. Always running like they were going *toward* something instead of running *from* something.

"Nothing wrong with my hearing," Sherm said.

His beady little eyes looked like licorice cough drops stuck between his wrinkles. Not even sixty but looked like ET's twin.

"Maybe you dreamed it then," I said, smiling. "Maybe you're *still* dreaming."

The waitress brought the Bloody Mary, a tall thin glass with a stalk of celery sticking out of the top.

"I know someone who's been losing sleep over finding you," Sherm said, his voice even-steven. "And he's willing to pay some fine cash for your head. How's it feel to be so popular?"

"Feels peachy."

Sherm leaned across the table, almost knocking over his Bloody Mary. He grabbed onto the glass to keep it from spilling. "I have put up with your bullshit, your sob stories, your fucking cocky attitude for years. Now, if you got something cooking and you don't let me in on the action, I'm gonna make sure this person not only gets your head, but your fucking balls. Let's call it an exact set. A *perfecta*, if you will."

I pulled the swizzle stick out of my glass and downed the last of my drink. I crunched on a piece of ice. "Tell me what you already know, then maybe we'll talk."

"Tell you what, asshole. You tell me what's what, and then, maybe... *maybe* I'll tell you what I know."

Shit. Not even a slight buzz from the drink. Too many hash browns soaking up the scotch.

"I don't know nothin'," I told him. "I swear."

"Okay. You gonna play this game? Here's what I know: that you reneged on a deal you had with Roly Polchecki. That you're a piece of shit, treating Charlie the way you did up until he died. Using the guy, playing on his I-don't-have-a-daddy-and-you-don't-have-a-son sympathies." Sherm stirred his drink with his stick of celery then stuck it in between his crooked teeth and took a bite. After he swallowed, he said, "And I know all about that brother of yours."

I stopped breathing. Stopped blinking. My heartbeat throbbed behind my Adam's apple.

The waitress came by the table to check on us, but when she saw Sherm's red face, she did a quick pivot and went back to the bar.

"I might look as old as a fucking brontosaurus," he said, "but I'm a lot further from being dead than you'd like. So tell me what you got going on, leaving out the crap you're so famous for, and I'll be sure to spare your balls."

I told him what I thought he needed to know, based on what I believed he already knew. About Roly-Poly's plan to have me kill a racehorse. About my running away for fear that if I got caught I'd be hung, or, if I refused to do it, be worse than hung. I told him about my kid brother coming to live with me, about how a crazy fucker had broken into the apartment and beat the shit out of him, how that beating was meant for me, and it was time to get the hell out of Dodge.

"If you're so afraid, why are you still in town?" Sherm asked.

When I didn't answer, Sherm smiled. A couple of teeth on the bottom row were missing.

God, Sherm, I thought, *why don't you buy some dentures or something?*

He said, simple and clear, like he was teaching me my first word, "William."

My mind did a double-take. Backtracked over the information I'd told him. My exhausted brain started to fizzle. I could almost hear the electricity bouncing around in there.

I had never mentioned William's name.

"How do you know—"

"How does anybody know anything?" Sherm said. "You ask, that's how. You ask until you get answers."

"He's not important," I told him. "You don't need him for nothing. He's just a—"

"Retard?"

Shit!

"I know way more than you think," Sherm said. "Where your mama lives. How your real daddy abandoned you. How you abandoned your brother, out cold, bleeding on the friggin' floor. How you bailed on the job for Roly so your brother had to fill in for you."

"Fill in?"

"Turns out he makes the perfect stable hand."

"What?"

Sherm laughed. "Your kid brother got a job at your home away from home. How could you not know that? Jesus Christ, which one of you is the idiot?"

I knew William'd gotten a job, but I figured it was cleaning toilets at a gas station or sweeping up construction sites. How the hell did he get hired at the track?

My stomach rumbled. I was pretty sure Sherm could hear it. My eyes darted to the bar's exit sign. I could run. Just like I'd thought about doing that day at the church with Roly-Poly. No way would Sherm be able to chase me. Wouldn't be able to get up fast enough with those rickety knees. I'd be up the alley before he had a chance to think about it. And the old guy didn't carry no gun.

But he had a shitload of buddies who did.

Up on the screen, my pony came in fifth. I'd bet my last dime. I couldn't afford a bus to the train station where I'd stashed my clothes. I wasn't wearing clean underwear. For some reason, this made me sadder than anything else.

Sherm grinned as I caved. My shoulders fell forward. My hair hung in my eyes. For a split second, it felt good to give in. A relief to let someone else pull the ropes, make the decisions. The throbbing in my neck disappeared.

"Okay," I said.

"Okay what?"

"I'm yours."

"Yippee for me," Sherm said. "I'm glad you're mine. But there's something else."

"What?"

"If we're gonna work together, Donald, there's gotta be a certain amount of honesty."

I stared at him.

"You left out an important detail in your story," Sherm said. "I'm sure it was an oversight, and this time I'll forgive you."

"I didn't leave nothin' out."

Sherm chewed on the rest of his celery stick. He took his time, not saying a thing until he finished every inch of that damned stalk.

The lower half of my body was cramping bad. If I didn't hit the bathroom in a matter of minutes, there could be a very embarrassing accident. My intestines were responding to Sherm's statement, even before he said it.

I couldn't let him see me freak. I could pretend he was a great uncle, asking me about my life, like he was interested in the real me, wanted to know me better, take me on a round of golf or to a monster truck rally.

But Sherm wasn't no uncle.

He said, in a voice that matched the fucking claws on his hands, "Tell me about the lottery money."

Chapter 60

On the desk in the small dark room they practiced. The only sounds were the occasional snort of a horse or the scratching of a nearby rat, making his nest out of leftover straw in the rafters, even though rodent traps were set up everywhere. A needle in, a needle out, over and over, until it was almost comical.

Of course, there was nothing funny about it at all.

I tried talking to William about what Manny's plans might be. When that didn't work, I tried taking him back in time.

You don't dream about it anymore, I told him. *Have you forgotten how things were before that day? Before we stopped breathing and flew into the air? Before the ambulance took us away? Before the doctors told Mom and Dad we would never be right again? The little things, like dates and math problems and parts of the alphabet don't matter so much—but how can you forget who we used to be?*

Sometimes I would carry on for hours at a time, which was exhausting.

And for every memory I tried to conjure up for William, an inch of me would disappear.

He knew something was wrong, he just wouldn't admit it. Like our memory of almost drowning, of being thrown into the bottomless pit, he refused to accept the reality of it. But I could feel it in him. Each time his aim with the needle improved, an inkling from somewhere deeper than his mind told him that what he was about to do wasn't right. And each time that needle slid in and out of the orange's dimply skin with precision, his pride smothered any feeling of doubt.

Neapolitan knew something was wrong as well. She had begun showing her temperamental side again. Each time I followed William past her stall, she'd close her eyes and turn her snout toward the ceiling, stretching her neck back and nodding her head up and down.

"What's wrong, Neon?" William would ask, patting the spot between her eyes, trying to stop her head from bobbing. After a moment she'd relax, her eyes would open again, and she'd allow William to gently stroke her nuzzle. But right before her eyes closed, she'd look at me. Just like the first day we'd met, as if I were really there—as if she could really see me.

Two evenings after Manny started William on the oranges, a package arrived by way of special courier. Manny stepped into the barn office with the box and came back out without it, shutting the door behind him.

He approached William, speaking in a serious voice like someone had died: "Tonight is the night."

William shuffled his feet. "Tonight?"

"Do not be nervous."

"I'm not," William said as he looked at Neapolitan and wiped his palms on his dirty jeans.

"Go and take your break, William. Thirty minutes. Then we will do what needs to be done."

Chapter 61

The beautiful pijon cooed like she was perfectly content to be sheltered in a cardboard box. In the barn office, I lifted the lid and stroked her tiny head. "You do not look sick to me, small one," I whispered. She didn't look sick, but still I wore a thick pair of garden gloves, and latex ones underneath, as instructed.

The evening arrived warmer than usual, a night sky full of clouds. The air had no movement. All was as still as a graveyard.

Except for the cooing of the pretty white bird.

The package also held a canvas sack. The sack was filled with everything we would need that evening.

William went to the break room each evening halfway through his shift, and tonight I made sure his schedule was no different. He would get himself a bag of chips or a package of cookies. But I could not think about food for myself. Instead, I sat on one of the crates in the makeshift office, surrounded by dried-up oranges, my knees supporting the open box which held the pijon.

Trying to imitate her birdsong, I rolled my tongue and hummed at the same time. Her response was beautiful and unexpected. For nearly thirty minutes we did this, talking to one another. I did not know what I was saying, but she did not seem to mind if I said the wrong things. She only wanted someone to keep her company.

Perhaps we had something in common.

In my waistband I felt the small hunting kouto with the mother-of-pearl handle, rubbing against my skin.

I will kill her quickly, so William will not hear.

The thought entered my brain like a bullet, but I caught it and threw it away. I would not allow myself to think of these things until it was necessary. I had to stay focused.

My throat was closing. I took a swig from my bottled water. I had gone through four bottles in as many hours.

How is it that it had come to this? How had my life become one where Debt's ghost haunted me? If only there was another way to release myself from this web. Something else that could be done to satisfy all parties.

I placed the box on the desk and closed the lid, ignoring the pijon's request for more conversation. I looked inside the canvas sack for the tenth time to see the tin filled with needles, a bundle of rags, a folded glad trash bag, and extra gloves. In a matter of minutes the needle would be filled.

I took another gulp of water. I breathed deeply. Then I waited for the sound of William's footsteps to come back to me.

Chapter 62

I put my stained work uniform in the washer, got into my robe, and put some water to boilin'. A cup of tea—maybe that would help my sour stomach. Mercy. You'd think that findin' out your son is alright woulda helped. But my shoulders were so tense I barely slept most nights.

The tea was nice and hot as it made its way into my empty tummy. Hadn't been able to eat nothin' all day. I pulled some saltines from the pantry and nibbled on a few. I felt like a mouse. A sad little mouse in a house too big and too quiet.

My swollen knuckles were aching. Didn't know how much longer I could scoop Sloppy Joe from the pans, mop up spills from the cafeteria floor, deal with whinin' children who never said "please" or "thank you" no more.

Carryin' the mug with me, I stepped onto my back porch. More of a stoop, really. A small square, 'bout five by five. Had wrought iron railin's on the sides where I'd hung some pots with new begonia seeds. Those would be sproutin' soon. I looked up at the sky. The back of my neck was hot and sticky, and it wasn't even summer yet. More rain comin'. Clouds moved in overhead makin' it almost too dark to see the trees edgin' the property a few yards away. The moon poked itself through every now and then. I could have turned on the back porch light, but I found it soothin', standin' there in the dark with my cup. I breathed in the smell of tea roses startin' to bloom next to the house, and the wild honeysuckle on the side fence, remindin' me of summers gone by. Billy pluckin' each and every honeysuckle blossom he could find, stickn' the pointy end in his mouth and sippin' nectar. Such sweetness, those flowers.

Such sweetness, my little Billy. Like a little hummin' bird himself—

A noise from the backyard came tumblin' over the grass, like someone was sharin' the yard with me. I never was good at tellin' distances, so I wasn't sure where it came from exactly.

There it was again.

I couldn't see nothin' in the pitch black, 'specially without my glasses. I'd bought them mainly for drivin' at night, and they seemed to help, but I wasn't doin' much drivin' at night these days, 'cept that night I drove downtown.

I cupped my hand over my eyes as if that'd help me see better. I wasn't afraid. There wasn't no problems out here in the country like they had in the cities. No robbers or drug pushers or nothin' like that. And anyways, if there was someone that shouldn't be there, I could make a quick call to that Officer Powers and he'd be at my house lickety-split.

"Who's there?" I called out, usin' the stern voice that sometimes worked with the ornery kids in the cafeteria.

A scrapin' noise, like a box slid'n across a plywood floor, came from the tree house. If it was some neighborhood kids with nothin' else to do, I worried about 'em, climbin' that ladder in the dark. What if one of 'em fell? Broke an ankle or somethin' worse?

I put my tea cup on the stoop, walked down the steps to the grass, and wrapped my bathrobe more tight around me. I didn't mind none if a young boy saw me in my robe, but no reason for him to see my nightgown underneath.

"Who'all ever's up there, y'all need to come on down. That tree house belongs to my boy."

Well, it used to, but that wasn't nobody's business.

I walked across the damp grass in my slippers toward the elm tree, wonderin' if I should go back into the kitchen and get a flashlight or keep goin' forward. I remember Frank wantin' to put up floodlights, but like so many other things the last year he was with us, he never got around to it.

The bottom of my robe all of a sudden tripped me. My left knee hit the ground and I let out a small yelp. I counted to thirty before standin' again. Brushin' the dirt offa my robe, I stared at the tree house again. Too dark. I had to go back and grab a flashlight. But what if while I was inside, whoever all was up there ran away?

Well, then, that would be for the best.

After limpin' back to the porch, I picked up my mug from the step and went inside. The flashlight was kept in the middle kitchen drawer. Only used it every so often. In the drawer were packs of matches, a few plastic spoon-forks—*sporks*, I think they call 'em—and a dozen skewers we used for our *shish kabobs* once in a blue moon. I dug around in the drawer, thinkin' the flashlight had somehow gotten crammed beneath all the junk. But I was wrong.

I opened all the other drawers in the kitchen. No sign of the flashlight.

In the middle of the room, I rubbed my throbbin' knee while thinkin'. I decided to light up my small lantern, the one in case of a hurricane, that I kept on the floor of the pantry. After makin' sure the glass cover protected me from gettin' burnt, I headed back outside.

All was quiet except for some crickets, chirpin' away like the whole neighborhood was already asleep, and it wasn't barely eight o'clock.

More careful this time, holdin' my robe offa the ground with one hand, the lantern danglin' from my other, I headed back to the tree house. At the bottom of the ladder, I peered up into the darkness. Couldn't barely make out the blue sign William and Donald had painted on the front: *MEN ONLY.* Stephanie had been the exception.

"Who's up there?" I called.

The only answer was the cry of a baby mockin'bird, probably callin' out in his sleep.

My eyes took in that long stretch of ladder, a mile up it seemed. My knee was still achin'. What if I made it up there and couldn't get back down? How long would I sit up there, with spiders and maybe even bats, waitin' for someone to notice I was missin'? Worse yet, what if I got to the top and someone *was* up there? What if it was a stranger? And what if the stranger wasn't a kid after all, and he was mad I'd found him? What then?

I listened as good as I could, but no more noises came down at me.

I'm gettin' feeble-minded, I told myself. *First I think there's someone up in the tree house, then I trip like my feet were bought on sale at the Rite Aid.*

I let out a sigh and went back to the house.

After blowin' out the lantern, turnin' out the lights, and double checkin' that everythin' was locked up tight, I went on to bed. I must not have been scared about nothin' since I fell to sleep quick.

I slept fine at first. Billy came to see me like he did sometimes, his yellow hair shinin' like a summer dandelion, laughin' and playin' and runnin' all over the place, a regular shirtless boy wearin' cutoffs, the bell bottom jeans that he'd cut into mid-thigh shorts when his legs grew.

That's how he was dressed in the dream. He was settin' on top of a large white mare, the kind in a fairy tale, white enough to be a unicorn but without the funny horn. No saddle. Just settin' on that smooth white back. Then he took off! His body leaned forward like he was one of them jockeys, his bony fingers grippin' onto her neck. I was an eye in the sky as my son rode that beauty over hills and through valleys, to the ocean, to the mountains, to the city sidewalks.

But sometimes dreams turn on you just when you're feelin' happy.

Fog rolled in. I couldn't see the horse or Billy no more. The fog rolled in around my legs. I couldn't see my own feet. Sweat dripped down the back of my neck and into the plush of my robe. I called out to Billy, but there wasn't no answer. I called again, with anger in my voice, to show him I wasn't kiddin' around. That's when the fog started rollin' away fast like a giant snowball, leavin' behind what it wanted me to see.

The beautiful white horse had turned into a different horse altogether, with black matted fur like she'd been dipped in tar, mangy skin, clumps of hair on the ground around her hooves. Her tongue hung far out of her mouth like a stretched out piece of pink taffy. Her eyes rolled up into her head. I felt sorry for the animal, but at the same time she terrified me.

Where was Billy? I had to find him, but I couldn't take my eyes offa that poor creature. Foam dripped from her mouth and snot ran from her nostrils. She let out a pained whinny and fell onto her hindquarters. That baby was dyin', I could see that clear as day. I wanted to help her, but my feet wouldn't obey.

Billy? I called.

Yeah, Mom? he shouted from somewhere beyond the walls of my dream.

Oh, I felt such relief at hearin' his voice. I said, *Your horse is dyin', son. Come tend to it.*

She ain't my horse no more.

Well, for goodness sake, who does she belong to? Someone has to help this poor animal…

A person that wasn't Billy stepped out of nowhere and stood next to the horse. He was covered in a dark cloak, like that Darth Vader character all the boys had paid good money to see over and over again at the movies. And even though I couldn't tell exactly who was under that hood, I could make out the blond sideburns with the bit of gray and the blond stubble along his jaw line.

And that familiar face was all smiles.

Chapter 63

William munched on potato chips as we made our way back from the break room. As I followed him across the greens, the sun was dropping on the other side of the track, leaving nothing behind but the darkened bleachers, the quiet stables, and the occasional whinny of a horse. The barn lights looked ominous in the distance.

Manny's words from earlier drifted between us: "Tonight's the night."

Please, listen to me, I begged William. *I don't know exactly what's going on, and you don't either. All I know is that if we leave now, we'll be safe. Ask Officer Powers for help. You won't be held responsible for anything.*

"I'm responsible," he said.

Outside the barn doors, I warned him, *If you don't stop this now, your life is over. You'll be blamed for whatever it is that Manny has planned. Do you understand? You're being used. You'll end up in prison. Alone.* I stared at my missing feet. *Even I won't be able to visit you…*

We entered the dim barn. William put on his work gloves and headed over to where Manny stood next to Neon's stall.

I stopped in the barn's doorway, half of my body present, the other half who knew where. My fear of vanishing was great, but my need to save William from himself was greater. Neon's head drooped submissively over the stall door, her eyes peering at me like she was begging me to do something.

There was only one person I knew that might be able to help. She'd be getting ready for bed now. Most nights she'd eat a light dinner, have a cup of tea, and hit the sack. Back in the early days of the coma, I'd slipped into Mom's dreams from time to time. But that was before William had grown into a man. Before I had become the only link between him and his memories.

Time meant nothing to me, but it was everything to William and the people around him. Maybe time was one of the anchors keeping me tethered to his world, even though I didn't care about it. But I had to make myself care. For William's sake. Because right then, time was the enemy.

It helped my confidence knowing that Neapolitan was aware of me, and that the little boy on the bus had spoken to me. I closed my eyes and blocked out the conversation between William and Manny, concentrating on my breathing. I was thankful that even though half of me floated in limbo, I was still able to hear my own breath. I concentrated on the warm, humid air and the smell of hay and manure climbing into my nostrils, then exhaled the same air back through my mouth. I did this over and over again, until I felt myself rocking with lightheadedness.

Soon, I floated next to Mom's bed. She was sleeping on her back. Her lips moved, like she was whispering to someone. Her breath was stale tea lying just beneath Colgate toothpaste. Her eyelids fluttered. Her hands twitched, one of them grabbing onto the sheets, then letting go again. I leaned in closer to her face. The soap she used smelled like lilac.

I'd never forget that smell.

I reached out to touch her face, but I was only a fraction of a body now, a skinny naked torso with a neck and a head. I allowed myself to tumble into Mom's mind, into her dreams.

As soon as I did this, my whole body came back again: calloused hands, clumsy feet, knobby knees, peachy barely-summer body, hairless chest. In the dream, I stood in the shadows and saw what Mom could see: a beautiful white mare, silently asking me to climb onto her back. She was like a mythical beast right out of the Greek mythology books from social studies. I went to her. Her fur felt soft and thick under my hands as I pulled on her mane to help me onto her back. She sighed with relief once I sat on top, as if she'd been waiting all this time for me to find her—to ride her.

As I rode, the sun rose and set, the shadows stretching or shrinking. Plains of wheat stretched ahead for miles as the horse carried me through fields, the tassels on the tops of the stalks whispering past my ankles.

I'm not sure how long we rode together when a fog as thick as the wheat wrapped around the mare's legs and crawled up around my legs as well, then around my body, my neck, my head. A searing pain spread through me like alcohol in a giant wound. The poisonous fog reached my eyes. I tried to scream, but no sound came.

The horse began to tremble, like a great earthquake beneath me. I looked for Mom, but I could see nothing through the fog. I tried to move the horse, believing that if I could get her to outrun the fog, we would be safe. But she didn't budge.

My legs started to cramp, then my arms and hands.

The horse started to buck. I was thrown to the cold and impersonal ground. I felt no pain from this but could tell that the hard earth didn't want me there.

I didn't belong there.

Mom called my name. My lips moved, but still no words came out. I stood up and went to reach for the horse, but my hands found only space. The fog was so thick I couldn't tell if I was right side up or upside down.

Something else entered the fog. I could feel it. *Him.* The smell of disease and contamination wafted around me. My skin crawled.

Mom's voice found me: *Someone has to help this poor animal, Billy…*

Had something happened to the horse?

Of course it had. Because the presence of evil was there in Mom's dream, the same way it was there in William's life, hovering over his head like a black cloud…

Go away, Mom was saying from somewhere in the distance. *You're upsettin' everythin'. Leave us alone.*

The person she spoke to did not answer.

You're hurtin' my heart, don't you see that? My heart aches…

Mom? I called, running in the direction of her voice.

No! Don't come here, Billy. No need for you to see this.

See what?

The horse's painful whinny seeped through the fog.

I pumped my arms and legs like I was in the final inches of the hundred-yard dash, and just as suddenly as the fog had appeared, it vanished.

Mom lay on the ground, her hand clutching her nightgown below her left collar bone.

Mom? I knelt beside her.

Donald, she said.

No, Mom, it's me, Billy.

Donald, she said again. Then she looked into my eyes. *Please hurry.* As soon as she said the words, she began to fade. I reached out to touch her face, but by the time my fingers made it to her cheek, she had disappeared.

Closing my eyes, I pictured her bedroom, the texture of her bedspread, the flowered pattern on the pillow cases, the valance fanned out on the top of her curtains. I opened my eyes again and found my limbless self floating above the foot of her bed. She was on the telephone. She hadn't disappeared!

"Two-eleven, Stoneybrook—" She choked on the words. "He was right here. Right here..."

I glanced around the bedroom. I didn't see anyone, but something was different...out of place...

Mom groaned as she leaned over the edge of the bed, barely holding on to the telephone. "Yes," she breathed into the phone just before it fell from her hand. Her head dangled loosely over the bed, her graying hair touching the floor.

A woman's voice on the other end of the line seeped from the earpiece. "Hello? Mrs. Baker? An ambulance is on the way..."

My eyes darted around the room again and stopped at the wall a few feet from the bed. On the television stand, a large clean rectangle outlined in dust was all that remained.

The soothing voice on the other end of the telephone line was still speaking. "Stay put, ma'am. We're sending an officer to look for the intruder."

PART V

Chapter 64

I was rubbing Neapolitan's snout when William came back from the vending machines thirty minutes later. He had a synchronized clock in his brain, ticking away, waiting. Why did that clock always have to be so precise? Why couldn't the seconds have fallen behind, like the rest of him, just this once?

As he walked over to me, he put on his work gloves.

"You have some crumbs," I told him, pointing.

He wiped the back of his glove across his chin.

"Are you nervous?" I asked him.

"About what?"

"You do not remember?"

The thought of William forgetting the task frightened me more than the task itself.

Well, almost.

"I remember now," William said, smiling. "Give Neon her shot. Then go home to sleep."

"That is right. Home to sleep. Just like any other night."

The horses already slept. Except for Neon. She was wide awake. I could not look at her directly. Karma had settled into her dark eyes, plainly accusing me: *In the end, you will be the one the universe blames. In the end, you will be the one to carry the debt. It does not matter who gives her the shot. Karma sees right through you...*

"Let us get started," I told William, my vocal cords working hard not to crack as I pushed the intrusive words from my head.

William started to follow me to the office where the bird slept soundly in her box. I put out my hand. "Stand with Neon and make sure she is comfortable."

William whispered softly to the horse as I stepped into the small room.

I opened the lid of the box. The dove napped in a feathery ball, her breath quick but rhythmic. I rubbed the top of her head. She cooed in her sleep.

I set the box on the table and pulled the tin of needles from the canvas sack. I opened the lid and removed a needle, held it up to the dim light coming from the yellow light bulb.

It was time. Time to take this plastic mosquito and transfer the infected blood from one animal to the clean blood of another. The power I held in my hands was overwhelming. The fear that consumed me made me sick. I took a swig from my water. A belch escaped from me, low and guttural, depositing the taste of acid in my mouth, that morning's coffee mixed with bile from my stomach.

I looked over at my thermos of stale coffee on the desk, at the packets of sugar and the powdered creamer used to disguise the bitterness of cafeteria coffee. Such ordinary things which showed a normal life, lived by a normal man. A cup of coffee with cream and two sugars. A cup of coffee defining America, defining me, soon to be an American.

Chapter 65

I worried that the blood would rush to Mom's head from hanging over the edge of the bed. Outside of her dream, without hands, it was impossible help her.

An ambulance arrived. The EMTs stormed through the house until they found Mom in the bedroom. They moved her body from the bed to the stretcher in seconds. Her face was incredibly smooth. The wrinkles across her forehead had softened, the bags under her eyes flattened. She looked so peaceful.

The same kind of oxygen mask I had worn sixteen years before covered Mom's face. In the ambulance, her eyes fluttered from time to time, and her hand tried once to take off the mask, but it was too weak and fell back to her side.

The EMTs pushed their way through the hospital doors, wheeling her into the ER. Nurses and doctors poked her with needles and sent her to another floor for tests. She remained unconscious. I didn't know if she would ever wake up again.

Once in her hospital room, she breathed more steadily, but only with the mask's help. The monitor by her bed kept tabs on her heart. Two bags of liquid hung from poles. A young nurse came in, rearranged the blankets, checked the IV in the back of her hand, and went out again.

We were alone.

Mom?

The monitor beat faster, but she didn't move.

I closed my eyes and tried to get into her mind again, but it was no use. My powers, if that's what they ever were at all, were nearly drained. My naked torso floated across the room. I stared at the moon outside the window.

What would happen if I gave up? Who would know? Who would give a rat's—
"Billy?"

I drifted to the bed and leaned over her.

Mom?

An oxygen tube sent air into her nose as she forced the words out.

"Oh, Billy. My baby boy…"

She stopped breathing for a moment and squeezed her eyes shut.

What can I do, Mom?

"You need to stop him," she whispered.

William. I had nearly forgotten about him. How long had I been absent from his side? I had lost all track of time. What was he doing right now? What if I went to him instead of staying here? I couldn't be in two places at once. I was barely connected to the real world as it was.

I began to cry.

Mom's fingers went through my forever wet hair. Her lips no longer moved as she spoke.

Go, Billy. Many are depending on you, even if they don't know they are…

I looked into her eyes which were now open. Her glowing shadow sat up and smiled, leaving her physical body lying on the bed beneath her.

You will always be my boy. Please take care of things. I trust you.

She grew fainter, slowly turning into what looked like a photograph, faded from too much sunlight.

What do I do, Mom? William doesn't listen to me anymore.

It's not William you should be worried about, son.

Then who?

Your brother…

Donald?

But her ghostly image was gone. All that remained was her motionless body, her eyes closed, the bleep of the machine now a single noted drone, a flat line across the bottom of the screen.

I stared at her relaxed face. A single tear slid down one cheek. I wanted to wipe it away, but I had no hands to do it with.

A pair of nurses ran to Mom's side.

Her words rose within me: *Please take care of things…I trust you…*

No time to think. I closed my eyes and waited. I opened them slowly, but I was still in the hospital room. I closed them again and squeezed them tight, as if it would help. The hospital room walls still surrounded me. I moved to the window and placed my forehead against the cool damp glass. Closing my eyes one more time, I wished like I have never wished before, like I would probably never have the strength to wish again.

The smell of antiseptic vanished, replaced by the smell of manure and damp earth.

I found myself hovering just inside the barn doors. Crickets jumped across the shadows. The night air crept across my face, and phantom shivers ran through my invisible arms and legs.

In the middle of the barn, Manny and William stood side by side. Both wore gardening gloves. William had his back to me as he reached his arm into Neapolitan's stall.

Manny's voice sounded like it was coming from far away, echoing in my ears like he was speaking from the bottom of a well. "That is it, William, pinch the skin lightly. Go easy…right there…that is the way…"

No! I screamed, but the only one who heard me was Neon. She turned toward me, her eyes wide and frightened, and took a step back, leaving William standing on the threshold of the stall door with the needle in his raised hand.

"Relax, Neon," Manny said, reaching out to grab the horse by her mane and nearly pushing William into the wall. "Now, William," he ordered. "Do it!"

William stepped farther into the stall with Neon, who whinnied with defiance. She stomped her back legs alternately a few times and bobbed her head up and down.

William patted her side, took a hold of some skin on her neck, and bunched it together. "It's okay, Neon. This'll make you strong..."

I floated to the stall, dragging my invisible appendages with me. But I was too late. As I reached Neon, the needle's tip burrowed in between the folds of the horse's thick neck—

You're going to kill her! I shouted. *She's going to die! You'll be her murderer!*

For an instant William's eyes met mine, but the moment vanished when Manny patted a gloved hand against William's back.

"Good work, William. You did exactly as instructed."

William smiled and patted Neon on the head. Her nostrils flared wide and she let out a contemptuous snort.

"Good girl, Neon," William said as he rubbed her snout.

Manny helped William close and lock the stall then walked with him toward the stable doors. He held out a brown paper bag. "Drop that in here." William let the empty needle fall from his hand. "Give me your gloves," Manny said. "You deserve a new pair. For all your hard work." William handed Manny his gloves. "Why not leave a little early? Get some well-deserved sleep. It has been a long night."

"Yessir!" William said. "Bye-bye Neon." He patted her on the snout and took off across the grass toward the tunnel.

I stayed behind for a while to see what Manny would do next.

He dropped William's gloves into the bag and rolled the top edge over a few times, until the stuff inside was compact. He pulled a faded bandana from his back pocket and patted his damp face. Then he went into the little room he'd used to practice on the oranges.

"Come here, my love."

I looked around curiously to see who Manny was speaking to. He pulled a box out from under the desk, opened the lid, and peered inside. A white dove appeared in his folded hands.

"You shall be rewarded for being so patient."

He pressed her against his chest and walked to the entrance. In the barn doorway he stood for a moment before raising his hands into the air. The dove took off, her white wings coming to life after being folded up in the tiny box. Into the dark sky she flew, disappearing around the corner of the barn.

In the distance, William's shadow entered the employee tunnel. As I floated out of the barn to follow, pulling my nearly nonexistent self with me, Manny's voice came to me, a whisper in the night.

"Go free, my *swazo*, my pijon," he said. "I will not be responsible for your death tonight. Your spirit, your imprisoned *lespir*, shall fly free."

Chapter 66

Officer Powers

The call came into dispatch just as I was settling into a late dinner at my desk. The word "Baker" drifted in from the other room. I put down my fork and wiped the spaghetti sauce from my chin. We were dealing with low staff with everyone trying to get their vacation time in before the spike in warm-weather crime.

I got up and stood in the doorway. Evelyn sat at her desk with her earpiece on, the side of her head leaning against her hand. When she saw me, she held up a finger.

"Do I need to send backup?" she said into the mouthpiece.

She waited while the person on the other end answered.

"Let me know when you're en route." She turned halfway in her swivel chair. "Hey, Chuck."

"What's up?"

"Probable heart attack," Evelyn said. "Francine Baker. Out on Stoneybrook, over by—"

"I know who she is."

"EMTs have arrived, and Scotty's cruiser was nearby, so he's heading over."

"Why did you ask if they needed back up?" I asked.

"She reported an intruder."

"Before or after the heart attack?"

"Not sure."

"Did you get a description?"

"She apparently passed out before 911 could get any details."

"Thanks, Evelyn."

I had a three-ring choice to make here: I could go to the hospital and interview Mrs. Baker, presuming of course that she was alive and coherent; I could drive to her house to assist Scotty, even though he was capable of handling things; or I could find William and inform him.

Or, I thought selfishly, I could finish my dinner and go home to my wife at nine o'clock like planned.

But cops don't get paid to be selfish.

My half-eaten plate of spaghetti was getting cold. Two out of the three meatballs still sat on top of the pile.

Someone had to let William know. Especially if there was a chance he could lose his mother.

"Evelyn, I need to run an errand. Would you do me a favor, besides holding down the fort?"

"Sure."

"Call me as soon as you find out anything about the Baker woman. Keep in touch with the attending physician once she gets to County General."

"No problem."

"I also need you to get a hold of the Dellshore Racetrack. Try to locate William Baker for me. That's the woman's son."

"Will do," Evelyn said.

I wrapped foil over the top of my dinner and shoved it into the small Coleman fridge, grabbed my coat, made sure my gun and stick were secure, and headed out.

A few minutes later, as I was driving down the highway, Evelyn called on the radio.

"Hey, Chuck. Only got an answering machine over at the track."

"I'm heading over there right now. Keep me posted on Mrs. Baker."

I hung up the radio, turned on my flashers, and headed more quickly down the highway.

Chapter 67

The flapping of her wings could be heard long after she was gone. To where she had flown I did not know. Perhaps to be with other doves, perhaps to die soon, perhaps defying odds.

I was about to close the barn doors when someone came up behind me. My instinct was to spin around swinging, but there was something so distinct about the way his shoes sounded on the dirt that I knew it was not a hit. I knew it was a cop before I saw him beneath the floodlight.

Over my shoulder, I slung the small backpack holding the paper bag with the dirty needles, the flattened shoebox, and the gloves. He glanced at my pack. A slight glance, but it was there all the same.

"Can I help you?" I asked.

"Officer Powers," he said, touching his badge. "I'm looking for William Baker. I understand he works here."

"Yes, sir," I told the policeman, keeping my voice even, my accent deeply buried. Was this the same policeman who had stared down at me from William's apartment? Horror stories of how the law treated *les imigrans* in the United States were rampant in my apartment building. "But he has already left for the evening."

"What time did he leave?"

I noticed that the cop did not write down what I told him. This made me even more nervous, the fact that he so trusted his memory.

"I believe it was around…" I looked at my watch. "Eight-fifteen…perhaps a little earlier?"

"Doesn't he have a set schedule?"

"Yes, sir. But sometimes he stays late. To spend more time with the horses."

As I finished my sentence, Neapolitan let out a loud whinny.

The cop peeked around me into the dark stable through the three-foot gap in the middle of the barn doors. He brought his eyes back to me.

I was mad at myself. I did not need to give this officer answers to questions he did not ask. I would have to be more careful.

"Did he go straight home?" he asked.

"I do not know. I assume so."

Officer Powers looked up into the night sky. "Sure can see a lot of stars way out here."

"Yes, sir."

"Mind if I walk with you?" He looked between the stable doors again. "You are leaving?"

"Yes, sir." I closed and latched the stable doors.

We walked together across the wet grass next to the track, the officer on my left, my backpack slung over my right shoulder. Even though the cop was only a few feet from me, I was relieved he had stopped me from throwing the brown bag into the Dumpster next to the main building. Wiser to throw it into a random trash bin on the way home. I tried to carry the satchel as nonchalantly as possible, an ordinary backpack anyone would use for their lunch or gym clothes, not filled with needles and gloves. Every so often it slipped from my shoulder, and I quickly hiked it back up.

"Has William done something wrong?" I decided to ask, otherwise the officer might wonder why I was not curious.

"His mother had a heart attack this evening."

"Oh. Did she—"

"No details yet. She's in the hospital."

Then I asked, even though I already knew the answer, "Do you know where William lives? To tell him about his mother, I mean?"

"Yes. I know a quite a bit about your coworker."

Sweat ran down my back between my shoulder blades.

"That is good" was all I could think to say.

As we approached the tunnel on the backside of the main building, a cooing sound came from behind us. We both looked toward the sound, and there, on the tallest post on the fence surrounding the grounds, sat the pijon.

It was time to end our conversation.

"I need to clock out," I said. "It has been a long day."

"I should get to William's anyway," Officer Powers said. "He may need a ride to the hospital."

"He is lucky to know someone like you."

"I hear the same about you, befriending him, landing him a good job."

William had shared that with the cop?

"Yes," I said. "He's a hard worker."

Silence.

"Well," I told the officer. "If there is anything else I can do, let me know."

"You can count on it."

"I will keep his mother in my prayers," I added.

The officer nodded before heading toward the security gate.

I walked down the tunnel to the employee lounge, counting my steps, tempted to look back again, especially when I heard his police radio crackle in the distance. But I kept my eyes focused straight ahead, the dark walls on either side of me acting as blinders, not so different from the ones worn by a horse when she races.

Chapter 68

On the bus, William ignored the world around him as music blared through his headphones: a bum picking his nose in the back seat, a hooker re-applying her lipstick in a tiny hand mirror, the bus driver, barely keeping his eyes open as he drove through the dark streets.

Mom's gone, do you understand? You will never see her again. How does that make you feel? Huh? HUH? And you hurt Neon. Your beautiful pony. What the hell is wrong with you?

He didn't hear me. We rode in silence until we got to the apartment. Upstairs, I watched as William performed his ritual: locked the door behind him, took off his sneakers and placed them by the front door, turned on the lights, first in the living room, then in the kitchen, then in the bathroom. As if by turning on the lights he wouldn't feel so lonely. He switched on the television, staring at the fuzzy screen until he remembered that the cable had been disconnected. He clicked it off again.

William took off his shirt and pants, dropped them on the floor outside the bathroom, used the toilet. He washed his face and hands in the sink, dried them on the ratty towel, and headed for the kitchen. He took the half-gallon container of milk from the fridge and poured himself a glass, then grabbed a package of Oreos from the top of the refrigerator. He sat at the kitchen table, munching on the cookies, occasionally dipping one into the milk. After a dozen or so, he put the cookies away, washed out his glass, and went to the apartment's only closet located in the living room. Two empty suitcases sat on the closet floor below his clothes. He pulled his light blue polyester shirt from the hanger and put it on. Slowly, he closed each button, except for the top three. After slipping the headphones over his ears, he took his hands and smoothed out the front of the shirt. He closed his eyes and began to sing, like he did every night.

"Uh-huh, uh-huh, you do it good, girl, uh-huh, uh-huh...I like the way you move, uh-huh, uh-huh..."

His backup singers popped into the room and stood behind the sofa bed under their disco ball. With his eyes still closed, William turned around in a circle, pointed his finger in the air, and thrust his hip out to the left.

"...shake it like this, shake it all around...yeah, what you do to me..."

A knock at the door.

His two backup singers paused and then disappeared. For a moment, William was a statue in his underwear and shiny shirt, his arm extended skyward, his face deep in concentration.

The knock grew harder.

William turned off the music and slid the headphones from his ears. "Who is it?"

"Officer Powers." When William didn't respond, Powers added, "Remember me? The police officer you met out at your mother's house? I have to speak to you. It's very important."

William opened the door.

Officer Powers' eyes moved from the underwear to the blue sparkly shirt. "May I come in?"

William stepped out of the way as the officer entered the apartment and closed the door behind him. "I just got home from work," he said. "I take care of horses."

"Yes, you told me." Officer Powers sat on the couch. He took off his police hat and placed it on one of his knees. "Come sit down, William. I have something to tell you. Something very important."

William sat next to the officer. I stayed by William's side. I would be there for him. Even if I was mostly gone and he acted mostly deaf.

"Son—"

Another knock at the door interrupted Powers. A scratchy whisper came from the hallway. "Everything all right, officer? That man in there okay?"

Officer Powers opened the door. Sherri the landlord stood in her dirty robe, her hair six inches high in curlers, a collection of keys dangling from a large ring by her side.

"Everything is fine, Miss…"

"Sherri Lynne. You can call me Sherri. Anything I can do?" She tried to peer around him.

"No, thank you. We appreciate your concern, but everything is fine." He closed the door, leaving her standing in the hallway.

Her muffled voice seeped through the door. "Well, if you need anything…" The clanging keys drifted away.

Officer Powers didn't sit back down.

"William," he said slowly. "It's your mother."

William laughed. "That's not my mom. My mom works in a cafeteria."

"Yes, I know. William, your mother had to go the hospital tonight. An ambulance—"

William stood up. "What?"

"She had a heart attack."

I tried to tell you…

"Hospitals are bad," William said. "She'd never go there."

"Your mother called 911 and—"

"You're a big fat liar."

"Why don't you put on your trousers and come with me—"

"She would never go there! She wouldn't, cuz she knows! It's bad there. She might end up like m-m-me!" He grabbed the officer by the wrist and spit the words out. "She'll get eaten by the d-d-dark, and then she won't come out again."

But I did come out again—you just didn't follow…

Officer Powers pried William's fingers loose and gripped his hand. "Your mother has passed away. I got the call a little while ago. I'm so sorry—"

"You're lying!"

"The doctors did everything they could. Her heart was weak."

"No, no, no!" William fell back against the sofa. "No. She needs me. She n-n-needs m-m-me." Gagging sobs took hold of him.

Officer Powers went into the bathroom, came back with a wad of toilet paper, and handed it to William. He waited patiently as William's cries turned into sniffles.

"Get dressed and I'll drive you to the hospital."

After a moment, William did as he was told. He pulled on his slacks, double knotted his sneakers, and locked the door behind him as the two of us followed Officer Powers down the apartment steps.

Chapter 69

Roly waited for me outside the employee tunnel, his oversized body taking up space on a narrow concrete bench next to the overflowing ash trays.

"Good evening, Emmanuel."

I shifted the backpack on my shoulder. I was sure he could smell my fear. Just as a man can smell a woman's perfume before she walks across the room, and long after she leaves.

Roly's breath turned thick as he used the bench to help him stand. "Security tells me a friend of yours dropped by to see you."

I knew damn well who he thought my "friend" was.

"I only met the officer for the first time tonight," I said, working hard to keep my voice smooth.

"What did he want?" he asked.

I could not tell him that William's manman had just died. This whole affair had begun when Donald lied to Roly about Charlie being his dada; a lie in which I did not get involved. Roly knew that Charlie's wife had died a long time ago, and he knew that Donald and William were brothers. How could their manman die twice?

"I do not know what he wanted," I lied. "Only that he needed to speak to William."

"What did you tell him?"

"I explained that he had already left for the evening."

The doors behind us swooshed open and a pair of female janitors came out. We nodded to them and they nodded back as they headed toward the employee parking lot.

Roly lit a cigarette and blew the smoke into the night air. "So there's nothing else to the story? Something you aren't telling me?"

"No, sir."

"Don't you find it odd—let's say a coincidence—that a cop starts snooping around the same night you took care of business?"

"I do not think he was snooping."

"You don't *think*—" Roly's red face matched the tone in his voice. "What you *think* and what that cop may *know* are two different things."

I did not know how to respond. For a moment, the two of us stood in silence under the lights. Moths fluttered around the bulbs over our heads.

Roly said, "I have always given you choices, Emmanuel, no matter what the situation. Isn't that right?"

"Yes, sir."

"So here is your choice: either William disappears, or you and your family will."

"But—"

"You knew that some aspects of this job would have to be erased. No reason for it to be you. Now, for starters, why don't you get rid of the evidence you have in your bag before that dead bird begins to smell."

I looked down at the bag but said nothing.

"There were problems?" Roly asked.

"No problem whatsoever, sir. She did not feel a thing."

"*She?*"

"It."

Roly held my stare a moment. "Get rid of *it*," he said. "Then get rid of *him*. And be quick about it. The faster you are, the sooner your mama can hang the American flag from her front porch."

Chapter 70

The abandoned barn was pitch black and all I could smell was dust and dried-up manure. My back was screaming from carrying that damn television through the woods. I near about dropped the thing when I crossed the creek. Now it sat on the barn floor between me and the buyer, a five-foot-nothing asshole wearing a pair of wedged shoes to make him look taller. He shined the flashlight in my face.

"Look, dude," I told the loser. "You said fifty bucks. It's like brand new. Brand fucking new."

"You said it came with a remote," he whined in a nasally elf voice. "I don't see no remote. Remotes are what make a TV worth something."

"I couldn't find the remote."

Actually, I was pretty sure it was buried underneath Ma's covers. My Ronald Reagan mask had really freaked her out. And then she screamed like I was gonna murder her or something. I told her to shut up, or I would shut her up myself, so she'd think I was a real robber. I'd thought about saying it like Ronald Reagan, I used to do a pretty good imitation, but it wasn't fucking *Star Search*. She grabbed the phone and called 911, just like in the movies. I didn't have time to mess around. That television was heavy, and sirens would be in the neighborhood within seconds. Total freak-out moment, man.

"Too bad for you," the elf was telling me now.

"What's too bad for me?"

The flashlight's beam hit the television screen. "That you went through

283

the trouble of jacking this nice television, and you forgot the remote."

"I told you, I couldn't get it!"

"Twenty bucks." He held up the twenty and shook it.

Shit.

I grabbed the crappy bill, buried it in my back pocket, and watched through the barn's doors as the elf drove off with the TV in a brand new fucking Jeep, leaving me standing in the dark.

Chapter 71

Manman was sitting on the plaid couch in our apartment watching television. A plastic Safeway bag filled with knitting supplies was tucked beside her. Her needles wrapped themselves around the light blue yarn. I do not know when or where she learned to knit. It seemed as though it was something she could always do, like singing church hymns or playing solitaire.

I leaned over and kissed her on the cheek.

"Turn down the television," she said in our homeland Creole. She often promised that one day she would learn to speak English in a real classroom.

I grabbed the remote from the coffee table and did as she asked.

"Anthony went to sleep early," she said. She still wore her full-length apron from making supper. On the front was a picture of the Statue of Liberty. I think wearing it made her feel like a real American woman. "He picked up a cold, though I do not know from where. Maybe from the white boy down the hallway. Every time I see that child, he has at least one finger in his nose. I bought medicine from the store on the corner."

"Does he have a fever?" I asked.

The anguished face of my Haitian prison friend came to me, his eyes pleading for me to use the knife, to end his suffering.

"No," Manman said. "Just something the man at the store called 'sniffles.'"

I walked down the short narrow hallway to Anthony's room. More like a closet, really, but at least he had his favorite things with him. A worn out

Beanie Baby lay tucked under his arm, and a Ninja Turtles poster hung crooked on the wall over his floor mattress. I would have given anything to furnish Anthony with a real bed. The kind that looks like a race car, or a captain's bed with the drawers built into the side.

On the room's only window I drew the blinds closed, then pulled the faded blanket up around Anthony's neck. Two small streams of dried snot stretched from his nose to his lips—the same beautiful lips as my sister, Angelina—but I felt no fever as I placed the inside of my wrist against his forehead.

"I would do anything for you," I whispered to my nephew. "Anything."

I closed the door and went back into the living room.

"Did you eat?" I asked my manman.

"I made some beef patties. Anthony begged for french fries but we do not have any. We had corn instead. You?"

With all that had happened, eating had not been a priority.

"I ate a good meal at work," I lied.

"Come here and we will watch the television together. It has been so long since you sat with me."

"Yes," I said, sitting beside her on the couch.

She patted my arm and went back to her knitting. I turned up the volume with the remote and together we watched as Bill Cosby and his perfect black family joked their way through some problem or another. I thought, *Monsieur* Cosby, you do not have a clue what problems lie in wait for a black man just come to America. What trouble there is for a black man with no American blood flowing through his veins.

The *Cosby Show* disappeared from my sight as my mind turned to other things.

Thirty minutes earlier, I had thrown the paper bag into a Dumpster behind a Chinese restaurant six blocks from our apartment. The trash men would come tomorrow, lessening my worries.

Most would be surprised to find that I had never killed anyone, other than my sick friend in Haiti. And he had begged me, to relieve him of his misery and pain. To kill for the sake of killing was incomprehensible. The thought of slaughtering that tiny pijon stopped my heart; the thought of a dying horse choked my breath; the thought of killing a kind person such as William was beyond my capability. Beating someone up was nothing since the body healed, the bruises and scratches disappeared over time. That I knew from firsthand experience.

Officer Powers jumped into my head. Most likely he was already at William's. Would the cop find it necessary to ask William about me? Then I wondered, what was there to ask? His only concern was telling William about the death of his manman. William's mind would snap the second he heard the news. The least of his thoughts would be about horses. But if I followed Roly's orders, wouldn't Officer Powers be curious about what had happened to William? Taking a few days off was not the same as never coming to work again. And the cop knew where he lived. How close were the tabs he kept?

And how far would I go to see that my family found happiness?

I knew answers to none of these questions as I stood up and went to the door.

"Where are you going?" Manman asked, barely taking her eyes away from the television. She loved that talking box almost as much as Anthony did. She had seen televisions in Haiti a few times, displayed in the glass windows of department stores in the city when she had to take a bus there for one reason or another. Her excitement had been that of a child, wishful face pressed against a toy store window. Of course, we never owned our own television in Haiti, nor did our neighbors. We did not even have electricity.

"I feel like taking a walk," I said. "I can use the exercise."

She looked up from her program. "You are healthy already. Strong. Like Hulk Hogan."

Manman loved watching the WWF on Saturdays.

"Sometimes the body needs to walk," I told her.

"I will be going to bed soon. Take your key." She turned back to the television, her needles swiftly clicking together.

I stepped out into the smelly hallway that led to the front lobby doors and wondered where the hell I planned on walking to.

Chapter 72

The hospital waiting room sat nearly empty at ten o'clock. I stood beside William next to the row of chairs. The on-duty doctor wore thick glasses that magnified the dark circles under his eyes. His tired demeanor was matched by his words.

"She never would have made it through the night," the doctor explained. "Too much scar tissue. I'm sure the autopsy will show the same."

William stared at the doctor with contempt. "Mom should be alive."

Officer Powers, who stood over by the coffee machine, said, "William, her heart was sick for a long time, even before she came to the hospital. She would have died at home if she hadn't died here."

"Someone needs to ID the body," the doctor said.

William looked at Officer Powers, confused.

"We need to go downstairs to the morgue," Powers said. "You can say goodbye this way."

William's shoulders slumped as he and I followed the two men to the elevator. The doctor pressed the button marked "B." The elevator doors shut, and opened to a smelly hallway: antiseptic mixed with the scent of something heavy and thick—the smell of death. I remembered the smell like it was yesterday.

We moved down the dimly lit corridor to a set of steel double doors with "Authorized Personnel Only" marked across the front. The doctor lifted the ID clipped to his pocket and swiped it through a small slit to the right. The doors opened and the four of us stepped through. The light in this room was different than in the hallway. Six rectangular fluorescent lights hung from the ceiling, suspended by chains. Three gurneys, each one under a separate light, lay empty, with clean white sheets draped over them. Behind the gurneys sat a long wall, completely filled with what looked like a file cabinet, only with bigger drawers.

William stared at the drawers and started trembling.

My invisible arms and legs were chilled.

A moment later, another doctor came through a door in the back of the room. He extended his hand to Officer Powers.

"Chuck," the doctor said, "good to see you."

"You too, Sean."

"This must be Mr. Baker."

"William," Officer Powers said, "this is Doctor Sean Satrino. He's the coroner."

William pointed to the cabinets. "Is my mom in there?"

"She's finally out of pain, son," the doctor told him. "She is peaceful."

"I want to see her so I can say goodbye." He bit down hard on his lower lip. "Now."

"Of course," Doctor Satrino said. "Please follow me."

The first doctor remained near the door as the rest of us followed Satrino to the far end of the wall. Satrino leaned down and opened a drawer level with his hip, sliding it along its tracks. It moved easily, like it had been greased with WD-40.

Doctor Satrino folded back the crisp white sheet to Mom's chin, exposing her face.

William leaned over her. "Mom?" The room was silent except for William's voice. "I gotta say goodbye, Mom. The doctor told me so. Cuz you're peaceful now. So, goodbye. Goodbye…"

As Doctor Satrino started pulling the sheet back up, William said, "Wait." He put his face close to hers and whispered, "You were the best mom ever."

A tear slipped from William's eye and fell onto Mom's cheek. Again, he looked up at the light hanging overhead and said nothing as the sheet was pulled over Mom's face and the drawer closed. We left Doctor Satrino behind and followed the first doctor back up to the waiting room. Officer Powers helped William fill out the necessary paperwork.

It was after midnight when Powers dropped us off in front of the apartment building. He handed William a business card. "Here's my number again," Powers told him. "Put it in a safe place. And call me if you need anything, understand?"

William slowly nodded.

"You sure you'll be alright by yourself?"

William nodded again. "Tonight was sad and happy. Sad cuz I had to say goodbye to Mom, but happy cuz I got to help Manny with a special job."

I froze, waiting to see if Powers would ask him what he meant.

But the officer only said, "You'll need some time off from work, William, to plan a funeral and all the other things we deal with when someone dies. I've already spoken with Manny. He knows what happened. I'm sure he'll give you a few days."

"Manny likes me," he said.

"I know."

"He trusts me. I get to be responsible. The horses need me."

That's it...tell him what happened...what Manny made you do! Maybe it's not too late!

"Especially Neon," William went on. "She needs me the most. Even if she doesn't like getting shots."

"I'm sure the horses will be fine," Powers said. "Don't go back to work until you're ready, got it?"

William got out of the car and stepped into the chilly night air.

No! I shouted to the cop. *Don't go!*

William closed the car door and headed across the sidewalk toward the apartment building. I tried shouting one more time.

Officer! Please! You need to ask about Neapolitan! You need to ask about Manny!

Officer Powers turned in my direction, and my hopes soared. But then I realized he was looking *through* me, watching William as he opened the double doors.

I started crying as Powers put the car in gear and drove away.

I cried because Mom was gone, because my body was almost gone, because I could no longer do anything to help William and had no clue what the hell I was still doing here. I cried because limbo was worse than any pit.

As the front doors closed, I slipped between them. Later, I watched as William undressed, crawled under a blanket on the unopened sofa bed, and slept through the night without movement, without dreams disturbing him, as still as a corpse.

Chapter 73

Six o'clock in the morning ought to be outlawed. I'd been sleeping like a hibernating bear when the phone rang. Still half asleep and with my eye mask still on, I felt around for the cordless on my end table.

"Hullo?"

A woman's voice. "Will you accept a collect call?"

My stomach clenched. A few years back, my stepfather had popped into town and telephoned me in the middle of the night, looking for a place to crash. My bed, to be exact.

"From who?" I asked.

"William Baker."

I pushed my eye mask onto my head and turned on the end table lamp. "Yes, I accept the charges."

The operator said, "You are connected, Mr. Baker."

"William," I said. "Is that you?"

"My m-m-mom is gone."

"What do you mean? Where'd she go?"

"She's dead. She had a h-h-heart attack. I said g-g-good-bye at the hospital."

"Oh, honey." I got out of bed with the phone against my ear. "I'll come right over." From the dresser, I grabbed a bra and panties and my jeans and a sweatshirt, and worked to get dressed with one hand. "Where're you calling from, William? I hear traffic."

"A phone booth. Like S-S-Superman. I d-d-don't have no phone any m-m-more on account of Donald didn't p-p-pay the bill." A cry of sorrow shot through the line and through my heart.

"Are you near your apartment?"

"S-s-sort of."

"How sort of?"

He gave me some landmarks. I told him to walk toward the stone chapel, turn right onto East Street, and go two blocks to a greasy all-night diner called Flo's.

An hour later, we sat across the red Formica table from one another.

William ordered oatmeal and I ordered a strong cup of coffee. His eyes were bloodshot and he had those crusty white things in the corners of his mouth.

"Did you sleep at all?" I asked him.

"Nuh-uh." He sprinkled cinnamon on top of his oatmeal and stirred some cream into it.

"Do you need someone to help you with everything?"

"I don't know," he said, dropping his spoon into his bowl. "I d-d-don't know what I'm supposed to do. I know I'm supposed to d-d-do something, but I d-d-don't know what. I can almost see it in here..." William tapped a fist against his forehead. "...but the harder I t-t-try to remember what to do, the harder it is to s-s-see it. Help me, Cecilia."

I pulled his arm away from his forehead and placed my hands on top of his. "There needs to be a funeral," I said calmly. "Your mom deserves one, right?"

He nodded.

"And we need to find you a good lawyer—I know a few—to see about any will. Do you know what a will is?"

"I think I do...I used to." William's cheeks turned red with shame as he stared at his oatmeal.

"Why don't we start with that buddy of yours?" I said.

"Lance?"

"Let's get a hold of him and take it from there." I downed my coffee.

"What are you gonna do about your job?"

"I dunno," he said. "I wanna go home. Not Donald's apartment. Back to *my* house. *My* home. But I have to go to work."

I pushed my empty coffee cup to the edge of the table, hoping the waitress would catch the hint. "Tell Manny you want to quit," I said. "I'm sure they can find someone else. I mean, how hard can it be to brush a couple of dumb ponies?"

"No! I have a responsibility. Manny showed me how to do it on the oranges, and then I got to do it on the horse!"

"Quit shouting, William."

"I did the oranges perfect," he whispered.

"What oranges?"

"The ones I practiced on. With the needles."

"I don't know what you're talking about." Maybe the death of his mama, along with lack of sleep, was making him delusional. I'd read about delusional people in my Psych 101 book back when I went to the community college. I probably could have been a psychologist.

"I practiced with Manny on the oranges first," William said. "Then Neon. That way I wouldn't hurt her or make her scared. Sometimes they kick when they get scared, and you don't want that to happen."

"Of course not. But I don't understand what you were doing with needles in the first place. Is the horse sick?"

"No!"

"Lower your voice."

William dropped his voice to a whisper again. "I gave her the shot so she'll stay strong. But you can't tell no one. It's a secret."

The word *secret* gave me chills. Again, I put my cool hands on top of William's.

"William, how many other horses did Manny tell you to—give a shot to?"

"Neon's the only one," he said. "We gave her a vitamin so nobody turns her into Elmo's glue."

"Did Manny tell you what kind of vitamin you were giving her?"

"No."

"Why didn't he give her the shot himself?"

"He wanted to give me responsibility." William sat up straight and pulled his hands from mine. "He trusts me."

The waitress finally came by with the coffee pot and refilled my cup. As I stirred the sugar in, I said, "Don't tell anyone else, William. If Manny wants you to keep it a secret, then you need to do that. Okay?"

"Okay."

If naïve William was mixed up in something criminal, he could wind up in prison, regardless of his IQ. I'd watched enough cop shows and read enough John Grisham to know what a scapegoat is.

William stirred his cereal and put the spoon to his mouth. "It's cold."

"Want them to reheat it for you?"

"I thought I was hungry. But I'm not."

He slid the bowl to the center of the table and pushed his overgrown hair out of his eyes.

I waved my hand to the waitress cleaning a table across the room. "Since you're not hungry, William, let's get out of here."

"Where are we going?"

"I think we ought to pack up your things."

"Did I do something wrong?" he asked in a frightened whisper.

The sun was up now, shining across the table. I pushed my thick hair from my face and cupped my hand around my eyes to see him better. "I don't know, William. I'm not sure."

"I wanted to save her from the glue factory!"

"Settle down."

"Manny trusts me. He said I'm his best worker. He said he likes m-m-me."

The waitress brought the check.

"Don't worry, William," I told him, leading him by the wrist to the cash register. "I'm sure that everything will be fine."

But even as those words crawled out of my mouth, I wasn't all the way convinced I was telling the truth.

Chapter 74

Our midnight manager hurt his back, and there was no one else but me willing to take his spot. Hell, the money alone was good enough reason. Had a backyard deck I wanted to build over the summer, and this was just the extra push me and Julie needed. Plus, it was sorta nice to have a change of pace. Though I did miss Jules and the kids something awful.

At a quarter past midnight, a voice over the intercom called me to the plant office. I pulled off my hard hat and headed up the steps. My heart got stuck between my ribs as I reached for the phone. If something had happened to my wife, or one of the kids, well, I woulda left work in a split second. But the bad news turned out to be Mrs. Baker.

I told Officer Powers I'd head to William's as soon as I finished my shift. It wouldn't be until around seven that morning, but the officer thought that would be fine. We both agreed that William needed someone to help with the funeral arrangements.

When I called Julie to tell her what happened, she said, "Don't worry, babe. I'll help with everything. You know how great I am with planning parties—not that this is a party, I didn't mean how that sounded..."

My wife was an expert at organizing baby showers, birthdays, Superbowl parties, so I knew what she meant. William would be in good hands.

I didn't have a chance to think about it much while I worked. Had to keep my eye on the machines and the fingers running them. But as I jammed my card into the time clock at seven on the dot, it hit me that, except for me,

William would be all alone in the world. His pop had left, his brother didn't count for nothing, his childhood sweetheart had gotten married, and now his mama was gone. Driving down the highway, I breathed in deep to get rid of the lump clogging up my throat.

With the spare key I'd made, I let myself into the apartment as quiet as possible, not wanting to startle him, especially after what happened to his mother and all. But the sofa bed was all made up, the pillows sitting on either end, the blankets folded on the chair near the door. I listened for running water but couldn't hear nothing. I went into the bathroom anyway. Empty. Kitchen was the same. Dishes stacked in the drain, table and counters wiped clean.

In the living room, I stuck the phone to my ear. You only get that kind of silence when the phone's been cut off.

I opened the closet door. Two oversized suitcases sat on the floor, and a few of William's things hung on wire hangers. I pulled out a white satin shirt. The collar was made up of two large triangles, pearly buttons down the front. Two pairs of bell bottoms, one denim and the other white polyester, hung side by side.

As I put the satin shirt back, I remembered all the times William and me went to those school dances, all the times he requested disco songs from the local rock bands and deejays. I'd hide on the other side of the school gym and pretend I didn't know him, asking those redneck boys to play Donna Summer instead of AC/DC. So many times I tried to get William to come out and hear some bands that school friends got together in their garages, or to drive with my older brother and me to see a rated R movie. He only wanted to hang out with Stephanie, twirling her around down in her club cellar, teaching her one of his new moves, like the pretzel or the slippery slope. The human body ain't supposed to be twisting around like that, especially a boy's. But William made it look easy.

I shut the closet door and found a pen in the kitchen. I laid out a paper towel on the table. I had just begun writing a note when the front door opened. Through the kitchen doorway I saw the creepy landlord, standing in the middle of the living room. She'd traded in her robe for a pair of tight white jeans and a yellow sweater that showed her nipples through the knitted material. Wild curls sprung out all over her head. She still wore her dirty slippers.

"What are ya doing in here?" she asked, closing the door behind her.

"I should be asking you the same question."

"I'm Sherri. The person in charge around here. Y'all got no right to be in someone's apartment unless you live here."

I stepped into the doorway between the kitchen and the living room. "Being a landlord gives you no right to be letting yourself into other peoples' homes."

"Wanted to see if Donald came back yet," she said. "Asshole owes me money."

"I thought the rent was paid up," I said.

"Owes me for something completely unrelated. Something personal."

"Then take it up with him when he gets home."

"Oh? Is he fixin' to come home?" Sherri picked up some bills on the end table and started sifting through them. "Sometimes the mailman delivers my mail here by mistake."

"I think you need to leave."

"You think so?" She held an envelope up to the light.

"I only ask nice the first time." I moved to the side of the couch.

"Why is it that I look after the welfare of my tenants, and uppity people give me their fuckin' attitude? You ain't no different than Donald or that black man who come snooping around."

"What black man?"

"Oh, now you wanna talk. Huh. Funny how *that* works." She tossed the envelope back onto the table.

I tried again, softening my voice. "What black man?"

"The foreigner. Dark and good looking. The man who's taken a liking to your freaky friend, the retarded one."

I held my tongue. "Do you know where William is?"

"No. I get wore slap out taking care of this dump and all. I can't keep track of everyone."

I sat on the couch. "Tell me about him," I said, as nice as I could under the circumstances. "The black man, I mean."

Sherri pulled her tight white jeans out of her crotch and sat on the ratty chair across from me. She kicked off her slippers and crossed her skinny legs on the seat. "I don't know him too good. Not like I do Donald." She squinted at me. "That's some great hair. You in a band?"

"No."

"Married, huh? I see the wedding ring. Probably got five kids in diapers."

"What does my family have to do with anything?"

"Can't a person make conversation without it being attached to something? Besides, you haven't given me a reason why I should tell you squat."

"William's mother passed way," I told her, hoping that by offering information, she'd do the same. "He needs me to help him sort things out."

"My own mama died two years ago. Lung cancer. She begged me to keep her in my apartment till she croaked. Can you imagine that? Her sleeping in my bed? Changing bed pans like I'm a fucking nurse? No way, José. She died in a hospital like you're supposed to."

Ignoring her rambling I said, "Do you know where William might've gone?"

"I'm not his babysitter." She leaned forward, her greasy bangs falling into her eyes. "You got any smokes?"

"No." I looked at my watch: eight-fifteen. The sun was now shining through the living room blinds.

"Anyways," Sherri said, chewing on a dirty pinky nail, "that black dude is nice looking, but you wouldn't catch me sleeping with a man like him. Not cuz he's black or nothing. I got no problem with color. 'Specially with muscles like his. But he's bad news. Why that retard would want to hang out with him is beyond me."

"Stop calling him that."

"Call 'em as I see 'em."

I wanted to kick her out of the apartment. But I needed her, at least for the moment.

"Tell me why you think this other man is bad news."

"He's sneaky as all get out," Sherri said. "He's got something going on that he don't want nobody to know about. Not sure what. I see a rat, I call him a rat. And I've known plenty of—"

The sound of a key suddenly entered the lock. I stood up fast. Sherri jumped off the chair and pressed a pillow against the front of her like she was naked.

The door opened. William stepped through. Cecilia, the stripper from the club, followed behind.

"Lance!" William said. He ran toward me, almost knocking me over as he grabbed my hand and shook it. "Whatcha doing here?"

"I—"

Cecilia interrupted. "William called me a few hours ago to tell me—"

"My mom's dead," William said.

"We know, honey, and we're so sorry," Sherri said, sliding into her slippers. "How did it happen?"

The three of us turned to Sherri but said nothing.

"What?" she asked.

"William and me need some time alone." I said this to Sherri, but I was hoping the stripper would get my meaning too.

"Only offering my sympathy is all," Sherri said. "There a crime against that?" When no one answered, she said in a huff, "Try to be helpful and what do you get? A load of nothin', that's what. I'm going back to my cave, as if any of you give a rat's turd." She threw the pillow onto the chair and slammed the door behind her.

After a moment, William said, "Cecilia took me to breakfast, Lance." He whispered, "I did something wrong."

"You did something wrong at breakfast?" I asked, confused.

"Look," Cecilia said before William had a chance to answer. "This has been a long night for everyone. Let's figure out what William needs to do next. You know, about a funeral and all. And the will, or insurance, or whatever it is that needs to be taken care of."

I turned to Cecilia, "William and I have known each other since the first grade, and even I've never asked him about a will."

The stripper said, all snotty-like, "I'm just trying to keep him on track, since he drifts off sometimes."

Cecilia was dressed in a sweat shirt and sweat pants, and her face looked freckly and ordinary without makeup. Her thick red hair was pulled back in a barrette, and she wore a pair of tennis shoes. A plain Irish Jane. But even without the flashy do-dads, she was still what she was.

I told her, "William's interests need to be protected."

"Yeah," William said. "Protected."

"I see," Cecilia said. "Well, William, I'm glad you felt close enough to me to wake me up before the fucking rooster crows; so glad I could be there for you. Take care. Call me again sometime, huh? Let me know how things turn out." She stepped through the door and shut it behind her.

The door had barely been closed for five seconds before it opened again.

"Oh yeah," Cecilia said, winking at William. "Keep me up-to-date on that *poor little pony* you messed with. And let me know how the *injection* works out." She closed the door again.

I ran to the door, opened it back up, and held it wide. "God bless it," I told the pain-in-the-ass stripper. "Get back in here."

Cecilia smiled like I'd just asked her to the senior prom.

Chapter 75

Officer Powers

Cops aren't supposed to give in to suspicions that defy the facts. But there it was: the keen sense I'd missed something.

Linda, my wife, sat up with me in the stove-lit kitchen until midnight, trying to help me uncover that missing piece. And even though it worked sometimes, bouncing off my wife, this time it did not. Nothing budged.

But, as I've always said, light bulbs can turn on at the most unexpected times.

A few days after Mrs. Baker died, Linda left for her part-time job at the children's museum, and I was standing in front of the mirror shaving. The volume was turned up on the TV in the bedroom. Even on my days off, I craved the news. Community goings-on were as much a part of me as my blood.

As I rubbed shaving gel between my hands, the Channel Eleven News reporter was saying something about the Dellshore Racetrack:

"Neapolitan, who some have endearingly nicknamed Neon, has been pulled from one of the largest purses in Dellshore racing history. While there is no comment yet from racetrack officials, an employee stated that the tri-colored Pinto is currently undergoing observation by a team of equine veterinarians who are working together with the CDC. In an interview yesterday, Neapolitan's owners said they will follow the state law to keep her quarantined until a diagnosis and subsequent prognosis can be determined. Neapolitan is the granddaughter of Sterling, an Alabama-bred—"

Something suddenly banged hard against the bathroom window, and I nicked my chin with the razor. Tiny beads of blood dripped into the sink. I grabbed a tissue and patted it against my chin while examining the window. A large red splotch was smeared against the other side of the glass. I thought, *Damn it, if I leave that blood out there, it'll bake in the sun.*

I finished shaving, stuck a tiny band-aid on the cut, and dressed in torn jeans, a sweatshirt, and my dirty Reeboks. In the garage, I shoved a rag into my back pocket, grabbed the aluminum ladder from behind the Lawn Pro mower and a gazillion rakes, and dragged it to the spot below the second floor bathroom window. I'd been so concerned about the stain on the glass, I'd nearly forgotten about the poor bird that had caused the mess in the first place. After positioning the up-righted ladder against the siding, I bent over and spread apart the branches of our knee-high boxwoods.

A small white bird lay unmoving at the base of the house. Broken neck, by the looks of it. Didn't make me too sad, since I'd hunted mallard and pheasant since the age of twelve. Odds were that the little dove never felt a thing.

I grabbed the rag from my pocket and picked up the dead bird by pinching the feet together. I held it up to my eyes.

Never saw any white doves around the neighborhood before. More likely to find a dead finch or a robin. Coincidentally, this was the third dove I'd seen in a handful of days. The first one was sitting on the fence at the track that night I went to find William Baker. The second was a dead one I'd nearly run over in the station parking lot two days ago.

What were the odds?

Linda would have told me to look at the bigger picture, the spiritual side of things. That maybe the universe was trying to tell me something. That seeing three white doves was *God*-incidence not *co*incidence. But that was Linda. That was not me. She waited for the universe to hand her signs, while I looked for signs to hand to the universe.

I walked to the side of the yard with the bird extended and lifted the trash can lid. Just as I was ready to toss the body inside, I noticed something. A cop is always noticing things. It's almost a curse, because it really can take the fun out of having a day off. The dead bird's eyes were shut, but they were bulging, like it had suffered from hypothyroidism. I could have thrown it into the bin and forgotten about it, but that's where the curse comes in.

I placed the lid back on the container and put the bird on the ground, checking to see if any of my neighbors were watching, but most folks were at work. I took the rag and carefully opened one of the eyes. What I saw didn't look like a normal bird's eye. It looked like the eye of a bullfrog or a Chihuahua. I turned the bird onto its belly and spread the feathers apart. The skin beneath the ruffles looked normal, but I'm not a vet, and I'm hardly an animal expert. I hadn't owned any pets since losing Sasha, our sweet black lab, gone five years. I turned the dove over to see the eyes again, and that's when I noticed the beak. The tiny nostrils, or whatever you call them, were plugged up with crust, like the animal had had a bad cold.

Do birds get colds?

I placed it next to the trash can, covered it with a rag, and hurried back into the house. I scrubbed my hands with dish liquid, then I grabbed the phonebook, looked up a number, and picked up the cordless in the kitchen.

The phone rang twice before a young woman's voice came on the line: "Southside Veterinary Clinic, how may I help you?"

"Doctor Yingling, please."

"He's just arrived at the office. Who's calling?"

"Chuck Powers."

"One moment, please."

Johnny Cash sang through the line as I took the cordless phone from the kitchen to the living room, glancing out the bay window. I could barely make out the small bundle lying next to the trash can.

A man's voice came on the line. "Chuck?"

"Mark, how've you been?"

"Can't complain," he said. "Work is busy, Donna's fine, kids are insane. You?"

"Overworked, underpaid, you know the drill. Listen, I have a question for you, not that I don't want to be sociable, but—"

"Once a cop, always a cop?"

Back in the kitchen, I poured myself a cup of coffee, holding the cordless in between my neck and shoulder. "I've found something odd, at least from my perspective…might not seem like anything strange to you, being a vet and all."

I stirred a spoonful of sugar into my coffee.

"What's going on?" Mark asked.

"A bird hit my window this morning."

"Ah, spring time. Poor birds think their reflections are rivals, or prospective mates. Lots of horny dazed birds flying around—"

"No," I said. "Not *dazed. Dead.*"

"Well, Chuck, they don't usually know what hit them if that's what you're—"

"I'm not worried about whether the bird felt anything. It's something else."

The sound of a truck turning onto my street made the glasses in the kitchen cabinet jingle. I headed back into the living room, carrying my coffee mug in one hand and holding the phone against my ear with the other. The weekly trash truck pulled up out front.

"What are you worried about then?" Mark asked.

"This bird," I said, "a white dove—I think it had something wrong with it before it ever hit the window."

The trash man jumped from the side of the truck and reached down to grab our trash can.

"What do you mean *something wrong*?" Mark asked.

The garbage man placed the lip of the garbage bin on the edge of the truck, pulled a lever, and a mechanical arm reached down, picked up the can, and dumped the contents into the truck's belly.

I was relieved to see the small bundle still lying on the ground.

"There's something wrong with the eyes," I explained.

Mark said, "Once a bird dies it doesn't take long for the eyes to dry up and sink. A normal part of expiration. Happens to all creatures. You should know—"

"That's not what I'm talking about."

The trash man placed the can back where it was and jumped onto the side of the truck. The truck inched forward. The man shouted something to the driver, the truck stopped, and he jumped off again. He came around the side of the trash can and knelt down.

"Then what *are* you talking about?" Mark asked.

I stared out the window and said under my breath, "Leave it there."

From the phone: "What?"

"Mark, hold on a sec." I threw the phone onto the sofa and in a rush sat my coffee on the end table, spilling some of it onto my hand. "Shit." I opened the front door with the back of my hand in my mouth and ran down the driveway.

The trash man was holding the rag I'd used to cover the bird.

"Don't take that bird," I ordered.

The man looked at the dead dove and then back to me. "Is not this trash? I pick up for you."

"No, not trash. Mine." I patted my chest with my palm. "Mine."

He shook his head solemnly. "He is dead."

"Yes, I know. Please leave it."

"But he is dead," he said again.

"It's on my property and I want you to leave it here."

I wondered if he knew I was a cop, the way he put his hands up in the air, palms facing out, at shoulder height. "Okay, no problem." He stood up and hoisted himself back onto the side of the truck. After signaling the driver, the truck slowly moved to the next house.

I ran back inside and picked up the phone from the couch cushion.

"Mark?"

"I've gotta get to work, Chuck."

"I'll bring it to you. I'll put it in a box and bring it to you."

"The bird? Why?"

"I don't know why. I only know you have to see it."

"Alright. But do me a favor: wear rubber gloves when you pick it up and try not to touch the bird itself. Put it in a plastic baggie. I have a busy morning scheduled, so tell my receptionist when you get here. I'll let her know you're coming."

"Thanks, Mark."

"If you're concerned about this bird, then I'll have a look-see. The day Chuck Powers worries about a little birdie is the day I worry too."

Chapter 76

The hood of the abandoned station wagon was covered in bird kaka. The interior looked like someone or some*thing* had lived in it for a long time. Soiled McDonald's bags sat crumpled on the floor in the front and back, dirty mismatched socks were clumped together on the dashboard, and some kind of white animal hair covered the back seat. The windshield wipers held onto a thick stack of parking tickets. It was the perfect blockade for me, since I needed something to hide behind while watching.

The three of them—William, his friend with the pony tail, and the stripper—moved suitcases from the apartment complex to an old truck parked out front.

I had little time before Roly knew what I had or hadn't done regarding the tasks I was expected to do. It was time to make a plan. A plan I would have to stick to. Perhaps I could move my family to some other city, where we would hide out until the dust had settled. I knew some Haitians who lived in Miami. But Manman often mentioned wanting to see snow for Christmas. It snowed in Chicago. And New York City. Perhaps we could head west to Los Angeles, where it is a known fact that a person can visit both the snow and the sea in the same day.

From the moment I stepped on American soil, I had tried to stay one step ahead of Roly. Hiding beneath a detached piece of linoleum in our apartment bathroom, next to the toilet, was an envelope holding two thousand dollars. For eighteen months I had saved every penny I could. But America is the land of the rich. Was two thousand enough for Manman and Anthony to start over? Perhaps not. Roly would not give me the rest of what he owed me until all evidence had been disposed of. And that evidence included William Baker.

Questions crashed into one another in my mind: Who was I to turn William into an unknowing martyr? Who was I to play God? And how and when would the universe see to it that I pay back the debt?

I thought about William's lottery money. Even a fraction of that money could change a life in an instant. Who else knew about it besides me? Did that whore trick him into giving her a share? If William disappeared, would the government put their greedy hands on it? Would Donald, being the closest living relative, come out from beneath his rock to claim it? If I had a way to get some of William's money, I would not need to take his life. Receiving a piece of his windfall could buy my family a way out without having to follow orders. Perhaps I could reason with him; ask for a loan…

I found myself wishing it had been Donald who had performed the task after all, because erasing him would not make a difference to me.

But a wish is not the same as reality.

Behind the dirty station wagon, the afternoon sun shone down on my shoulders. I watched as William and his friend got into the truck and headed northwest. The whore got into a car and headed in the other direction. I assumed William was heading home. Where else would a man in mourning go but back to the place where his manman had raised him? I closed my eyes to remember the address I had seen in his wallet the day I found out who he was. I pictured the numbers: "One. Two. Nine…" I shook my head and tried again. "One. Two. Seven. Yes." I was gaining confidence. "River. No. Stone…something…" I could not remember the street name, but I was not worried. I would use the phonebook to fill in the gap. Of course, if I found his house and the courage to do as Roly demanded, it would prove difficult now that William was surrounded by his *entourage*, but I would cross that bridge when I reached it.

William was a lucky man, even if he did not realize it. It must be like floating in a perfect dream every day, without ego ruling decisions; without fear that an evil fat man will suddenly grab a pair of scissors and cut the strings to another's life. It would be like heaven, living a life without worry that the sun will rise the next day, or the day after that, because the most wonderful thing is knowing that the sun is up *now*. The sun is up now and forever shining.

Chapter 77

I was a modern-day Goldilocks, except that Goldilocks didn't use a spare house key hidden inside a fake rock. I grabbed it the night I took the television. That's how smart I was. Now I could come and go as I pleased. If it was safe to. Which it probably wasn't.

It's all good, I told myself. Food in the fridge, a warm bed, a hot shower. Ma wouldn't be back for a couple of days at least. The hospital would run a bunch of tests she didn't need and charge her insurance company. No need to sleep in that damn tree house anymore. If she came home while I was still in the house, I'd hide in the attic. She'd never know I was up there as long as I stayed quiet. It'd be worth the wait. But there were black widows and brown recluses hiding in the corners, and it's not that I'm afraid of spiders, I just didn't wanna be bothered by 'em is all.

Making a devil's deal with Sherm wasn't so bad when thinking of the alternatives. I would pull out a hundred thousand for that snaggle-toothed loser. In exchange, he would let me live. Why Sherm didn't want more cash for himself was beyond me. Maybe he thought he was too old to have time to spend it all. Made me sign a promissory note. Asshole.

I wasn't an idiot. There was over half a mill in my brother's account. Whatever was left after Sherm's cut, I'd take for myself. Tell the bank, *Thanks for your help, it's been nice doing business with you*!

I was also excited knowing inside information about a pony I'd never seen up close. Neapolitan could've been a chunk of meat wrapped in cellophane as far as I was concerned, a dash of A-1 to drown out the salty flavor.

My future was finally looking good, and it was about time. The world owed me after all the suffering I'd been through. No more scrounging from day to day, not knowing if the bills were gonna get paid, not getting my share when I was the one who helped Woody win that money on the *Lotsa Luck Show* to begin with. Making sure he was stylin'. That he dressed and spoke like a real human being, not some fucking idiot. Letting him come and live with me, for chrissake. Eating me out of house and home, crashing on my damn sofa bed, wearing out my only bath towel.

Ever since that day at the pond, poor baby Billy got the world handed to him on a silver platter and my life was nothing but mother-fucking shit.

It was time for me to get what I deserved.

Chapter 78

Thirty minutes after the truck drove away, I was sitting at a bus stop close to William's apartment when Roly called me on the mobile phone he had loaned me. Nothing he gave was truly a gift. The television set, cable, some pretty blue earrings my manman wore, Anthony's Reeboks, all on loan. In the beginning, I believed Roly to be my American savior. It is funny how a man's perspective can shift without his awareness.

The phone kept ringing. I wanted to ignore it. Ideas were forming in my head, and I did not want to be taken away from it. But I had no choice.

Roly breathed heavily in my ear. "Have you taken care of things?"

"Not everything. But do not worry. I am playing my cards right."

"*Your* cards? Oh, Emmanuel. You haven't held a deck of cards since you arrived in this country. In fact, you don't even *own* a deck of cards. I own the cards, I shuffle the cards, I deal the cards. You, my friend, merely sweep them up from the floor when they fall."

I did not respond to his sarcasm because he was wrong. I had my own deck of cards hiding up my sleeve, and some had already been played. More ideas tried to form, even as I listened to the fat man's threats.

"I know where your family lives," Roly said. "Do not forget that."

"No, sir, I will not."

"That's good. Especially now that our pony is out of action."

"Out of action?"

I tried to remember what I had done exactly. What William had done. I tried pulling it up from the deep well, but the memory had drowned there, or at least it was holding its breath there, unable to surface at the moment.

"I've brought in a groom from the equestrian center until you return," Roly said. "There is a list of employees the CDC has received, and William is not on it. You are on the list, of course. I told them you were out sick, that you'd be back in a day or two. Please, Emmanuel, tell me if there is anything I can do to help speed up the process."

"I have it under control."

"That's what I like," Roly said. "A man who does his job without being micromanaged. Call me as soon as you have expedited the matter."

As soon as I hung up, my hunger came back to me with ferociousness, a sign that confidence would soon follow. I stopped at a corner deli, then took the bus home and shared lunch with my family.

"Why aren't you at work today?" Manman inquired.

"Every once in a while, a man is rewarded with a little time off. For working hard."

"Well," she said, patting my arm, "you work harder than any man I know."

The three of us ate together, Anthony, Manman and me. I listened to my nephew tell knock-knock jokes that are so popular among American boys, and laughing through a mouth filled with mustard and bologna on white bread.

Afterward, I showered, shaved, dug city dirt out from under my nails, pressed my shirt, polished my shoes, made sure my thin flashlight had proper batteries, and sharpened my shiny kouto before tucking it into my waistband. Then I pulled back the bathroom linoleum and stared at the envelope. My insurance policy for my family. Just in case William's money was not an option. In case things went awry.

I spent another hour sitting with Manman and Anthony on the sofa as she clicked the stations back and forth between that Oprah lady and that loud-mouthed judge. Finally, I put on my denim jacket, wrapped a knitted scarf around my neck, and kissed my family goodbye.

PART VI

Chapter 79

I was lying on my brother's twin bed, dead to the world, when the kitchen door slammed in its frame, throwing my neck into spasms.

Voices. Below me. In the kitchen.

In my socks, I tiptoed to the top of the stairs. Through the hallway window, the sun was just setting behind the trees. I stood on the landing like a ghost and listened to two people talking.

Neither voice was Ma's.

But one of them was Woody's.

"I just wanted to see the house again," he said.

The other man, who sounded vaguely familiar, said, "I understand."

For a few minutes I couldn't hear anything. Then the man said, "We could ask Officer Powers to send a police cruiser to keep an eye on things."

Police?

"Would that make you feel better?" he asked.

I couldn't hear anything, but I could picture Woody bouncing his head up and down like a freakin' Jack-in-the-box.

"Come and stay at my house tonight, and we'll come back later to settle things."

"Okay, Lance."

So, that's who the other person was: I-work-in-a-factory-cuz-I'm-too-dumb-to-do-anything-else Lance.

"In the meantime," Lance said, "let's go through the house and make sure it's locked up tight."

I slid across the landing into the bedroom, scrambled to get my jeans on, and crammed my feet into my double-knotted sneakers. Next, I snuck into the closet and as quiet as I could, cuz the damn thing had five-thousand-fucking-year-old hinges, squeezed through the tiny door and up the narrow staircase, keeping my fingers crossed that the vermin in the attic had found another home.

Chapter 80

I could feel his presence the same way I could feel that something had been wrong with Mom, or that William needed me.

Donald was in the house.

I floated behind Lance and William. In the kitchen, Lance checked the knobs on the stove, making sure all the burners were off. Then we went down into the basement, where he pulled hard on the latch that held together the cellar storm doors. Back upstairs, we made our way through the living room, double checking the turn-locks on all the windows and the lock on the front door. Lance turned on the end table lamp.

"Makes the house feel more lived in," he told William.

We followed him out of the room. In the hallway, Lance opened the narrow closet door, separating the coats with his hand. He stopped for a moment, his head cocked a bit to the side, his eyes turned up toward the ceiling.

"There's no windows in there," William said from behind him.

"Just making sure there aren't any boogie men waiting to throw a party after we leave."

This made William laugh, but the serious look on Lance's face told me he had the same gut feeling I did.

He pushed back the shower curtain in the small bathroom next to Mom's bedroom. The window above the tub was open a crack. It was too tiny for the average person to crawl through, but Lance locked it tight just the same. In

Mom's room, he flipped on the overhead light. He looked at the sheets which lay in a pile on the floor next to the bed. Silently, he and William remade the bed together, folding the top sheet over the bedspread and fluffing up the pillows.

As William grabbed the last pillow, something hit the bedroom floor with a loud clack.

"What's that?" Lance asked.

William picked it up. "The remote," he said. He walked to the pressed wood TV stand against the wall.

Do you see?

"It's gone," William said.

"What is?"

"Mom's TV."

Lance and William searched the room with their eyes, as if there were some way the television could have ended up in another place.

"Maybe she gave it away," William said.

"I doubt she'd get rid of it without the remote," Lance told him.

The three of us stared at the clean spot on the stand.

"Maybe you're right," Lance said finally. "She probably gave it away." He took the remote from William's hand and placed it on the empty stand. "Let's check out the rest of the house." Lance patted William on the back and followed him through the doorway, glancing once more behind him as turned off the overhead light.

On the way to the staircase in the kitchen, I noticed that Lance pulled his Swiss Army knife out of his pocket and opened it, holding it close to his side. William and I followed him up the narrow stairway. We looked in the tiny, windowless bathroom off the landing and headed into our old bedroom.

Lance opened the closet door. He pushed apart some of the hanging clothes William had left behind, along with hiking boots, goulashes, and pairs of sneakers lining the floor. He started to close the door again when he froze.

"Did you hear that?" Lance whispered.

It's not Merle! I warned William.

"That's Merle," William said.

"Who?" Lance asked.

"Merle the squirrel. He lives in the attic. Him and his family. Me and mom never went up there on account of there are rabies everywhere."

"Merle the squirrel," Lance said smiling. He folded up his knife and shut the closet door. "Sounds like a circus name."

No! I shouted. *He's here*! *Can't you feel him*?

I moved to William's side.

Look at the bed! *You made it before you left*! *How come it's all messed up again*?

Lance and William checked the latches on the bedroom windows.

I stared at the closet door.

He knows we're here.

Reluctantly, I followed Lance and William back downstairs.

Lance locked the kitchen door behind us. From the passenger seat in the truck, William stared at the house, then at Mom's car sitting in the driveway.

"You okay, buddy?" Lance asked.

"Just miss Mom is all." He looked toward the wild roses starting to bloom along the worn fence. "Wanna give her a good funeral. With lots of flowers."

"I think she'd like that," Lance said as he steered the truck out onto the evening road.

Chapter 81

In the attic, I sat cross-legged on an itchy blanket in the dark, my pants still unbuckled, praying that I didn't get bit up by any black widows, when the sound of scratching made me freeze even more than I was already froze. The rodent, which I was pretty sure was a rat and not a squirrel, sniffed at my foot and headed across the floor to the other side, where it chewed on its dinner of dead cockroaches or whatever it is that vermin eat.

"Keep the freakin' hell away from me," I whispered. If he knew what was good for him.

Outside, an engine revved. I looked through the third-floor window and waited until the truck disappeared up the road. In the dark, I made my way out of the attic, through the bedroom, and down the steps to the kitchen. Yellow light from the living room came through the archway, but it was still too dark to see good. Turning on more lights was probably a dumb idea. It took ten minutes to dig through all the drawers to find a dinky flashlight. Then I rummaged through the fridge for something to eat.

I was feeling sort of lucky, sitting down to a hot dog and Fritos dinner, figuring that with Ma still in the hospital, I'd finally have a sweet meal, even if it was mostly in the dark.

The plan was to take the bus to the bank the following morning. It had already been a couple of days, and the *Lotsa Luck* check would have cleared. I was hoping to get Sherri's car, but I'd already kissed my apartment goodbye and good riddance. Could have looked for Ma's car keys, though I'd be a bigger idiot than my brother if I stole the Buick, seeing as how Lance had already spotted it in the driveway. The meeting with Sherm was supposed to take place at an empty building about a mile from the bank. But I'd changed my mind. The new plan would give me enough time to take a detour to the airport instead.

Fuck you Sherm, you ol' brontosaurus. I've worked my ass off for this money. I don't owe you nothing.

I still had my own driver's license, but my connection had made me an ID with William Baker's name. He also made a second fake ID and a passport to match with the name Robert Jones. I was good to go. Living south of the border would soon become a reality. Man, I could already taste the Margaritas.

I got up off the kitchen chair and wiped my mouth with the dishtowel. For the next two hours, I kept the flashlight in my hand as I snooped for some cash so I could take the bus instead of hitching. I pulled out end table drawers, picked up lamps, dug through shoe boxes and cookie jars. I held Ma's hat boxes upside down and shook them, then pulled out the stinky lace hats and did the same. Took the few books that sat on the shelf next to the fireplace and opened 'em up, leafing through the pages to see if something would fall out. Even looked in the ancient Bible. Finally, I dug under the sofa cushions and came up with over a dollar in change.

All that searching made me hungry again. A container of Chunky Monkey ice cream sat in the freezer and a bottle of Hershey's chocolate syrup sat in the refrigerator door. I grabbed a bowl from the cabinet and pulled a spoon out of the drawer. I scooped three huge lumps of ice cream from the tub and left the container sitting on the counter, in case I decided to go for more.

Chillin' out in front of the fridge, I ate my ice cream while moving the flashlight across gobs of old photos stuck to the refrigerator door with those ugly plastic flower magnets. One was a picture of my brother when he was a kid, not even five, I'm guessing. The picture was sort of foggy, his face and hair the color of Brussels sprouts. Another showed him when he was maybe ten, on his fugly horse that wasn't really his horse to begin with but some stupid unmarketable pony pawned off on our family by a neighbor who couldn't afford to feed it. Dad gave it away while Woody was in the hospital. In another photo, my brother stood in his track shorts holding up a ribbon from a middle school relay race. Pictures of my brother covered near about every inch of the damn refrigerator: Christmas morning opening gifts; standing on the porch in a Snoopy Halloween costume; crying while sitting on the Easter Bunny's lap; laughing while being pushed on a swing. Swimming. Dancing. Sitting on a log. Eating a Dairy Queen hot dog, for chrissakes.

I skimmed over the pictures to find one of me. It'd be easy to miss one. We looked like twins when we were little. It would have been easy for a stranger to mix me up with my brother in those pictures.

But *I* wasn't no stranger.

And there wasn't no *me*.

Get over it, I told myself.

But I couldn't. My face got hot. My throat clenched. I took a bite of my melting ice cream, but it barely made it down. The circle of light got wider as I stepped back with the flashlight. *First he scares away our dad, then he hogs the whole fuckin' fridge. What am I? Invisible? How could Ma—*

In the middle of my anger, something happened. An angel—I swear to God that's what it was—came right down from heaven and whispered in my ear. It said, *Take a closer look, Donald ol' boy.*

My eyes zoomed all over the fridge.

Don't you see it? Hidden among the pictures? It's right there, right in the middle of the fucking Woody shrine.

I moved closer. The flashlight narrowed in on the center of the fridge. And then I spotted it, laying flat beneath a chipped daisy magnet. Not a picture, but a small beige envelope that looked like some kind of fancy invitation.

But I knew it didn't hold no invitation the same way I knew that Chunky Monkey would give me gas.

I placed the bowl of ice cream on the counter, licked my lips, and slid the envelope out from behind the magnet. I turned it over. In Ma's handwriting, it said, "William."

"Fuckin'-A," I said to the empty kitchen.

I put the envelope on the table and stared at it as I finished my dessert. Suddenly there wasn't a problem getting the ice cream down. I liked this game, guessing what was inside that envelope. The anticipation of maybe getting something more or something better than what I had at that very moment.

I dug the rest of the ice cream from the container and dumped it into the bowl. I doused it with another gallon of Hershey's. Then I clicked off the flashlight, put it back in the drawer, and took my bowl and the envelope into the living room.

No reason I shouldn't be comfortable, after all I'd been through.

Under the living room lamp, I placed the bowl of ice cream on the end table beside the recliner and kicked off my sneakers. I took my wallet and passport out of my back pocket and put them next to the bowl, then sat back in the chair, popping up the foot rest. I was stylin', like a king opening a scroll. I did it real careful, like I was holding a fucking flower. It was poetic, I can tell you that. I unfolded the letter and began reading:

My Dearest William…

Chapter 82

Three buses later, I stepped off the dirty number forty-eight. With the help of my flashlight, I reviewed the crudely drawn map and started walking the half mile. It was past dinnertime. The street was silent. The houses, all sitting on an acre or more of land, were separated by long driveways and thick trees, enough to hide behind. Even so, I glanced nervously behind me. No *nwa* families lived in any of these big houses, that was for sure. These were white families, generation after generation of them.

My manman used to say, "White folk may be smart enough to buy a house, but most are too stupid to know how good they have it."

What if William was not home? What if he never returned? What if he was already at his house, but he was not alone? What if he was alone but refused my request for a loan? What if someone had already taken the money from him? What then? Would I move forward with Roly's brutal plan?

These questions were not intellectually driven. They were my conscience's way of punishing me, of trying to drive me mad.

I kept walking.

Soon I found the address on the mailbox. The gravel crunched under my work shoes as I hurried to the top of the driveway. A pair of dead headlights, like they belonged to a sleeping dragon, stared at me from a green Buick. The hood was cool to the touch. I assumed it had belonged to William's manman. I turned the corner of the house and stood against the back wall for a long moment, listening to the sounds of the countryside. Tiny chirping of baby birds, somewhere high up in the trees. A bat's rubbery wings slapping above the elms and pines. A large mosquito or other bug zooming past my head, its buzz echoing in my ear and sending a tickle along my neck.

And then the sound of something else: a drawer slamming shut, a cupboard door clicking.

Someone was in the house.

Was it William? A relative or a friend? Lance's truck was not in the driveway, and I could not imagine he would have abandoned William just after his manman had died.

After a few minutes, I made my way up the porch steps and peeked into the house through the door window. A dim light from another room showed me an empty kitchen. Quietly, I jiggled the knob. Of course, it was locked. The whole house was probably locked up tighter than a Haitian prison.

I stepped off the porch and moved like a cat along the back of the house, careful to keep the flashlight beam close to the cinderblock foundation and not up near the windows. The house seemed enormous to me but was most likely small by American standards.

As I approached the front side of the house, I clicked off the light. Two large windows on the first floor faced the street. I hid behind a tree. By the yellow lamplight, I could see a man sitting in a big chair, looking down at something in his hands.

The man was not William, but there was no mistaking the same round face, same thick blond hair, same peachy white skin.

I rubbed my chin, thinking, smiling.

So then. Perhaps fate had something else in mind. A new idea was blossoming in my head. I could nearly smell its beauty.

Sorry, fat boss-man—your way does not work for me anymore.

I would *tell* Roly I had erased William. Take a lock of Donald's hair for proof. There was a good chance Roly would not realize the switch until Manman and Anthony and I had already escaped to another state. There was even a chance he would never know. I would quickly collect what was owed, and my family could start our lives of freedom.

I had to slow down my excitement. No reason to be rash. I had come this far, and I would need to be careful. There were to be no mistakes. My family could not afford even one.

Below the large windows behind the bushes, I sat on the soft ground. Thirty minutes passed by the time I had worked things out in my mind.

I made my way to the back of the house again, mostly crawling, looking for a way in. My flashlight caught its reflection in a small basement window, barely noticeable behind some shrubbery and low to the ground. One piece of wood separated the top pane from the lower. Termites had done their damage. It would be easy to break and perhaps just as easy to climb through.

I leaned for a moment against the side of the house. Crickets sounded all around me, and the occasional chirp of a bird made its way through the thick trees along the property's edge. But the evening was windless, and there was nothing in the way of automobile traffic. I was used to sirens and horns blaring at all hours of the night, couples fighting in the apartments surrounding us, children screaming, footsteps endlessly echoing up and down the stairwells.

The silence out here in the countryside unnerved me. I had not heard this much quiet since after the flood had poured through Haiti, before I moved to the busy Port au Prince and then to America. I had always felt more secure in the city. Could blend into the woodwork with all the other hopeful men of color. Disappear at a moment's notice. People were too busy in the city to notice if someone was or was not there anymore.

Bending down, I held the flashlight tightly in my fist. The first crack came as I barely tapped it against the glass. I sat on my bottom and struck the window, shined the flashlight through the square hole, and listened. Not a sound. The smell of damp earth rose to my nostrils, reminding me of harvest time in Haiti, radishes and onions and potatoes being pulled from the thick soil. As quick as a fox with a chicken in its mouth, I squeezed through the opening and jumped to the cement floor.

The basement walls were aged stone. A furnace sat near one wall, a washer and dryer leaned side by side against another. Next to the third wall sat a large freezer chest, which hummed through the otherwise quiet basement. To the left of the freezer, a staircase led up a flight of steps. I turned around to shine the flashlight behind me and caught sight of another staircase, this one leading to the outside. I scolded myself for not having looked around the entire perimeter of the house more carefully before choosing the window as my point of entry.

No matter, I told myself, brushing the dirt and splintered paint chips off my jeans. I would be much more observant in the future.

Chapter 83

William barely spoke while spooning beef stew into his mouth. Lance's pretty wife, Julie, moved between the kitchen, the dining room, and finally the bonus room over the garage, where her kids were finishing up their homework. She made it look easy as she removed the dinner plates and replaced them with small dessert dishes, a Pepperidge Farm assortment of cookies on a platter in the table's center, and coffee on the side. Then she ran up the stairs each time one of the kids called to her about where his sneakers were hiding, or can she borrow Mom's pink button-down the next day.

Finally, she glided into her seat at the dining room table, holding her cup of coffee between her hands as if she'd been relaxing with us all evening. She said, "Did y'all meet with the funeral director?"

"We did," Lance said. "William withdrew money from the account where he deposits his paychecks. He still can't touch the other account for a few more days. But it was enough to put a down payment on a casket."

William whispered, "I chose the brown one."

"I'm sure it's beautiful," Julie told William. "Now don't you worry about anything else. I've already talked to your pastor."

"Jules wants to call the newspaper," Lance said, "but doesn't know what to say for the obituary."

William looked up from his dessert. Cookie crumbs fell from the corners of his mouth.

Julie placed her cup on its saucer. "It's the newspaper's way of saying something nice about your mom, so everyone in town will see it. It also lets friends and neighbors know the details of the funeral. You know, time and place and everything."

"Mom was really nice," William said. "We could tell them that."

"Okay," Julie said, casting a smile at Lance. "Anything else? Wasn't she a teacher?"

"She worked in the school cafeteria."

Julie got up and went to a kitchen drawer, returned with a pen and a stack of Post-its, and sat again. "What did your mom like to do when she wasn't working?"

"Um…" William looked into his empty coffee cup. "She liked to watch *Home Improvement* and *Roseanne*, and read romance stuff, and plant flowers. Our yard always had more flowers than anyone on my street. And she…took care of me."

Julie scribbled on the paper. "That's perfect, William. Now, how about relatives? I can make the calls tonight before it gets too late. Is there anyone who might not read the paper that you'd like to have—"

"Mom!!" Her daughter's high-pitched voice interrupted from upstairs. "I can't find my Social Studies book! I have a test tomorrow!"

Julie started to stand, but Lance touched her wrist. "I'll get this one."

"Thanks, babe."

Lance left the dining room and ran up the stairs.

"Donald is my brother," William said.

"You want him to come to the funeral?"

"I dunno where he is."

"Well, is there anyone else? Cousins or aunts?"

"Aunt Bernice. She lives in Cranston. She's my dad's sister. But I haven't seen her in…lots of years."

Julie wrote on the pad. "Is that it?"

William nodded. "My family is small." He started to cry.

Julie came to his side of the table, stood behind him with her arms wrapped around his neck and whispered, "It'll be alright William. I promise. You'll be fine. We'll help with everything."

"But I don't have no one anymore. I don't have no one."

Julie hugged William tighter.

I floated to William's side.

Whether you realize it or not, I whispered in his other ear, *you still have me.*

Chapter 84

I'd dozed off on the living room recliner with my windbreaker tied around my waist, my sneakers on the floor beside me, and the ice cream bowl sitting in a ring of water on the end table.

That's gonna leave a mark, I thought as I rubbed my eyes.

Except for the end table lamp, the house was in total darkness. I couldn't see the clock across the room on the mantle, but it felt like hours had gone by. My mouth felt sticky. I'd had two bowls of ice cream, had near about finished off the Hershey's, and I was dying of thirst. As I pushed against the footrest and stood up, a piece of paper floated to the floor. I looked down.

The letter.

Before falling asleep, I'd read it ten times. The words were still in my head. Would *always be* in my head. I bent down to pick it up—

Glass shattered from somewhere below me.

What the fuck?

I shoved the letter into my front pocket.

The basement steps creaked.

I grabbed my sneakers.

The words "You're a dead man" entered my brain.

A can hit the pantry floor. I held back a scream.

In the kitchen, the pantry door hinges squeaked. I heard giant footsteps crossing the linoleum, the grunts of an animal, my own yelp as I tripped over an iron rabbit doorstop while reaching for the front door. My hand grabbed the bolt and turned it. The door swung open. I didn't look behind me. Didn't want to see—

Just move forward, I told myself. *Keep running, even if pebbles and gravel dig into your feet, even if you step on broken beer bottles, or scraps of tin cans, run like a fucking jack rabbit...*

I tore down the front porch steps, positive I could feel breath on my neck, eyes digging holes into my skull.

At the bottom of the hill, I spotted a car coming up the road. I ran fast into the headlights, waving my arms like a madman, a sneaker in each of my hands, not caring if the sonofabitch hit me. Probably easier to deal with a couple of broken bones than what was gonna happen to me in the house.

The Cadillac stopped. I ran to the passenger side and opened the door.

"Someone's after me!" I shouted to the old man behind the wheel as I got into the car. "He's got a gun!" I didn't know that for sure, but I woulda bet my bus money on it.

"Calm yourself down, son."

With his foot on the brake, the man hit the automatic lock buttons and turned on his high beams.

"Why aren't you going?" I shouted.

"Just checkin' things out."

The long road stretched into the darkness ahead. The dust I'd kicked up floated in front of the headlights. We looked from side to side and into the shadows.

"I don't see no one," the man said. "You sure someone's after ya?"

"Yes," I said, cranking my neck to see up the slope of the yard. "Yes," I said again, not as convinced.

"Son, I'll give you ten seconds to put on your shoes, then you can go on and git out of my car." His old-man eyes stared at me over a pair of wire-rimmed bifocals. "You on that heroin, son?"

"What? No. Dude. I'm telling you, there's someone in my house."

"Which one's yours?"

I nodded with my head so I could use my hands to tie my shoelaces.

"That house up there?" the old geezer asked. "That's the Baker place. That

Missus Baker, she died a few days ago. Knew her for years. Know her son too. That boy's brain damaged, seen him myself. And you ain't him."

Ma was dead?

Wheels began to turn in my head. Spinning wheels, like the kind you find on a race car when she's gunning and blowing smoke before she's good to go.

"Git out of my car," the man said again. "Go on now. These neighbors all know each other out here, and all's I gotta do is tell 'em there's a crazy guy on the loose, they's gonna be all over ya. I can promise ya that."

The man leaned past me and opened the door.

I grabbed the man's arm. "But I *am* William Baker." I real quick put on the goofy Woody mask. "I can show you."

"Y'all don't gotta show me nothin'. Just git out of the—"

"No, wait!"

I shoved my hand into the back pocket of my jeans. I froze. Panic and Chunky Monkey rose up in my throat. Both back pockets were flat as griddle cakes. No wallet, no IDs, no house key, no nothing.

"I think you need to do as I tell ya, son. *Now.*" The man slid a hand down to the underside of his seat.

I didn't want to know what he had under there.

I slammed the door behind me as I got out, heard the automatic locks, and watched the car drive off down the road.

No time to think. With my tennis shoes barely tied, I made a bee-line for the woods where I'd played hide and seek and hunted for treasure as a kid. Back when Ma and Dad were together, and doing monkey business without getting caught was the only thing to worry about; back when I was little and life was sweet and things were just like they were supposed to be.

Chapter 85

A dark-skinned man running in the night after a white, all-American redneck is a dangerous affair.

In the kitchen, I picked up the house key from the table and put it in my front pocket. In the living room, I closed the front door, started to lock it, then changed my mind. Better to make it easy, should the chicken kaka decide to come back. Then I smiled. Of course he would be back. On the end table sat a wallet. The wallet held three ID's: Donald Baker, William Baker—I could clearly see the resemblance between them—and someone named Robert Jones. Beneath the wallet, a passport also said Robert Jones, but, of course, it was Donald who stared at me from the photo. All of these documents I put into my own back pockets. Underneath the melted bowl of ice cream, a wet mark had begun to whiten the wood. I wiped it dry with the hem of my T-shirt and carried the bowl to the kitchen sink. With my flashlight, I headed into the basement with a broom to sweep up the glass.

As I finished this task, my stomach growled. Back upstairs, I picked up the knocked-over can of tomato sauce that had given away my surprise and put it back on the shelf among the other cans. It was a small but full pantry.

"Can you imagine building a special room to store extra food?" my manman had asked more than once. She had never had extra food in her entire life.

The smell of hot dogs hung in the air, so the choice for dinner was made. After three filled my stomach, and the dishes were cleaned and put away,

I called my manman on the mobile telephone.

"Manman," I said. "Turn off the television and listen to what I tell you." When she came back on the line, I said, "There is some cash hidden in the bathroom..."

She listened quietly as I explained there was a chance she and Anthony would need to take a Greyhound bus.

"To where?" she asked. Her voice came through the line without worry. Manman had dealt with enough in her lifetime that fear was no longer a part of her makeup.

"New York," I told her without thinking.

"I will look it up on the map."

"Do not pack anything until you get my call."

"My suitcase has been packed since we arrived," she said sadly. She put Anthony on the phone.

"I have a knock-knock joke for you, Uncle."

"Tell it to me."

"Knock-knock."

"Who is there?"

"Boo."

"Boo who?"

"Aw, what are you crying about?"

Anthony laughed and I laughed with him.

"Say your prayers," I told my nephew.

"I will, Uncle Emmanuel. And I will say a special one for you."

"Yes, that will be good. A special prayer for me."

I said goodbye to my nephew.

Eventually, Donald would come back. He could go nowhere without identification. It could be that night, or the next day. No matter. I would be waiting for him. At that time, I would do what had to be done.

I closed the living room curtains, used lemon oil to fix the water stain on the end table, lay down on the small but comfortable couch, and placed my sharp kouto on my chest with a hand wrapped around the mother-of-pearl handle. Soon, I was dozing with a smile that, no matter how I tried, would not leave my lips.

Chapter 86

Officer Powers

"What did you find?" I asked my vet friend, Mark Yingling, over the phone.

It was ten PM and my wife was upstairs taking a bath before bed. I sat in the dark kitchen with the cordless against my ear. I imagined Mark's voice would sound anxious, but instead it was somber.

"I know what killed the bird," Mark said. "But if I share this news, Chuck, we could have a real panic on our hands."

"Why would I panic?"

"Not you. The whole state. Maybe the whole country."

"Explain."

"Your bird," he said, "did not die of natural causes. I'll have to notify the Center for Disease Control."

"The CDC?"

"What I've found I've only read about in journals. I've never visited the regions where something like this occurs."

"Are you saying the bird died from a virus?" I asked.

"That's my educated guess. A virus that is extremely contagious among birds. Possibly other types of animals."

"Like dogs and cats?"

"Who knows? Maybe sheep. Pigs. Monkeys. I have no idea. I only have so many resources available to me."

"What about humans?" I asked.

"Couldn't tell you. Every time there's a new strain of anything, scientists do a mad rush to find a vaccine. But for those animals already infected, it's too late. Your little friend suffered from an extremely gross form of encephalitis. I've dealt with encephalitis before, don't get me wrong. It's just that this case seems—different. The bird's brain was so swollen, that when I opened the skull it literally oozed out onto the table."

"Damn."

"Thanks a lot, Powers. I was supposed to play golf this weekend. Now it looks like I'll be answering questions for a bunch of suits."

"Sorry."

"Yeah, well," Mark said. "It is what it is. There's always a chance we'll nip it in the bud."

"You think so?"

"I have to believe so. Trust me. You don't want a virus that number one, doesn't have a name, and number two, can give you a headache mean enough to make you place that pretty black beauty you have in your holster against your temple."

We hung up. As I locked up the house for the night, Mark Yingling's word repeated over and over—*encephalitis*—until the word seemed imaginary. Images of a widespread panic soared through my brain.

Later that night, while sitting up in bed watching the news, my wife snoring softly beside me, the broadcaster spoke to me and anyone else still up at midnight. I was exhausted but having a difficult time getting to sleep.

A photo of a horse appeared on the television.

"The future is uncertain for a young horse pulled from the Dellshore Racetrack late last week," the pretty blond reporter was saying.

I turned up the volume with the remote.

"A team of state officials and veterinarians met today to discuss their findings. Doctor Edward Yates, with the CDC, has quarantined four other horses…"

My wife rolled over toward me and mumbled, "Turn that down."

"Shh," I told her. "This is important."

"What?" Linda tried to sit up but ended up laying her head on my chest.

The news reporter continued. "In a statement given today, the Dellshore manager offered a little more information."

The camera switched from the blond anchor to a fat man in a suit, who kept his hands folded neatly in front of him while microphones jabbed him in the face.

His voice was calm. "It is with regret to inform you that Neapolitan, our five-year-old Pinto, will not be competing in the upcoming race." The man stopped, closed his eyes a moment, then began again. "If it comes down to euthanasia, there will be an autopsy as mandated, and once the CDC has the information it needs, we will pass the details on to you."

The pretty blond girl came back on the screen. "Also in the news today, a small tornado threatened homes and schools in nearby—"

I turned off the television.

My wife sat up and pushed her pillow behind her head. "Chuck? What is it?"

"First the bird. Now the horse."

"You think the two are related?" she asked.

"I don't know."

"Wouldn't scientists have already figured that out?"

"I don't know."

"I'm sure they'll find out exactly what they're dealing with," she said. "You know how those G-men crack their whips over the backs of the CDC."

"It's not that."

Linda turned on the lamp. "What, then?"

"I was at the Dellshore less than a week ago."

"You were? What for?"

"Visiting a man who works at the stables. A foreigner. Slight accent. Maybe Haiti, or Jamaica…"

"You think this person brought a virus from Jamaica?"

"No. I don't. But there's something…" I couldn't finish the statement because I didn't have any answers.

Linda said, "I think you need to get a good night's sleep, and tomorrow you'll be able to put some pieces together—if this really is some kind of puzzle."

She kissed my cheek, turned off her lamp, and rolled over, pulling the comforter up to her ear. I turned off my own lamp and snuggled my body up against hers. In less than a minute she was sleeping, her breathing regular and smooth.

I, unfortunately, lay awake until nearly three, thinking of nothing but doves, horses, viruses, men with foreign accents, and the invisible string that somehow tied them all together.

Chapter 87

"Police Department," the woman on the phone answered. "How may I direct your call?"

I stared at my lovely sweet-as-pie birds and took a deep breath. "Officer Powers," I said, careful to add the word "please."

In less than a minute, a man's voice came on the line.

"Powers here."

"Hi. My name is—I gotta tell you my name?"

I sounded like an idiot. I'm sure he had ways of knowing where I was calling from. I should have called from a phone booth. I was so tired from not sleeping right, I couldn't make a good decision to save my life.

The cop said, "That depends on what you have to tell me."

"Um…I have this—friend—and something's happened to him…"

"Maybe you should call 911."

"No. It's not like that."

"Is he missing, or hurt?" Powers asked.

"No. Neither. He's sort of—um—being framed. I think. Shit. I don't know what I'm talking about. It sounded so good when I explained it to the others. Maybe I'll let his best friend call you. He's better with words than me…"

"Take your time."

"No, really," I said. "I'm no good until I've had at least three cups of coffee, and here it is almost ten in the morning and I've only had one. I haven't even read the morning paper yet. Besides, what do you care if some girl calls you up and tells you about her friend who may or may not be framed, and it turns out that it's only a coincidence that one of the horses he works with might die, and that the only thing I really know for sure is that—"

"William Baker."

I about stopped breathing.

"Am I right?" he asked.

"Yes."

"I'm stuck at the station all day," Powers told me. "Why don't you come on down so we can talk in person?"

"In *person*?"

"We still have some bagels left from this morning. And super strong coffee, if you're into super strong."

I poked my finger through the slat in the cage and let La Toya nibble on my nail. "Damn it," I said to La Toya and the cop at the same time. "As if I haven't done enough for that man."

Officer Powers sat at a large desk on the other side of the counter. He stood up and shook my hand like we were friends. A firm but sensitive handshake says a lot about a man.

"Come on back, Cecilia," he said after I told him my name. "There's a room we can use that's private."

A large metal table with a metal chair on either side were the only things in the room.

"Have a seat," he said. "I'll get you a cup of coffee. Cream and sugar?"

"Black. Thanks."

He came back a moment later, placed a bagel covered in cream cheese on a paper plate on the table, and handed me a Styrofoam cup filled to the top with black coffee. He sat on the chair opposite me, opened up a small pad of paper, and licked the end of his pencil.

He didn't waste any time.

"How do you know William Baker, Cecilia?"

"We're friends," I told him.

"How long?"

"Not long."

"You know about his challenges?"

I nodded.

"Did you know his mother just passed away?"

"Yeah. I knew her too."

"I'm sorry."

"It's not like I was a daughter to her or anything." I took a nibble of stale bagel and sipped some lukewarm coffee to wash it down. "Look, it took a lot to get up the courage to talk to you. I'm not so comfortable with cops. Nothing personal."

"I understand," Powers said. "So, let's talk about William. What do you know about his job at the Dellshore?"

"He helps in the stables. William's sort of a broken record when it comes to horses."

"How did he get the job?"

"A guy named Manny hired him."

"Without sounding offensive, why would Manny hire someone like William?"

"That's the question of the hour," I said. "Maybe he thought he owed him something after he beat the shit out of him."

"What? When did this happen?"

"A few weeks back. And then he left him crumpled up on the floor in his apartment. I was the first one to find him."

"You didn't call the police?"

"No. I know I should have. But William totally freaked out when I suggested it. He didn't want to go to the hospital. I think he's afraid of doctors."

Officer Powers nodded as he scribbled on his note pad. "Do you know the reason Manny beat him up?"

"Thought William was his brother, Donald. I guess they sort of look alike.

But I've never met him. Which is fine by me, from what I hear."

"What have you heard?"

"That Donald treats William like a piece of shit. I'm pretty sure he forced William to move into his apartment so he could get a hold of his lottery money—William won on the *Lotsa Luck Show*. But someone got pissed off at Donald for something or another, and Manny mistook William for his brother. At least that's what Lance and I have put together."

"You and Lance are friends as well?"

"He's the reason I'm here," I explained. "He's helping William take care of the funeral stuff, and I'm taking care of things at this end. Though I'm a little bit behind." I took another sip of my coffee and held the Styrofoam cup between my hands. "Like I said, I'm not real good with cops. I'm definitely not the type of person who strolls into police stations offering information about people I hate. If that were the case, I'd keep you guys busy all day. This is about a nice guy who never did no one any harm. I'd like to see his brother face to face so I can spit in it. I'd like to see Manny get his ass kicked out of the country, back to wherever it is he's from. But to hear William talk about him, you'd think Manny was a god. And then, there's the weird thing William told me…"

It took a few minutes, but I explained everything William had shared, about the needles and the oranges, how upset he was over leaving his mama, everything I could remember. Well, everything except for the personal stuff, since that was no one's beeswax.

I added, "I'm not the smartest girl in the world, but I think Manny is using William to hurt the horses. And William just happened to be sweet enough to do what he was told. Without knowing what he was doing, of course. I don't want him to get into trouble."

Officer Powers scratched a gray sideburn. "Do you know when the funeral is?"

"Tomorrow. Lance said it was important that William get closure. But you know, I'm not so worried about William getting over his mama's death. I'm way more worried about William's money."

"Has he talked to you about it?"

"Not really. He mentioned something about depositing it, but he never told me the name of the bank or anything."

"You're sure you don't know where his brother is?"

I shook my head.

"Well," Officer Powers said, "I think William's a lucky man to have friends so concerned about his welfare."

"Yeah. He's one of the good guys."

After I said it out loud, I realized how true that statement was.

Powers smiled. "Don't worry, Cecilia. I'll sit down with William as soon as the funeral is behind him. We'll look into things."

We stood up and he shook my hand again.

"I'll walk you out," he said.

I left both my home and mobile phone numbers at the front desk. A moment later we stood in front of the police station.

After thanking me for my time, Powers said, "You know, you look somewhat familiar to me."

I twisted my ponytail into a bun and clipped it high on my head. I told him, smiling, "Guess I have one of those girl-next-door faces."

I started down the street, headed in the direction of the Jumping Java. After spending the better part of an hour at a police station and drinking the worst cup of coffee in the whole U.S. of A., I deserved a double caramel espresso, with the perfect touch of cinnamon on top.

Chapter 88

Without any IDs I was beyond nervous, and with no money to leave town, I was trapped. Sherm would be looking for me. I could feel him somewhere out there, watching, biding his time, like a hunter waiting in the bush for a deer.

I was so stressed out from not sleeping, I looked pale and confused without even trying, like my brother on a good day. But just because the reflection in the grimy gas station mirror looked like my brother, there was no telling what the bank teller would think. Plus, without a razor, my five-o'clock shadow was almost a beard. I had to get the face down pat, like last time. I stuck out my bottom lip, slouched my left shoulder, and ran my fingers through my greasy hair until it sort of looked feathered.

I stepped into the lobby imitating Woody's walk as I shuffled over to the rectangular table in the middle of the bank. In scratchy handwriting, I filled out a withdrawal slip while glancing up to locate the chesty gal who had helped me before. There she was on the far left, behind the bullet proof glass. It was still early. Only one person waited in line in front of me. My stomach cramped with hunger and nervousness.

My girl, Gina, called out, "Next in line…"

It's go time.

I smiled his crooked smile and walked his stupid walk to the window. I placed the slip in the scoop.

"Mr. Baker," Chesty Gina said, reading the withdrawal slip, "is it possible you added too many zeros?"

I gave her the dumb ol' Woody stare and crinkled up my forehead.

"Are you sure you want this much cash?" she asked, like I had just asked her to sleep with me. Her eyes got all big and her lips curled up at the corners like she was freakin' full of herself.

"Yes, cash," I mumbled. "In an envelope, please."

"Mr. Baker, I can't hand you this much money."

"You said when the check cleared—"

"Yes, I know. And the check did clear. First of all, you have it in a very specific account. We need to get manager approval anytime funds are withdrawn. And, of course, he'll ask to see your identification, and forms will have to be signed…"

I forced myself to stay chill. "Oh, yeah. My ID." I fumbled around in my pockets and looked up at the gal with watery eyes. "I d-d-don't have it." My lips trembled like a lost kid. "I think I left it at my m-m-mama's house."

"Let me get my manager, I'm sure he'll—"

"No!" My spit hit the window. She stared at the drops.

Careful homie…don't go postal…

"I need to b-b-bury my mama. She died. I gotta pay for the funeral." I knew Ma would come in handy at some point in time. Weird that it would be *after* she died.

"I'm so sorry," Gina said. "I understand about your mother, but I still can't—"

"If I don't get my money, she won't get a g-g-good burial. I wanna buy her the biggest and most beautifulest casket you ever seen in your l-l-life."

"But I can't allow *any* withdrawal transactions without an ID. Especially such a large amount."

I glanced at the sign posted to the right of every teller's window: *Proper identification is required for all bank transactions.* Then I read a larger sign hanging behind her, but this one I read out loud, nice and slow: "At Southern States Bank & Trust, we take pride in knowing our customers by name."

Gina only stared at me.

"You *know* me," I told her. "I'm William B-b-baker."

She leaned closer to the window and lowered her voice. "I cannot hand over this much money without a manager's approval. We don't do things that way. Even if you were my brother, I couldn't do it."

Crying for real was starting to get easier. "Please," I sniffled. "If I don't get any money, my mama will stay in the ref-f-frigerator at the hospital. I don't want her to be cold anymore. I want her to c-c-come home."

The gal was weakening. Without that hater monster mask she started to look sort of okay again. And with that blouse she was wearing, she sure didn't mind letting you know her on a personal level, if you get what I'm saying.

"Calm down," she said, glancing right and left and lowering her voice so I could hardly hear her. "Let's look at your other account. It shows here that you recently withdrew a few hundred, but you still have about a hundred dollars left. Why don't you take out fifty? Maybe that'll help a little. When you find your ID come on back. You can talk to our manager then. He's really nice, and I'm sure he'll help you—"

"Fine. I'll come back later. Whatever."

Fifty dollars wasn't enough for a Greyhound bus ticket or a week's worth of food. I didn't give a shiznit about sounding like Woody anymore. My choices were all but used up. I was tired and hungry and needed a fucking shower.

Gina counted out two twenties and a ten, put them inside an envelope, and had me sign the slip.

"Please don't be offended, Mr. Baker," she said, smiling that fake-ass smile, sliding the envelope into the metal scoop. "Our primary goal is customer satisfaction. Come on back later today with your ID, and I'm sure the manager will do everything he can—"

But I was already halfway across the marble floor. I had to pee, and underneath my jacket, my too-small T-shirt was digging into my armpits, which were sweaty and in need of deodorant. I headed out onto the sidewalk, looked both ways, then crossed the street to a greasy spoon. First the restroom and some chow in my empty belly, then back to the house to get my wallet. If it was still there.

And if whoever wanted me dead wasn't.

Chapter 89

Stephanie

I spent a large part of the morning holding back tears, partly because my stomach was so nauseous, and partly because I was missing Mrs. B's funeral.

Gerald was bunking at the firehouse for a few days. The television played the *Today* show with the volume down. As I lay on the couch with a cold washcloth against my forehead and a bucket nearby, I wasn't thinking so much about Mrs. B, when I probably should have been. I was thinking about someone else. As a young boy. His skinny-minnie arms and knobby knees, his tan summertime skin, his pretty blond hair, always feathered to perfection like he was preparing to perform a live show. And those blue eyes, crystal blue, like if there'd been sand in them you'd be able to count the grains.

On Saturday nights, when the only movies playing in town at the two-movie cinema were *Star Wars* (which we'd already seen seven times) or *The Exorcist* (neither of us was allowed to see that one even once), we'd head to my basement, which my daddy had loosely named "Pop's Groovy Club Room." As if having a wet bar in the corner, plastic cups on the bamboo bar, and green indoor-outdoor carpet covering the cement floor would constitute a club room. The rest of the room looked like all our other friends' basements, complete with small windows at ground level, a staircase that led up to the kitchen, fluorescent lights that hung over the washer and dryer, and two used plaid couches my parents thought were perfect for the basement when our living room upstairs got that nifty Brady Bunch remodel.

We'd turn on the hi-fi, stacked with as many records as that poor metal arm could hold, and turn up the volume just loud enough for us to hear but not enough to make my mama or daddy come storming down the stairs. Then William—Billy back then, of course—would plug in the disco party light we'd bought together by saving our allowance for three months. We'd move the dusty couches against one wall to give us room.

In the dark, by the bouncing light, I turned into the dancing queen:

Billy takes my hand and twirls me around in that strangely graceful way he has, and I glide my way across the floor, his garden-calloused hand in mine, his eyes never leaving my face, his sneakers like ballet slippers on his feet.

His right hand clutches my waist for a moment, our free hands connect, and our arms stretch out as we twirl. Then his right hand leaves my side and reaches for my left. Facing one another, we are only inches apart until he spins away from me. Like a Chinese dragon, the rest of me follows, sliding through arms filled with loops and turns, over and under, a fancy square dance, really, but you wouldn't have caught me comparing our moves to a square dance out loud. I'd have been banished from the disco floor. Exiled from dancing with my one and only.

We twist in and out of a pretzel, and he suddenly grabs my waist in both hands, small hands hanging at the ends of monkey arms, and then, suddenly, I'm flying through the air, his arms lifting and swinging me side to side on each of his hips, then continuing without my feet touching the floor while his arms swing me forward, my legs knowing what to do before I do, straddling Billy, then legs flying out again before sliding along the floor underneath him, my hair spraying out behind me. He steps over my body. His arms catch me in an embrace as the song ends, and he methodically and brilliantly tilts me back into the moment that will forever be etched in my memory: my back arched, my hair sweeping the thin green carpet, Billy's face only inches from my youthful belly. Ever so slowly he brings me up again, just in time to hear my mama call that it's time for soup and sandwiches.

My young girl's voice floats up the basement steps, "Coming," as Billy reaches his hands around the back of my neck, his fingers digging into my hair, his lips pressing against mine, hard and soft at the same time.

I was his dance partner, never his lover. But William, in his heart's recollection, believed I was his only. And even though I had fallen in love with him all those years ago, it wasn't me who stayed in love.

Often times I wondered, what would have happened if that unlucky day at the pond had never happened? Would William and I have stayed together? Would we be the ones having a baby? How many things would be different?

The possibilities were endless, like the universe. Endless and overwhelming and uncontrollable.

Chapter 90

Sherm found me in the restaurant's restroom, taking a wiz. Fucker had built-in radar when it came to money.

"Nothing like peeing together to turn men into equals." That's what he said to me, all of a sudden the smart-ass philosopher.

I didn't say nothing back. Didn't even look at him as I finished my business and washed my hands in the sink. I held the door for him. Cuz that's the kind of guy *I* am.

"Where're you headed?" Sherm asked.

"Hungry."

"Me too."

We slid into a booth in the back of the restaurant in the smoking section, the only table available. About a hundred truckers and construction workers ate their bacon and grits while smoking at the same time.

"You fucking with me?" Sherm asked after the waitress took our order.

"No," I said, trying to look anywhere but directly into those foggy old-man eyes.

"Not planning something behind my back?"

"No," I lied. "I swear."

"My patience is wearing thin, Donald. And that makes me cranky."

"I'm taking care of it."

"Too vague."

"Later today," I said.

"Name the time."

"Three o'clock," I told him without blinking. "That's when the funds will be ready."

Of course, the real plan was to somehow nab my fake IDs and get back to the bank by noon. That would give me more than a three-hour lead. Sherm would show up while I was on my way to Mexico. I'd salute him from the airplane as it flew over the bank.

We finished our meal in silence, except for the sound of Snaggletooth Foggy-Eyes slurping his biscuits and gravy.

When we were through breakfast, he said, "My treat," and snatched the bill from the table. "Don't want you thinking I'm an animal."

As Sherm paid at the register, I headed outside. I was already sitting on the bus by the time he stepped onto the sidewalk. I slumped down and peeked through the window. Sherm's dinosaur head was turned in the other direction.

Hasta la vista, baby.

Chapter 91

A breezeway separated the First Baptist Life Center from the church. After the service and the burial, bored kids zoomed around the large room in the life center, dodging under tables, in between grownups, and down the hallways. Some parents scolded, others ignored. It felt more like a cheap wedding reception than a funeral.

William didn't notice the children bumping into him or people shaking his hand. He smiled politely when people we hadn't seen in years spoke to him. Friends of Mom's from the middle school, a handful of neighbors, a few people we'd known as kids, who, of course, were all grown up now. But William's blue eyes remained blank, his memory of those people suspended in a void. He needed a lifeline but had no idea how to ask for one, or even that there was one. He drifted among the guests as they offered hugs or patted him on the back, then walked away murmuring under their breath, "Poor William." I drifted along beside him. He was as lonely and confused as the day he'd come home from the hospital, stuck in that wheelchair for eight months, his eyes darting around to each object in the house, searching for something recognizable, something he could remember and hold onto. Looking as lost now as back then, when he woke up each morning and had to be reminded of where he was, or *who* he was.

Standing next to the casserole-covered table, William looked like any normal man, attending anyone's funeral. The true William wasn't obvious unless he opened his mouth to speak.

"William!"

A heavy-set woman wearing a black dress with purple trim and a wide purple hat with daisies on the brim suddenly stood next to us.

"William, honey, I am so sorry about your mama. My oh my how you've grown. I haven't seen you since you were about this high, just a skinny little grasshopper."

William said nothing.

"You don't remember me? I'm Miss Trudy."

William stared at the jiggling flowers dangling from the brim of her hat and shook his head.

"Well, honey, I'm the one who was there with you twenty-four-seven when you came home from the hospital. Remember? Your live-in aide? From the state? I was the one who tried to help you remember things. We spent months together. I slept at your house three nights a week and took you out every morning into the garden to help you recall the names of flowers. Remember?"

She continued even though William didn't answer her.

"First, you'd remember the daisies, then forget them the next day and the next, then you'd remember them again, then forget again, then one day you came screaming into the kitchen, oh, you scared the life out of me and your mama! I thought for sure you'd gone and done something to yourself, you'd only been out of the wheelchair a few weeks, but you came limping in screaming, 'Daisies, tea roses, jasmine, vinca, daisies, tea roses, jasmine, vinca' over and over again, till I thought you'd forgotten everything else it the world but the names of those flowers!"

A small crowd was forming behind the large and grinning Miss Trudy. Her voice gained momentum in her excitement, and the small size of the room only made her seem louder.

"Oh, I remember how you loved playing your music," she said with enthusiasm. "And dressing in your funny little outfits. You were so cute! You really did make us all laugh, in a sad and funny sort of way."

Julie and Lance made their way to William's side. Guests at the buffet had stopped sorting through the lunch meat and cheeses and were turned in our direction.

"But we didn't always laugh," Trudy said. "There were some days when your mama cried. Like the time you swallowed that poison you thought was your Kool-Aid, and the time you fell down the basement steps while walking in your sleep, and, of course, after your daddy left." Trudy shook her head like our daddy had been her own kin.

William stared at the daisies on her hat. "I don't remember," he said quietly.

"I'm sorry, honey, I didn't hear what you said."

William moved his eyes to meet Trudy's. He repeated more loudly, "I don't remember."

"Don't remember what, honey?"

"Nothing." His lip started to twitch. "I don't remember nothing."

"Well, it's perfectly alright if you don't remember me. That was a lot of years ago, and you'd just had your accident."

William's voice grew. "I don't remember *nothing*. Not you or mom crying or dad leaving. I don't remember the accident or the net or how to set the t-t-table."

Trudy's mouth opened and closed, like she was about to say something but changed her mind. A circle of people, with plates of sweet potato fluff and chocolate cake in their hands, gathered around the small group.

"I don't remember," William said, his face growing red with frustration. "I don't r-r-remember n-n-nothing. Just my eight-tracks and Stephanie and Lance and my t-t-tree house and my h-h-horse. My horse! My horse!"

William's backup singers appeared in the back of the room, excited to have been called to action. They crouched down low, legs crossed, hands on knees, under the wavering lights of blue and red, waiting for William's cue.

William squatted down and pressed his fists against his eyes. He started chanting, "Shake it, shake it, that's the way you do it, uh-huh…"

His backup singers performed the electric slide, their white pleather shoes sliding effortlessly across the linoleum.

Julie placed a hand against William's back.

William stood up fast and slapped her hand away. "No!" he shouted to the room. "No! Shake it shake it shake it! That's the way you do it, uh-huh, uh-huh!" He ran his fingers through his hair. Tears ran down both cheeks.

William's singers froze in place, waiting.

Then, as if he were in our bedroom again, all those afternoons, all those years, with his eight-tracks playing KC or Sister Sledge or the SOS Band, he pointed his index finger to the ceiling, stuck out his hip, and said, "Shake it shake it shake it!" He spun in a circle and touched the ground in a near split, then bounced back up. He undid the tie that Julie had helped him with, pulling the loop over his head and throwing it to the floor. His backups did the same, happily following William in perfect imitation, their afros bouncing up and down with the beat. "Shake it shake it shake it!" William panted as he said the words, his face red and anguished, his hips swaying to the music churning in his head.

Then he took a wide step toward Trudy. She placed a hand on top of her hat like she thought it might fly away.

William shouted, "Shake it, uh-huh. Shake it!" He put his nose two inches from her face. He whispered, looking directly into her eyes. "Shake it shake it shake it...don't you see?"

He grabbed her by the arms and started shaking her. Not viciously, but rough enough for Lance and another man to yank William's hands from the blubbery arms of the poor woman, her face filled with fear and confusion.

William dropped his hands to his sides. He turned to Lance, his lips quivering, his hair in his eyes. He whispered angrily, "Y-y-you never told me!"

His backups sang happily, "You never told me, you never told me..."

"Told you what?" Lance asked.

But William didn't give him an answer. The roomful of people watched as he disappeared through the double doors that led to the Sunday school area. It was all I could do to catch up with him and his personal dancers as they tore down the dimly lit hallway and through the emergency exit door.

A block away, as William waited for the bus, I could still hear the ringing of the life center's alarm.

Chapter 92

Stephanie

A couple of saltines and a small glass of ginger ale, and lo and behold, my tummy finally settled. It was already after ten. I'd missed the funeral, but it was important I tell William in person how much I'd cared about his mother. It was also something I wanted to do in private.

I showered and dressed in one of my new spring dresses from Sears, tied a sweater around my shoulders, then stopped at a corner flower shop for a mixed bouquet. I wrote a note in the card and signed it.

The old neighborhood hadn't changed much since my high school days. Trees were taller and wider, and a handful of newer homes dotted the countryside. Other than that, it still looked the same, even though it didn't really feel the same. I passed by the house I grew up in, a typical split foyer, amazingly popular back in the seventies. Complete with ugly shag carpet, cheap light fixtures hanging from stucco ceilings, and an above ground pool we almost never used, since the pond was a little ways up the trail that wound through the cypress and red oaks. The house used to be tan, but the current owners had painted it white.

I couldn't keep up with all the thoughts flooding my mind as I neared William's house. Memories of racing in bare feet along dirt roads; riding bikes to the feed and seed place a mile away to get an ice cold cola from the machine they kept on the porch; hanging out in William's tree house, even in mid-summer when it was a hundred degrees; messing around in the pond to cool off.

I shook my head. That last memory had no right pushing away more important thoughts.

William might not be at the house yet, but I pulled my car in the driveway just the same. It was like entering a ghost town, the house looking so still, and that old green car in the driveway like a memorial to Mrs. B.

Parking my car next to the Buick, I turned off the radio, then the engine. The silence was almost deafening, and it was unnerving to step out of the car and hear my flats crunching the gravel. I leaned in and grabbed the bouquet then saw the horse necklace hanging from my rearview mirror. I unclipped it from the mirror, closed the car door, and walked to the back porch. That kitchen door must have opened and closed fifty times a day when we were kids, always running in and out. I stared up at the roof line. The house seemed lonely, its lifeless windows peering down at me, begging me to come inside, liven up the place.

Standing on the back porch, I looked out over the yard. Birdsong rained down into the yard from every tree. It was like standing on the edge of an aviary. Pansies, roses, and honeysuckle vines would be in full bloom soon, and the grass would grow in thick and lush. Tulips were already making their way through the dirt.

I knocked on the door, knowing nobody was there, but heartbroken all the same when no one answered. From the plastic sleeve in my wallet, I dug out the spare key. Mrs. B had given it to me the same day William came home from the hospital, as a safeguard. Lance got one too, though I don't know if he still had his. But I never got rid of mine.

The house smelled the same as always, like celery and chicken soup, mixed with an underlying scent of something summery—what was it? It took me a second as I closed the door behind me to realize it was hot dogs. My stomach churned a moment before settling again.

Way back when, the Baker house had so much life in it. Two growing boys bouncing around, racing through the kitchen on the way to the bus stop or a local ballgame, or to hang out with their buddies. Even Donald had a sprinkling of friends in those days. But Billy, of course, had been the popular one. Always waiting for an adventure. Always happy.

Now, with the door closed again, the house seemed to hold its breath as if expecting something. I placed the flowers on the kitchen table and laid the necklace next to it. After finding a vase in a cabinet, I filled it halfway with water and carefully dropped the stems inside. I fluffed the petals out and placed the small sympathy card on its plastic stand. I centered the bouquet in the middle of the table and stepped back. It seemed out of place, this pretty dash of color in the middle of a vacant kitchen.

A scraping noise fell into the room. I cocked my head to the side, straining to hear it again, but there was nothing.

Squirrels, branches, old house sighs, ghosts of my childhood.

I breathed a laugh at how nervous I was. So many things had happened in the last few months. So many.

But not all of them terrible.

The house was chilly. I untied my sweater from around my neck and put it on, buttoning the top three. I stepped into the living room and then walked back to Mrs. B's bedroom. I wasn't snooping. I was trying to feel a little more at ease, as if seeing her things might make me feel better. But I felt intrusive. I didn't belong in the Baker house alone. I had no right being there without William.

And yet I couldn't leave.

I opened the blinds and looked out through the bedroom's back window toward the woods behind the house. Beyond the edge of the yard and through the trees lay the narrow path, probably grown over after all this time. I was sure that William didn't go back there anymore. Not since that fateful day.

If we kids took our time along the path during the warmer months, we could get a bellyful of black raspberries that grew in abundance all the way to the pond. Our hands would be stained purple for days, and fresh jam would be spread on toast all summer long.

My mouth watered. There wouldn't be any berries growing this early in the spring, but I was curious to see if the path was still there. Curious to see if the way I remembered it was really the way it was.

An overwhelming craving to see the water suddenly came over me. We were so happy back then, with nothing to fear but getting caught making out in the tree house, or skinny dipping by the moonlight during sticky August nights. Those memories, like so many others, were hiding down that long narrow path once trampled on by growing feet. Feet belonging to other people, in a different season, in another time.

Chapter 93

Officer Powers

Thomas Wells led me to his office in the back of the brick building. The thirty-something bank manager was a walking stereotype, and even if his degrees weren't framed on the wall, I'd have known he was an MBA graduate in accounting. He had long bony fingers perfect for pressing calculator keys. Most likely a hall monitor back in middle school; headed up the high school math and chess clubs; scored a pretty wife because of his Lexus and stock portfolio.

"How old is this bank?" I asked, mostly to make conversation.

"Seventy-five. One of the oldest banks downtown. We still use the original safe. Of course the bullet-proof glass is all new."

His office was uncluttered. Two silk plants sat on a black file cabinet, and a gold-framed photo of a young woman holding an infant sat on his desk.

"What can I help you with, officer?" Thomas sat behind his desk, folded his manicured fingers in front of him, and nodded for me to sit, which I did.

"I need to know if you've heard either of these names before."

I slid a piece of paper across the desk, turning it around for him to read. The manager looked at the two names, written out in my best printed hand.

"The name 'Baker' rings a bell," Mr. Wells said. "We open six to ten new accounts every day, so forgive me if I don't recall specifics."

"I understand," I told him, leaving the paper on the desk between us. "Is there any way you can tell me if either of them has an account here?"

"I really can't do that, sir, not without a search warrant—"

"Of course. Privacy and all that. I could get one, but in the time that takes, someone could wind up in a lot of trouble."

Thomas Wells didn't respond.

I tried a different tactic. "Would it be possible for me to interview one of your employees?"

"Anyone in particular?"

"Gina."

"Gina Marsten?" he asked. "The teller?"

"Is that your only Gina?"

"Yes, sir."

"Well, then," I said, "she'd be the one."

"I'll get her for you," Thomas said, standing. "It is company policy that as her manager I sit in on your meeting. If there's anything I feel shouldn't be disclosed, I will say so. At least not without an attorney present."

"That's fine," I said smiling. When a cop smiles, the whole world notices.

The manager returned a thin smile. "Be right back."

A few minutes later, a young buxom woman came into the office. Thomas closed the door behind her.

The girl looked very worried.

I stood up and shook the girl's hand. "Officer Powers."

She looked from me to her manager and twisted one of her dangly earrings.

"It's alright, Gina," Thomas said. "He just needs to ask you a few questions."

"Did I do something wrong?"

"No, not at all," I told her. "As a matter of fact, I think you may be able to help me." I grabbed the piece of paper from the desk and held it out for her to see. "Either of these names look familiar to you?"

"Yes," she said, hesitantly pointing to the first one.

"The other name doesn't mean anything to you?"

"Donald? No, sir. Only *that* one. William Baker. You just missed him."

"He was here today?"

The same day as his mother's funeral?

Gina looked at her manager, who shook his head ever so slightly.

"Look," I told them both. "If you want me to get a search warrant I will, but I only want to know—"

Gina cut me off. "Why do you need a search warrant?"

"We're not sure exactly," I told her.

"But he seems so sweet," she said. "How could he have done anything wrong? I mean, he's slow and everything. I can't imagine—"

"So, you'd remember him if you saw him again?"

"Oh, you can't forget him. He has this weird way of looking at you, and sort of slurs his words. He gets pretty confused sometimes."

"What was the last transaction Mr. Baker made?"

Thomas piped in. "Gina, you don't have to tell him anything else."

I said to the girl, "What you tell me won't get William into trouble, Gina. It's to help him."

"He wanted to withdraw a chunk of his lottery money this morning, and I told him he'd have to sign some forms." She looked at her manager. "He wanted to take out five-hundred-thousand dollars, if you can imagine. His mother just died, and I tried to explain to him our policy and everything, how it would take a while to get him that much money and all, but he's slow, you know, so I had a hard time getting him to understand what I meant, and he left in a huff. I felt really bad. He was so confused." She told her manager, "I was going to let you know the second he came back in." Then she bit down on her bottom lip and looked at her shoes.

"There's something else?" I asked.

"He forgot his ID."

Thomas Wells said, "And?"

"I—I gave him fifty dollars from his other account. I know they aren't allowed to withdraw money if they don't have their ID, but I did recognize him, even with his beard growing in, he has that funny face and walk, and I'd know him anywhere, and please don't fire me, Mr. Wells, I have my little girl to worry about and my ex is God-knows where, and Mr. Baker *promised* he'd go back to his mother's house and get his wallet, and it was only fifty, not even enough to bury his mother, who just died…"

"Gina," Thomas said, "why don't you go take a break?"

Gina's lips trembled. "Our policy is customer satisfaction," she said. "Customer satisfaction."

"Gina," her manager said again, "please go take a break."

"He's really sweet," Gina said. She was crying now, and I felt sorry for her. "And he's slow. I told him to come back later today, so I know he will. Y'all can talk to him then."

Just as she opened the door to leave, I latched onto something she'd said. Damn cops and their memories.

"Gina?" I said. "Where did you say he was headed to get his wallet?"

She wiped a hand across her cheeks. "His house."

"You mean his *apartment?*"

"He never said the word *apartment*, I'm sure of that. He said his mother's *house*. Even though she's dead and all he wants to do is give her a decent burial." She left the room sobbing. A few personnel gathered around her at the end of the narrow hallway as Thomas Wells came around the desk and closed the door.

"Well?" he asked, and not so nicely either.

"I'll be back in a little while," I said.

"With a search warrant?"

"I won't need one."

"I think you should—"

"I won't need a search warrant because the search will be over the moment Mr. Baker comes back to complete his transaction."

Chapter 94

In the morning, I called Manman again to make sure she and Anthony had not been sent back to Haiti while I waited for the scumbag to return. Manman assured me they were fine, that no one had come to the apartment and no one had called but me.

But what if Roly believed I had abandoned him? With every tick of the cuckoo clock, seconds slipped away. Each time the little wooden bird came out of its hole, I became more aware of the space around me. Perhaps I had been foolish thinking the situation was under control.

Donald had not yet come back for his things. No one came to the house. Not even William. It occurred to me that the house had been abandoned; maybe no one would ever come. But there was food, fresh water, and a hot shower, and for those things I was grateful. I was also able to occupy some time cleaning up after myself, so if I left in a hurry, it would not be suspected that a stranger had been squatting in the Baker home.

So it was that I was sitting in the silent living room when a car door slammed and footsteps treaded gently across the gravel. I ran through the short downstairs hallway. There had been plenty of time to discover a few good hiding places.

But I was not prepared for the arrival of a woman.

For a brief instant I thought maybe William's mother had not died after all and was returning from a senior bus trip to Atlantic City or a BINGO hall. American senior citizens are always traveling to somewhere glamorous on buses.

But the footsteps were not the sound of an *older* woman.

In the downstairs bedroom I ducked behind the bed. I listened intently as she opened and closed a kitchen cabinet and ran the tap water. I felt her moving through the downstairs, held my breath, pressed my body against the floor, and squeezed underneath the bed as she stepped into the bedroom. Blinds suddenly opened, spilling sunlight across the walls. She lingered there a moment, closed the blinds again, and exited.

I listened as the back door opened and shut once more. After waiting a considerable amount of time, the sound of an engine turning never came to me. I got up from my belly and crouched beside the bedroom window. I pulled back the lace curtain and peeked through the blinds. I could see the backyard, but not the side of the house where the driveway sat. My hand started to lower the curtain when the back of the woman came into view. The edge of her flowered dress moved in the breeze, and she wore a sweater which covered her arms. She stopped a moment, stared up at a tree house, and continued toward the back edge of the property. She reached up to move some branches out of the way, then disappeared into the thickening trees behind the house.

Who was she? And where was she going?

Wondering these things made me realize how little I knew about William, other than his lack of intellect and the fact that his mother had died. And, of course, his brother's antics. I had rooted through William's things, the music collection in his room, the tin box filled with hundreds of used lottery scratcher tickets, the horse ribbons and trophies. But I did not truly *know* William, just like I did not know this woman who had come to visit.

Was someone expected to meet her? Perhaps someone I had not bargained on? And why would she be walking into the woods, dressed like she should be sipping tea at a restaurant or getting her nails manicured?

I let the blinds fall back into place and walked into the kitchen. A large bouquet of mixed flowers sat in a glass vase in the middle of the table, spilling the scent of springtime into the room. I reached for the card and pulled it out of the envelope.

William: I am so sorry about your mom. She was just like my own and will be sadly missed. I am heartbroken I was unable to make it to the funeral. I'm sure it was beautiful. Please let me know how I can help. Love, Stephanie.

It came to me, even stronger the second time, the feeling that there was a whole world William was a part of that I had never known. A world that included home-cooked meals, a manman who had loved him, and a pretty friend named Stephanie who brought him flowers.

Now I knew *why* she had come.

The question was *Where did she go?*

In the hall closet I found a dark green hunting cap, the kind with ear flaps, placed it on my head, put on my sunglasses, and went through the back door. I pulled my jacket collar up around my neck. Except for the blue Honda's clicking engine and the chirping birds, the neighborhood felt like a silent tomb, the acre of lawn like a graveyard not yet filled.

Quickly, I made my way across the sprouting grass and dashed for the trees which lined the back of the property. I entered the woods, the shade dropping the late morning temperature by at least ten degrees. A chill ran up my neck as I quietly followed behind the girl.

Chapter 95

Stephanie

I had revisited the pond only twice since 1978. Once was with the police the day after the incident. The other time was a few months after William had come home from the hospital. His therapists asked Lance and me to take him back to the pond. Just like riding a horse, they'd said. But we never had the courage to drag him back there, and besides, William could barely walk at the time. He used a wheelchair and didn't switch to a walker until almost year later.

Lance and I had ventured out beyond the path one chilly autumn evening, after Mrs. B made us dinner. William was getting ready for bed. He was nearly sixteen then and was going through a growth spurt, and it took his mother a half hour or more to get him into his nightclothes and brush his teeth.

For an hour, Lance and I stood on that wooden plank, listening to the water as the cool breeze pushed the tiny waves up against the pylons, thinking about whatever it is people think about in moments like those. Wishing, maybe, for another chance. Praying in our own way for forgiveness. Wondering what our lives would become if we'd done something differently.

On our way back to the house, Lance had grabbed my hand. We stopped on the path.

"We can't tell him, Stephanie," Lance said. "Ever." His face was nearly invisible, darkened by the pines blocking the sunset and the rising moon, but I could imagine his serious eyes matching his tone.

"We owe it to him," I said, knowing what he meant without him explaining.

"It wouldn't matter," he told me. "He probably won't remember nothing anyways. Let it be, Steph. No reason why we gotta add more grease to the fire. What's done is done."

Lance seemed so grown up then, using phrases the way my daddy did, making me believe that his way was the best way.

And maybe it was.

In the end I never told William. Neither of us did. And we never told the authorities the truth because William would have been dragged through all kinds of police muck and maybe even court, and there was no way we'd do that to him. We didn't tell Mr. or Mrs. B either. Who were we to tear a family apart? Hadn't they already been through enough? We kept that secret as close to our hearts as a mama would a newborn baby.

And here I was, once again walking along the path, heading to the place that changed our lives forever. Only this time I was alone with the memory tagging along behind me, breathing heavily, working hard to catch up.

The path was not so terribly overgrown that it couldn't be followed. Trees with new buds draped their branches out over my head like the ribs of an umbrella, and I had to swat no-see-ums and early spring mosquitoes away from my face.

My feet remembered the path, gracefully leading me along the dips and grooves and bends, over the same spots where roots had clawed their way through the dirt and reached up to trip the feet if a person wasn't careful. But my feet knew what to do even before my mind did. On either side of the thin trail were thick bushes filled with either fruit buds or birds nests, gearing up for warmer weather. A stream trickled to my right, parallel to the path for twenty yards or so, then zigzagging its way to the east. The smell of moss rose thick in the air, the green fuzz clinging to the sides of tree trunks.

A squatting rabbit froze in the center of the path. I stopped to watch him watch me, his nose twitching and his ears poking straight up, and for a few seconds our eyes held like we were friends. And in that moment of standing, waiting to see who would move first, me or the bunny, I heard a loud snap behind me.

I turned with a jerk, placing my hands firmly against my slightly rounded belly, the protective mama bear in me having unexpectedly evolved. I peered into the thickness. Tree limbs and trunks and ivy and brambly bushes cloaked the path. For a moment I could hear the distinct sound of heavy breathing, then shook my head as I realized the breathing was my own heavy panting, proof I hadn't used my legs for much more than sitting, spending the last few years parked on my rear amongst stacks of veterinarian science books in the library. I smiled for my silliness and turned back to the rabbit, but it had disappeared into its sanctuary in the underbrush.

I went another ten yards, and the clearing appeared. I stepped out of the trees and onto the damp earth that stretched out before me about fifteen yards or so.

Beyond the mud and loose brown grains of rock lay the pond, lifeless on this spring day.

I stood on the edge of the clearing only a moment before I slipped off my flats and walked with them in my hand to the dock, stepped onto the cool weathered wood, the rough texture of dried lumber rubbing against my bare feet.

I could easily see to the other side. Had the pond always been so small? For years, in the part of my brain that holds onto all of my childhood memories, I was convinced the pond was of mammoth proportions. A huge wet monster waiting to chew up and spit out any children who dared to enter. As an adult, however, I could see how minuscule it really was. Amazing that what had given me nightmares for most of my adolescence was so small I would have been able to swim across if I'd jumped in right then. Well, maybe not in my current condition.

Even without dipping my toe in I knew how cold the water would be; I'd had plenty of experience with springtime wading. At the end of the dock, I crouched down, pulling my hair back with one hand as I looked over the splintery edge. Fragments of itty bitty scars still dotted my shinbones as evidence of that awful day.

The face in the water stared back at me, my reflection smooth and clear without the disturbance of summer wind or splashing children. But then my image on the pond's surface disappeared, and I could see beneath the brown eyes staring back at me; could see all the way down to that exact place.

The day after Billy almost drowned, Mr. Baker had taken his hunting knife and cut out the net. I'm not sure what he did with it, but I had a feeling he burned it with the other garbage on trash day.

Now, I stared into the cool darkness of the pond, down to where the pylons dug into the muck under the water, where eager boys and one eager girl on a sunny day so long ago held destiny in their promising hands, where all my childhood dreams drowned along with the love I used to have for a young boy named Billy Baker.

Chapter 96

With my hand against the hood of the light blue Honda, I stood looking up at the windows of the house I grew up in. The hood was warm, so that meant the person had only shown up a while ago. A chick car. Maybe stolen.

I had two choices: go inside and instantly get killed by Roly's hitman, or don't go inside and eventually get killed by one of Sherm's guys. I'd thought about calling the police anonymously, telling them there was someone in the house. But my tight ol' brain stayed one step ahead of me: if the cops took down the guy in the house, they'd grab the IDs as well.

I was between a mother-fucking rock and a hard place.

On top of everything else, I'd lost my pocket knife somewhere between the bus stop bench and the house. But I'd always been a creative dude, if you hear what I'm saying. The Honda was parked with the driver's door on the opposite side of the house. I peeked inside the car window. The locks were in the up position. I opened the door and slumped down in the driver's seat. In the glove box I found a county map, a couple of pens, a pair of sunglasses. I rubbed my hand along the carpet under the seat but found nothing. Then I won the prize for being so freakin' smart. My hand came across a black leather bag on the floor behind the driver's seat.

The clasp was simple enough to undo, but I was confused by what was inside: a stethoscope, two thermometers—one normal size and the other so big you could lose it inside an elephant—gauze and alcohol, blood pressure cuffs, and a bunch of freaky-looking rubber tubes and black rubber bags.

There were also a pair of goggles and two pairs of rubber gloves. I pulled out a sealed plastic bag and read the words.

"En-do-trach-e-al tubes."

What in the hell were endotracheal tubes? Maybe this wasn't the same dude that had beat up my brother. Maybe this was someone who got off on torturing his victims.

No time to guess, no time to have a freak out. I dug my hand back into the bag and BINGO! A pair of scissors. Not the most lethal weapon in the universe, but I could see jabbing someone in the neck if I was forced to.

The letter from the fridge sat folded up in the front pocket of my jeans. The words were festering, giving me an edge, keeping me postal. No matter who was in the house, there wasn't a fucking thing at this point in time gonna stop me from getting that money.

Chapter 97

William took off his suit coat and slung it over his shoulder as the afternoon sun beat down against his head. His tie was left behind at the life center, and he looked like a sloppy but eager butler as he skip-walked up the old neighborhood road.

I floated by his side, trying to keep up with his quick pace. My invisible feet felt like they were made of lead.

You got a fire in your pants?

He sang, each step accentuating every few words: "Out on the disco floor, I see you dance around, it makes me want you more and more, my heart makes not a sound…"

He turned his face toward the sky. His private performers were a few paces behind us, moving in sync.

As we approached the house, he kept singing: "So I dance with you, we shake our stuff, not one but two, and girl, that's enough…"

Next to the mailbox at the bottom of the yard, William froze. I followed his gaze up the driveway. A blue Honda was parked next to Mom's green Buick.

"Stephanie," William whispered.

His backups vanished.

William put his jacket back on and tried to make sense of his long feathered hair by brushing it back with his fingers.

"Stephanie?" he said again, this time as a question, as he stood at the bottom of the drive. He cocked his head to the side. The Honda's driver's side door was open. But Steph was a careful girl. A smart girl. She never would have forgotten—

Don't go! I warned. *Head to a neighbor's house! Call the police. Something is wrong—I know you feel it.*

But if William did feel it, he never let on. He started up the driveway, slowly, deliberately.

And for the very last time, I followed.

PART VII

Chapter 98

The Kitchen was empty and clean. Pine-sol clean. Had I done that good a job of cleaning up after myself? Homey didn't think so. In the middle of the table sat a vase of fresh flowers. Next to it was a gold necklace with a horse's head on it. But I didn't give a shit about Pine-sol or flowers or some cheap-ass necklace. The only things I cared about were my life and my money.

I listened. The bastard could be anywhere. I held the scissors tight in my fist, thinking that if I had to use 'em, I wouldn't be able to let go of the handle after. I tiptoed into the living room to grab my wallet and passport from the end table, even though odds were stacked against me.

I was right about the odds. Along with my IDs, the bowl of ice cream I'd left sitting on the table was gone. I rubbed my finger across the wood and held it to my nose: Lemon Pledge.

Did Roly hire someone with a fetish for flowers and household products? This idea freaked me out more than my missing things.

In Ma's room, the bed was made with the pillows tucked away underneath the ugly granny bedspread. I jumped onto the bed and kicked the covers around, making it look like it did the night I'd stole the television, when she'd let out that awful scream. I jumped hard, hoping to crush or at least surprise the bastard who might be hiding underneath.

No one appeared. I dropped to the bed on my belly and hung down over the end, pushing the bed ruffle out of the way to get a look, the scissors ready for action. All that stared back at me were a pair of slippers and a couple of dust bunnies.

The closets, the bathroom, all empty.

But the car…

The bastard was here, somewhere, and there was a good chance he wasn't planning to leave.

Fuck it then, cuz neither was I.

With the scissors held out in front of me like a sword, I made my way upstairs and into the attic. Nothing but the same shadows and cobwebs in the corners, and that stupid vermin living in the wall.

Back downstairs, through the pantry, and down to the cellar.

I stood in the center of the basement, tapping the chain that hung from the overhead bulb, back and forth, wondering. Maybe the guy got bored and decided to go exploring. Maybe he was sitting in the tree house this very minute, reading the carvings in the wood or counting beer bottle caps in the old turtle shell.

My next thought really fucked with me: maybe there never *was* anyone else. I had only *imagined* the psycho chasing me. I mean, the geezer who picked me up in his Cadillac never saw a thing. Was it possible that stress had wiggled the old marbles around?

But my things were missing. There was a car in the driveway. And a warm engine.

Then, while standing in the cellar, I noticed the hollow window frame. Broken clean through. But there weren't any glass fragments. Spotless. Like the kitchen.

I wasn't sure what to do next. Without any ID, where would I go? Even if I found Ma's car keys and took the Buick, the fifty bucks I got from the bank wouldn't get me very far, and if I got caught in a stolen car…

All the good luck in the world had been wasted on Woody. Just tumbled past me like the invisible man I'd always been and made a straight shot for my brother.

I reminded myself that miracles happen every day. Ponies you thought would lose end up wining. Lottery scratchers sometimes give you magic numbers. Always someone gonna lose, but someone gonna win too. And right when I was thinking this, my luck changed.

Upstairs, the kitchen door slammed. A familiar voice called out. A voice that most times made me angry enough to shoot a dog, but in that moment made me feel like a little sunshine was finally peeking through.

"Stephanie?" the voice called. "Stephanie, where are you?"

So. The car belonged to Steph. Roly's henchman hadn't stuck around after all. Dealing with my brother would be a piece of cake. Even if Stephanie was somewhere nearby, she'd be easy enough to scare away.

Heavy footsteps clomped across the kitchen floor over my head. The clomping moved up the staircase and across the second floor landing.

"Where are you?"

Clomp, clomp, clomp!

As I made my way up the basement steps, I pictured Woody with his oversized feet, walking like a circus clown through the house, calling for his namby-pamby Stephanie. As if she gave a crap. She married a fireman, whoopdie-do. Duh. She wasn't stupid, getting benefits if he burned up in a fire and all that other junk girls think they deserve.

A stupid teenage crush was all she'd ever had for Woody, but everyone made it sound like some freakin' Hollywood love affair. Even if it had been more than a crush, what did it matter now? Way too fucking little, way too fucking late, is what I always say.

My excitement and confidence grew as I stepped through the basement doorway into the pantry, my hand holding tight to the scissors. I shook all over like a contestant on *The Price is Right*.

Stephanie or not, hit man or not, plan or no plan, I was gonna get my fucking comeuppance.

Chapter 99

Stephanie

I sat on the dock with my feet in the water, creating large circles until the ripples blocked me from seeing anything below the surface. I tried to think of happier days, but the only memory that kept coming back to me was the one I didn't want to remember.

The cold seeping through my swollen ankles felt soothing at first, but then my toes grew numb. A shiver ran through my core. I pulled my legs up over the edge, pressed myself up from a seated position, brushed my dress flat, picked up my sandals, and turned. There, in the clearing, stood a man with dark skin, wearing a hunting cap and sunglasses. Even with the sunglasses, I could tell he was staring at me. Startled, I took a step back, but there was no step to take. Under my foot was air, then water. My hands clutched at invisible ropes as I tumbled over the wharf's edge, but not before I let out a scream as the stranger came running toward the dock.

My imagination had been playing cruel tricks on me since my first trimester, like seeing weird lights at night and odd shadows during the day, so I convinced myself the man in the hat was only in my mind, and blamed my lack of equilibrium on the pregnancy.

The icy water attacked my bones. I used to be a strong swimmer, but I hadn't jumped into a pool, and certainly not the pond, in a very long time. I wasn't afraid of drowning, but my limbs were growing numb, and I'd have to get out and dried off before I froze to death. It was still springtime and hypothermia would happen fast. This thought is what drove me back to the dock. The possibility of the man actually being real didn't occur to me until I bobbed up. There he was, on the edge of the dock, towering over me. He had removed his sunglasses.

Pushing my bare feet hard against the rough pylons, I flung myself away in a backstroke, kicking like a wild woman. The man said something, but I couldn't hear him with the water splashing. I looked toward the other side of the pond. It seemed a lot farther from this perspective than it had from the dock.

I doggie paddled about twenty yards out, but I was shaking uncontrollably, unable to make any more headway. If I did not get out now, I would die.

"What do you want?" I shouted.

"I want to help you!"

"I don't need any help—I can get out by myself."

The shivering grew worse.

"Miss, you need to get out *now*." He looked behind him through the trees, then back to me. "You need to leave. Do you understand?"

For some reason, a part of me did understand. At least I understood that what he was saying was the truth, though I don't know how. Perhaps intuition takes over when it needs to. Perhaps we believe in possibilities when there is no other way.

"I'm…freezing," I told him, crying, my teeth chattering painfully together.

The man took off his jacket and held it out. "Come out of the water, Miss."

"You…might…hurt…me."

"Why do you think that? Because I am black? Because I am foreign?"

My mind tried to wrap itself around the fact that I was having a conversation about stereotypes while doggie paddling in the same pond that had destroyed William's life. And in that moment, I remembered something so clearly and intimately that it took my breath away, nearly causing me to stop paddling. It was in the slight movement of the wind through the tall trees which stood behind the stranger; the way the sun fell across my forehead; the sound of the water as it lapped against the posts.

How could I have forgotten *that*?

Donald, sitting on the horse blanket, his beach towel wrapped around him, watching the paramedics work on Billy, watching the rest of us as we cried and prayed and tried to save his life; Donald grinning, like he'd discovered the secret to a magic trick. And then, in that horrific moment of near-death and despair, came the shattering sound of Donald's snickering, cutting its way through time and piercing my eardrums.

Maybe William wasn't the only one who had chosen what to remember, what to forget…

"Come out, Miss," the man coaxed from the dock. "William's brother may come back. He may already be here. You must leave."

Words were just about impossible to form now.

"Wh-wh-who are you?"

"I will explain later," the stranger said. "You are not safe right now."

It was either try to make a swim for the other side or stay afloat. Either way I would surely die.

And I had a lot more to worry about than just me.

As I neared the dock, my fingernails already blue, as I knew my lips were, the man extended his hand. With much effort, I reached up my own frozen one and let the dark stranger pull me to what I prayed was safety.

Chapter 100

Like Casper the ghost, I followed William as he ran down the stairs two at a time, skipped the last one, and jumped onto the kitchen floor.

In the middle of the room stood Donald.

"What up, dog?" Donald said. His left hand was buried in the front pocket of his jeans. His right hand remained behind his back.

"Donald!" The name popped out with a tinge of fear in it. "What are you doing here?"

"I should ask you the same question."

"Mom's dead," William said.

"Yeah? Too bad."

William looked around the room. "What do you want?"

"I hear you've been a busy dude, chillin' at the Dellshore and all."

"It's—my job."

"Doing what? Killing racehorses?"

"I don't kill horses. Never ever."

"That's not the word on the street."

William nervously walked over to the narrow archway between the kitchen and living room to create some space between them. Donald narrowed the gap.

"I clean the stalls and feed them," William said. "I take care of them."

"You mean the way you took care of Neapolitan?"

"She's my favorite."

Donald either didn't notice the defensiveness in William's voice, or didn't care. He moved closer, until the two of them stood three feet apart.

"How can a dying pony be your favorite?" Donald asked.

William held onto the doorway frame between the two rooms as if trying to ground himself. "She's not dying. She's the best—"

"It's all over the news, brother. All over the fuckin' television. How sad that I gotta be the one to tell you. Breaks my heart, it does."

"You're a liar."

"Turns out you gave your Pinto a little something in that needle, and now she's on the ground, foaming at the mouth."

"You're a big fat l-l-liar!" William began to cry.

"Call me that one more time, and I won't tell you how we can save her."

William wiped his eyes with the cuff of his suit jacket, and even though his lips trembled, he stopped crying. "I want to save her," he whimpered. "Not turn her into glue."

"Sure you do, buddy," Donald said. "But it's gonna cost a lot of money to do that. And the only one I know with any money is you."

"My money is at the bank."

"Well," Donald said. "Let's say you give me your state ID card, and I make a quick trip to the bank for you. Then I can get your money and save your poor little pony."

William didn't respond.

"Every minute you stand there like an idiot is another minute your precious—"

"Why weren't you there?" William asked.

"What?"

"At the funeral?"

"Someone forgot to send me an invitation."

"You shoulda been at the funeral," William told him. "It would've made Mom happy."

"Yeah? Well, Ma's not here to feel anything one way or the other is she?"

"You shoulda been there."

"What for?" Donald said. "*I'm* not her favorite son."

"Mom loved us both."

Donald's ears and cheeks turned red. He moved forward in a heated rush. He placed his face five inches from William's, pulled a piece of paper out from his pocket, and shook it in the air. William flinched, but his feet stayed planted.

"Bullshit," Donald said.

"You were *Dad's* favorite," William said. "Dad loved *you* b-b-best."

"Yeah? Well, good ol' Daddy up and left. How's that for fatherly devotion? And I didn't make it to the top of his list until after—"

"My accident," said William, looking down at the ground, ashamed.

"You know, every time you say the word 'accident' it takes the blame away from you, doesn't it? It was *your* fault that day, homey. *Your* fault Dad left. *Your* fault Neapolitan is dying. *Your* fault Ma's dead. So quit calling it a fucking accident!"

Donald's face was purple with rage, yet William stood quietly staring down at his polished faux leather shoes. I couldn't hear what he was thinking, but I didn't need to. He decided to say it instead.

"I don't remember."

"You don't remember?" Donald's voice jumped up an octave, like a little girl's. "I d-d-don't r-r-remember anything. It's all a b-b-blur to me." He shook the piece of paper until it opened. William stared at the scissors dangling from his other hand.

Donald read out loud: "'My Dearest William. I know you gave that CD player to your brother, but I truly wanted you to have one, so humor your mom. Your new player is in the pantry behind the soup cans, so if your brother comes a calling he won't see it and take it for hisself. The man at that superstore picked out some new CDs he thought you'd like, the ones popular with kids today. I haven't been feeling good lately. So I've been doing some planting to help me feel better. The poinsettias will be up by Thanksgiving. I want you to know that—'"

Donald stopped and swallowed. Hatred swam in his eyes.

"'—that you're my favorite son, my William. You always have been and always will be. That's why I have recently—'"

He stopped again. Into William's face he breathed, without looking at the letter, as if he'd memorized it.

"'That's why I have changed the will so you have the house solely...'" Donald grinned like a gargoyle. "'Solely,'" he repeated. "Know what that means, Wood? She left you the house. Her favorite son gets the house. Isn't that totally dope? Aren't you the luckiest guy in the world? You get to live in this!" Donald spun around in a circle, arms straight out, the scissors a silver blur. "All of this! Woo-hoo-hoo!"

The heavy table stopped his spin as he tumbled into it, knocking a chair to the floor. He laughed, loud and long, like a wolf celebrating its first meal after weeks of starvation.

As Donald leaned with his rear against the table, tears streaming down his cheeks, choking on his laughter, something big and entirely destructible became unleashed in William as he let go of the doorway and took a step forward.

Chapter 101

Officer Powers

Things were moving at warp speed. While prepping at the station, I quickly telephoned my wife. I told her there was something going down at a local bank, how the FBI was now involved, how excited everyone at the station was. I couldn't tell her all the details, just the ones to let her know why I loved being a cop.

"That's fantastic, honey," Linda said. "But how would you like to hear some *super* good news?"

"That wasn't good enough?" I asked, as I put the phone against my shoulder and checked both my guns.

"This news will blow your socks off."

I'm always game for having my socks blown off. "Trouble and Treasures come in threes. Tell me."

"I started spring cleaning today, and I was hanging up our summer sheets outside on the line to dry…you know, to make them smell good, plus there's a chance it'll rain later today, and you know how much of a pain it is to have to take down laundry when it rains…"

My wife has a lot of unleashed energy and tends to ramble when she's excited. I let her finish about the sheets and waited patiently while staring at the second hand on my watch.

"Well," she said. "The news came on the radio. You know how I love to keep the little Sony on the picnic table while I work outside, in case a tornado might be spawning close by, or a thunderstorm might be coming. And I about froze when I heard the reporter mention that horse…Neapolitan."

My stomach flipped. "Neapolitan? What about her?"

"She was misdiagnosed," Linda said. "Some German epidemiologist hired by the CDC had originally diagnosed it as a strain of encephalitis. But he was wrong. Looks like the eager beaver will be looking for a new job. Had a whole bunch of suits doing a panic dance for nothing. Neapolitan's going to be fine, Chuck. It was all a mistake."

A mistake? I thought. *What about the birds? What about Manny, or what William had told Cecilia?*

"Did you hear what I said?" Linda asked.

"I think so."

"What do you mean you think so? You haven't stopped talking about that horse and those birds—"

"Doves."

"—for days. Now all you have to say is you think so?"

"What else did they say?"

Linda said, "Something about it not being a virus, that the symptoms are stress related—maybe the trainers pushing her too hard, or something like that. They say there's a chance she could race in two weeks, but even if she doesn't, her owners are ecstatic she's going to be okay. At least they think she'll be okay. They're still not positive about everything, but at least she's standing, which is supposed to be a good thing, though I don't know why. When I'm stressed out I'd rather lie down more than anything, but I suppose horses are different…"

"This doesn't make any sense," I told my wife. "Two days ago they were going to put her down. Now they're saying she might actually *race?*"

"Some idiot made a mistake is all."

"What about the birds?" I asked.

"Obviously, Chuck, there's no connection. You only thought there was. I even thought there was, by the time you were done convincing me."

"But—"

"In all honesty," Linda said, "I'd rather it not make sense if it means a horse is healthy again. Don't you think?"

I said nothing. I rubbed the tiny scar on my chin, a reminder of the nick I gave myself shaving when the bird slammed against the bathroom window.

"Chuck? You there?"

"Yes."

"Aren't you relieved that your theory was wrong?"

"Of course I am."

But there was a trade to be made for those few moments of relief, and the trade was the curse of knowing that another more intricately wired bomb had yet to go off.

Chapter 102

Something was happening. Donald no longer frightened me. My invisible arms and legs and body didn't frighten me anymore either. My energy emanated from a place deeper than my limbs or my chest.

William's energy was growing too. He nearly glowed as he took another step toward the table. His blue eyes grew large and clear, matching mine.

"I remember," he whispered.

Donald snorted some lingering giggles as he slowly regained his composure. Mom's letter lay on the table. His fist still clutched the scissors.

"You remember what?" Donald said. "How to tie your shoelaces? How to wipe your ass by yourself?"

For sixteen years, William had been holding onto feelings he didn't know how to tap into. Sadness and anger had been lying side by side, as deep and dormant as beasts. But it was the anger that rose to the surface first. Anger coming from recognition. William still couldn't see it clearly like I could, but his rage was helping it become something tangible; it was filling his lungs, keeping him standing, moving him forward.

Remember, I coaxed.

William shook his head like he was clearing water out of his ears.

The pond…the music…the net…

The fog behind his eyes was beginning to lift.

Yes, yes, yes—remember! That's it…

William chose his sentence carefully. He worked extra hard not to stutter.

It was important he say the words without sounding like the imbecile Donald believed he was. His eyes met his brother's. For the first time in sixteen years, William felt strong in his mind. *Even if I hadn't been a part of him, the part he hadn't let go of completely, I would have recognized that strength.*

"You were there," he told Donald.

That's my boy!

"I was where?" Donald asked.

"Holding the net."

The net. Yes.

"You're losing it, little brother."

William took a quick glance at the scissors in Donald's hand. Sadness rose to the surface, not replacing the anger, but again sitting next to it. "You left me."

Oh, he did more than leave you.

"You were showing off," Donald said.

"You should have stayed."

"Stayed for what?"

"You knew. You—"

William closed his eyes. He tapped a hand against his forehead as if to knock the life back into the memory that had been without life for so long.

"You've lost it, man," Donald said. "Just give me your fucking ID and I'll get out of here. A quick trip to the bank, then off to save your little pony. A fair trade."

I stood next to William.

You've always known. Tell him.

William's eyes opened. He glared at his brother. He said, in a voice that was both calm and frightening, "You looked in my eyes. And you laughed."

"That wasn't me. Must have been a fish."

On the bank. We saw you.

"I saw you on the bank."

Donald smirked. "What the fuck are you talking about?"

"I saw you laughing. You were laughing at me."

He wanted us dead. He left us in the apartment. He left us in the pond.

"Why, Donald? Why did you leave me?"

Tell him what you remember.

William turned slightly in my direction. "I can't."

"Can't what?" Donald said.

"I can't remember!" William beat his fists against his head.

"You are fucking psycho."

It wasn't an accident!

William moved his fists away from his head. He stood a foot away from the man who looked like William but was as different as a brother could be.

"Not an accident," William said.

"That's right," Donald said. "It was your fault. Now you're catching on."

At the same time, William and I both shouted, "No!"

Donald seemed unaffected by William's outburst. He said, "Every damn day of summer you'd dive into the pond, holding your breath for as long as it took to prove you were better than me."

"That's not true," said William.

"Of course it's true. Pussy showoff."

William looked like he might resign. Might give in to what Donald was telling him.

The fishing net! I screamed.

William said, "The fishing net. I couldn't hold my breath. It was too long—"

"You were flailing your arms like a water ballerina."

"You tricked me," William said.

"Uh-huh."

He was laughing!

"You laughed at me, Donald. I could see you."

"*See?*" Donald laughed. "What could you *see?* You were busy doing a water dance!"

We floated.

"I...I floated. I swallowed water and I floated...into the air...I did loop-de-loops..."

"Holy Crap," Donald said. "Your brain has finally gone zippo!" The scissors moved through the air for emphasis.

We saw you!

"We saw you," William said. "You were on the bank, laughing. I couldn't breathe. You knew I couldn't breathe. The men had to come and breathe for me."

He left us. Alone. To die.

Donald let out an exaggerated sigh. "None of it matters. Only thing that matters is what you are now. It doesn't matter what you were like before."

But he remembers.

"I remember."

"What do you remember?" Donald snapped the scissor blades open and closed at his side.

"I remember what it was like."

"I'll bite. What *what* was like?"

Before.

"Before," William said. "Before I drowned. I r-r-remember everything." A lonely tear dribbled down William's cheek and onto the lapel of his crisp white collar. He worked hard not to stutter. "How smart I was…"

Yes, yes, yes!

"Yeah, right," Donald said.

"I was good at math and reading…"

"There's something to be proud of."

"I ran fast and rode horses and swam and—" He stopped abruptly.

"And what?" Donald asked. "Don't leave me in suspense!"

William looked at the ground and whispered, "Stephanie loved me."

"You see," Donald said. "This is the part that keeps me trippin'. How you could think a crazy thing like that. You know Stephanie always had the hots for your big brother, she just didn't want to hurt your feelings. Everyone knows she never loved you, she only felt pity for you—"

William lunged forward, pushing Donald to the table on his back, and using the weight of his arm to press against his throat.

"You did this to me!" William screamed. "You let me drown! I almost died! I *did* die! And then I came back again! Like this!"

Donald tried to move William's arm from his throat but was too weak for him. His right hand still held onto the scissors, but the left side of William's body kept his arm in place.

"You're wrong, man," Donald squeaked. "That coma made you *loco!*"

Tell him! I shouted in William's ear. *Tell him what he did to us!*

William's tears fell onto Donald's face. "You wanted me to drown so you wouldn't have me around anymore. I—got stuck and I can't get out—I g-g-got st-st-stuck—" His body shook with his sobs, each tremor crushing down on Donald's throat.

"You wanted attention and that's what you got," Donald choked. "Everyone coddles Billy. Poor Billy. Always gotta change the program for Billy!"

"You made me this way!" William screamed.

He took his weight off his brother, grabbed him by the shirt, and flung him across the kitchen floor. The scissors flew from Donald's hand, crashing into the baseboard a foot away from where he landed near the pantry.

William towered over him.

"You're just looking for someone to blame, man," Donald told him, pushing his long hair out of his eyes. "All I can tell you is, if I had to do it all over again, I wouldn't save you."

Instantly, the fog of confusion entered from behind William's eyes.

No! I screamed.

"*I'm* the one who saved *you*," Donald said, staring up from the floor. "I came in after you, untangled you, and saved your lousy ass."

"I thought Dad—"

"Dad only pulled you out of the water *after* I untied the line. Do you remember now?"

I could barely peek inside William's hidden memory, could barely make out the murky water, the sound of air bubbles leaving his nose, Donald's laughing face appearing, then disappearing, then blackness.

William didn't remember everything after all.

But you remember enough! I screamed.

"No," William said, shaking his head. "No, Donald. You pulled on the net—"

"To *un-tie* you."

No! That is not what happened. Tell him you know!

"You pulled on the net to—to—"

Tighten it.

"To tighten it. To trap me there. F-f-forever."

A car door slammed. An engine revved, and tires crunching the gravel disappeared down the driveway.

William turned toward the door. "Stephanie?"

It only took a split second for Donald to see his window of opportunity. He crawled to his right, grabbed the scissors from the floor, and slashed through the space in front of him. But the scissors cut more than air. William's right leg was slightly bent. His calf faced Donald, who still lay on the floor. The gush of blood pouring through the slice in William's trousers was instantaneous.

As William bent down to tend to his wound, Donald brought his knees up to his chest and with one strong double-legged kick, sent William flying, bashing his head into a table leg. He fell into a slumped pile on the floor. His eyes fluttered, but before they closed, he had a chance to see his older brother, the once mischievous, loud-mouthed boy who had turned into a monster of a man, descend upon him.

Chapter 103

My lower back screamed as I slid Woody's unconscious body toward me. He'd put on weight since working at the stables. Muscle weight. His biceps bulged under my fingers. Blood seeped through his pants, leaving a red trail on the floor.

This was his house now. He could clean up the mess himself.

My hands worked to get underneath him so I could grab his wallet. As I rocked him onto his side, I felt the lump in his front pocket. I slid my hand inside and smiled as I pulled out the keys. One for the back door, one for the front, one to my apartment, and one to Ma's car. Ta-fucking-da! It would be easy enough to dump that piece-of-shit Buick in long-term parking at the airport, but I had to move fast. I shoved the keys into my pocket and kept rolling him. When I pulled my hand away from the back of Woody's head, I spotted the sticky blood on my palm. Shuddering, I wiped it on his dress shirt. I noticed the hairline split in the table leg. Maybe his head really was made of wood! I held back a nervous giggle.

As soon as he was on his side, the wallet slid out of his pocket like it wanted me to own it. I opened it and looked inside: fucking sweet. A state ID card fit for a king. I shoved the whole wallet into my back pocket.

I was still in a crouched position when I heard the floor squeak behind me. I felt a pair of stranger's eyes ripping holes through the back of my skull. Turning around without screaming or peeing my pants would take skills I didn't have. Moving fast to the door made more sense. If the dude had a gun,

I would try to outrun the bullets. I didn't come this far to get assaulted by one of Roly's thugs with nothing better to do than kill a small-town nobody.

My unconscious brother rolled onto his back as I stood, my shoulders chillin' like I had no clue someone was standing behind me. My heart pounded in my ears. I was sure the bastard could hear it. I pretended to fiddle with the zipper on my windbreaker while my eyes darted toward the baseboards. I couldn't see the scissors anywhere.

Fuck. I'd have to make a run for it without a weapon.

I took in some air, then real slow let it out, counted to three, and made a beeline for the back door.

But I was no match for whatever animal had been sent out to the boonies to hunt me down.

My body slammed into the refrigerator and then the floor. My arm was yanked hard against my back. I heard the crack as my wrist snapped.

"Ouch, fuck, fuck!"

The snap sent a shooting pain from my thumb to the top of my shoulder. The side of my face smashed against the kitchen floor. Lemon scented cleaner from the linoleum swam up my nose.

"Don't kill me, man, don't kill me," I said. "I can get you cash. Lots of cash."

"I do not want your money, ugly white boy. I want your ass."

I still couldn't see his face as his wet breath touched my ear, like a Quentin Tarantino character.

"Do you know the difference between green cash and a white ass?" he asked. "A white ass will never be worth anything." His weight pressed down on me as he laughed. "That is an American joke. I saved it just for you."

"You're a real stand-up comedian."

He pulled harder on my arm and I screamed.

"Where do you get all this money you brag about?" he asked. "You have a supersized piggy bank, Donald Baker? No. You do not have a piggy bank. I think you steal the money from that one over there."

He yanked my hair and turned my head in William's direction, near about breaking my neck in the process.

I groaned. "He owes it to me."

The man let go. My face fell to the floor again, splitting my top lip as my front teeth dug in.

"How much does this man owe you?" he asked.

More than what's in the bank, I thought to myself. "A lot," I said.

"Well, then, why do you beat him up? Why not ask him for it? Why do you take his wallet? Is that where he keeps the money he owes you?"

I said, "I know Roly sent you."

The man laughed again, crushing my lower spine to pieces as he leaned back. He was making himself comfortable, sitting on me, like I was a human boogie board.

"Roly did not ask me to come after *you* this time. He asked me to come after *him*." I could feel the man nod toward William, still out cold. "But this is a much better situation, yes? What you Americans love to call *irony*."

"I don't understand…"

"You fucking *zidòl*. All you ever had to do was the job your brother ended up doing for you. All you had to do was follow orders. But you could not even do that. Now you beat him up, after all he did for you."

His last statement fueled me. Even with his weight squashing my lungs, I shouted, "Did for *me*? He made my life shit! He deserves nothing, but gets everything. He should have been stuck in an institution, not take over the house like it was his private hospital ward. Things were perfect before he was born. He took away everything I ever had! He fucking stole my childhood, and I'll never get it back!" My wrist throbbed, and my hips screamed from the pressing weight. Snot ran out of my nose.

"Well, now," the man said. "Sounds to me like money is the least of what he owes you. Sounds like you deserve a whole new life."

"Fuckin'-A."

"You deserve a clean slate."

"Word up."

My spine relaxed as the man stood.

"Get up," he demanded.

I got to my knees real slow. I rubbed my wrist and held it against my chest as I stumbled and then stood. Shaking my dirty hair from my forehead and wiping the snot from my nose, I finally faced the man who was sent to kill me.

"So," the comic book villain said, his dark eyes peering out of his dark face, the gun pointed in my direction. "I will give you the opportunity to start over." He held out his free hand. "Give me the wallet."

"What for?"

The man still held out his hand. "Give it to me."

I'd never had a gun pointed directly at me. It ain't a good feeling, I can tell you that.

Even so, I told him, "No."

"What did you say?"

"Just let me go," I said. "I'll leave town. You'll never see me again. No one will. I promise."

The man's gun held steady.

"This is my only way," I begged. "Don't you see?"

"All I see is a sniveling man with more axes to grind than there are axes in his pathetic world."

Hearing him talk about axes made me remember the scissors. There they were on the floor, halfway between me and the kitchen table, about three feet away. But what could a pair of scissors do that a gun couldn't do faster?

Sometimes, I have found, when you're in the middle of a sticky situation, God or whoever the hell is up there gives a hand to the powerless. He shows a little compassion, gives them an extra second or two here and there to help them out.

In that miraculous couple of seconds, a car crunched along the gravel in the driveway. I didn't know who it was, but it made Roly's henchman look toward the window over the sink. It took less than a second for adrenalin to catch up to my idea.

I dove for the scissors and grabbed William's wobbly head in my hands, the sharper of the two blades against his neck, so close to his Adam's apple a hiccup would cause a mess.

The man placed his other hand against the gun and pointed it down at me.

"You kill me," I said, "and these scissors will do their job."

"You are too chicken kaka to kill your brother."

A car door slammed outside.

"I could put him out of his misery," I said.

"You mean out of *your* misery."

"He almost died when we were kids. He was *supposed* to die."

"So, you should take it into your own hands and decide his fate? Fate that should have happened, but did not?"

"Damn straight," I said, staring up at the end of his gun, about ready to pee my pants.

"What about *your* fate, Donald Baker?"

"*This* is my fate. Getting what's owed me."

"Nobody owes you anything," the man told me. "You are a sad excuse of a man who waits for others to give him handouts. You do not deserve anything."

"Don't fucking tell me what I do or don't deserve!" I shouted, pressing the blade harder against William's throat. A speck of blood appeared. "You don't know me! You don't know anything about me!"

"No, but I do know your brother."

I was shaking hard. "Yeah. My brother, who can't tell the difference between a knife and a fork. My brother, who still wears polyester like it's fucking 1978!"

The man glared at me from the other end of the gun. "If I were on a sinking ferry boat in the middle of the sea, and I had to choose between you and William to help me make it to shore, the winner would not be you."

He took a step closer.

I gripped the scissors tighter. "I swear I'll slice his throat so fast—"

Now the man used two hands to hold the gun. His thumb pulled back the hammer. "Then we shall see who is faster. You, or—"

A shot exploded. My ears rang as the bullet zipped past my shoulder. I felt a sting. William's head fell back to the floor and the scissors flew into oblivion as I rolled under the kitchen table. A bullet hole appeared in the cabinet door under the sink. I put my good hand up to feel the wound, expecting to see my shoulder in shreds, but there was barely a graze under the rip in my jacket.

I crawled out from the other side of the table and tore out the back door. Another gunshot blasted. I screamed as I jumped off the back porch and ran to the Buick, dropping the keys in the gravel, picking them up again, trying to ignore my broken wrist. I opened the car door and shoved the key into the ignition. An empty police car was parked behind me. I drove across the grass, tore down the driveway, onto the street, and out of the neighborhood.

If there was no traffic on my way to the bank and those gunslingers back there didn't stop their shoot-out to follow my ass, the next twenty minutes would change my life forever.

Chapter 104

Only the faces of my manman and Anthony were in my head as I toppled to the floor. Manman and Anthony, waiting for my phone call that would never come, getting a visit from Roly, then waiting in line at immigration, holding onto trash bags filled with their belongings, holding onto each other. Manman, covered by grief, like a black veil worn at a funeral, heading back to Haiti, a place that held no future for a dying dog. Anthony, crying for losing what he now believed was his home. I thought of nothing else, not my life or my death, only my manman and my nephew, who would have been better off never having come here, better off never owning their own television, eating McDonald's french fries and street vendor hot dogs, riding in buses that don't smell like chickens. If only they had never had a taste of what the free world had to offer. A person can not miss something they have never had.

I barely felt the pain in my side as my hands were cuffed behind me. Barely heard the words as the officer told me I had the right to remain silent. The right to an attorney. Just like on the cop shows Manman sometimes watched. Another officer joined him. The sirens were deafening.

William let out a moan as the ambulance men put him on the rolling bed. I turned toward him. His eyes were open. They were fixed on something across the room. His voice rose up, seeping through my pain.

"Please," William said. "Don't go."

From a place deeper than my wound, I understood he was not speaking to me.

I, too, was placed on a bed with wheels, my hands now cuffed to the bed rails. I slid in and out of consciousness while the ambulance monitor played my heartbeat, but I could think of nothing but Manman and Anthony, huddled together in a mob of despairing immigrants, going back to a home that was not their home anymore; going back without me.

Chapter 105

A parking spot right outside the bank's side door and no line inside. Yoyo, homey Jo, can you give me a hallelujah!

I pulled the ID out of my wallet and held it in my shaking hand.

But then the wrong bank teller called to me. An older lady I'd never talked to before.

"Can I help you, sir?"

I stayed behind the rope. "Um…I want to see Gina. She's my favorite teller."

The lady didn't seem hurt and politely asked me to wait a moment while she went into a back room. Gina came out and went to her window. Pushing my hair out of my eyes, I stepped up to the counter.

"I did what you told m-m-me," I said as slow as possible, even though my heart was freakin' out and I wanted to get out of there like the room was filled with poisonous gas. But I had to take my time. Pretend like I didn't have two brain cells to rub together. Pretend like time didn't matter, even though it sure as shit did. "I brung my ID."

I slid the filled-out withdrawal slip and my brother's ID under the window.

Gina smiled at me. "That's fine, Mr. Baker. All I need from you is your signature and we'll be on our way."

She placed a form into the dip in the window. I took the form and signed it, extra extra slow, and pushed it back to her.

Then I noticed three things that made my racing heart stop dead.

Number one: Gina never stopped smiling. Like her mouth was attached to wires and someone else was making her lips curve up that way.

Number two: even though I'd hid my bloody shirt under my windbreaker, she acted like she didn't notice my split lip or my swollen wrist the size of a baseball.

Number three: earlier that morning, Gina'd had a bitch fest about getting her manager's approval. But she wasn't getting her manager now.

Then number four popped into my head, smart dog that I am: the other tellers had disappeared. No customers. No tellers. Except for Gina.

"How would you like this, Mr. Baker?" Gina asked me, still smiling like a puppet.

"What?"

"How would you like your bills? I need to go to the safe to get your cash." She pulled a key out of a drawer below the counter.

I didn't say anything.

"Don't worry," she said. "I'll be sure to put it in an extra-large envelope. Why don't I get you a few thousands and a few hundreds? So it won't weigh so much."

"Yeah," I said. "Thousands…and hundreds."

"That's fine. Just give me a minute and I'll be right back."

I stood in the ghost town bank and waited. Time disappeared until she was once again standing in front of me, a large envelope in her hand.

"Here you go, Mr. Baker," she said, smiling. "I had my manager pre-approve it this morning right after you left. All of us here at Southern States Bank & Trust hope this helps with your mother's funeral. We offer our deepest condolences."

I almost slapped myself in the forehead. What a paranoid dope I was! Here was the envelope lying in front of me, filled with five-hundred grand in real live bills. I didn't have to kill no one, didn't have to rob a liquor store, didn't even care anymore about who owed me what. Because it hit me in that moment: I was a free man. Like a king, I'd eat lobster, do some fishing, bet a on a cockfight or two, spend quality time with those dark-haired hoochies.

Real tears came to my eyes. "Thank you," I told Gina. "Thank you." I meant it. I really did.

I spent a few seconds trying to get my jacket pocket unzipped with one working hand, then a few more cramming the envelope inside my waistband. Before walking away for the last time, I decided to tell that fine hottie Gina, with her pretty smile and super awesome boobs, to have a great day. After all, she was saving my life, even if she didn't know it. I turned back to the window.

Gina was gone.

In her place stood a tall man in a black suit, his right hip sporting a bulge.

I twirled around. Four more men, with poker faces and dark suits, stood blocking the bank doors like toy shoulders.

"That's him," a man's familiar voice said from behind the teller window.

I didn't have to look, but I did anyways. Standing next to the man who had taken Gina's place was none other than that old fucker, Sherm. His snaggle teeth stuck out beneath a grin.

"What?" I said.

No one answered.

My knees buckled and I fell to the marble floor, my damp hair sticking to my face, my wrist screaming in pain. A stampede of black shoes rushed toward me. Guns were drawn. Voices shouted, one on top of the other.

I did as they ordered. Put hands on my head. Kept my mouth shut. Froze every bone in my body.

As strong arms dragged me to my feet, my bladder let loose. I watched through my tears as the yellow liquid spread out across the marble, turning the light blue floor to an ugly green.

Epilogue

Cecilia

I only saw the boys one more time, and that was on a Tuesday night in the middle of summer, when it gets so hot you could grill a pork chop out on the street. But they didn't come to see me dance. They came to *thank* me. For how I'd helped William.

"Hey, no one needs to thank me," I told them.

But they handed me the check anyways and told me to quit my job and go back to school, not to the community college, but the university. Like I couldn't afford to pay for it myself, pa-leeze. And because I was paying for it in cash, they accepted me for the fall term.

It wasn't the money that made me sign up. It was them two knowing there was a better life out there waiting for me. It was them telling me I'm worth more than having men drool over my long hair and pretty toenails and other parts.

William kissed me on the cheek and whispered, "I'll remember you." It was the first time in my whole life I blushed.

I've got me a full schedule coming up. English 111, Biology, Biology Lab, Comparative Cultures, and Critical Thinking, as if I don't do enough of that already. My major? Well, business, of course. I'm setting my eyes on opening a club one day. Not a strip club though. Too hard to get all those licenses. A *real* night club, that smells like limes instead of men's sweat, with local bands and hot wings and happy hour, and tall windows that actually let in the sun now and then.

The university has a summer abroad program. You don't have to guess I've already looked into the different European cities they offer, and when I found out that Sicily is on the list, I about died from the ironicalness of it all.

Woops. I gotta scoot. Orientation's today and I gotta find a parking space before they're all filled up.

If you ever see a girl sitting on the grass in the quad with long red hair down to her ass and her nose in a book, that'd be me. But don't bother me, cuz a girl like me needs to stay focused.

Lance

It took a while, but the Baker house has finally come together. New carpet and roof, and lots of rose bushes, just like Mrs. B woulda loved, which are in full bloom after a summer of rain and sun. The hard part was putting up the barn. Had to convince William that in order to build one, we needed to get rid of the tree house. He finally agreed, and hung out at the bowling alley while the men tore it down so he wouldn't see.

The barn isn't huge, but it's big enough to hold his new pet, a paint horse named Rocky Road.

Sometimes we pull Rocky in the trailer to be with his sister, Neapolitan, to run around in the fields at her foster family's farm. She was retired from racing after all the hullabaloo. They seem more like mother and son, the way Neon nuzzles Rocky and eggs him on sometimes.

We all head over to William's every Sunday for supper. The kids have come to love him like an uncle. They all love Rocky too.

William was only in the hospital a few days after it all went down. He lost some blood, but he's a man who more than once has defied the laws of death.

That's all behind him now. Now he has a home to call his own, a horse to treat like his kid, and friends who have become his family.

Well, that part's never really changed.

Tonight we're meeting up with Stephanie and Gerald over at William's, for dinner and a movie. He bought a big screen TV and about fifty videos. His accountant gives him a pretty tight allowance but let him splurge on the television. Tonight we're watching *The Breakfast Club*. Still not quite into the nineties, but we're getting there. Maybe William'll be all caught up by the time he turns fifty.

Manny

America gets crazier by the minute. I share this thought with Manman, and she says, in broken English, "Crazy or not, I take it!"

Of course, I agree.

We brought Anthony to the drugstore for pencils and paper and erasers, and he got all of his required shots and never once cried, because he knows it is part of his education.

Manman loves to chat with her new Italian friends who own the deli downstairs. They told her yesterday that their part-time manager is quitting, would she like a job? You should have seen her excitement in the kitchen last night, bits of macaroni and cheese flying off her wooden spoon, talking about ham and bologna and Swiss cheese like they were precious jewels.

It is the first time Manman has a real job. To find one in New York is like winning the lottery.

The wound in my side healed quickly. I am strong, that is why. And because I carry no guilt. Guilt, I have found, is a silent killer.

There are many pigeons here in New York. Too many. But they leave me be and I them. Some people feed them in the parks, even though it is illegal. I have no problem with this. I befriended a pijon once, so I can understand.

Every once in a while I see a dead one in an alley near the trash bins or at the base of a tree in the park. I wonder if it has always been this way, maybe from the city's air pollution or the filth in the water. And as I begin to wonder if its death was from something unnatural, I stop myself. In my manman's village, it would have been considered bad luck, all of these dead birds. Here, they use science to explain things. But some things cannot be explained.

I deliberately do not follow the news.

Except in the case of William.

Lightning struck twice. First, Donald pleaded guilty to all charges—

perhaps he felt safer living in prison for twenty years than on the run for life—and then Roly had a heart attack. It took six paramedics to get him onto the gurney. He was already blue by the time an employee found him, a cigar clenched between his teeth. The match between his fat fingers had melted them together.

Roly's books were cleaned out, and if he had not died on top of his desk, he would have died in prison.

William and I write on occasion. He invited my family to come live with him. He says I can work in his barn. But I have had enough of sweeping up kaka.

My job as a taxi cab driver is exciting. I get to see the city from one end to the other. Get to drive past Central Park, through Manhattan, up and down 42nd Street and Broadway, past the Twin Towers and the Empire State Building. Pick up beautiful women and even more beautiful men. One man in particular, his name is Sammy, has taken me out to lunch once. But only once. He is married. It seems there is as much frustration to be who you are in the United States as there is in Haiti, or anywhere for that matter.

The skyline is magnificent. Some days, I climb to the roof of our apartment building and look out over the city. Squinting through the smog I see the beauty. There is constant movement and flow down below, like traveling rivers filled with eager fish.

I miss the trees, so a few days ago I planted a ficus tree on the roof, even though fall is nearly here. Next spring I will add vegetable planters and spread out my garden. A few of my neighbors want to do the same. Who says the city cannot be combined with the country? It is the best of both worlds.

As I have mentioned, I carry no guilt, but Debt's spirit still follows me. I owe William and Officer Powers more than I can ever repay. My plea bargain was simple: information in exchange for freedom. Freedom for me and Manman and Anthony. It was an easy choice because Donald was taken to jail and Roly is dead. Who else did I have to worry about?

Officer Power's gun was aimed at Donald that day, but I had stepped in the way.

He is a funny man, Officer Powers. He knew the truth before I told him.

Knew that William and I had not done anything cruel to Neapolitan, otherwise she would be dead.

When I explained what I had *really* done that night in the barn, he laughed.

"Very clever."

I told him, "When you have suffered for days without food or water, survival makes you creative."

And, of course, if William had not given my family such an incredible financial gift, we would still be living in that rat hole. Now we are still in a rat hole, but at least it is bigger and overlooks a park and has a good school district. And there is a McDonald's in walking distance, which makes Anthony quite content.

There is nowhere like America, the land of the free and the brave, and those endless golden arches.

Officer Powers

"This isn't a Hollywood movie," my wife tells me as she kisses the top of my head, more patronizingly than with love. I have just finished mowing the lawn for the millionth time this summer, and I'm ready for a nap. As Linda heads inside to make some iced tea, she adds, "You're not FBI." Before she closes the sliding glass door behind her, I hear her mumble, "Thank God."

But handing a file over to the government doesn't make a case invisible.

Fact: William injected Neon with sugar water, thanks to Manny.

Fact: The horse became ill due to stress.

Fact: Sherm had his own reasons for screwing Donald over, of which I care very little since he gave the Feds what they wanted.

Fact: Donald pleaded guilty to multiple counts of fraud, two counts of breaking and entering, one count of aggravated assault, and one count of grand theft auto.

Fact: Eager malevolent scientists are still out there, waiting for the dust to settle in order to continue their disgusting experiments.

Fact: Over the last few months, six dead birds have been discovered in our county.

Fact: Three counties away, a yearling at a nearby training ground died from encephalitis.

It doesn't take a genius to find correlations.

But as my wife reminds me almost daily, I am not FBI. Let them and the CDC handle it. I did my job.

I fall back in my hammock, turn up the classical music on the portable, and close my eyes for a moment. Birds chirp in the trees overhead as my mind reviews the latest conversation I had with Doctor Mark Yingling, my vet friend.

"It's out of my hands," Mark had told me solemnly. "A situation like this can't be dealt with by a small town vet. Or a small town cop. Let it go."

I open my eyes. Above me, two catbirds sit on a branch, their necks twisting sideways as they try to spot worms in the freshly mowed grass.

The man on the radio has decided to interrupt my Sunday afternoon with a bit of news. Thunderstorms in the vicinity. Hurricane headed toward the Virgin Islands. New satellite in space. Price of gas dropping a few pennies. Housing market on the up-swing. Missing child found alive. Man in West Virginia the first U.S. death in what is suspected as a bird virus—

I grab the radio, place it on my stomach, and turn up the volume.

"The forty-five-year-old man's body will be quarantined until specialists are satisfied with their findings. Saint Matthew's Hospital refuses to comment but says they will make a statement by Tuesday. And now, a quick word from our sponsor—"

I turn off the radio.

"Honey?" I call.

I see my wife through the kitchen window, but she can't hear me with the air-conditioning on in the house.

The world becomes silent. The catbirds fly away. No breeze rustles the locust leaves overhead, the cicadas are napping, thick muggy air wraps itself around me.

I close my eyes again.

Fact: West Virginia is too close for comfort.

Fact: I am a damn good cop.

Fact: I am not an investigator.

Fact: It is my day off and I refuse to let anything screw it up.

I force a heavy breath from my lungs, will myself to keep my eyes closed, and do everything in my power to convince myself that Sunday is still the best day of the week.

Stephanie

Gerald and I are heading to William's house for dinner and a movie. We've been trying to get over there once a week, which we did at first to make sure he was alright living by himself, but now we do it just because it's fun. Lance and Julie and the kids come too, so it's sort of turned into our weekly tradition.

I'm incubating a basketball. William asked to feel my stomach last week. I held his hand while he placed his palm against my belly, and when the baby kicked, his eyes lit up and he blushed, just like the day he won the 100-yard dash on the elementary school playground and I kissed him on the cheek.

I think a tiny part of him still doesn't quite remember how it all happened.

But a bigger part of him does.

Something happened to William that day—the day of the funeral, when Manny pulled me from the pond and I drove half frozen to the 7-11 to call the police. Something I can't put my finger on. He still speaks slowly, still sets the table wrong, still shudders when he sees the pink scar on his calf.

Lance thinks William's change comes from the fact that Donald is finally behind bars. But I think it's something more.

If you look at his face now, it seems less child-like. Like he grew up all of a sudden, no longer that little boy who used to twirl me around in my basement. Like we somehow flashed forward into the future, leaving Billy behind.

In the driveway, Gerald helps me grab the potato salad I made to go with the chicken. I showed William how to make country-style baked chicken, like his mama did, and now he cooks it every time we come over. Cooking that chicken makes him mighty proud. I'm proud of him too.

We walk up the back porch steps and into the kitchen, but when I call out to let him know we're here, there's no answer.

"Probably out in the barn," Gerald says.

William and Gerald get along like brothers now. William asks Gerald what it's like to be a fireman, and Gerald tells him stories of fire rescues and cats in trees and babies being saved from swimming pools. William tells Gerald all the time that if he'd been at the pond that day to save him, he wouldn't be the way he is now. Gerald tells him he's perfect the way he is.

I put the potato salad on the kitchen counter. As Gerald helps me off with my sweater, Lance and Julie come in the door.

"Hey, all," Julie says. "Brought some chocolate cream pie."

Gerald reaches for the pie, lifts the aluminum foil, and sighs.

All I'm thinking is how eating together once a week has made us like a real family.

"Where are James and Shelby?" I ask Julie.

"The barn," she says. "The kids go through withdrawal if they haven't seen Rocky for a few days."

I laugh and open the oven. "Chicken has twenty more minutes by what the timer says."

Footsteps thump outside, followed by panicked voices. James and Shelby come tearing through the back door.

At the same time they shout, "Ya'll gotta hurry! It's William!"

My throat clenches. "What is it? What's wrong?"

"He's going crazy," James says. "Y'all need to come quick!"

Together we follow the harried children, marching out the back door and hurrying across the wide yard, sure not to step on the violets William planted along the stepping stones. With the sun setting behind the barn, and an early evening fog swirling around it, I feel like I'm in the middle of a Thomas Kincaid painting.

Three feet from the barn, we come to a stop.

A deep base beat rocks the building.

Julie's daughter Shelby anxiously waves her arms, motioning for us to follow. The barn doors are closed, so she opens them a crack. We all take turns sneaking a peek.

I start laughing, and Lance follows. Gerald and Jules are used to our numerous inside jokes, so they only raise their eyebrows.

"What?" Gerald asks.

"Let's go in," I say.

Shelby opens the doors all the way. Hip-hop music slams us in the face. Rocky is standing in the corner of his stall, eating hay which is scattered about the floor. He seems oblivious to the deafening music or the fact that there are other people in the barn. I think to myself, *Maybe he's already deaf.* As a vet, this causes me great concern.

William stands in deep concentration behind a pair of record players on a table, their long cords crisscrossing the barn floor to the outlets. Two huge speakers sit in opposite corners of the barn. His finger doesn't point to the ceiling. His hips don't move from side to side. His feet don't slide across the floor. His hands are a busy blur moving back and forth between two records, both playing the same song, an early hip-hop tune from at least a decade ago. He scratches one record over the other like Grandmaster Flash.

I can barely see William's face behind the large round sunglasses. He has given himself a makeover. He's dressed in a bulky black leather jacket with a wide red stripe down each sleeve and a black T-shirt underneath. On his head sits a plain red baseball cap cocked to the side. His white bellbottoms have been traded in for an extra-long pair of straight, dark blue jeans, bunched at the ankles around a pair of black and white Adidas tennis shoes, minus the laces. A chunky gold necklace that must weigh two pounds hangs around his neck to the center of his chest. I smile when I notice he also wears the horse pendant.

I shout to William while pointing one finger to my ear and the other to Rocky, "Your horse will go deaf!"

He finally looks up.

I repeat my warning.

"Ear plugs!" he shouts back, grinning.

I spot the lime green plugs in Rocky's ears.

Gerald catches my eye as he suddenly moves to the center of the room. In his collared shirt and Dockers and dress shoes, he starts moving to the music, showing us his rendition of the humpty, and then the scissor, like Run DMC or Salt 'n Peppa. After a moment, his moves grow more elaborate, turning into the butterfly and then the running man. I am dumbfounded. Here I am with a baby on the way and still discovering things about my husband!

William stops scratching and lets the record play without his help. He goes to the front of the table and tries to imitate Gerald. The kids soon join in, giggling so hard they keep doubling over. Jules grabs me by the wrist. Me with my huge belly, and Jules holding onto her kids' hands, we dance until our feet ache from the cement floor. Lance stands in the corner, laughing, shaking his head. We must look like a bunch of patients receiving shock therapy. We try to outdo one another until the song ends, and it's time to head inside for dinner.

Later that night, after the barn is all locked up and we sit around the living room watching *The Breakfast Club*, none of us able to move an inch because we are way too full from chicken and chocolate pie, I glance over at William sitting on a large floor pillow, his back against the couch. Finally, I figure out what I'd been trying to put my finger on all night but couldn't, and it seems so clear to me now: William is a man at peace. In the light of the television, he smiles with contentment as if to say, *This is my life and it isn't half bad.*

I look around at my friends, put my hands on my belly, and lean into the crook of my husband's arm.

I think to myself, *I couldn't agree more.*

William

My friends went home around ten o'clock cuz I gotta get up early to feed Rocky. I might even train him some more tricks. I already showed him how to stomp his foot when I say, "Stomp, Rocky!" He's a good horse. And smart too.

I bend down and scratch the scar on my leg. Sometimes it itches, but other times I forget it's there.

Just so y'all know, I watched Billy leave that day when I was bleeding on the kitchen floor. I felt him say goodbye. Saw him disappear. He headed through the open kitchen door, like he was going out for a walk. Just went out and never came back.

I barely even had a chance to say goodbye.

Before he left he leaned over me and said, *That's it for us. You know that, right?*

I nodded cuz I did know it.

I have to let you be now, he told me. *You need to do the rest on your own. It's time to let go. Time to move on.*

"Please don't go," I told him. I don't know why I didn't want him to go. Maybe I thought he'd forget me. Maybe I thought I'd be lonely without him. Or lost. Maybe. But before I could say that stuff, he was already out the door. Just like that. Lickity split.

It's funny, him being gone, cuz I don't feel lost at all no more. I think he's still inside me somewhere, since sometimes at night when I'm sleeping, I play hide and seek with him, but he's such a good hider, I can't never seem to find him, even though I know he's nearby. We're a lot alike, me and him, like brothers, even though I know that's not what we are. It takes a lot more than a brother to know you good enough to make you see the truth. It takes a part of yourself.

Sometimes at night, I walk to the dock, hike right through them trees along the narrow path, past the tire swing that took me and Lance a whole hour to tie up. I put my shoes on the grass at the clearing and head down the dock to the edge and look into the water.

That's where I am now.

I take off my baseball cap. Tonight the moon is extra big. I can see its roundness wiggling in the pond. I see the moon and I see the stars and I see everything, even the stuff that isn't right in front of me. I can't do math. I can't remember the whole alphabet. And setting the table is crap. But I see it now. It's a good life, my life, the life I'm supposed to have, the one with my friends and my horse and my house and my self.

At first, after he left, I'd come out here, thinking for some reason this is where he was most likely to be.

"Billy!" I'd call. But the only thing that ever answered me back was an owl that has a nest high up in a tree on the other side of the pond.

"Hoo-hoo!" the owl says to me now.

I lean down and stick my hand in the water. Pretty warm. Warm enough for a swim even.

But not tonight.

I shout, "Hooty-hoo-hoo!"

The owl calls back, "Hoo-hoo!"

It feels really good to laugh in the dark under the moon with an owl that's been living here as long as me.

I stand back up and wipe my hand on my jeans. I put my baseball cap back on my head, sideways, the way it looks best.

As I'm halfway up the dock, cuz it's getting sort of chilly and I still gotta wash them dessert dishes, I think I hear something splashing in the water. I look over my shoulder, but the only thing behind me is the dark empty pond with the bright white moon floating in the center.

Author's note

Knock on Wood was originally written in 1997 as a full-length play, and the following year it was performed at California State Long Beach's Day Repertory Theatre. As the play's author and director, I had to chisel the ninety-minute script down to an hour in order to fit the allotted time frame. Back then, I had no idea the play would eventually become a novel, but I was hopeful that it would one day find its way to the stage again, in musical form. Hopefully, the process of adapting a novel into a musical won't take another twenty years!

Acknowledgements

This story would still be snug in its chrysalis if not for the incredible talents of the original cast and crew. I would like to take this time to thank each of them, respectively, as they have remained in my heart for over two decades: Jane Chung, Nathan Koval, Meira Perelstein, David Walker, Timothy Barnhart, Aaron Fry, R. Dylan Wasser II, Sarah Camp, Carrie Pettitt, Theodore "Mark" Martinez, Kari Serpa, Mario Leggs, Ryan Yoneyama, Shelly Cohen, Denise Cheng, Jason Enyart, Tandy Prosser, Leanna Haagen, Jason Rogel, Heidi Neidermeyer, John Zamora, Walter Nunez, Miki Ah Heong, Kerry Melachouris, Christopher Beamon, Alison Sever, Geovanna Finuzia, Ana Vuletic-Babun, Julie Tran, and Scene-shop Corey. An endearing posthumous thank you goes to Don Gruber, who taught me everything there is to know about set design, and a special thanks to Joanne Gordon, who trusted my work in her arena. I send, with love, a special shout-out to my then boyfriend, now husband, Jay Kenton Manning, for creating the amazing *Lotsa Luck* wheel used in the original play. Of course, Jay also designed my groovy book cover, so extra-special hugs and kisses to this master artist. Thanks to my sisters, Sandra Ferguson, Jennifer Argenti, and Angela Maurer, the best beasts who ever lived. I will get you all backstage passes to the musical! A thank you to infinity and beyond goes to my dear friend and literary agent, Uwe Stender, who has never once doubted me and works tirelessly on my behalf climbing up the rickety ladder of the publishing world. Thanks to the following incredible authors for helping to guide *Knock on Wood*'s transition way back in the beginning: Kathy Sartori, Ralph Hupka, Jan De Marco, and Frank Aranda. A HUGE thank you goes out to my earth angel beta readers, who took a chance reading a disco-filled, five-pound, multi-point-of-view book and gave me notes that made the work shine: Paula Gabier, Patty Howard, and Rick Romeo. A much overdue thanks goes to Clare Bazely, equine aficionado, for crucial information regarding racehorses; and to Kreyol.com, for bringing Manny to life. My deepest gratitude is sent to Josh Dasal, Emmy award-winning video and film director/producer/writer, for his notes regarding film adaptation. Countless hours of research went into this novel, and without these organizations, scholarly journals, and doctors, I would have been utterly lost: *Scientific American*; US Department of Agriculture; National Institute of Health; National Center for Biotechnology Information; *Journal of the American Medical Association*; and Dr. Daniel Barron, MD, PhD. Because music is such an important part of this story, I thank the numerous disco bands that kept me smiling and dancing when angst infiltrated my teen years; Sam Densler for moving his living room furniture around so we could practice the pretzel and other nifty moves back in high school; and Ashley at Hip Shake Fitness for her awesome old-school Hip Hop tutorials. Since every author needs a talented formatter, I send my thanks halfway around the globe to Jason and Marina at Polgarus Studio. Closer to home, I offer a big hug to Mary Jo Buckl at the Next Chapter Bookstore for supporting local authors. Last but not least, thank you to North Carolina's Wake and Craven County Libraries for including my books in their wonderful collections.

Please use the following discussion questions to enrich your reading of *Knock on Wood*. (Read the book first!)

1. How important is music in your life? Is it something you could live without? What are some of your specific memories related to a particular song or band?

2. With so many to choose from, who became your favorite character in the story? Your least favorite? Which character do you feel grew the most? The least? Are there any minor characters that stand out more than the others?

3. Discuss Lance's role in the story and his relationship with William. How does this relationship help move the story forward?

4. Even though William makes the decision to move out and get a job and become "independent," he tends to be a passive main character, a bit like a pinball trapped in a machine. Do you wish William had been a more active participant in the telling of his story? Were you satisfied that his personality came through mostly via the other characters' perspectives?

5. *Knock on Wood* briefly shows Billy a glimpse of heaven during his near-drowning experience. Do you believe in an afterlife? If so, how does your vision compare to Billy's? Have you or someone you know had a near-death experience?

6. I deliberately chose to omit an evident Haitian accent for Manny. Why do you think I did this? How effective or ineffective was this omission? Could you still hear his accent in your head?

7. What do you think are the most relevant themes (underlying messages) and motifs (repeated symbols or ideas) in *Knock on Wood*? How do some of these themes and motifs work together to tell the story?

8. William's backup singers pop into his head from time to time. How would the story have been different without these characters? How do they help express or hinder William's personality?

9. Discuss Stephanie and her long-time friendship with William. Is it possible to remain friends with someone you were once in love with? Is there a danger in this? How do Stephanie's engagement, wedding, and subsequent pregnancy help William grow?

10. While a minor character, Sherri the landlord plays an important role in the story. What is this role? Do you ever feel sorry for her? Why or why not?

11. In the very last scene, William tells the reader, "…I see everything, even the stuff that isn't right in front of me." What does he mean by this statement? Do you think he has come into his own by the end of the story? If so, what is the catalyst for this change?

12. William defies being stereotyped because there are many levels of traumatic brain injury and coma; the possibilities regarding the brain's response and outcomes are limitless. What are clues that William suffered a traumatic brain injury? What are clues that parts of his brain still function normally?

13. Sadly, while I was wrapping up the final edits of this book, the world of horseracing took top billing in the news when nearly two dozen thoroughbreds at a California racetrack had to be euthanized. A 2005 study by the US Department of Agriculture found that injuries are the second leading cause of death in horses, second only to old age. Do you feel horseracing is an archaic sport? Do you consider it a sport at all? Should it be legal? Why or why not?

14. Donald is the primary antagonist in the book. Despite his evil side, does he draw any empathy or sympathy from the reader? Does he get what he deserves? What is the true cause of Donald's anger, and how does it play out?

15. Some psychologists say it is vital we tap into memories that cause us pain, while others believe it is the brain's job to automatically protect us from harmful memories. Do you think it is better to invoke negative moments buried deep within our psyche, or is it better to forget? What does William gain or lose by eventually remembering the details of his tragic childhood experience?

16. Mr. Baker abandoned his family shortly after Billy's injury, leaving him without a father figure. Which character in the story represents a male role model to William? How would the story have been different if Mr. Baker had never left?

17. After Billy's near-drowning incident, he insists that others call him William. Why is this, and what does this tell us about him?

18. Like William Faulkner's *As I Lay Dying*, or Rebecca Wells' *Little Altars Everywhere*, *Knock on Wood* uses multiple points of view (POVs). Do you think this is a constructive way to tell a story? How does this particular novel work well with many voices? How does it weaken the story? Would it have been just as or more effective using one omniscient narrator?

19. When we first get to know Manny, he tells us, "Life is all about who owes who what. It is a world of debts. If Joe does me a favor, I owe Joe. If I overpay the favor to Joe, then Joe owes me a bit more. It goes on that way until the debt owed feels equal to both parties. But only then." Do you agree with this philosophy? How does Karma play a role in Manny's life? How does it play a role in your own life?

20. What is your favorite quote from the story and why?

21. What kind of future would William have had without a traumatic brain injury? Would he and Stephanie have married? What do you see him doing for a living? Would he have kept in touch with his brother? Would he still be fixated on music?

22. *Knock on Wood* is an extended adult fairy tale, like Winston Groom's *Forrest Gump* or Daniel Wallace's *Big Fish*. In what ways is this book like a fairy tale? In what ways is it different?

23. Does the story have a happy ending? Did you feel a catharsis? Do you wish it had ended another way?

24. Discuss who you believe the hero is in *Knock on Wood*.

25. In the book, the specific virus causing equine encephalitis is imaginary. Even so, I did intense research to find out how viruses spread and where/how they are most likely to incubate. While US officials are not concerned regarding a possible epidemic in America, there are known poultry virus outbreaks recently isolated in China, Nepal, Iraq, and Cambodia. Officer Chuck Powers has concerns because he has seen the effects of bird flu firsthand. Does he have a right to worry? Was Manny wrong to set the dove free? If the story were to continue, what chain of events could take place?

26. Discuss how Cecilia has a big heart. Why does she befriend William? What does she teach him? What does he teach her? What will her future be like?

27. Who is Billy? Is he William's soul? A part of his psyche? A memory of the person he used to be? Others can sometimes feel Billy's presence. Is this because they miss the little boy William once was, or is there something deeper going on?

28. All of the narrators in *Knock on Wood* have a back story. Whose back story stands out the most vividly? How does knowing a character's past help him or her come to life on the page? Is there any character you wanted to know more intimately?

29. Discuss Mrs. Baker's role. What are some of the trials she faces? What are her strengths and weaknesses? Is she a classic enabler or a mother who simply loves her son?

30. Can you envision *Knock on Wood* as a stage musical? Why or why not? What parts would work well while others would not?

Leslie Tall Manning with the original Lotsa Luck wheel
Photo by J. Kenton Manning, 1998

About the author

Leslie Tall Manning loves writing about teenagers stumbling into independence headfirst, and about grownups craving change and discovering it in ways they never expected. Her YA novel, *Upside Down in a Laura Ingalls Town*, is the proud recipient of the Sarton Women's Literary Award. She holds a BA in Theatre from California State Long Beach and is happily represented by the TriadaUS Literary Agency. As a private English tutor and study skills expert, Leslie spends her evenings working with students of all ages and her days working on her own writing projects. When she isn't clacking away at the computer keys or conducting research for her books, she loves traveling with her artist husband, laughing at life's idiosyncrasies, bingeing on the weirdest Netflix shows, or walking along the river in her historic Southern town. You can connect with Leslie on Facebook, Twitter, Instagram, Goodreads, or her website: www.leslietallmanning.com.

What readers have to say about *Maggie's Dream*:

"This is a weird and wondrous book! Don't let the deceptively simple beginning fool you: there are clues planted throughout the novel suggesting nothing is quite what it seems. The ending will surprise you and is worthy of the best psychological thrillers. It still haunts me days later..."
~ Clarissa Harwood, author of *Impossible Saints*

"Undeniably one of the most twisted...feminist...different... and at the same time amazing books I have read!"
~Net Galley Reviewer

"Leslie Tall Manning has created a world that is sometimes magical, sometimes terrifying, always entertaining."
~Padagett Gerler, author of *Invisible Girl*

"A fun ride and an imaginative journey both into the past and to a fantastical—and dangerous—land outside our reality..."
JD Cortese, author of *The Sound of a Broken Chain*

Enjoy the following excerpt of *Maggie's Dream*, a psychologically twisted tale combining post-WWII feminism, psychotherapy, and the hidden world of the 1940's tranquilizer epidemic.